LEGO LEGENDS OF CHIMA™

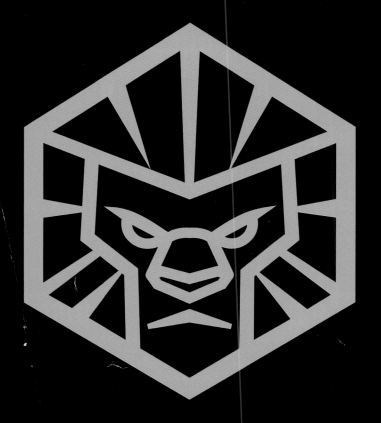

LEGO® LEGENDS OF CHIMA GRAPHIC NOVELS AVAILABLE FROM PAPERCUTZ™

LEGO
LEGENDS OF
CHIMA
ALL-NEW GRAPHIC NOVEL SERIES!
HIGH RISK!
PAPERCUTZ
#1 **"High Risk!"**

LEGO
LEGENDS OF
CHIMA
THE RIGHT DECISION
YANNICK GROTHOLT
COMICON
PAPERCUTZ
#2 **"The Right Decision"**

LEGO
LEGENDS OF
CHIMA
CHI QUEST!
YANNICK
GROTHOLT
COMICON
PAPERCUTZ
#3 **"CHI Quest!"**

LEGO
LEGENDS OF
CHIMA
THE POWER OF
FIRE CHI
YANNICK GROTHOLT
COMICON
PAPERCUTZ
#4 **"The Power of Fire Chi"**

LEGO
LEGENDS OF
CHIMA
WINGS FOR
A LION
YANNICK GROTHOLT
COMICON
PAPERCUTZ
#5 **"Wings for a Lion"**

LEGO
LEGENDS OF
CHIMA
PLAYING WITH
FIRE
YANNICK GROTHOLT
COMICON
PAPERCUTZ
#6 **"Playing With Fire!"**

LEGO LEGENDS OF CHIMA graphic novels are available for $7.99 in paperback, $12.99 in hardcover.
Available from booksellers everywhere. You can also order online from Papercutz.com.
Or call 1-800-886-1223, Monday through Friday, 9-5 EST. MC, Visa, and AmEx accepted.
To order by mail, please add $4.00 for postage and handling for first book ordered,
$1.00 for each additional book and make check payable to NBM Publishing.
Send to: Papercutz, 160 Broadway, Suite 700, East Wing, New York, NY 10038.

LEGO LEGENDS OF CHIMA graphic novels are also available digitally wherever e-books are sold.

Papercutz.com

FSC
www.fsc.org
MIX
Paper from
responsible sources
FSC® C006398

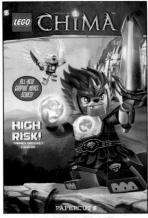

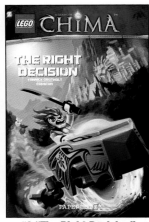

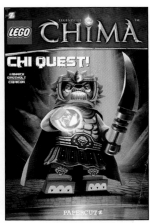

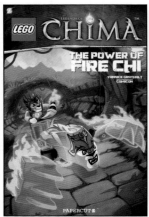

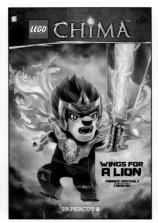

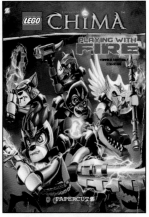

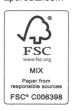

by Yannick Grotholt

Writer

Comicon

Artist

New York

LEGO ® LEGENDS OF CHIMA
#6 "Playing With Fire"
Yannick Grotholt – Writer
Comicon (Pencils: Miguel Sanchez, Inks: Marc Alberich, Color: Oriol San Julian) – Artist
Tom Orzechowski – Letterer
Asante Simons, Emily Wixted – Editorial Interns
Jeff Whitman – Production Coordinator
Bethany Bryan – Associate Editor
Jim Salicrup
Editor-in-Chief

ISBN: 978-1-62991-457-2 paperback edition
ISBN: 978-1-62991-458-9 hardcover edition

Printed in Hong Kong
January 2016 by Asia One Printing LTD
13/F Asia One Tower
8 Fung Yip St., Chaiwan
Hong Kong

Papercutz books may be purchased for business or promotional use.
For information on bulk purchases please contact Macmillan Corporate
and Premium Sales Department at (800) 221-7945 x5442.

Distributed by Macmillan
First Papercutz Printing

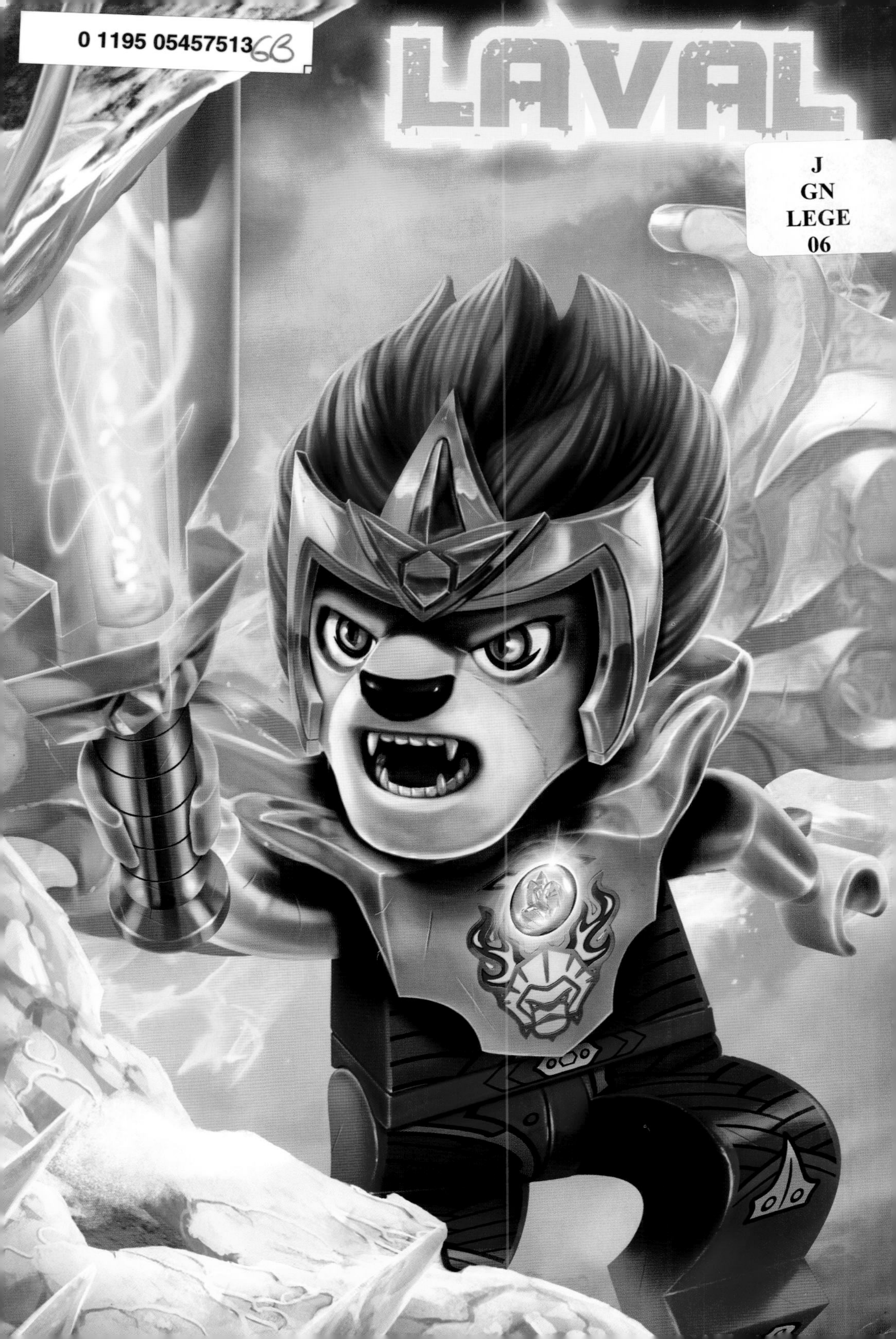
LAVAL

The Hunt for TORMAK

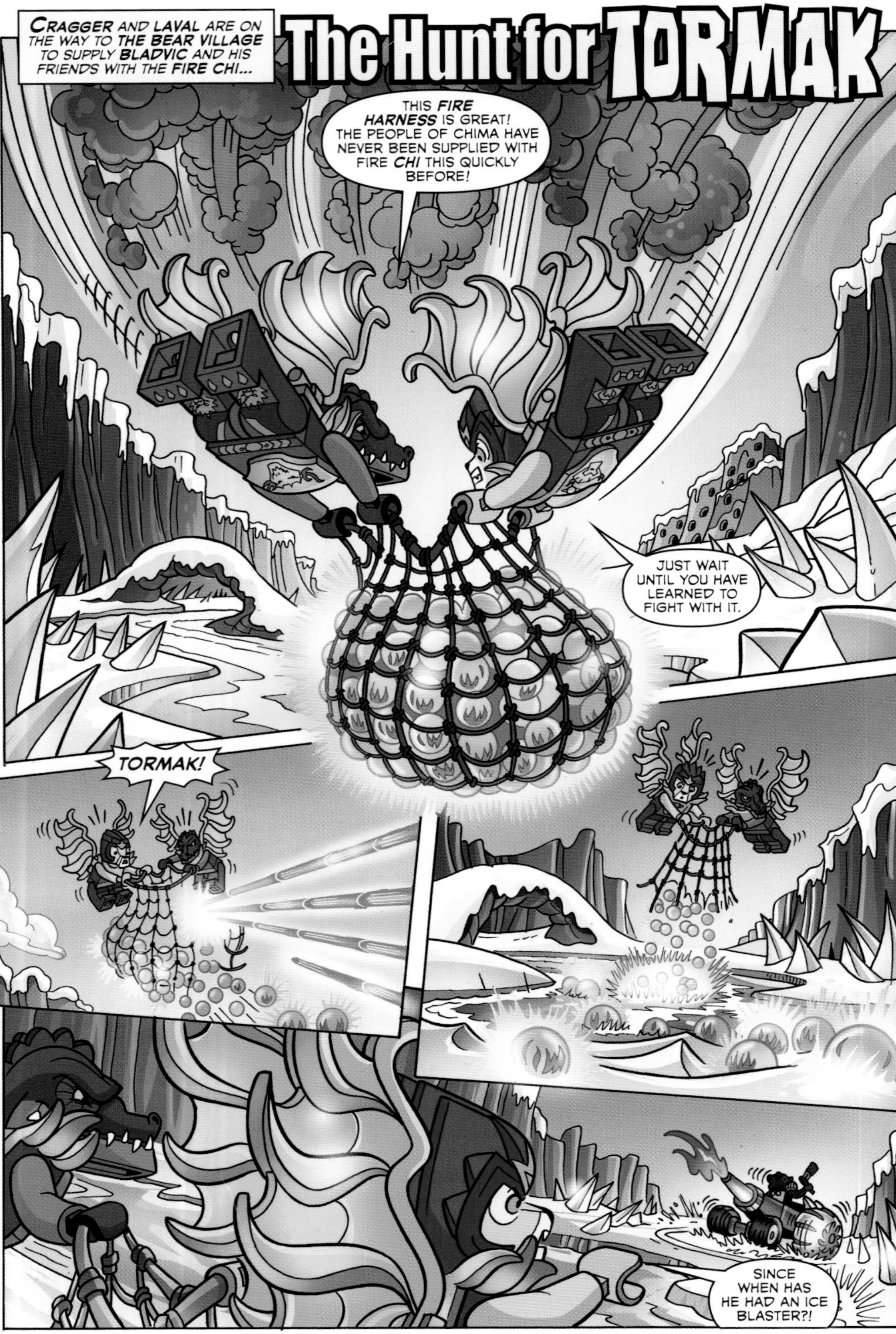

CRAGGER AND LAVAL ARE ON THE WAY TO THE BEAR VILLAGE TO SUPPLY BLADVIC AND HIS FRIENDS WITH THE FIRE CHI...
THIS FIRE HARNESS IS GREAT! THE PEOPLE OF CHIMA HAVE NEVER BEEN SUPPLIED WITH FIRE CHI THIS QUICKLY BEFORE!
JUST WAIT UNTIL YOU HAVE LEARNED TO FIGHT WITH IT.
TORMAK!
SINCE WHEN HAS HE HAD AN ICE BLASTER?!

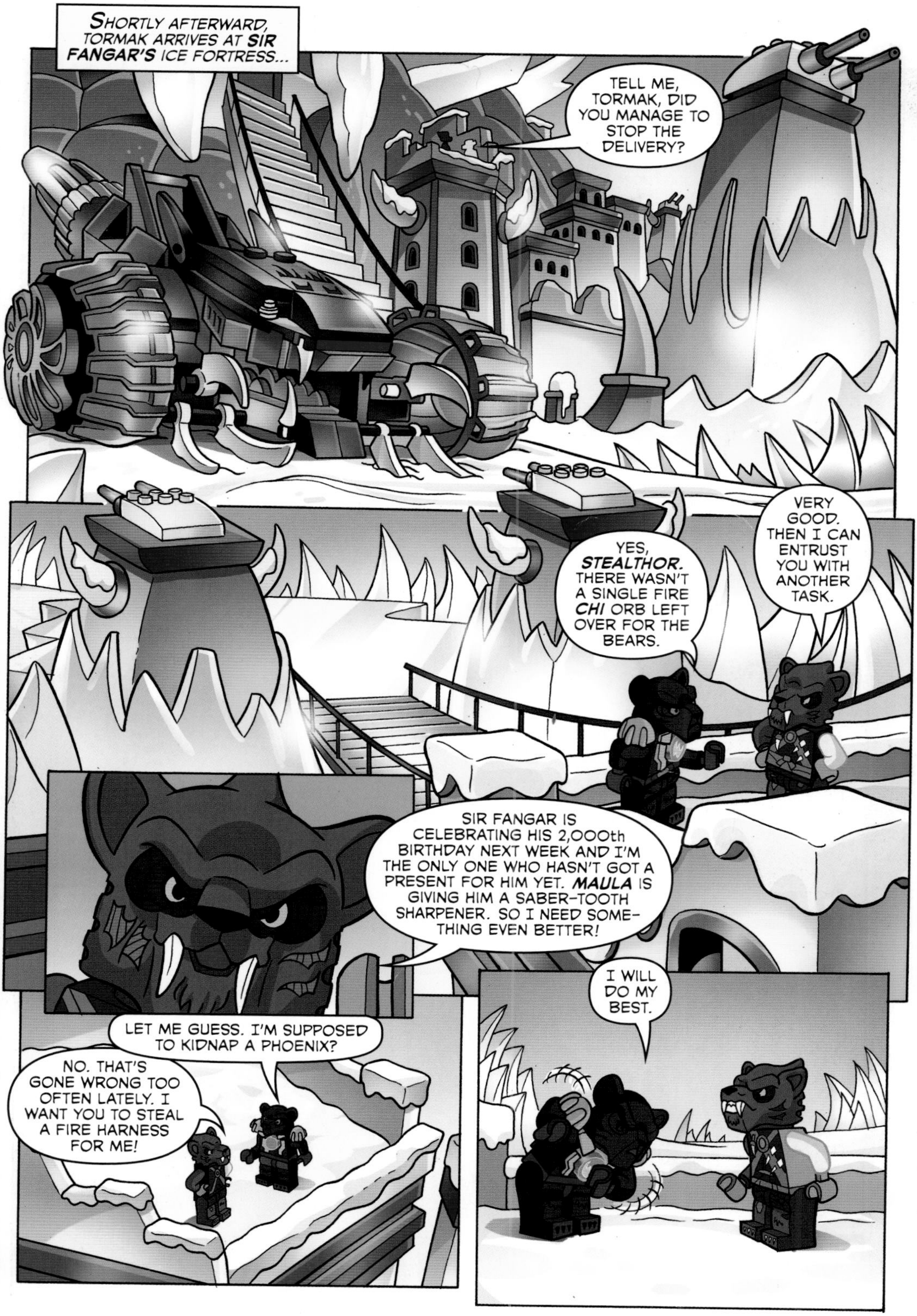

SHORTLY AFTERWARD, TORMAK ARRIVES AT SIR FANGAR'S ICE FORTRESS...
TELL ME, TORMAK, DID YOU MANAGE TO STOP THE DELIVERY?
YES, STEALTHOR. THERE WASN'T A SINGLE FIRE CHI ORB LEFT OVER FOR THE BEARS.
VERY GOOD. THEN I CAN ENTRUST YOU WITH ANOTHER TASK.
SIR FANGAR IS CELEBRATING HIS 2,000th BIRTHDAY NEXT WEEK AND I'M THE ONLY ONE WHO HASN'T GOT A PRESENT FOR HIM YET. MAULA IS GIVING HIM A SABER-TOOTH SHARPENER. SO I NEED SOMETHING EVEN BETTER!
LET ME GUESS. I'M SUPPOSED TO KIDNAP A PHOENIX?
NO. THAT'S GONE WRONG TOO OFTEN LATELY. I WANT YOU TO STEAL A FIRE HARNESS FOR ME!
I WILL DO MY BEST.

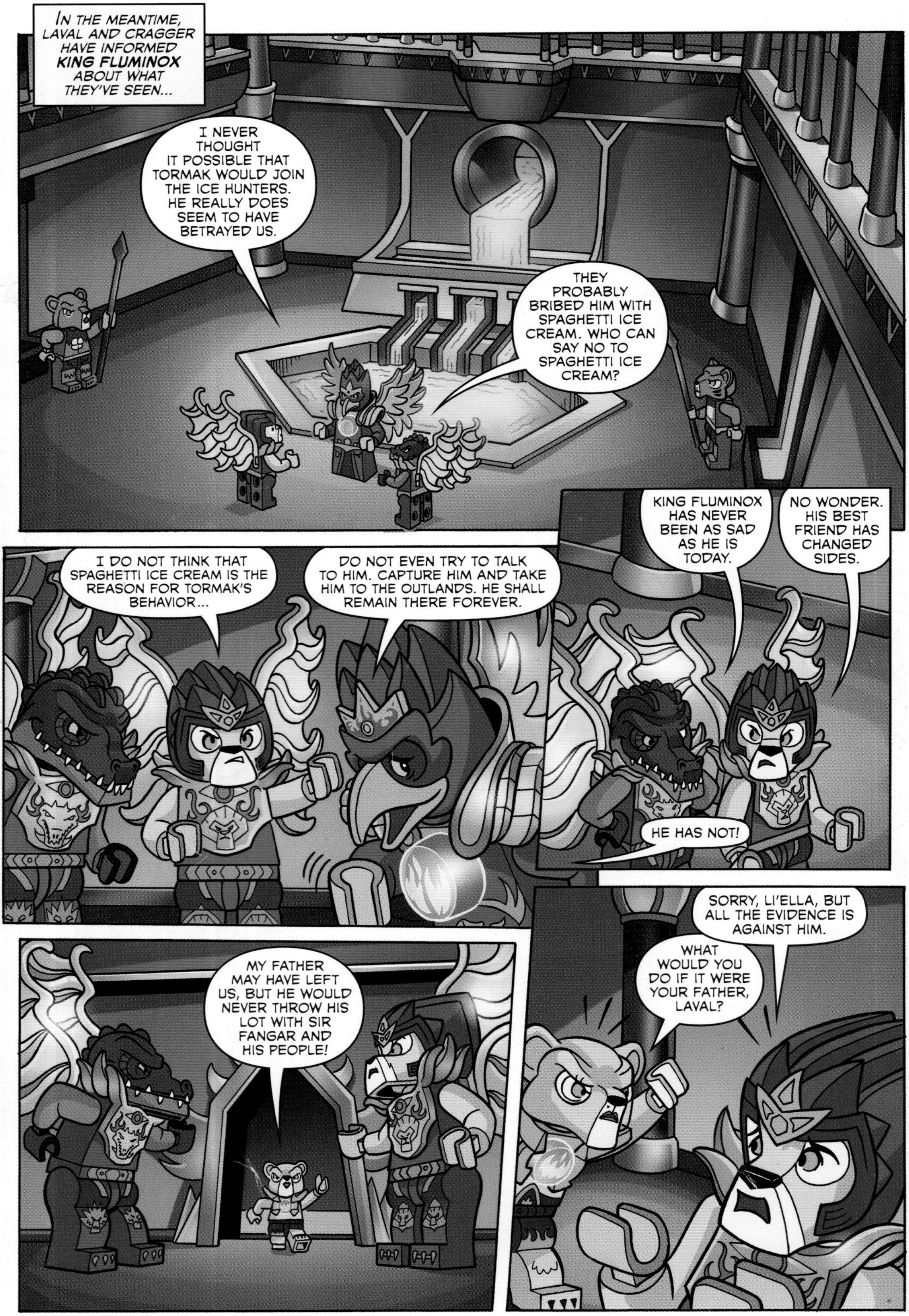

IN THE MEANTIME, LAVAL AND CRAGGER HAVE INFORMED **KING FLUMINOX** ABOUT WHAT THEY'VE SEEN...
I NEVER THOUGHT IT POSSIBLE THAT TORMAK WOULD JOIN THE ICE HUNTERS. HE REALLY DOES SEEM TO HAVE BETRAYED US.
THEY PROBABLY BRIBED HIM WITH SPAGHETTI ICE CREAM. WHO CAN SAY NO TO SPAGHETTI ICE CREAM?
I DO NOT THINK THAT SPAGHETTI ICE CREAM IS THE REASON FOR TORMAK'S BEHAVIOR...
DO NOT EVEN TRY TO TALK TO HIM. CAPTURE HIM AND TAKE HIM TO THE OUTLANDS. HE SHALL REMAIN THERE FOREVER.
KING FLUMINOX HAS NEVER BEEN AS SAD AS HE IS TODAY.
NO WONDER. HIS BEST FRIEND HAS CHANGED SIDES.
HE HAS NOT!
MY FATHER MAY HAVE LEFT US, BUT HE WOULD NEVER THROW HIS LOT WITH SIR FANGAR AND HIS PEOPLE!
SORRY, LI'ELLA, BUT ALL THE EVIDENCE IS AGAINST HIM.
WHAT WOULD YOU DO IF IT WERE YOUR FATHER, LAVAL?

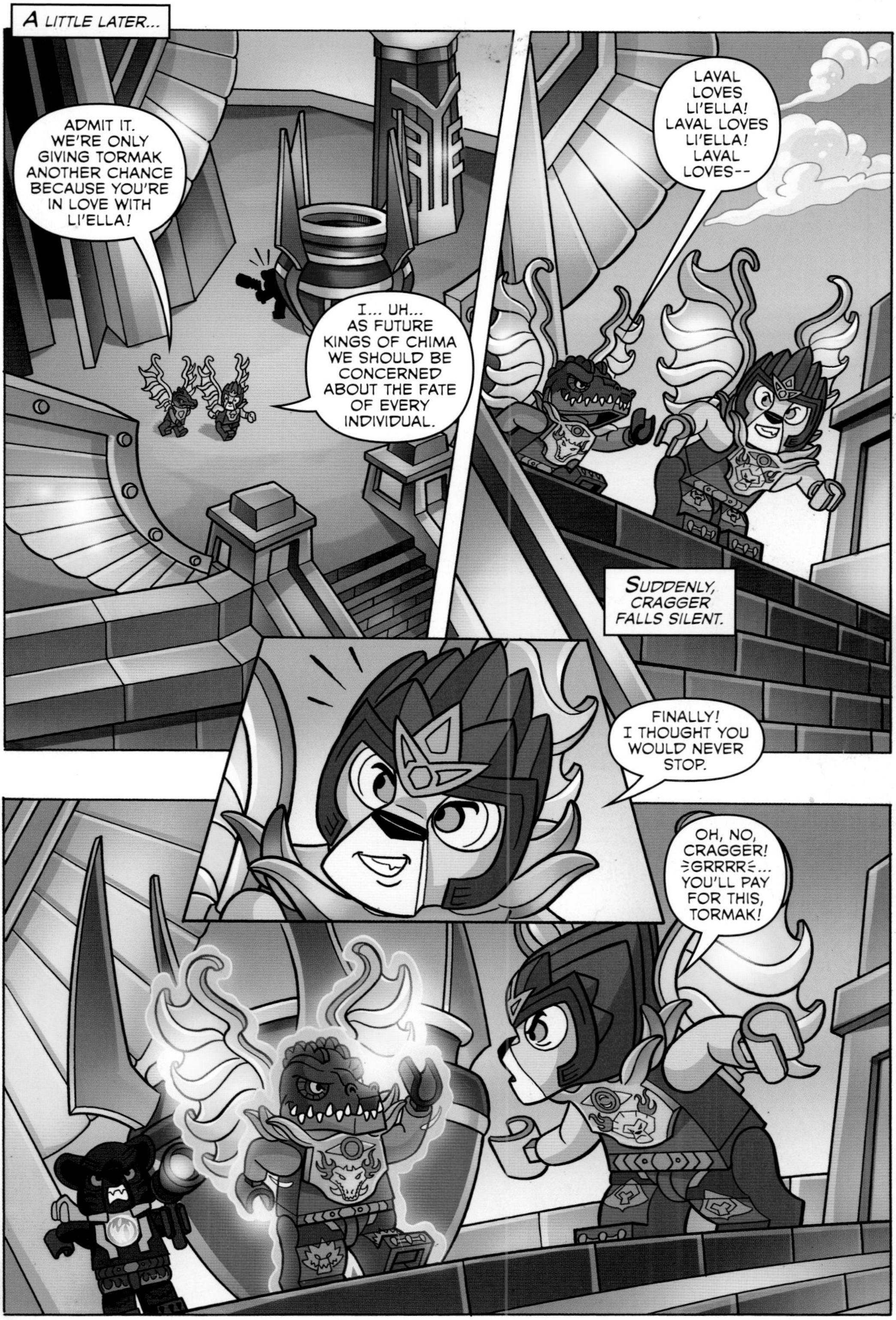
A LITTLE LATER...
ADMIT IT. WE'RE ONLY GIVING TORMAK ANOTHER CHANCE BECAUSE YOU'RE IN LOVE WITH LI'ELLA!
I... UH... AS FUTURE KINGS OF CHIMA WE SHOULD BE CONCERNED ABOUT THE FATE OF EVERY INDIVIDUAL.
LAVAL LOVES LI'ELLA! LAVAL LOVES LI'ELLA! LAVAL LOVES--
SUDDENLY, CRAGGER FALLS SILENT.
FINALLY! I THOUGHT YOU WOULD NEVER STOP.
OH, NO, CRAGGER! ≡GRRRR≡... YOU'LL PAY FOR THIS, TORMAK!

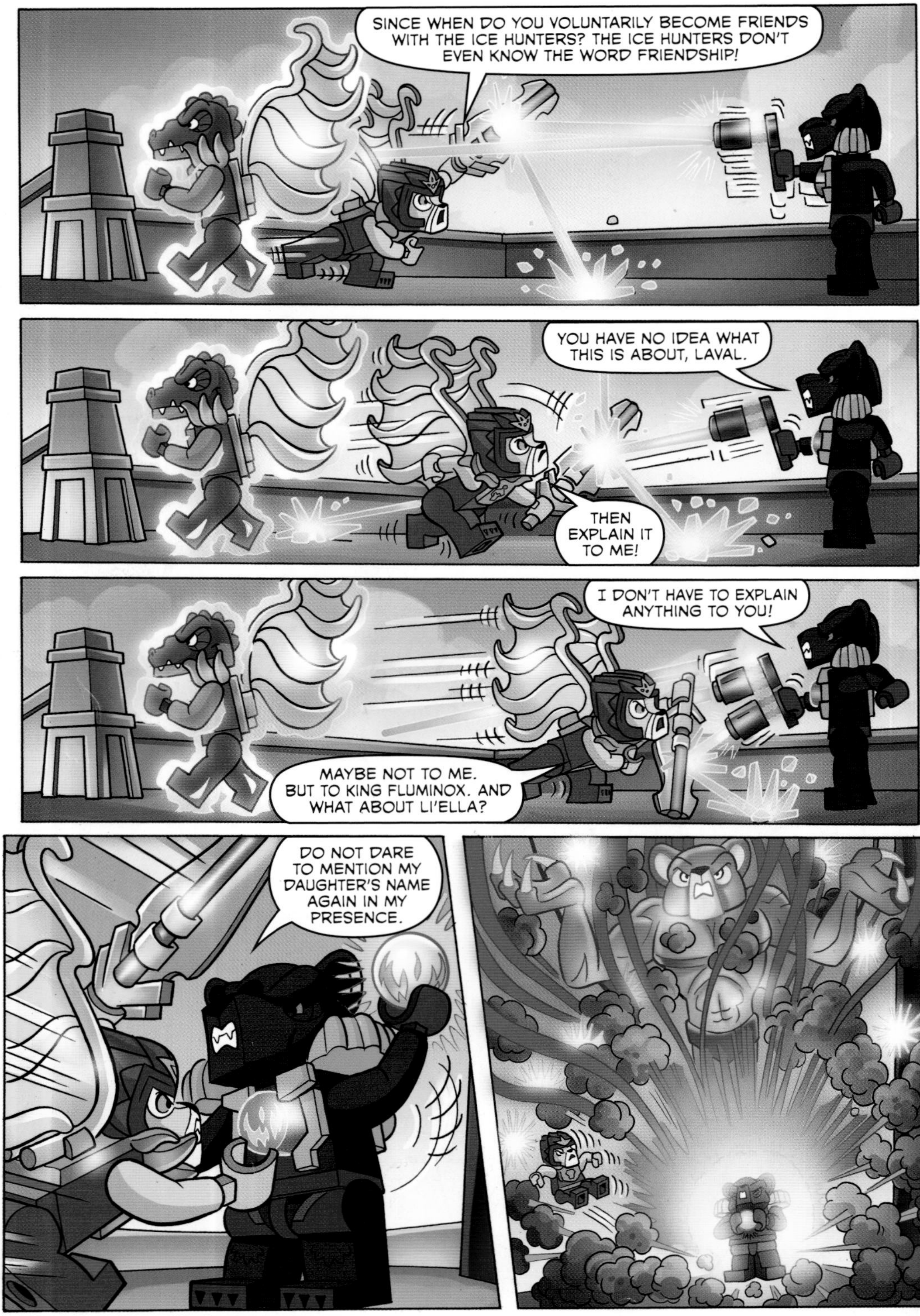
SINCE WHEN DO YOU VOLUNTARILY BECOME FRIENDS WITH THE ICE HUNTERS? THE ICE HUNTERS DON'T EVEN KNOW THE WORD FRIENDSHIP!
YOU HAVE NO IDEA WHAT THIS IS ABOUT, LAVAL.
THEN EXPLAIN IT TO ME!
I DON'T HAVE TO EXPLAIN ANYTHING TO YOU!
MAYBE NOT TO ME. BUT TO KING FLUMINOX. AND WHAT ABOUT LI'ELLA?
DO NOT DARE TO MENTION MY DAUGHTER'S NAME AGAIN IN MY PRESENCE.

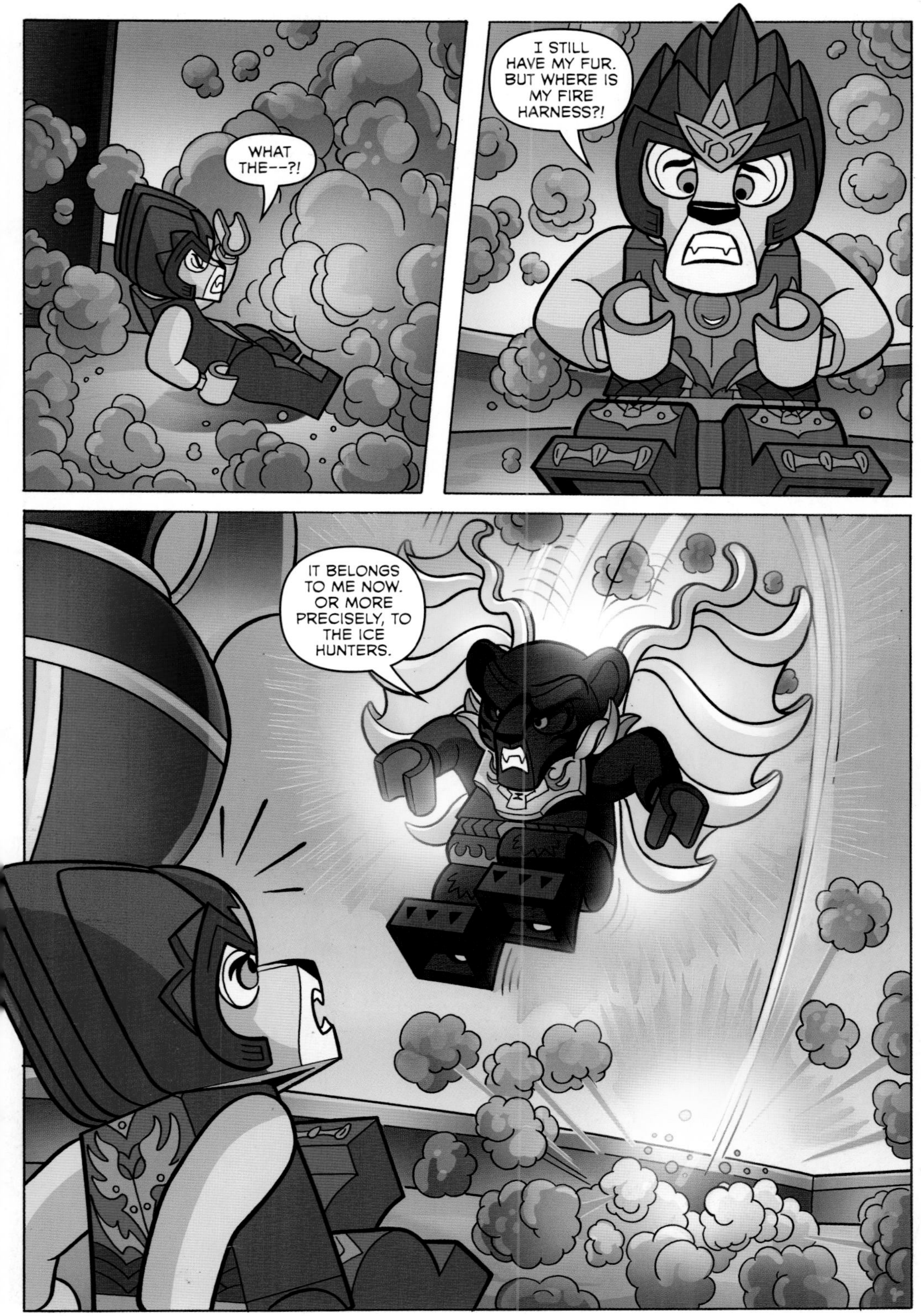
WHAT THE--?!
I STILL HAVE MY FUR. BUT WHERE IS MY FIRE HARNESS?!
IT BELONGS TO ME NOW. OR MORE PRECISELY, TO THE ICE HUNTERS.

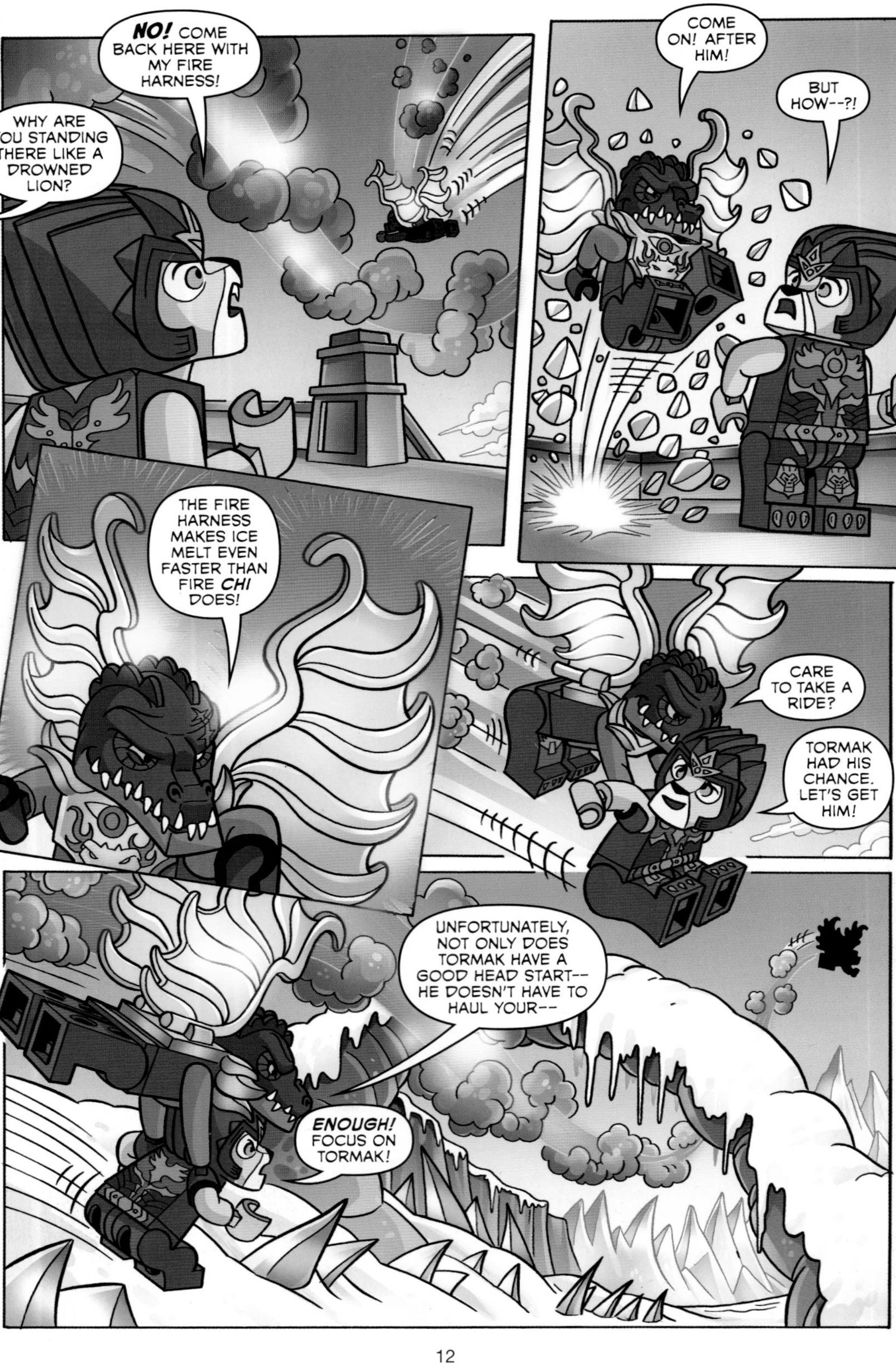
NO! COME BACK HERE WITH MY FIRE HARNESS!
WHY ARE YOU STANDING THERE LIKE A DROWNED LION?
COME ON! AFTER HIM!
BUT HOW--?!
THE FIRE HARNESS MAKES ICE MELT EVEN FASTER THAN FIRE CHI DOES!
CARE TO TAKE A RIDE?
TORMAK HAD HIS CHANCE. LET'S GET HIM!
UNFORTUNATELY, NOT ONLY DOES TORMAK HAVE A GOOD HEAD START-- HE DOESN'T HAVE TO HAUL YOUR--
ENOUGH! FOCUS ON TORMAK!

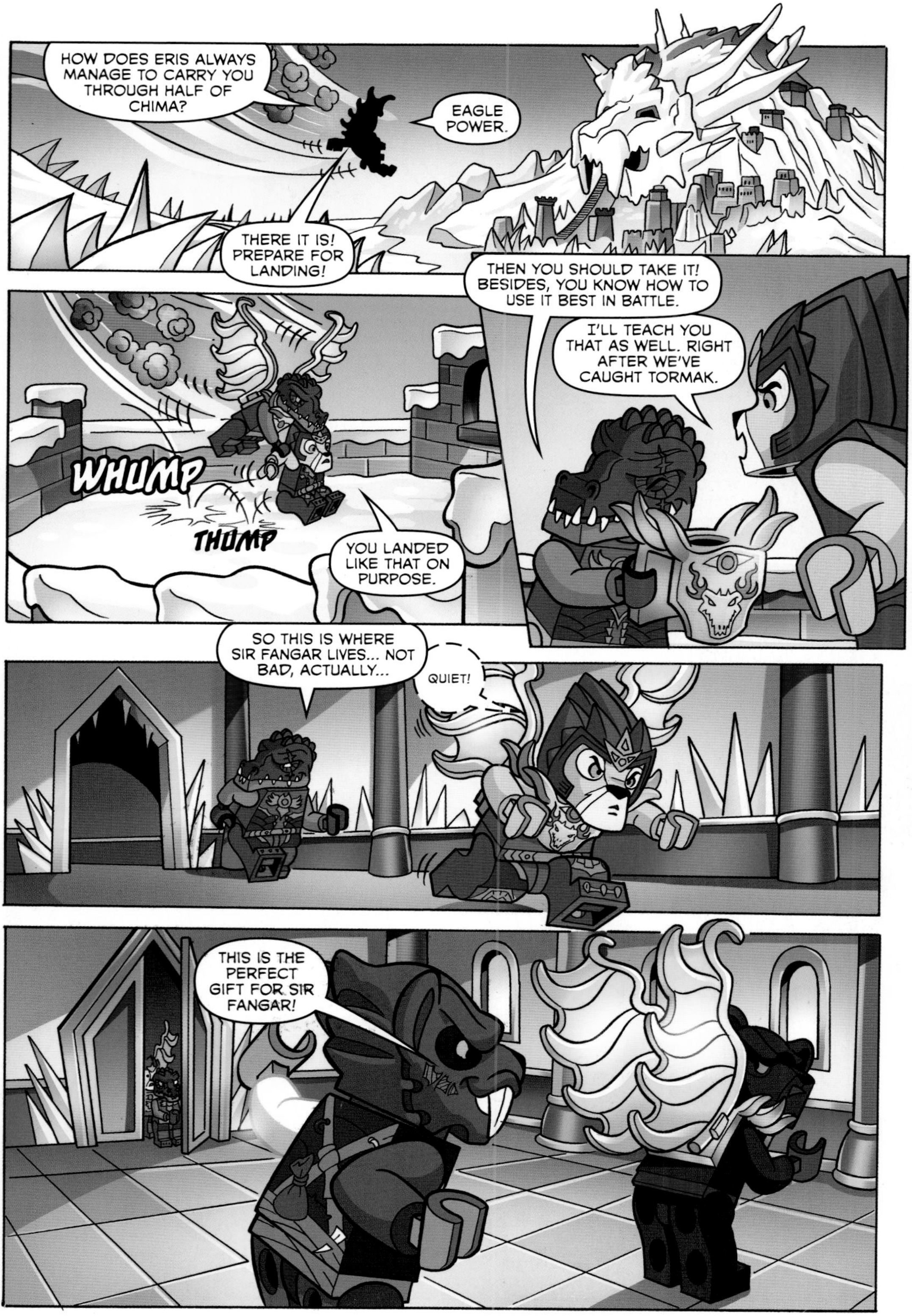
HOW DOES ERIS ALWAYS MANAGE TO CARRY YOU THROUGH HALF OF CHIMA?
EAGLE POWER.
THERE IT IS! PREPARE FOR LANDING!
WHUMP
THUMP
YOU LANDED LIKE THAT ON PURPOSE.
THEN YOU SHOULD TAKE IT! BESIDES, YOU KNOW HOW TO USE IT BEST IN BATTLE.
I'LL TEACH YOU THAT AS WELL. RIGHT AFTER WE'VE CAUGHT TORMAK.
SO THIS IS WHERE SIR FANGAR LIVES... NOT BAD, ACTUALLY...
QUIET!
THIS IS THE PERFECT GIFT FOR SIR FANGAR!

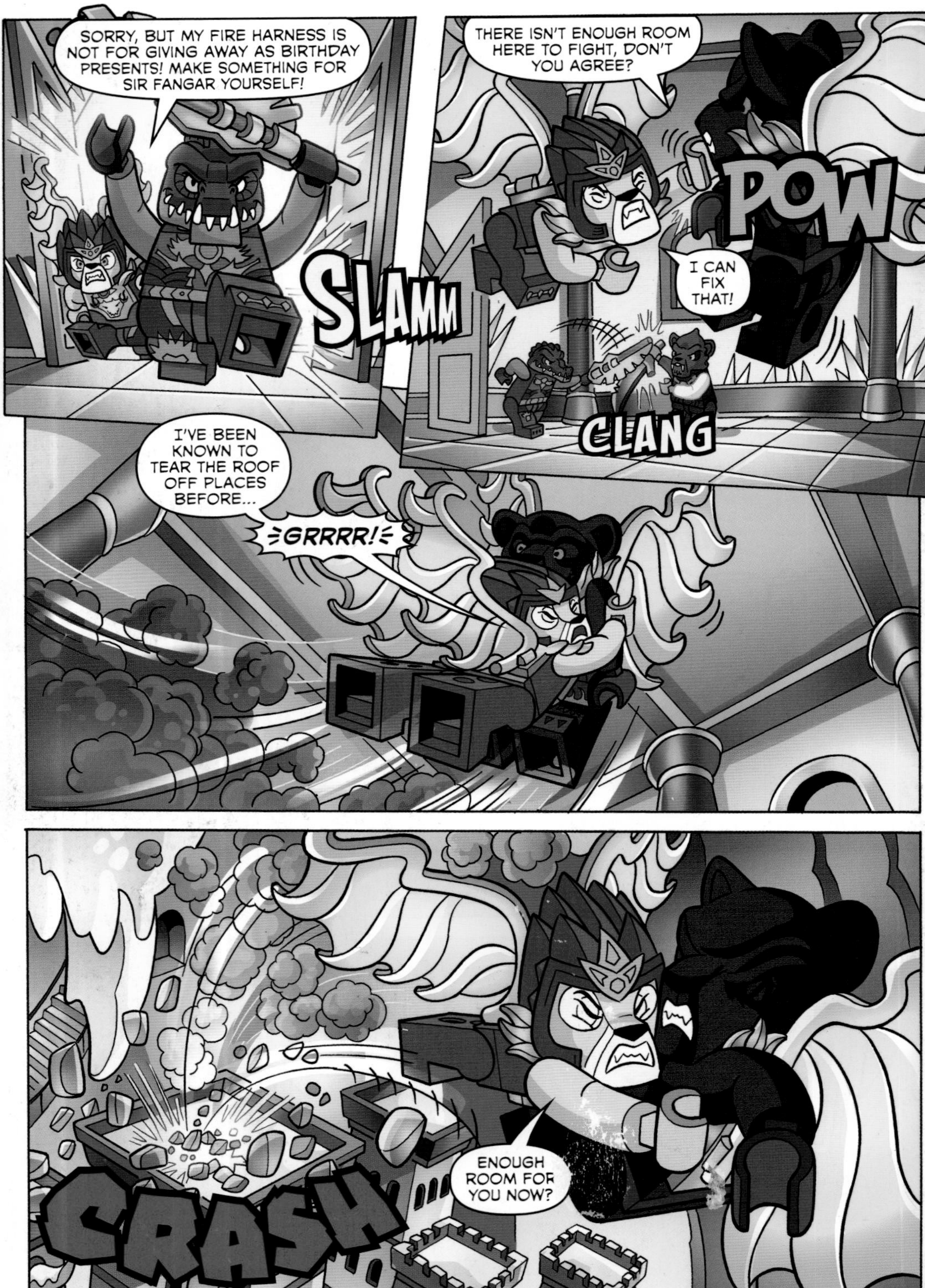
SORRY, BUT MY FIRE HARNESS IS NOT FOR GIVING AWAY AS BIRTHDAY PRESENTS! MAKE SOMETHING FOR SIR FANGAR YOURSELF!
SLAMM
THERE ISN'T ENOUGH ROOM HERE TO FIGHT, DON'T YOU AGREE?
POW
I CAN FIX THAT!
CLANG
I'VE BEEN KNOWN TO TEAR THE ROOF OFF PLACES BEFORE...
GRRRR!
CRASH
ENOUGH ROOM FOR YOU NOW?

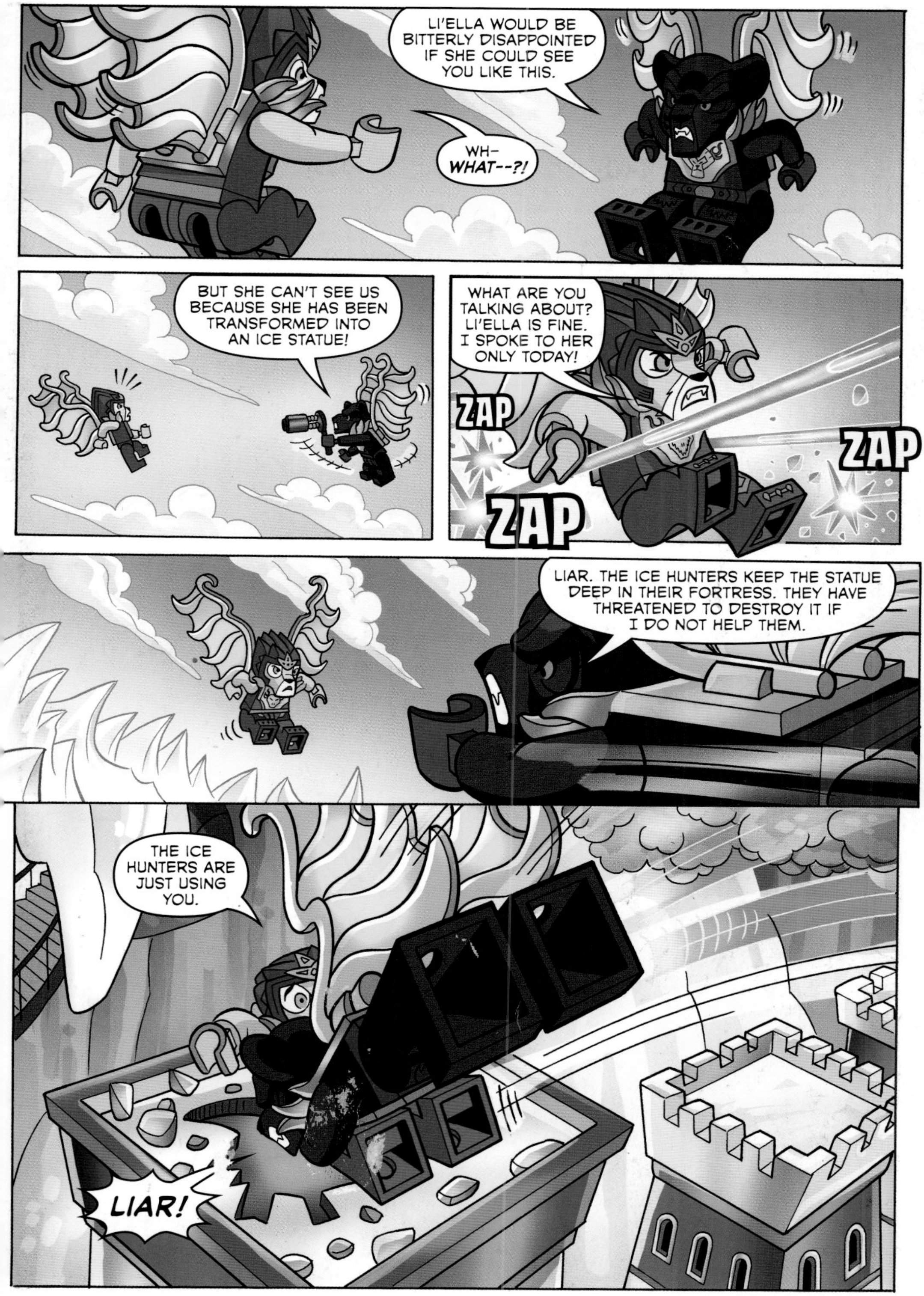

LI'ELLA WOULD BE BITTERLY DISAPPOINTED IF SHE COULD SEE YOU LIKE THIS.
WH- WHAT--?!
BUT SHE CAN'T SEE US BECAUSE SHE HAS BEEN TRANSFORMED INTO AN ICE STATUE!
WHAT ARE YOU TALKING ABOUT? LI'ELLA IS FINE. I SPOKE TO HER ONLY TODAY!
ZAP
ZAP
ZAP
LIAR. THE ICE HUNTERS KEEP THE STATUE DEEP IN THEIR FORTRESS. THEY HAVE THREATENED TO DESTROY IT IF I DO NOT HELP THEM.
THE ICE HUNTERS ARE JUST USING YOU.
LIAR!

TAKE A CLOSER LOOK. THAT IS NOT LI'ELLA!

WHAT... WHAT HAVE I DONE?

LAVAL, WE SHOULD GET OUT OF HERE. I ASKED FOR SPAGHETTI ICE CREAM, AND NOW THERE ARE TWENTY SABER-TOOTH TIGERS AFTER ME!

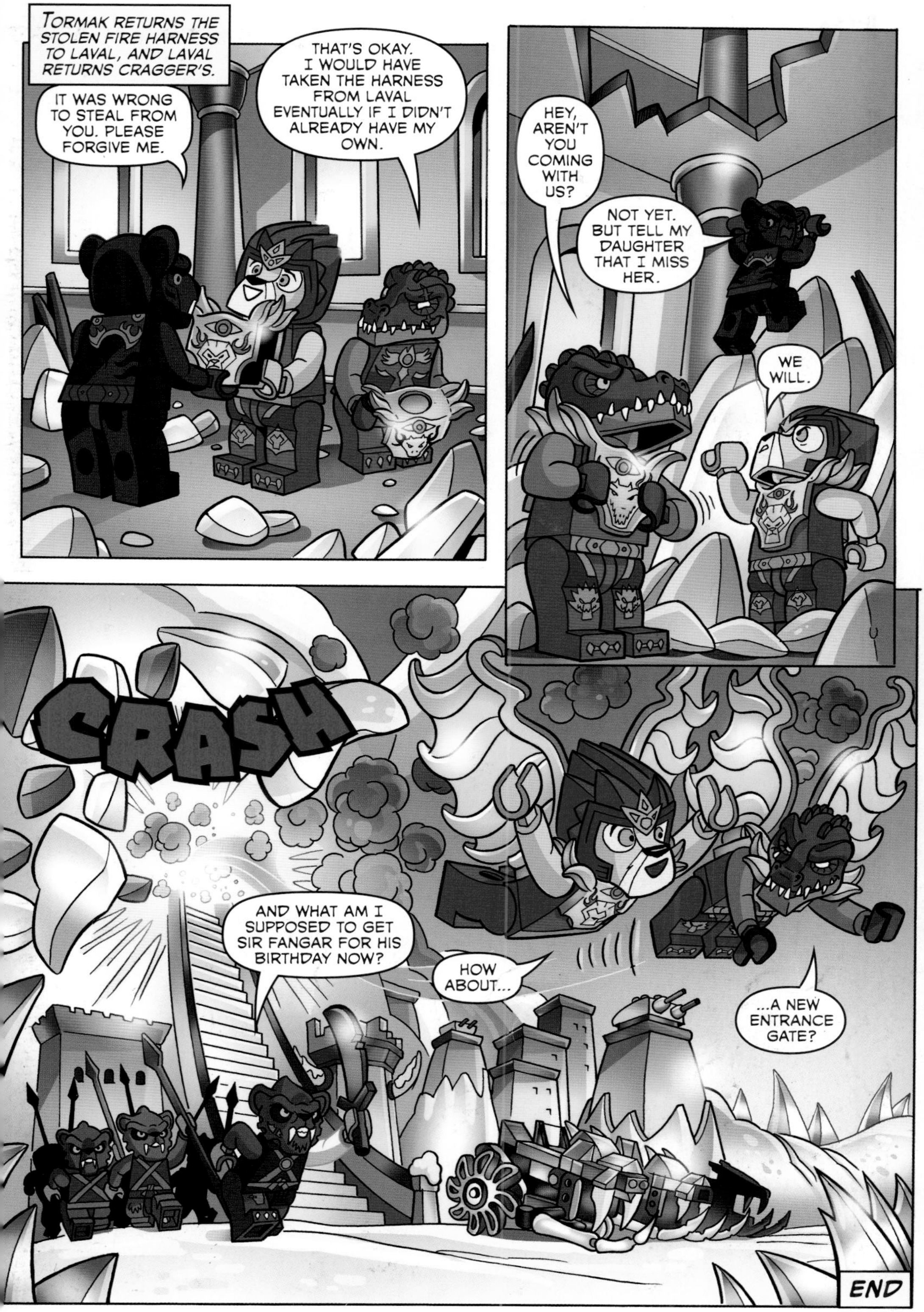
TORMAK RETURNS THE STOLEN FIRE HARNESS TO LAVAL, AND LAVAL RETURNS CRAGGER'S.
IT WAS WRONG TO STEAL FROM YOU. PLEASE FORGIVE ME.
THAT'S OKAY. I WOULD HAVE TAKEN THE HARNESS FROM LAVAL EVENTUALLY IF I DIDN'T ALREADY HAVE MY OWN.
HEY, AREN'T YOU COMING WITH US?
NOT YET. BUT TELL MY DAUGHTER THAT I MISS HER.
WE WILL.
CRASH
AND WHAT AM I SUPPOSED TO GET SIR FANGAR FOR HIS BIRTHDAY NOW?
HOW ABOUT...
...A NEW ENTRANCE GATE?
END

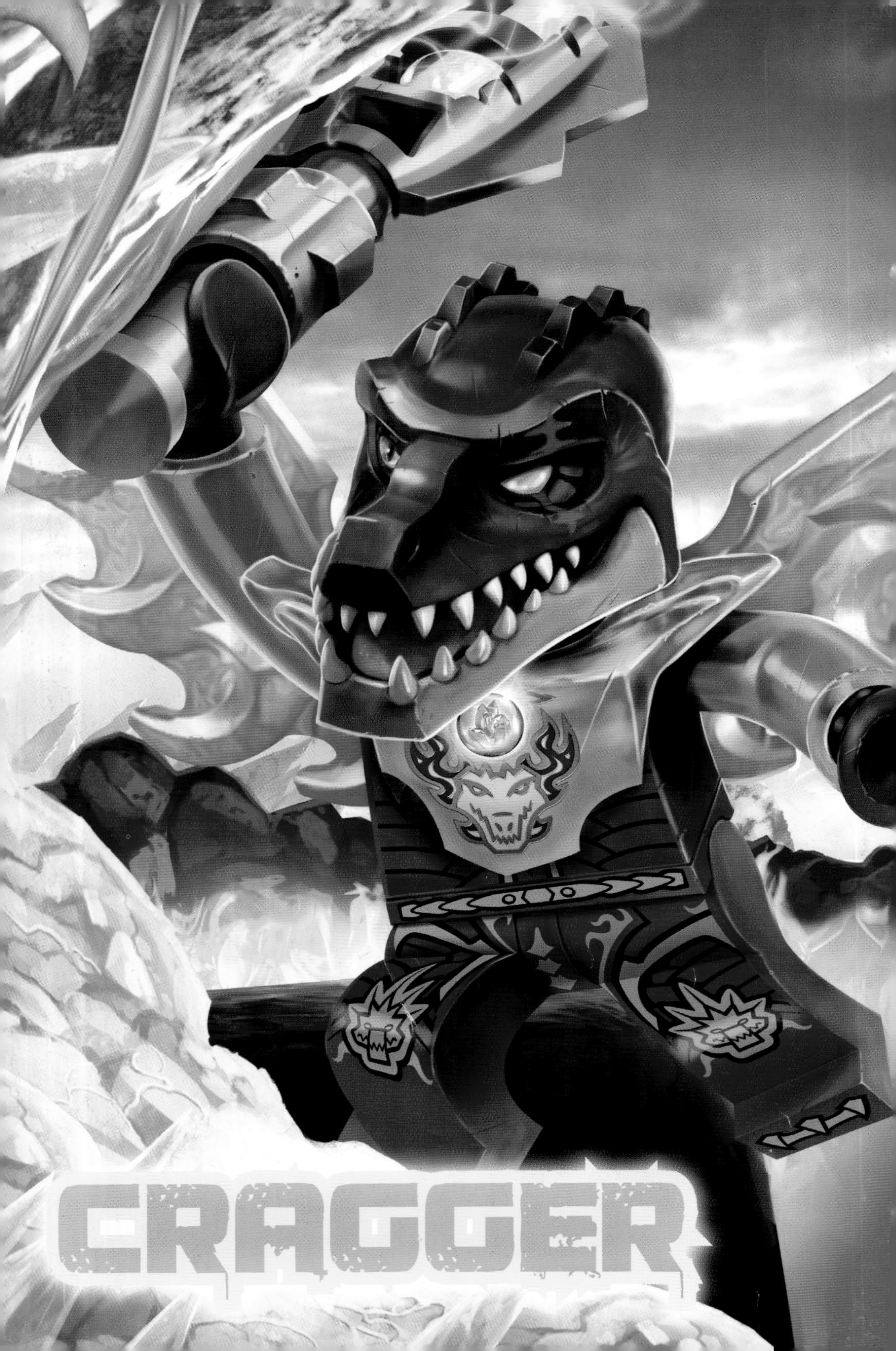
CRAGGER

The Great Illumination

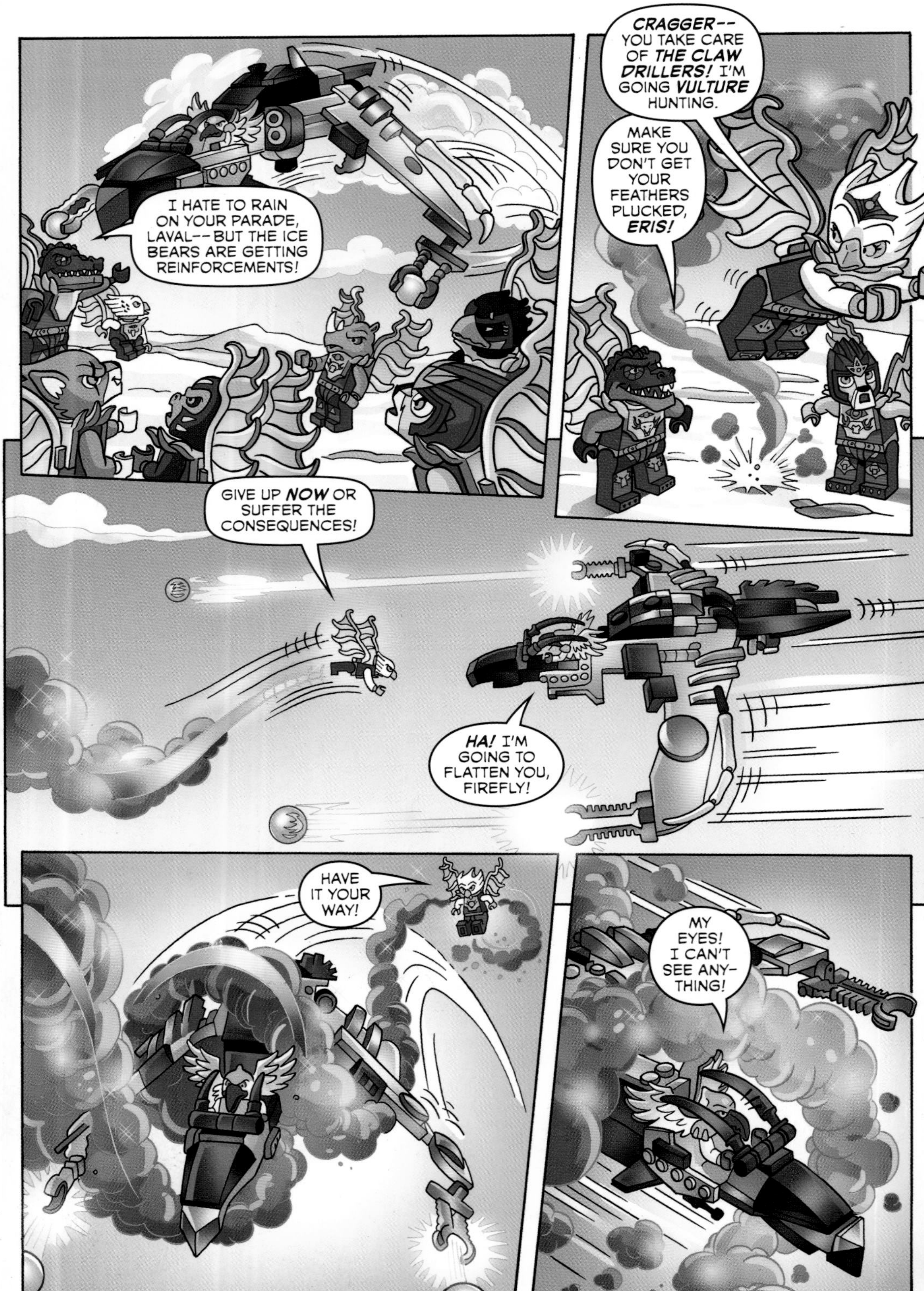
I HATE TO RAIN ON YOUR PARADE, LAVAL--BUT THE ICE BEARS ARE GETTING REINFORCEMENTS!
CRAGGER-- YOU TAKE CARE OF THE CLAW DRILLERS! I'M GOING VULTURE HUNTING.
MAKE SURE YOU DON'T GET YOUR FEATHERS PLUCKED, ERIS!
GIVE UP NOW OR SUFFER THE CONSEQUENCES!
HA! I'M GOING TO FLATTEN YOU, FIREFLY!
HAVE IT YOUR WAY!
MY EYES! I CAN'T SEE ANY-THING!

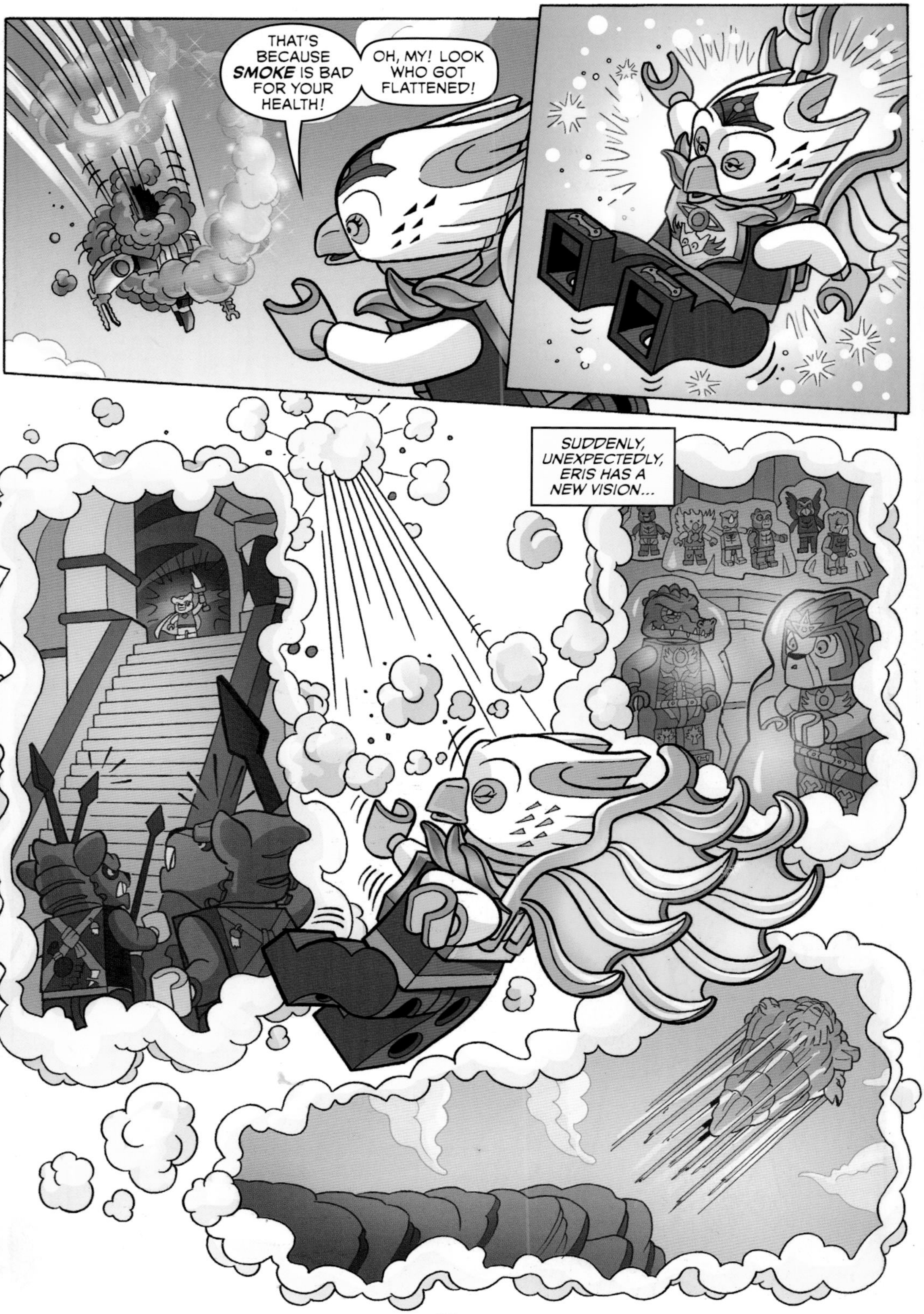
THAT'S BECAUSE SMOKE IS BAD FOR YOUR HEALTH!
OH, MY! LOOK WHO GOT FLATTENED!
SUDDENLY, UNEXPECTEDLY, ERIS HAS A NEW VISION...

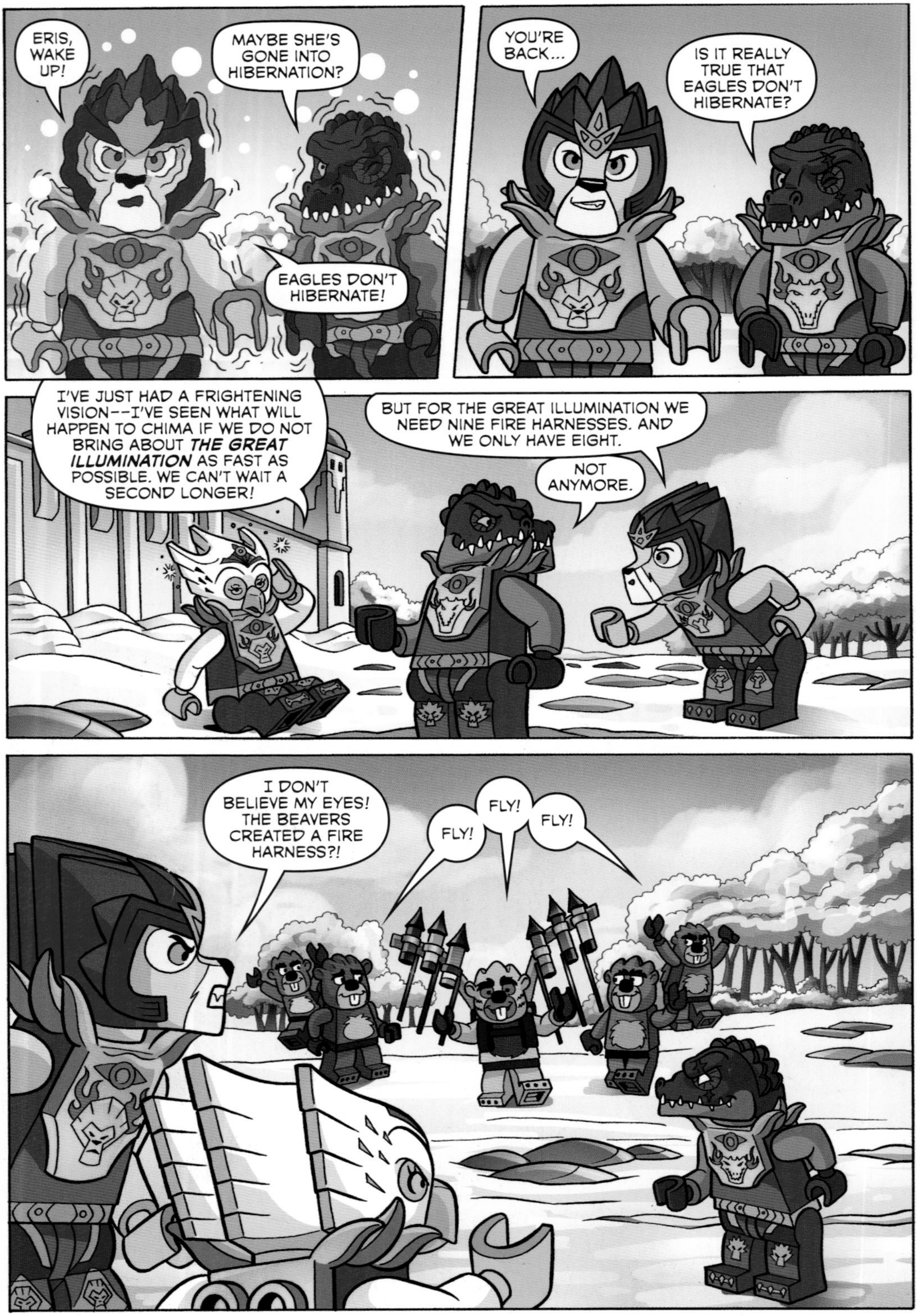
ERIS, WAKE UP!
MAYBE SHE'S GONE INTO HIBERNATION?
EAGLES DON'T HIBERNATE!
YOU'RE BACK...
IS IT REALLY TRUE THAT EAGLES DON'T HIBERNATE?
I'VE JUST HAD A FRIGHTENING VISION--I'VE SEEN WHAT WILL HAPPEN TO CHIMA IF WE DO NOT BRING ABOUT ***THE GREAT ILLUMINATION*** AS FAST AS POSSIBLE. WE CAN'T WAIT A SECOND LONGER!
BUT FOR THE GREAT ILLUMINATION WE NEED NINE FIRE HARNESSES. AND WE ONLY HAVE EIGHT.
NOT ANYMORE.
I DON'T BELIEVE MY EYES! THE BEAVERS CREATED A FIRE HARNESS?!
FLY!
FLY!
FLY!

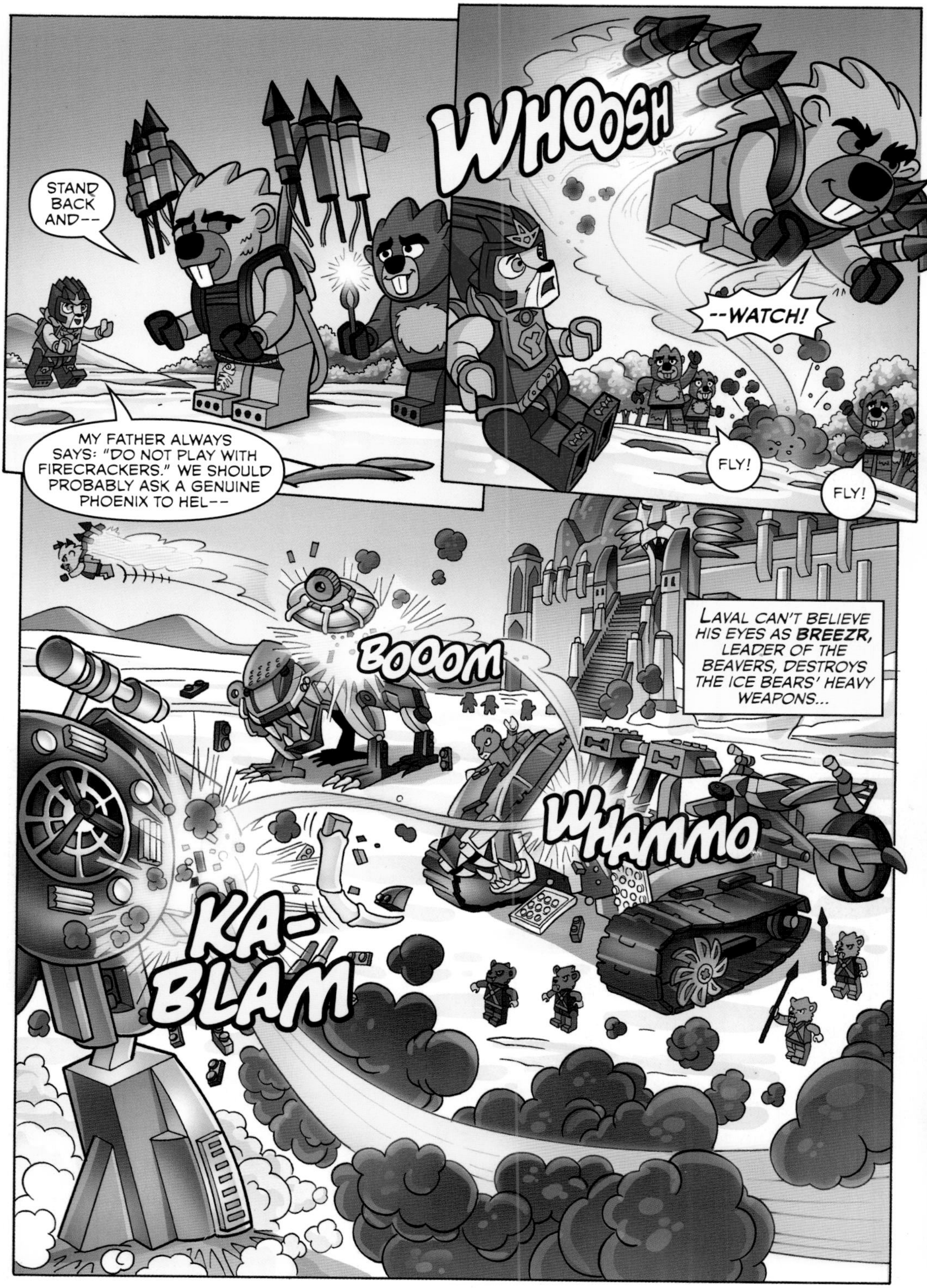

STAND BACK AND--
MY FATHER ALWAYS SAYS: "DO NOT PLAY WITH FIRECRACKERS." WE SHOULD PROBABLY ASK A GENUINE PHOENIX TO HEL--
WHOOSH
--WATCH!
FLY!
FLY!
LAVAL CAN'T BELIEVE HIS EYES AS BREEZR, LEADER OF THE BEAVERS, DESTROYS THE ICE BEARS' HEAVY WEAPONS...
BOOOM
WHAMMO
KA-BLAM

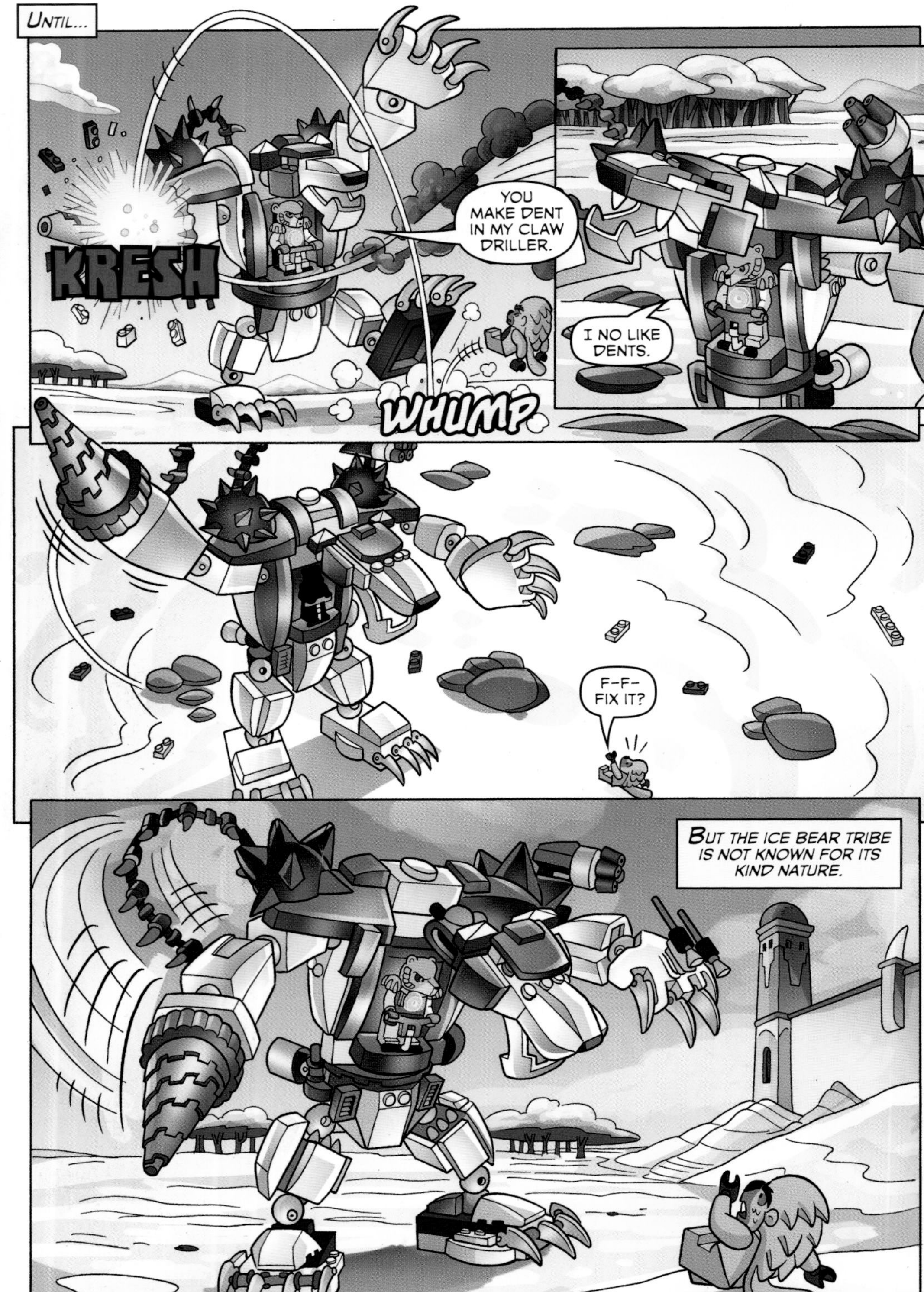
UNTIL...
KRESH
YOU MAKE DENT IN MY CLAW DRILLER.
WHUMP
I NO LIKE DENTS.
F-F-FIX IT?
BUT THE ICE BEAR TRIBE IS NOT KNOWN FOR ITS KIND NATURE.

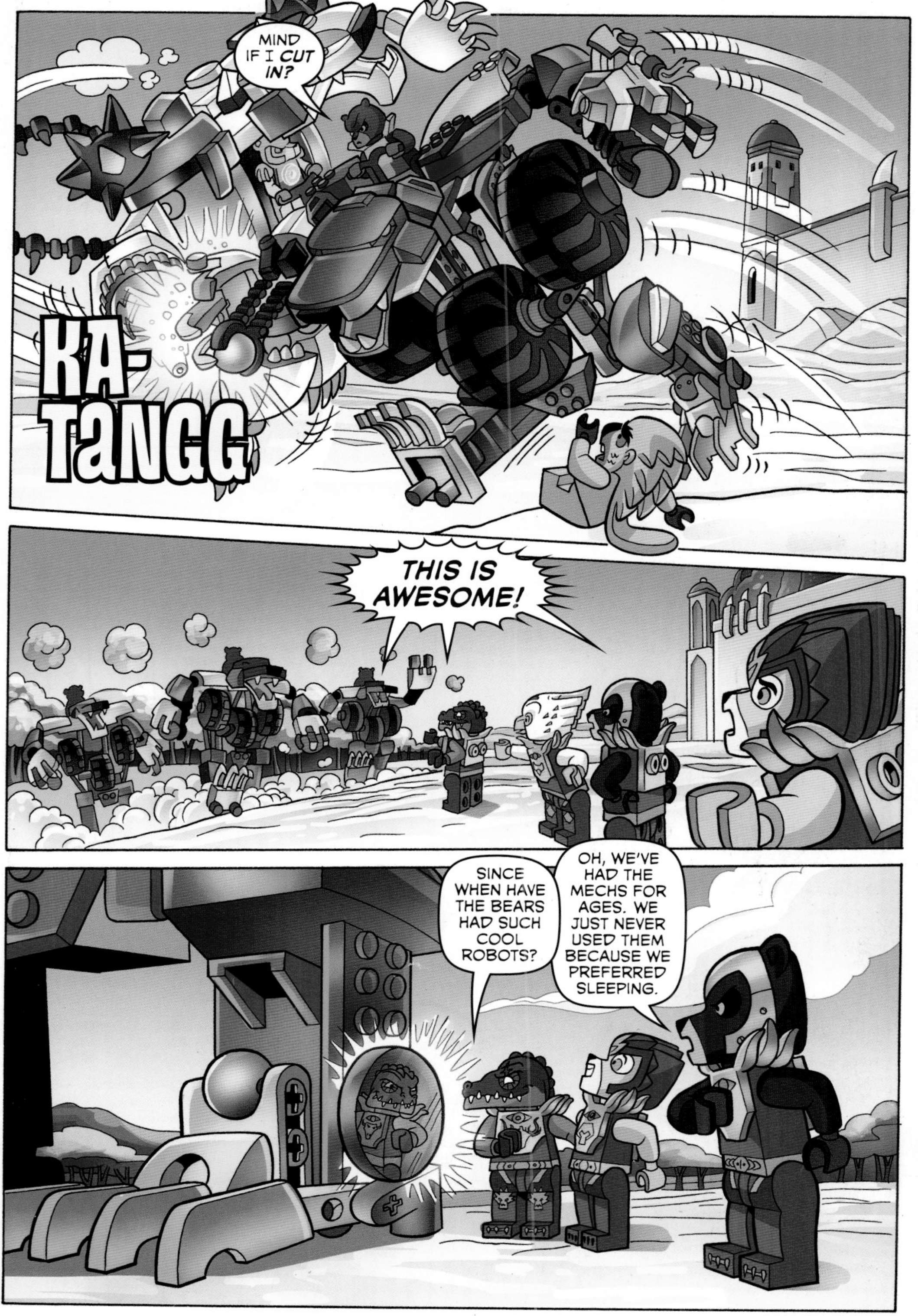
MIND IF I CUT IN?
KA-TANGG
THIS IS AWESOME!
SINCE WHEN HAVE THE BEARS HAD SUCH COOL ROBOTS?
OH, WE'VE HAD THE MECHS FOR AGES. WE JUST NEVER USED THEM BECAUSE WE PREFERRED SLEEPING.

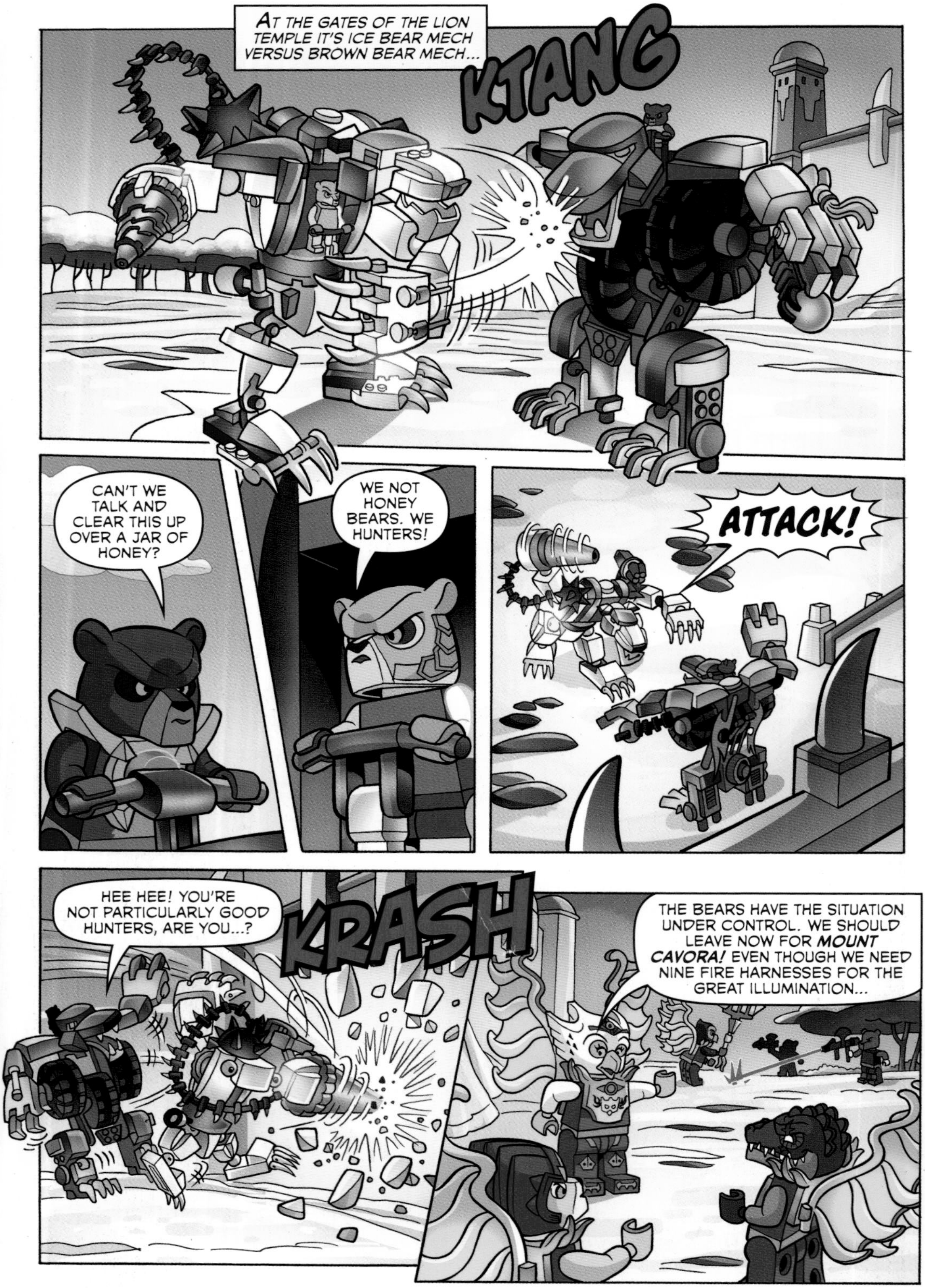
AT THE GATES OF THE LION TEMPLE IT'S ICE BEAR MECH VERSUS BROWN BEAR MECH...
KTANG
CAN'T WE TALK AND CLEAR THIS UP OVER A JAR OF HONEY?
WE NOT HONEY BEARS. WE HUNTERS!
ATTACK!
HEE HEE! YOU'RE NOT PARTICULARLY GOOD HUNTERS, ARE YOU...?
KRASH
THE BEARS HAVE THE SITUATION UNDER CONTROL. WE SHOULD LEAVE NOW FOR MOUNT CAVORA! EVEN THOUGH WE NEED NINE FIRE HARNESSES FOR THE GREAT ILLUMINATION...

"...WE SIMPLY HAVE TO MAKE DO WITH WHAT WE HAVE!"

SEE YOU ON THE OTHER SIDE, MY FRIENDS!

AAAAAHHH!

I WISH PHOENIX No. 9 WERE HERE NOW. THEN WE COULD FINALLY CLEAN UP PROPERLY!

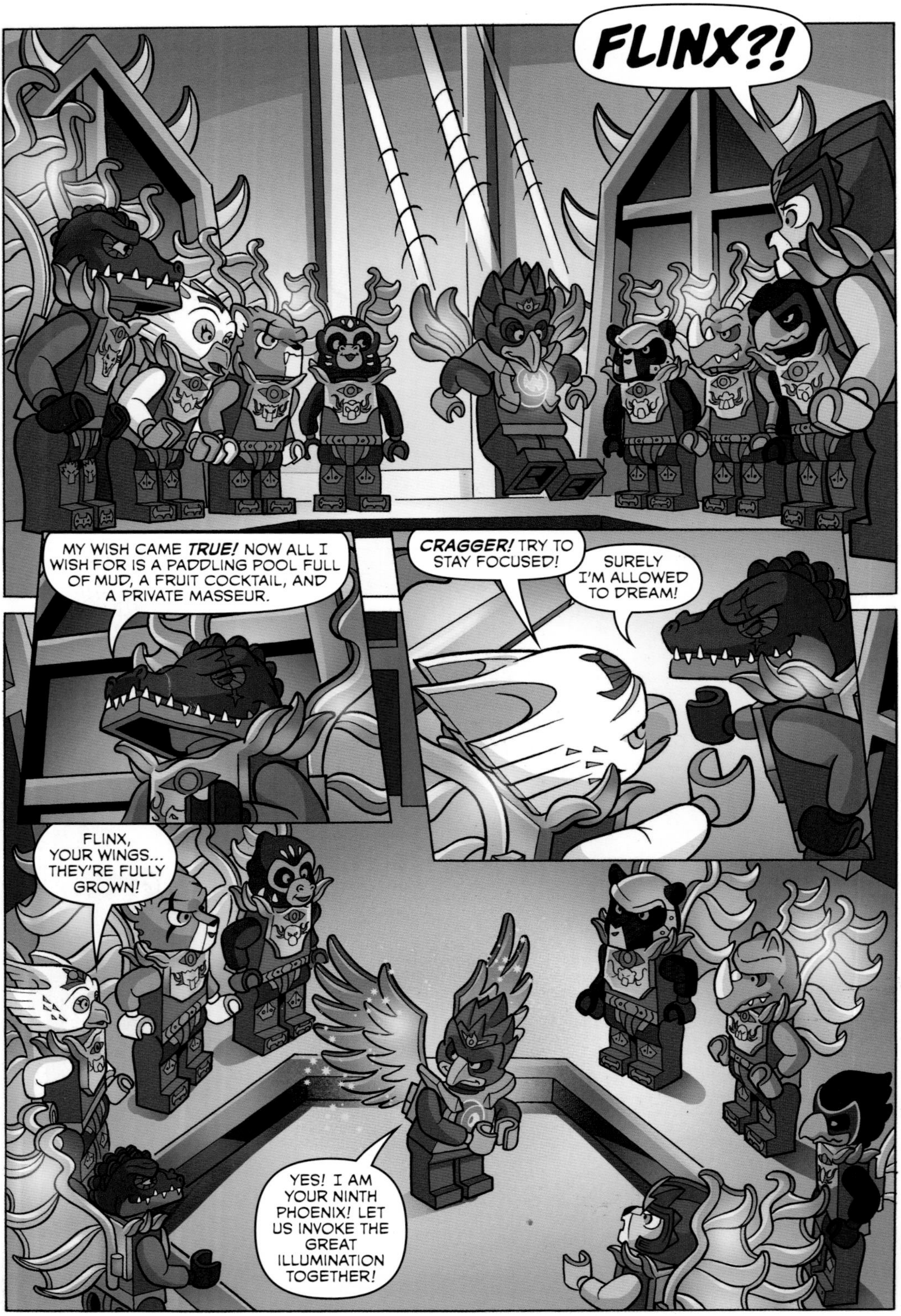
FLINX?!
MY WISH CAME TRUE! NOW ALL I WISH FOR IS A PADDLING POOL FULL OF MUD, A FRUIT COCKTAIL, AND A PRIVATE MASSEUR.
CRAGGER! TRY TO STAY FOCUSED!
SURELY I'M ALLOWED TO DREAM!
FLINX, YOUR WINGS... THEY'RE FULLY GROWN!
YES! I AM YOUR NINTH PHOENIX! LET US INVOKE THE GREAT ILLUMINATION TOGETHER!

TOGETHER WITH LAVAL AND HIS FRIENDS, FLINX INVOKES THE SPIRIT OF THE **LEGENDARY PHOENIX**...

...AND RELEASES CHIMA FROM ITS ICY PRISON.

THE WATERFALLS OF MOUNT CAVORA ARE FLOWING AGAIN...

...AND THE LION AND THE SABER-TOOTH TIGER JOIN HANDS.

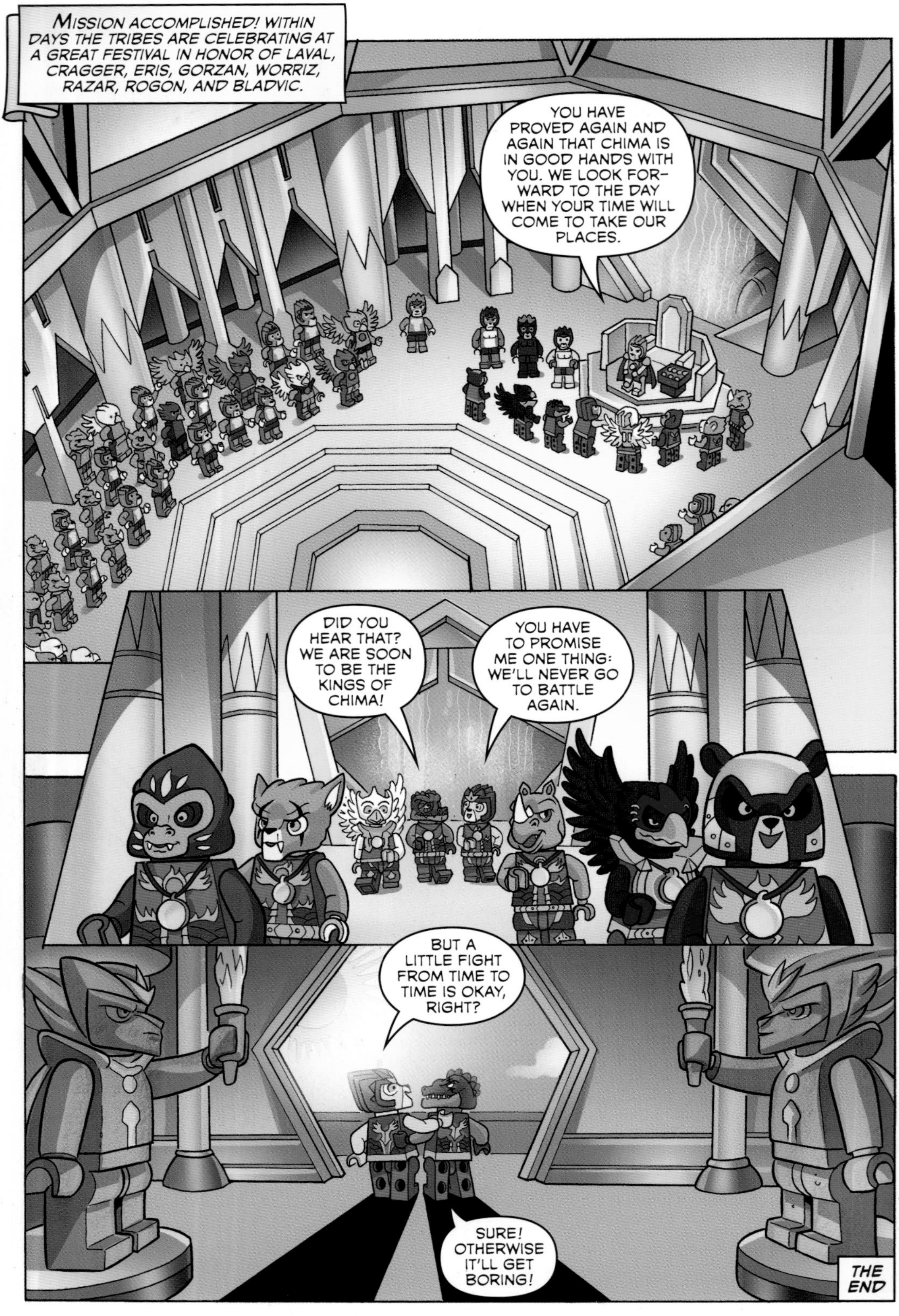
MISSION ACCOMPLISHED! WITHIN DAYS THE TRIBES ARE CELEBRATING AT A GREAT FESTIVAL IN HONOR OF LAVAL, CRAGGER, ERIS, GORZAN, WORRIZ, RAZAR, ROGON, AND BLADVIC.
YOU HAVE PROVED AGAIN AND AGAIN THAT CHIMA IS IN GOOD HANDS WITH YOU. WE LOOK FOR-WARD TO THE DAY WHEN YOUR TIME WILL COME TO TAKE OUR PLACES.
DID YOU HEAR THAT? WE ARE SOON TO BE THE KINGS OF CHIMA!
YOU HAVE TO PROMISE ME ONE THING: WE'LL NEVER GO TO BATTLE AGAIN.
BUT A LITTLE FIGHT FROM TIME TO TIME IS OKAY, RIGHT?
SURE! OTHERWISE IT'LL GET BORING!
THE END

WATCH OUT FOR PAPERCUTZ™

Welcome to the sizzling, yet somewhat shorter sixth and final (this time for sure!) LEGO ® LEGENDS OF CHIMA graphic novel, by Yannick Grotholt and Comicon, from Papercutz—those CHI-loving men and women dedicated to publishing great graphic novels for all ages. I'm Jim Salicrup, the slightly sobbing Editor-in-Chief and Greatly Illuminated! Why am I gently weeping? As George Harrison once sang, "All Things Must Pass," and unfortunately that applies to this series of LEGO LEGENDS OF CHIMA graphic novels as well. If you've read this column in the last two graphic novels, this won't be a surprise. We even thought it was all over with the fourth graphic novel, but the news of the LEGO LEGENDS OF CHIMA graphic novel series' end was a tad premature, and we survived for two more graphic novels. But, I'm afraid this is it.

But while Papercutz will no longer be publishing any new LEGO LEGENDS OF CHIMA graphic novels, we are publishing more exciting stuff than ever before. Just check us out on Papercutz.com for an idea of what other cool graphic novels we'll be publishing. Here's a short list of just the first few (A-C!) that are available now:

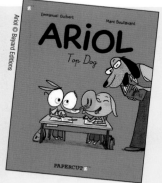

ANNOYING ORANGE – Based on the Internet sensation, enjoy comics by master cartoonists Mike Kazaleh and Scott Shaw!

ARIOL – He's just a donkey like you and me! This series is perfect for anyone who either is a kid or has been a kid at some point. Written by Emmanuel Guibert and drawn by Marc Boutavant.

BENNY BREAKIRON – From Peyo, the creator of the Smurfs comes a super-powered little French boy!

BREADWINNERS – Based on the hit Nickelodeon animated series. See SwaySway and Buhdeuce deliver bread in their rocket van. Written by Stefan Petrucha and drawn by Allison Strejlau and Mike Kazaleh. (And don't forget NICKELODEON MAGAZINE and the SANJAY AND CRAIG, HARVEY BEAKS, and PIG GOAT BANANA CRICKET graphic novels we mentioned in CHIMA #5.)

CLASSICS ILLUSTRATED and CLASSICS ILLUSTRATED DELUXE – Featuring Stories by the World's Greatest Authors!

Just to be perfectly clear, while Papercutz may not be publishing any further new LEGO LEGENDS OF CHIMA graphic novels, there are still plenty of new LEGO LEGENDS OF CHIMA products coming your way! Just keep an eye on LEGO.com for all the latest big announcements!

So while this is indeed the final graphic novel, clearly with everything Papercutz and LEGO has planned for the future, it's safe to say, that's not all, folks—the best is yet to come!

Thanks,

Jim

STAY IN TOUCH!

EMAIL: salicrup@papercutz.com
WEB: papercutz.com
TWITTER: @papercutzgn
FACEBOOK: PAPERCUTZGRAPHICNOVELS
FAN MAIL: Papercutz, 160 Broadway, Suite 700, East Wing, New York, NY 10038

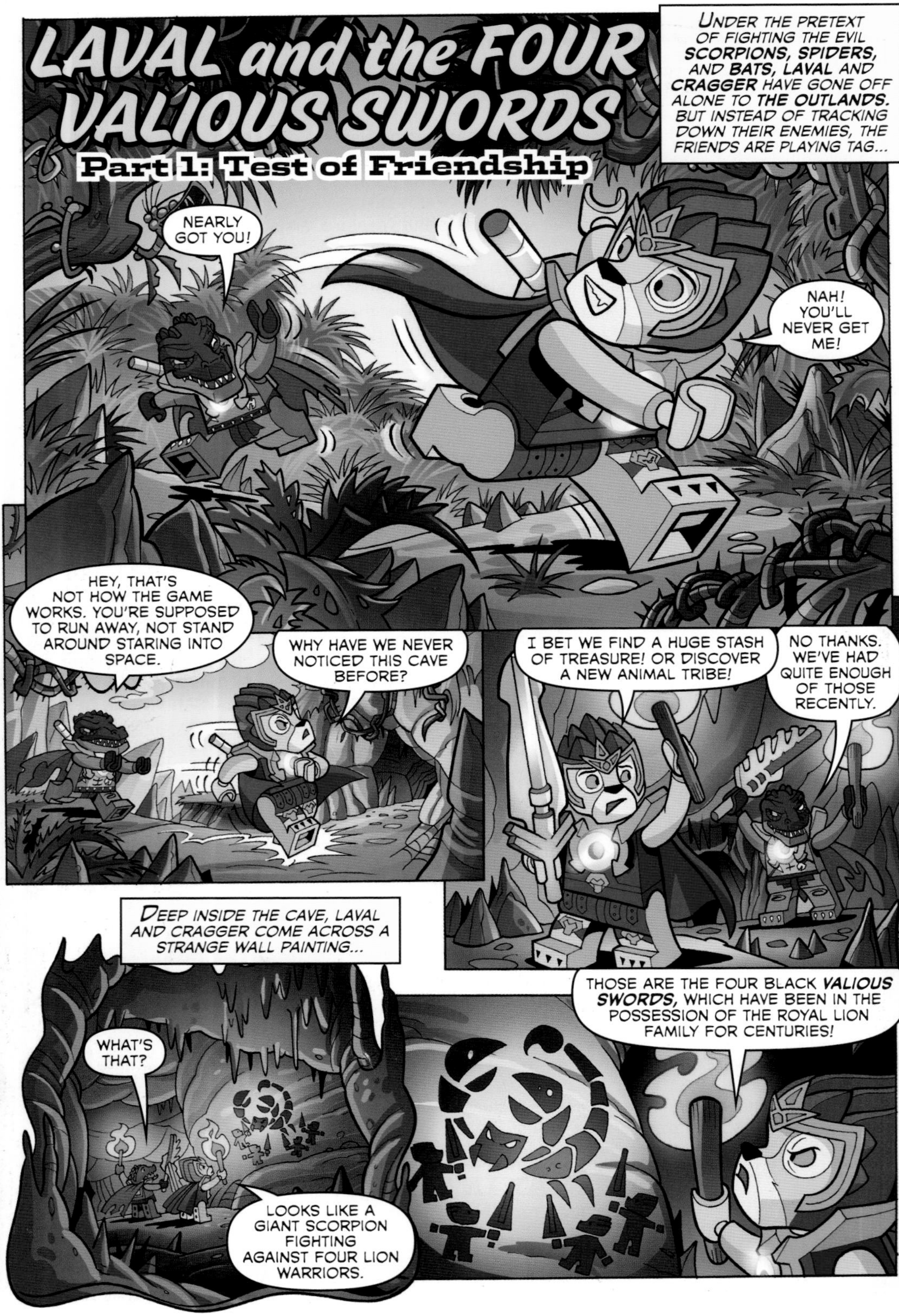
LAVAL and the FOUR VALIOUS SWORDS
Part 1: Test of Friendship
UNDER THE PRETEXT OF FIGHTING THE EVIL SCORPIONS, SPIDERS, AND BATS, LAVAL AND CRAGGER HAVE GONE OFF ALONE TO THE OUTLANDS. BUT INSTEAD OF TRACKING DOWN THEIR ENEMIES, THE FRIENDS ARE PLAYING TAG...
NEARLY GOT YOU!
NAH! YOU'LL NEVER GET ME!
HEY, THAT'S NOT HOW THE GAME WORKS. YOU'RE SUPPOSED TO RUN AWAY, NOT STAND AROUND STARING INTO SPACE.
WHY HAVE WE NEVER NOTICED THIS CAVE BEFORE?
I BET WE FIND A HUGE STASH OF TREASURE! OR DISCOVER A NEW ANIMAL TRIBE!
NO THANKS. WE'VE HAD QUITE ENOUGH OF THOSE RECENTLY.
DEEP INSIDE THE CAVE, LAVAL AND CRAGGER COME ACROSS A STRANGE WALL PAINTING...
WHAT'S THAT?
LOOKS LIKE A GIANT SCORPION FIGHTING AGAINST FOUR LION WARRIORS.
THOSE ARE THE FOUR BLACK VALIOUS SWORDS, WHICH HAVE BEEN IN THE POSSESSION OF THE ROYAL LION FAMILY FOR CENTURIES!

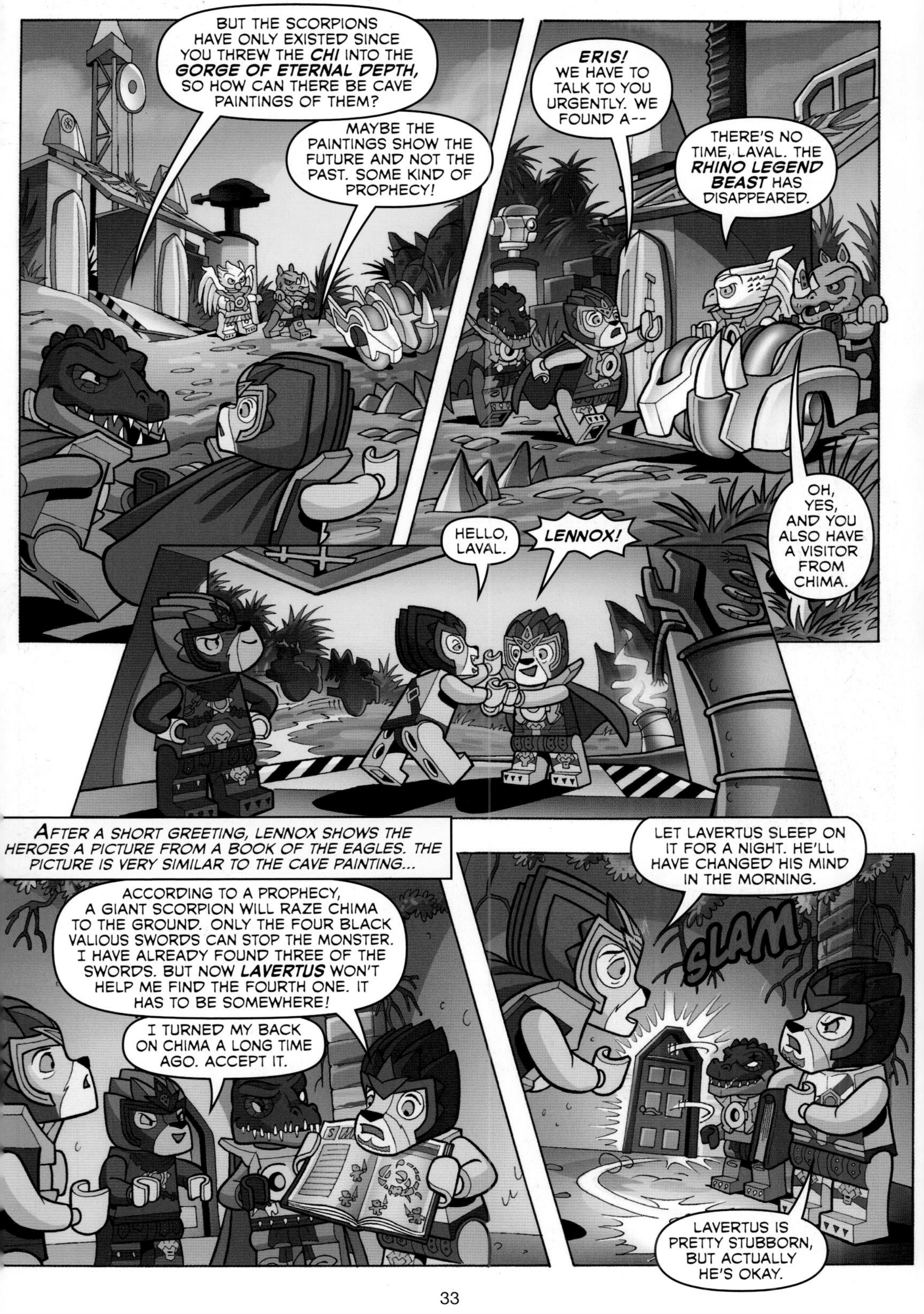
BUT THE SCORPIONS HAVE ONLY EXISTED SINCE YOU THREW THE *CHI* INTO THE ***GORGE OF ETERNAL DEPTH,*** SO HOW CAN THERE BE CAVE PAINTINGS OF THEM?
MAYBE THE PAINTINGS SHOW THE FUTURE AND NOT THE PAST. SOME KIND OF PROPHECY!
ERIS! WE HAVE TO TALK TO YOU URGENTLY. WE FOUND A--
THERE'S NO TIME, LAVAL. THE ***RHINO LEGEND BEAST*** HAS DISAPPEARED.
OH, YES, AND YOU ALSO HAVE A VISITOR FROM CHIMA.
HELLO, LAVAL.
LENNOX!
AFTER A SHORT GREETING, LENNOX SHOWS THE HEROES A PICTURE FROM A BOOK OF THE EAGLES. THE PICTURE IS VERY SIMILAR TO THE CAVE PAINTING...
ACCORDING TO A PROPHECY, A GIANT SCORPION WILL RAZE CHIMA TO THE GROUND. ONLY THE FOUR BLACK VALIOUS SWORDS CAN STOP THE MONSTER. I HAVE ALREADY FOUND THREE OF THE SWORDS. BUT NOW ***LAVERTUS*** WON'T HELP ME FIND THE FOURTH ONE. IT HAS TO BE SOMEWHERE!
I TURNED MY BACK ON CHIMA A LONG TIME AGO. ACCEPT IT.
LET LAVERTUS SLEEP ON IT FOR A NIGHT. HE'LL HAVE CHANGED HIS MIND IN THE MORNING.
SLAM
LAVERTUS IS PRETTY STUBBORN, BUT ACTUALLY HE'S OKAY.

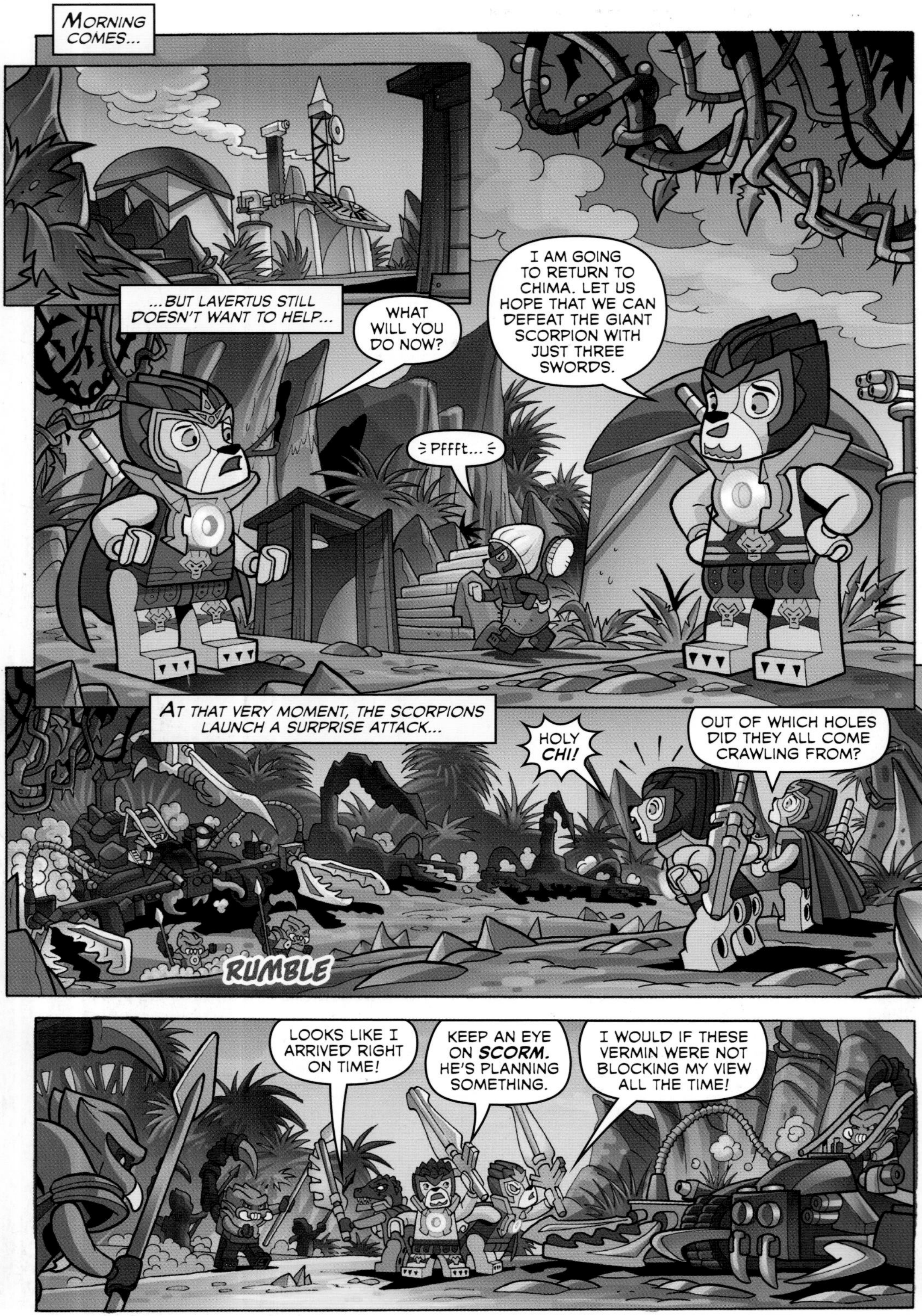
MORNING COMES...
...BUT LAVERTUS STILL DOESN'T WANT TO HELP...
WHAT WILL YOU DO NOW?
I AM GOING TO RETURN TO CHIMA. LET US HOPE THAT WE CAN DEFEAT THE GIANT SCORPION WITH JUST THREE SWORDS.
PFFFT...
AT THAT VERY MOMENT, THE SCORPIONS LAUNCH A SURPRISE ATTACK...
HOLY CHI!
OUT OF WHICH HOLES DID THEY ALL COME CRAWLING FROM?
RUMBLE
LOOKS LIKE I ARRIVED RIGHT ON TIME!
KEEP AN EYE ON SCORM. HE'S PLANNING SOMETHING.
I WOULD IF THESE VERMIN WERE NOT BLOCKING MY VIEW ALL THE TIME!

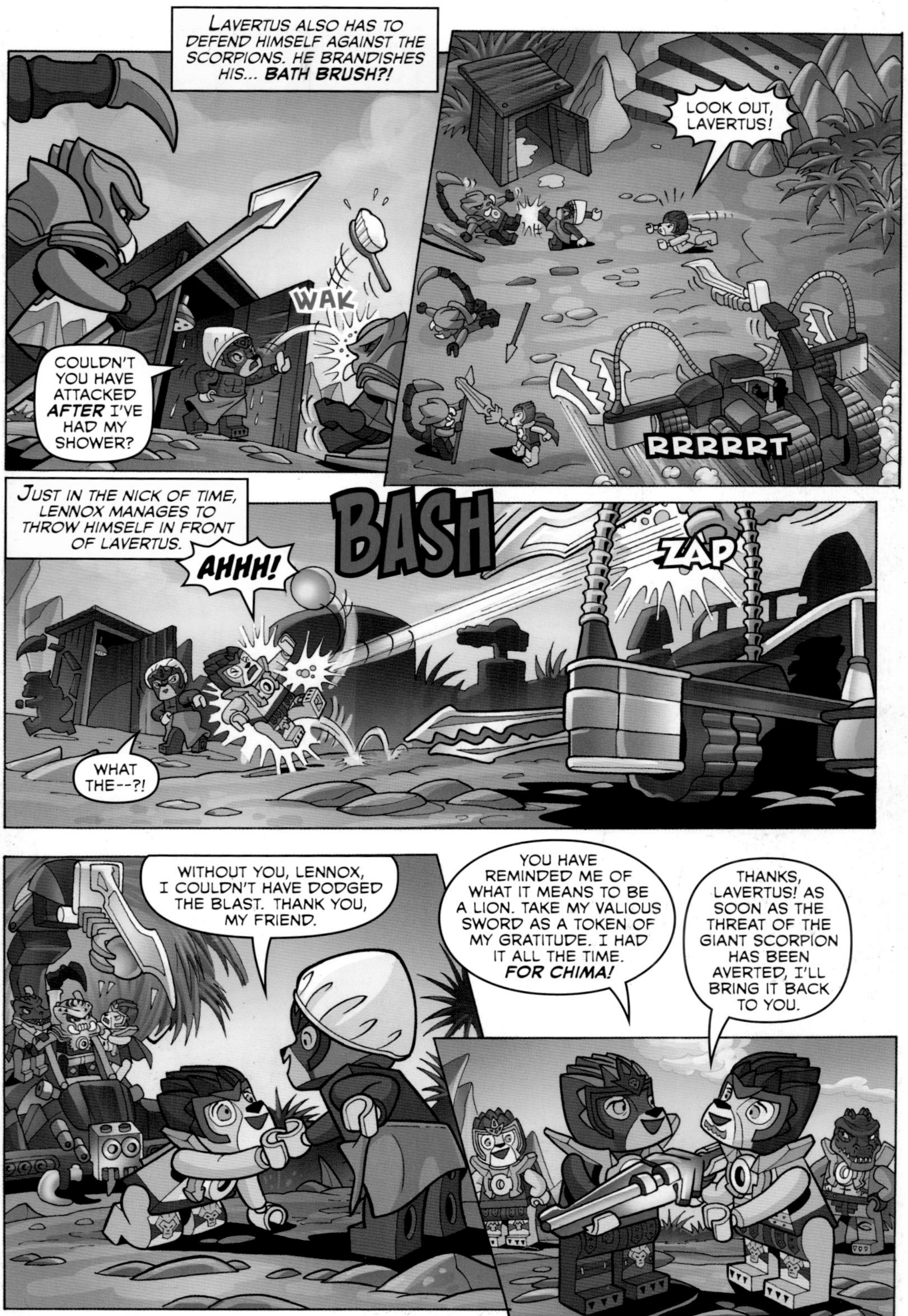

LAVERTUS ALSO HAS TO DEFEND HIMSELF AGAINST THE SCORPIONS. HE BRANDISHES HIS... BATH BRUSH?!
WAK
COULDN'T YOU HAVE ATTACKED AFTER I'VE HAD MY SHOWER?
LOOK OUT, LAVERTUS!
RRRRRT
JUST IN THE NICK OF TIME, LENNOX MANAGES TO THROW HIMSELF IN FRONT OF LAVERTUS.
BASH
AHHH!
ZAP
WHAT THE--?!
WITHOUT YOU, LENNOX, I COULDN'T HAVE DODGED THE BLAST. THANK YOU, MY FRIEND.
YOU HAVE REMINDED ME OF WHAT IT MEANS TO BE A LION. TAKE MY VALIOUS SWORD AS A TOKEN OF MY GRATITUDE. I HAD IT ALL THE TIME. FOR CHIMA!
THANKS, LAVERTUS! AS SOON AS THE THREAT OF THE GIANT SCORPION HAS BEEN AVERTED, I'LL BRING IT BACK TO YOU.

WHEN LAST WE SAW *ERIS* AND *ROGON*, THEY HAD HEADED OFF IN SEARCH OF THE *RHINO LEGEND BEAST*, WHICH HAS DISAPPEARED WITHOUT A TRACE...

PART 2: THE INNER RHINO!

ALTHOUGH THE SITUATION IS VERY GRAVE, I'M SO LOOKING FORWARD TO HAVING AN ADVENTURE WITH ROGON. I THINK I LOVE HIM!

OH, GREAT...

ROGON! WHY DON'T WE GO LOOKING FOR THE RHINO LEGEND BEAST TOGETHER?

SURE! THE MORE THE MERRIER, *RINONA!*

ERIS PULLS HERSELF TOGETHER AND TRIES TO MAKE THE BEST OF THE SITUATION...

SHOULD I TAKE OVER THE WHEEL?

I'M AT THE WHEEL.

≶SIGH.≷ AS AN EAGLE DO I EVEN HAVE A CHANCE WITH ROGON?

SORRY, ERIS, BUT ONLY RHINOS CAN DRIVE A *ROCK FLINGER.* AND, WELL, YOU'RE AN EAGLE.

36

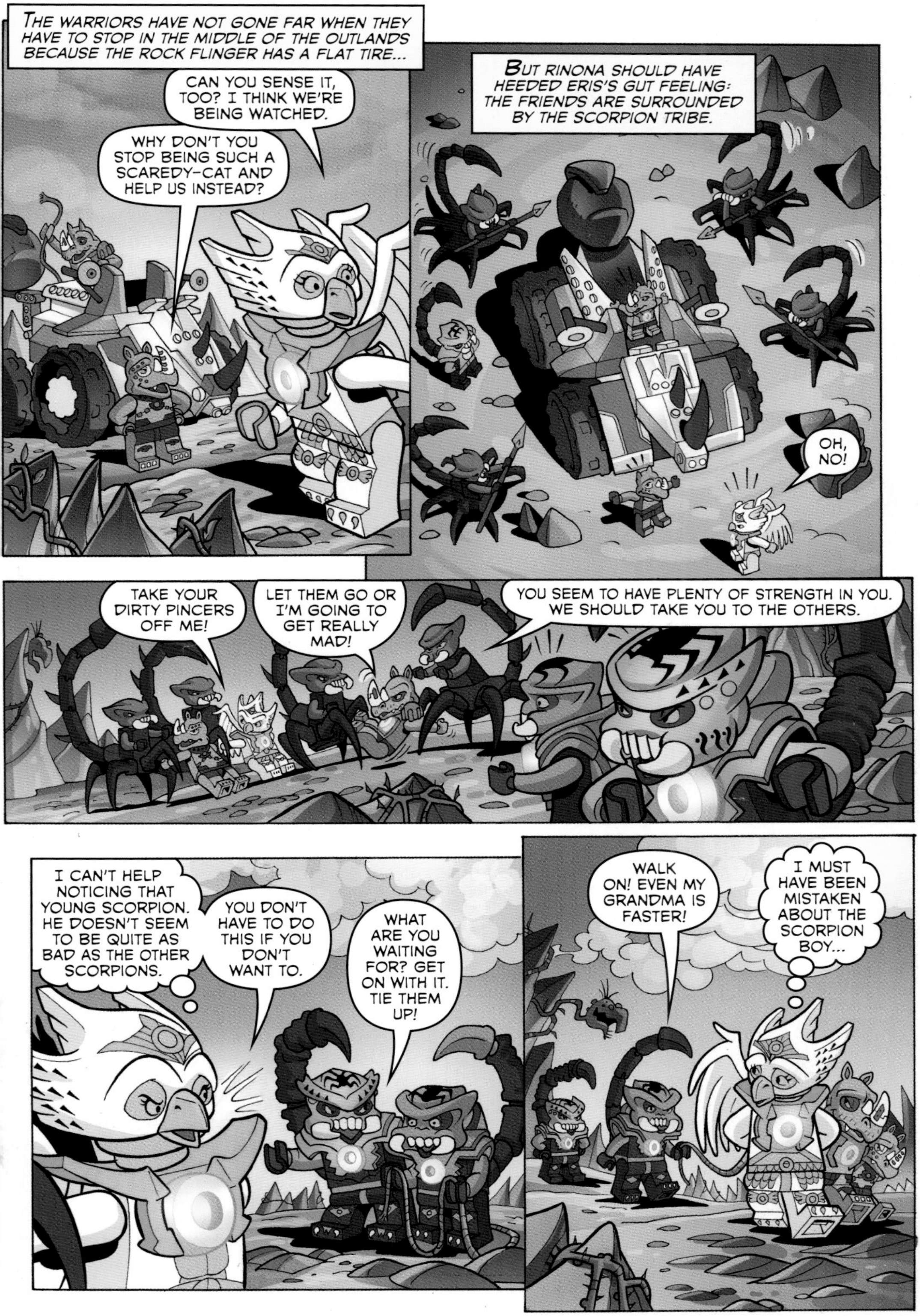
THE WARRIORS HAVE NOT GONE FAR WHEN THEY HAVE TO STOP IN THE MIDDLE OF THE OUTLANDS BECAUSE THE ROCK FLINGER HAS A FLAT TIRE...
CAN YOU SENSE IT, TOO? I THINK WE'RE BEING WATCHED.
WHY DON'T YOU STOP BEING SUCH A SCAREDY-CAT AND HELP US INSTEAD?
BUT RINONA SHOULD HAVE HEEDED ERIS'S GUT FEELING: THE FRIENDS ARE SURROUNDED BY THE SCORPION TRIBE.
OH, NO!
TAKE YOUR DIRTY PINCERS OFF ME!
LET THEM GO OR I'M GOING TO GET REALLY MAD!
YOU SEEM TO HAVE PLENTY OF STRENGTH IN YOU. WE SHOULD TAKE YOU TO THE OTHERS.
I CAN'T HELP NOTICING THAT YOUNG SCORPION. HE DOESN'T SEEM TO BE QUITE AS BAD AS THE OTHER SCORPIONS.
YOU DON'T HAVE TO DO THIS IF YOU DON'T WANT TO.
WHAT ARE YOU WAITING FOR? GET ON WITH IT. TIE THEM UP!
WALK ON! EVEN MY GRANDMA IS FASTER!
I MUST HAVE BEEN MISTAKEN ABOUT THE SCORPION BOY...

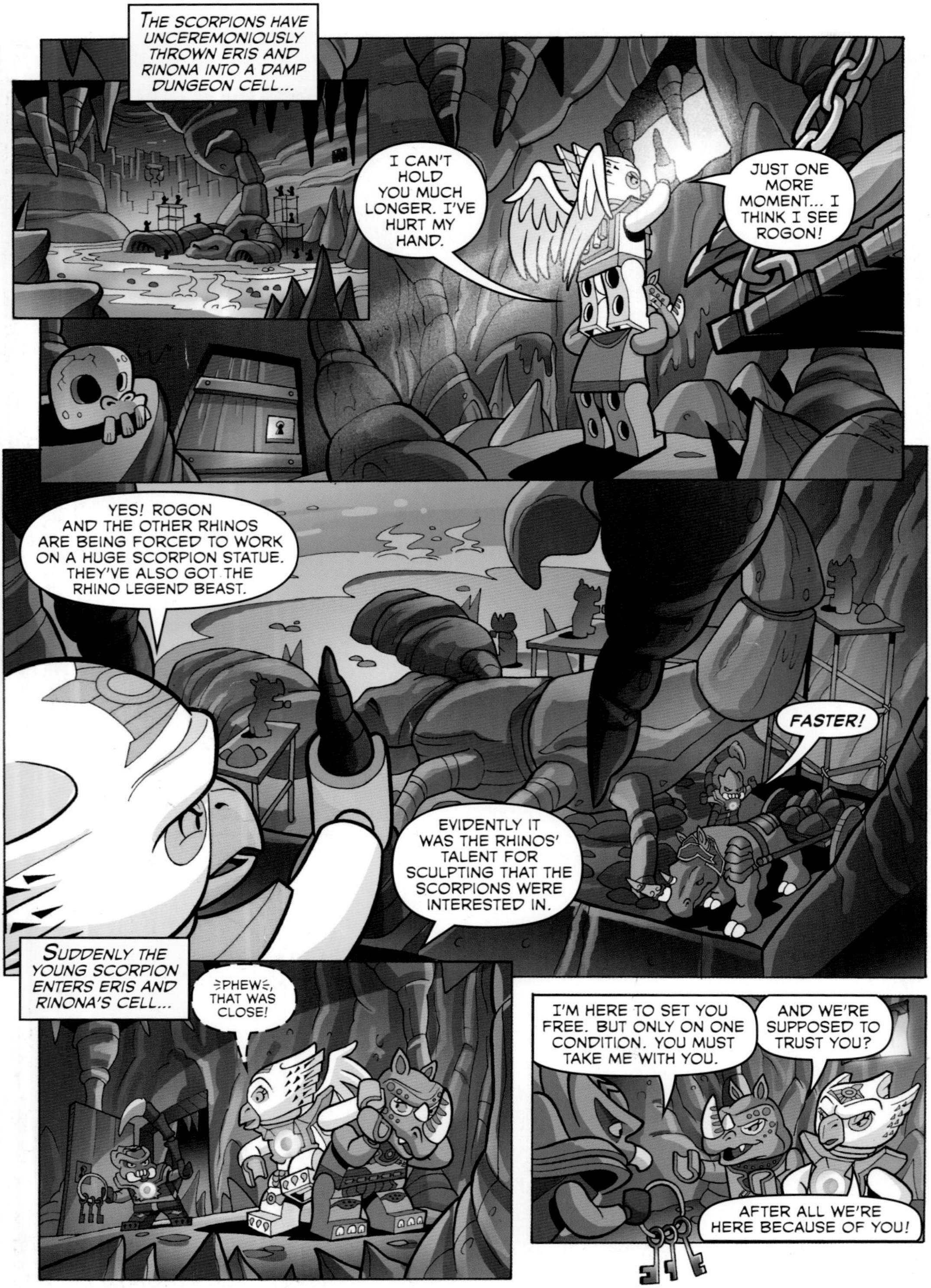

THE SCORPIONS HAVE UNCEREMONIOUSLY THROWN ERIS AND RINONA INTO A DAMP DUNGEON CELL...
I CAN'T HOLD YOU MUCH LONGER. I'VE HURT MY HAND.
JUST ONE MORE MOMENT... I THINK I SEE ROGON!
YES! ROGON AND THE OTHER RHINOS ARE BEING FORCED TO WORK ON A HUGE SCORPION STATUE. THEY'VE ALSO GOT THE RHINO LEGEND BEAST.
FASTER!
EVIDENTLY IT WAS THE RHINOS' TALENT FOR SCULPTING THAT THE SCORPIONS WERE INTERESTED IN.
SUDDENLY THE YOUNG SCORPION ENTERS ERIS AND RINONA'S CELL...
PHEW, THAT WAS CLOSE!
I'M HERE TO SET YOU FREE. BUT ONLY ON ONE CONDITION. YOU MUST TAKE ME WITH YOU.
AND WE'RE SUPPOSED TO TRUST YOU?
AFTER ALL WE'RE HERE BECAUSE OF YOU!

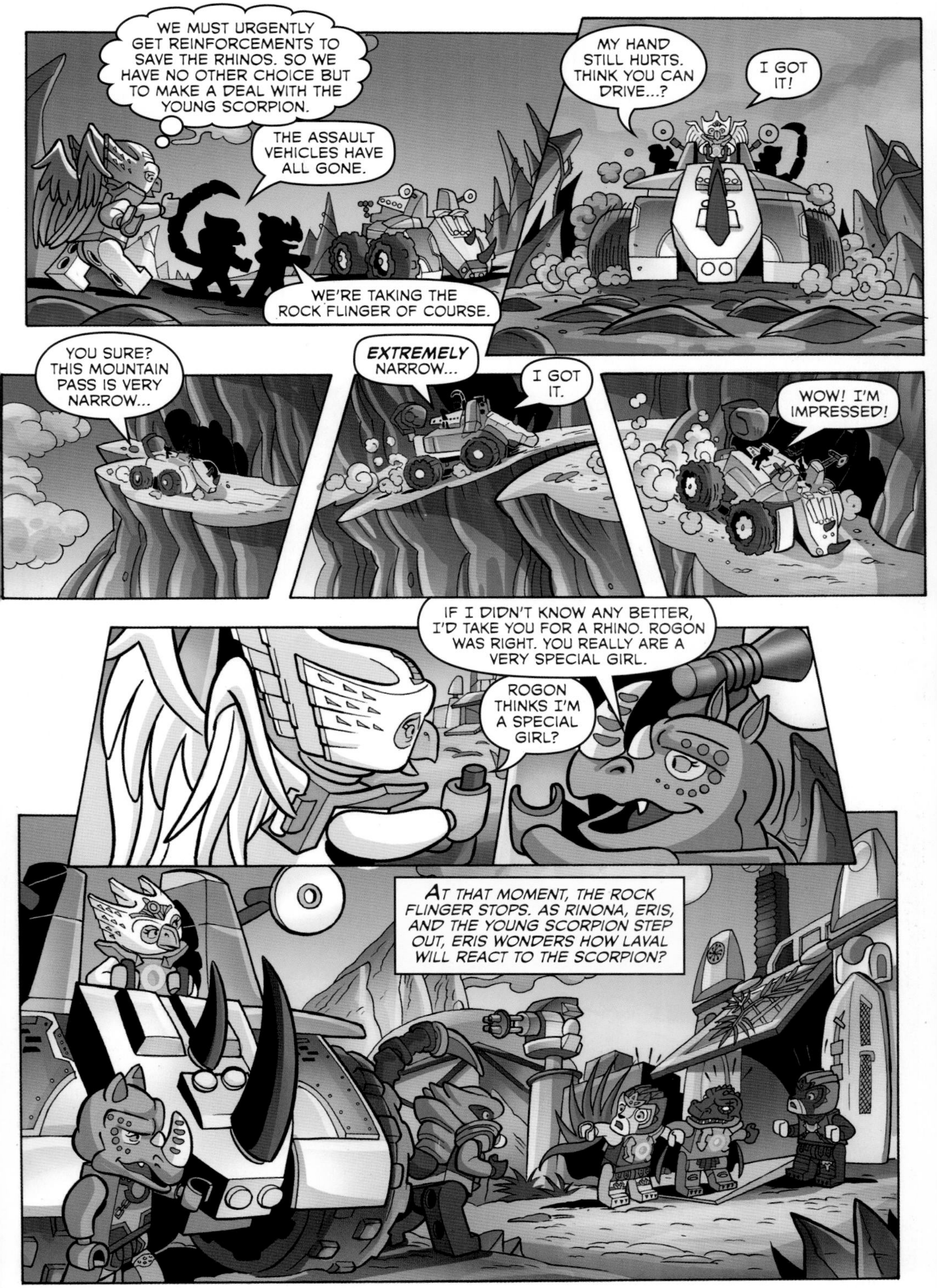
WE MUST URGENTLY GET REINFORCEMENTS TO SAVE THE RHINOS. SO WE HAVE NO OTHER CHOICE BUT TO MAKE A DEAL WITH THE YOUNG SCORPION.
THE ASSAULT VEHICLES HAVE ALL GONE.
WE'RE TAKING THE ROCK FLINGER OF COURSE.
MY HAND STILL HURTS. THINK YOU CAN DRIVE...?
I GOT IT!
YOU SURE? THIS MOUNTAIN PASS IS VERY NARROW...
EXTREMELY NARROW...
I GOT IT.
WOW! I'M IMPRESSED!
IF I DIDN'T KNOW ANY BETTER, I'D TAKE YOU FOR A RHINO. ROGON WAS RIGHT. YOU REALLY ARE A VERY SPECIAL GIRL.
ROGON THINKS I'M A SPECIAL GIRL?
AT THAT MOMENT, THE ROCK FLINGER STOPS. AS RINONA, ERIS, AND THE YOUNG SCORPION STEP OUT, ERIS WONDERS HOW LAVAL WILL REACT TO THE SCORPION?

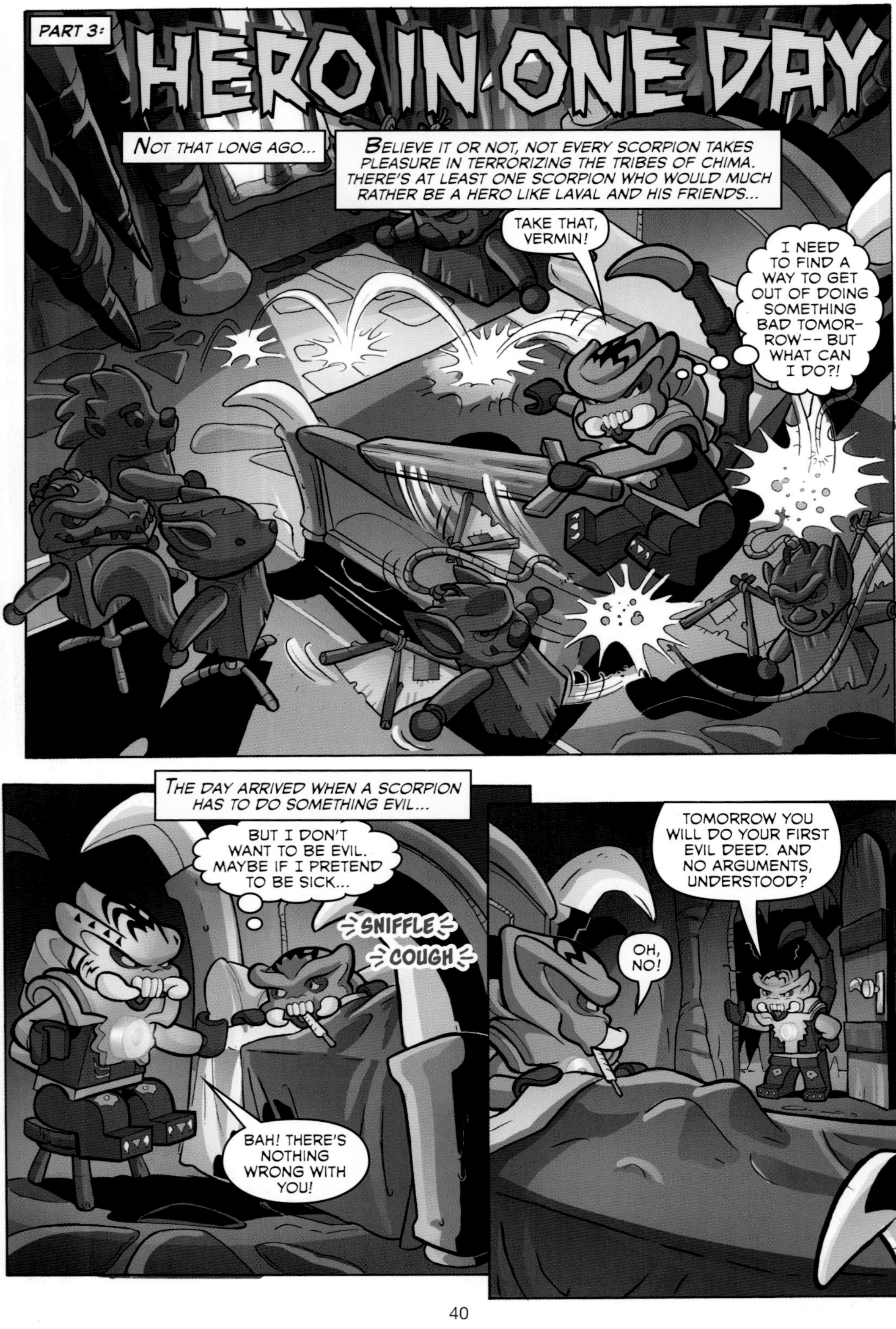
PART 3:
HERO IN ONE DAY
NOT THAT LONG AGO...
BELIEVE IT OR NOT, NOT EVERY SCORPION TAKES PLEASURE IN TERRORIZING THE TRIBES OF CHIMA. THERE'S AT LEAST ONE SCORPION WHO WOULD MUCH RATHER BE A HERO LIKE LAVAL AND HIS FRIENDS...
TAKE THAT, VERMIN!
I NEED TO FIND A WAY TO GET OUT OF DOING SOMETHING BAD TOMORROW-- BUT WHAT CAN I DO?!
THE DAY ARRIVED WHEN A SCORPION HAS TO DO SOMETHING EVIL...
BUT I DON'T WANT TO BE EVIL. MAYBE IF I PRETEND TO BE SICK...
SNIFFLE
COUGH
BAH! THERE'S NOTHING WRONG WITH YOU!
TOMORROW YOU WILL DO YOUR FIRST EVIL DEED. AND NO ARGUMENTS, UNDERSTOOD?
OH, NO!

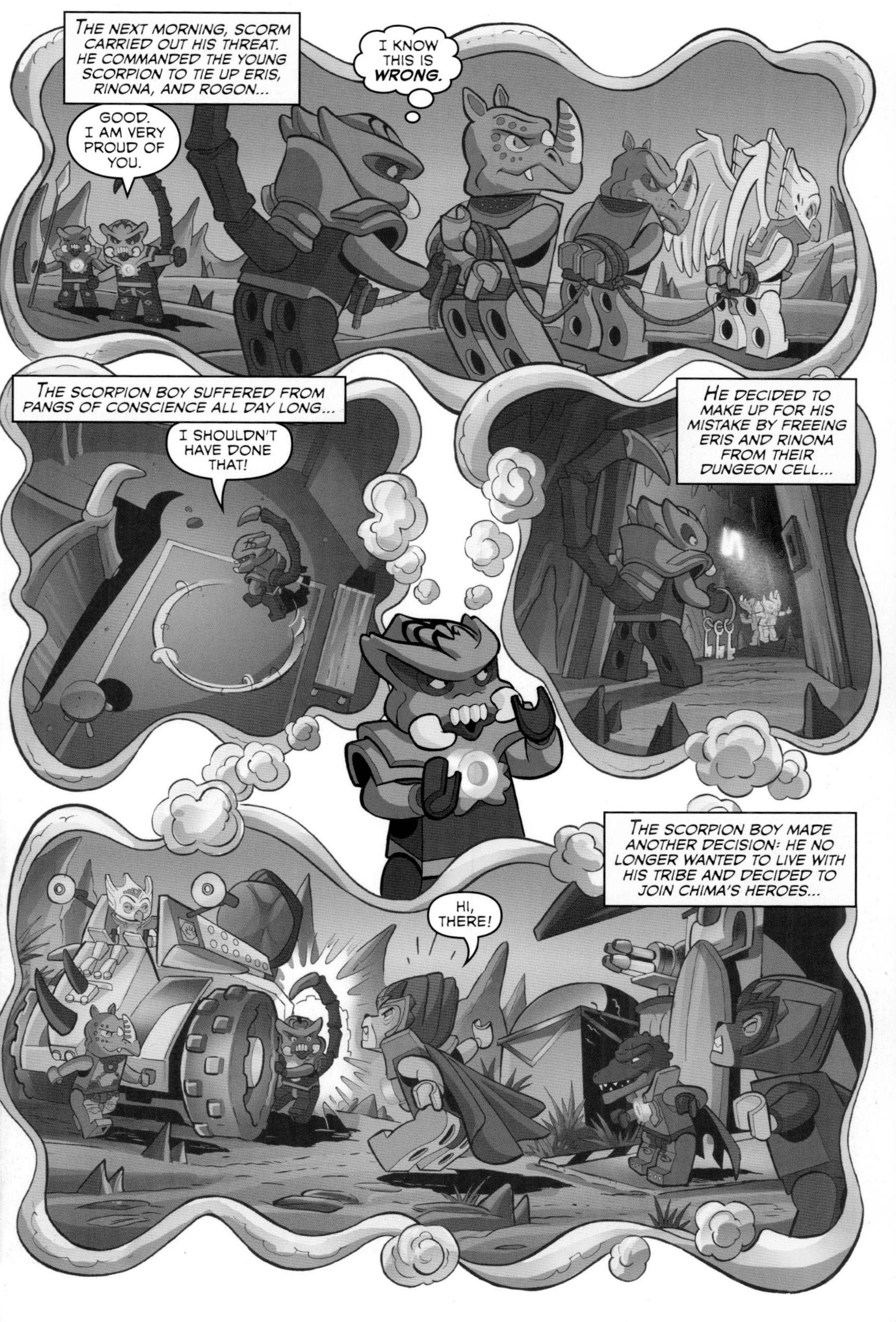
THE NEXT MORNING, SCORM CARRIED OUT HIS THREAT. HE COMMANDED THE YOUNG SCORPION TO TIE UP ERIS, RINONA, AND ROGON...
I KNOW THIS IS **WRONG.**
GOOD. I AM VERY PROUD OF YOU.
THE SCORPION BOY SUFFERED FROM PANGS OF CONSCIENCE ALL DAY LONG...
I SHOULDN'T HAVE DONE THAT!
HE DECIDED TO MAKE UP FOR HIS MISTAKE BY FREEING ERIS AND RINONA FROM THEIR DUNGEON CELL...
THE SCORPION BOY MADE ANOTHER DECISION: HE NO LONGER WANTED TO LIVE WITH HIS TRIBE AND DECIDED TO JOIN CHIMA'S HEROES...
HI, THERE!

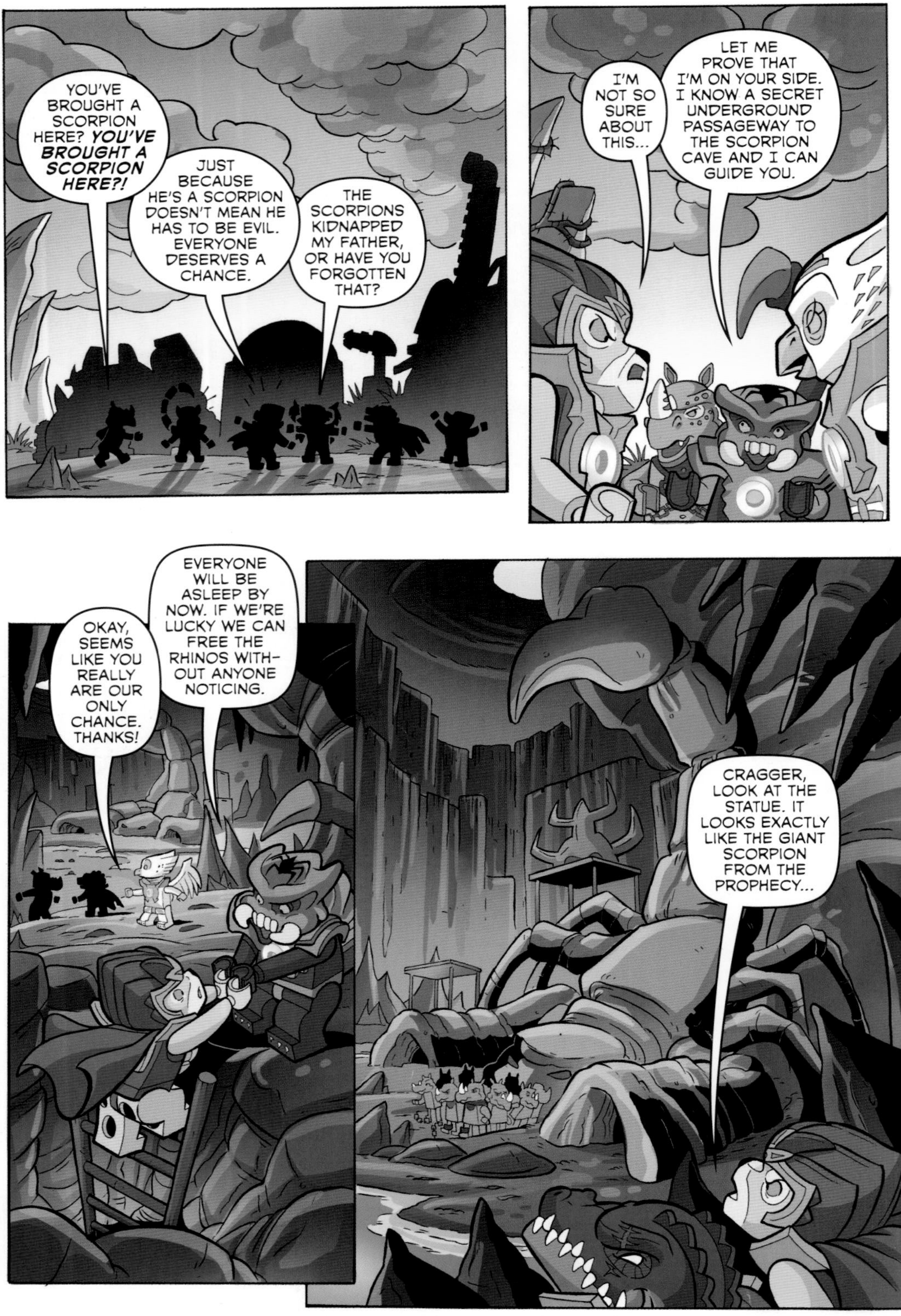
YOU'VE BROUGHT A SCORPION HERE? ***YOU'VE BROUGHT A SCORPION HERE?!***
JUST BECAUSE HE'S A SCORPION DOESN'T MEAN HE HAS TO BE EVIL. EVERYONE DESERVES A CHANCE.
THE SCORPIONS KIDNAPPED MY FATHER, OR HAVE YOU FORGOTTEN THAT?
I'M NOT SO SURE ABOUT THIS...
LET ME PROVE THAT I'M ON YOUR SIDE. I KNOW A SECRET UNDERGROUND PASSAGEWAY TO THE SCORPION CAVE AND I CAN GUIDE YOU.
OKAY, SEEMS LIKE YOU REALLY ARE OUR ONLY CHANCE. THANKS!
EVERYONE WILL BE ASLEEP BY NOW. IF WE'RE LUCKY WE CAN FREE THE RHINOS WITHOUT ANYONE NOTICING.
CRAGGER, LOOK AT THE STATUE. IT LOOKS EXACTLY LIKE THE GIANT SCORPION FROM THE PROPHECY...

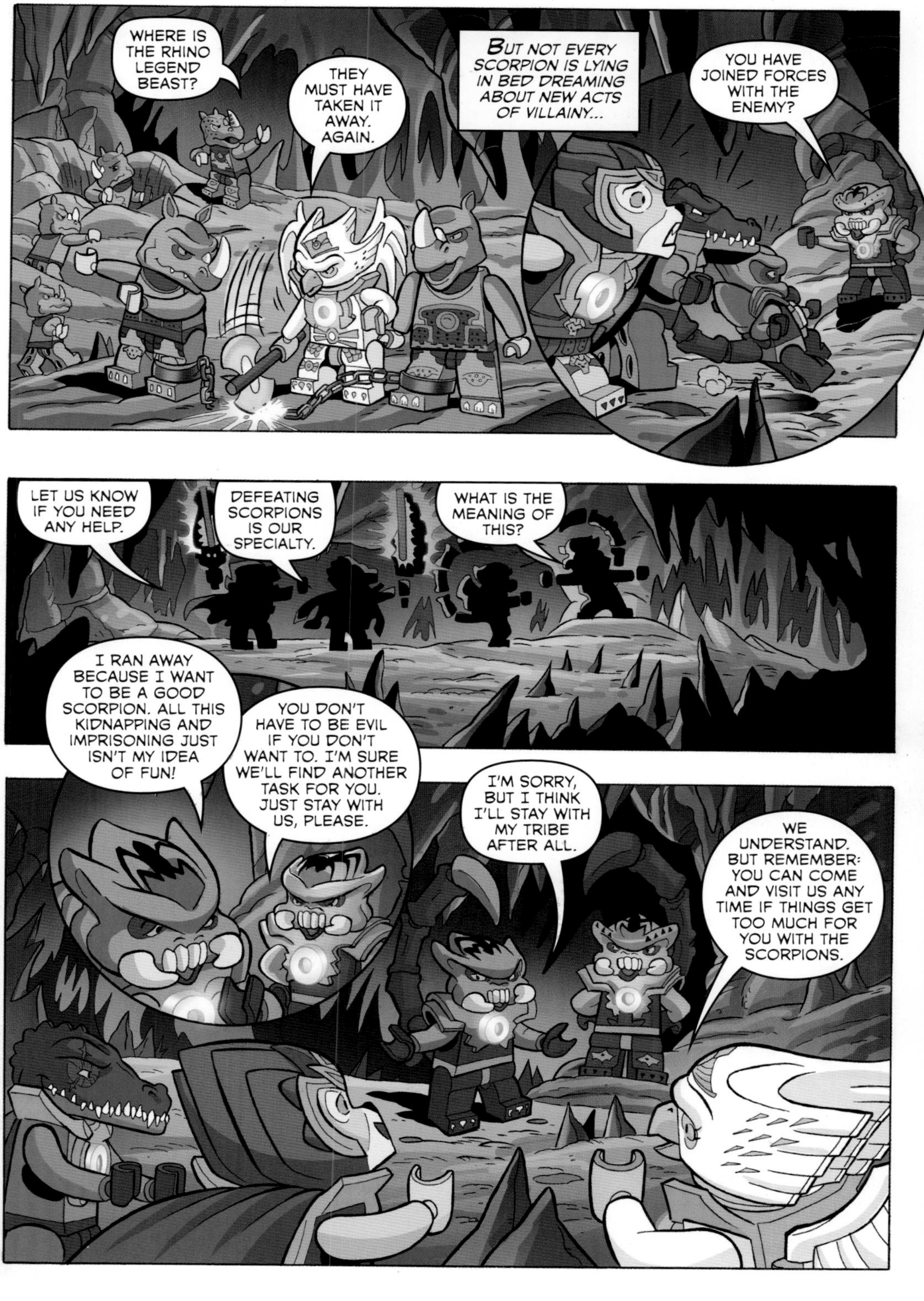
WHERE IS THE RHINO LEGEND BEAST?
THEY MUST HAVE TAKEN IT AWAY. AGAIN.
BUT NOT EVERY SCORPION IS LYING IN BED DREAMING ABOUT NEW ACTS OF VILLAINY...
YOU HAVE JOINED FORCES WITH THE ENEMY?
LET US KNOW IF YOU NEED ANY HELP.
DEFEATING SCORPIONS IS OUR SPECIALTY.
WHAT IS THE MEANING OF THIS?
I RAN AWAY BECAUSE I WANT TO BE A GOOD SCORPION. ALL THIS KIDNAPPING AND IMPRISONING JUST ISN'T MY IDEA OF FUN!
YOU DON'T HAVE TO BE EVIL IF YOU DON'T WANT TO. I'M SURE WE'LL FIND ANOTHER TASK FOR YOU. JUST STAY WITH US, PLEASE.
I'M SORRY, BUT I THINK I'LL STAY WITH MY TRIBE AFTER ALL.
WE UNDERSTAND. BUT REMEMBER: YOU CAN COME AND VISIT US ANY TIME IF THINGS GET TOO MUCH FOR YOU WITH THE SCORPIONS.

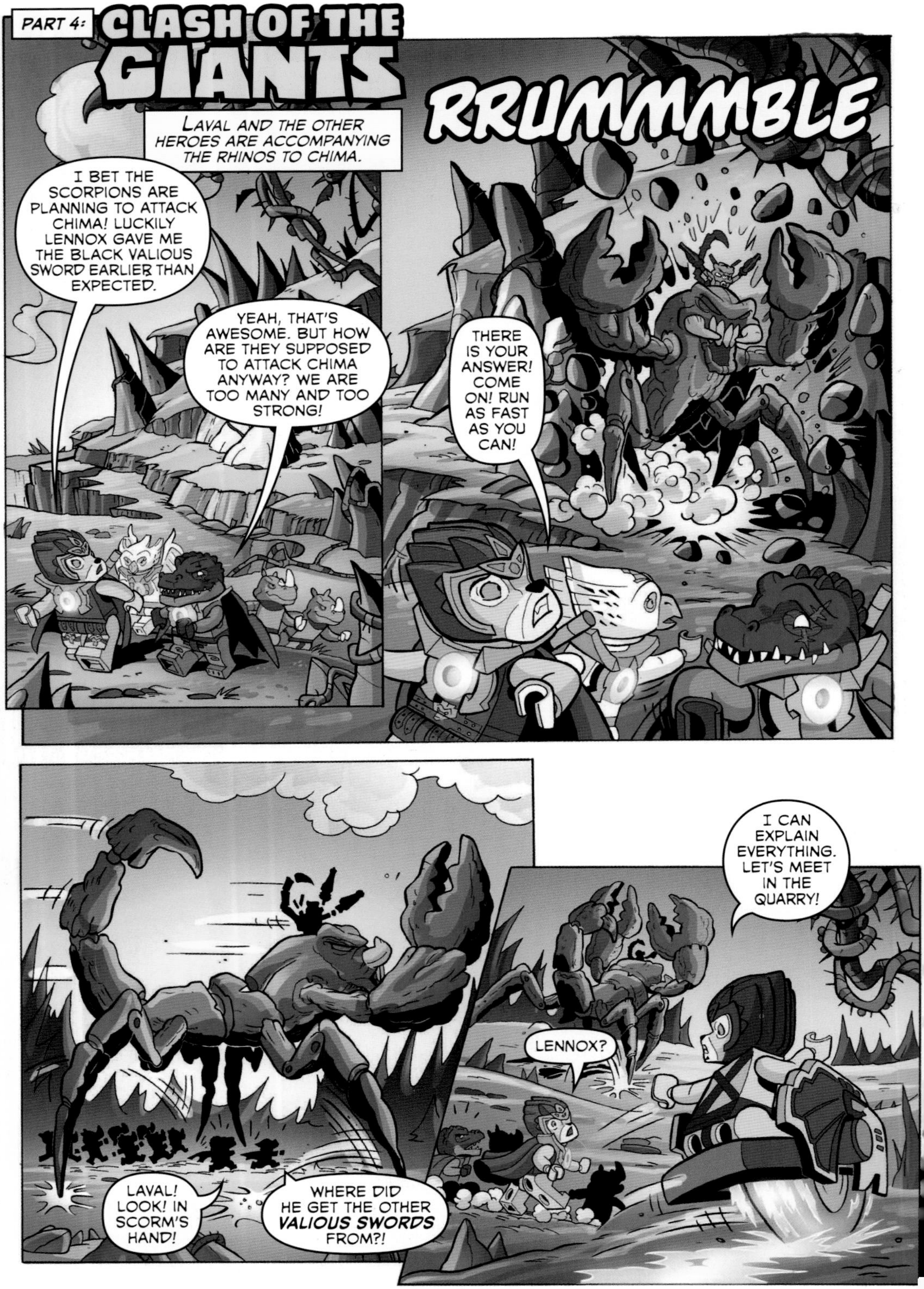
PART 4: CLASH OF THE GIANTS
LAVAL AND THE OTHER HEROES ARE ACCOMPANYING THE RHINOS TO CHIMA.
I BET THE SCORPIONS ARE PLANNING TO ATTACK CHIMA! LUCKILY LENNOX GAVE ME THE BLACK VALIOUS SWORD EARLIER THAN EXPECTED.
YEAH, THAT'S AWESOME. BUT HOW ARE THEY SUPPOSED TO ATTACK CHIMA ANYWAY? WE ARE TOO MANY AND TOO STRONG!
RRUMMMBLE
THERE IS YOUR ANSWER! COME ON! RUN AS FAST AS YOU CAN!
LAVAL! LOOK! IN SCORM'S HAND!
WHERE DID HE GET THE OTHER VALIOUS SWORDS FROM?!
I CAN EXPLAIN EVERYTHING. LET'S MEET IN THE QUARRY!
LENNOX?

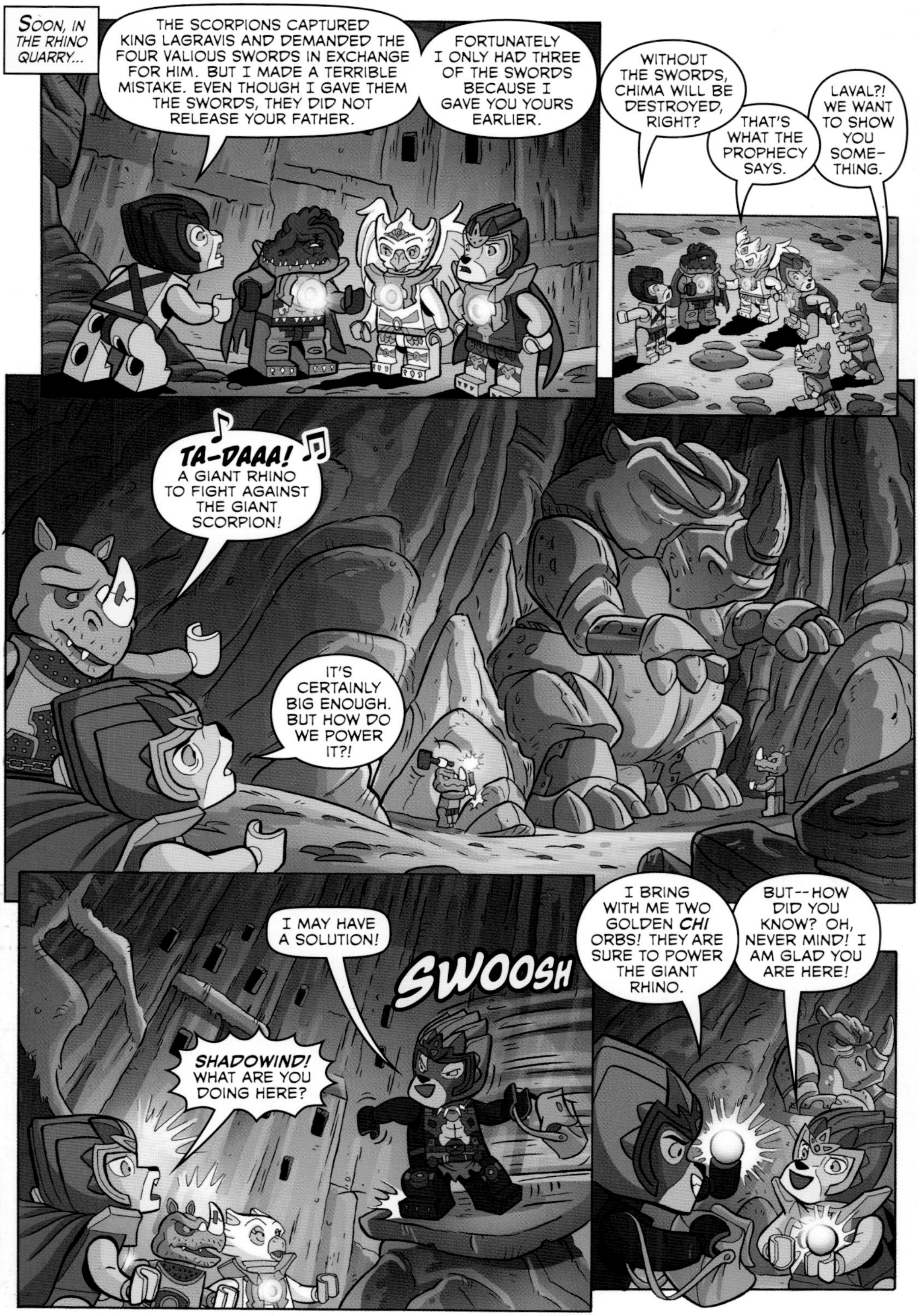

SOON, IN THE RHINO QUARRY...
THE SCORPIONS CAPTURED KING LAGRAVIS AND DEMANDED THE FOUR VALIOUS SWORDS IN EXCHANGE FOR HIM. BUT I MADE A TERRIBLE MISTAKE. EVEN THOUGH I GAVE THEM THE SWORDS, THEY DID NOT RELEASE YOUR FATHER.
FORTUNATELY I ONLY HAD THREE OF THE SWORDS BECAUSE I GAVE YOU YOURS EARLIER.
WITHOUT THE SWORDS, CHIMA WILL BE DESTROYED, RIGHT?
THAT'S WHAT THE PROPHECY SAYS.
LAVAL?! WE WANT TO SHOW YOU SOME-THING.
TA-DAAA! A GIANT RHINO TO FIGHT AGAINST THE GIANT SCORPION!
IT'S CERTAINLY BIG ENOUGH. BUT HOW DO WE POWER IT?!
I MAY HAVE A SOLUTION!
SWOOSH
SHADOWIND! WHAT ARE YOU DOING HERE?
I BRING WITH ME TWO GOLDEN CHI ORBS! THEY ARE SURE TO POWER THE GIANT RHINO.
BUT--HOW DID YOU KNOW? OH, NEVER MIND! I AM GLAD YOU ARE HERE!

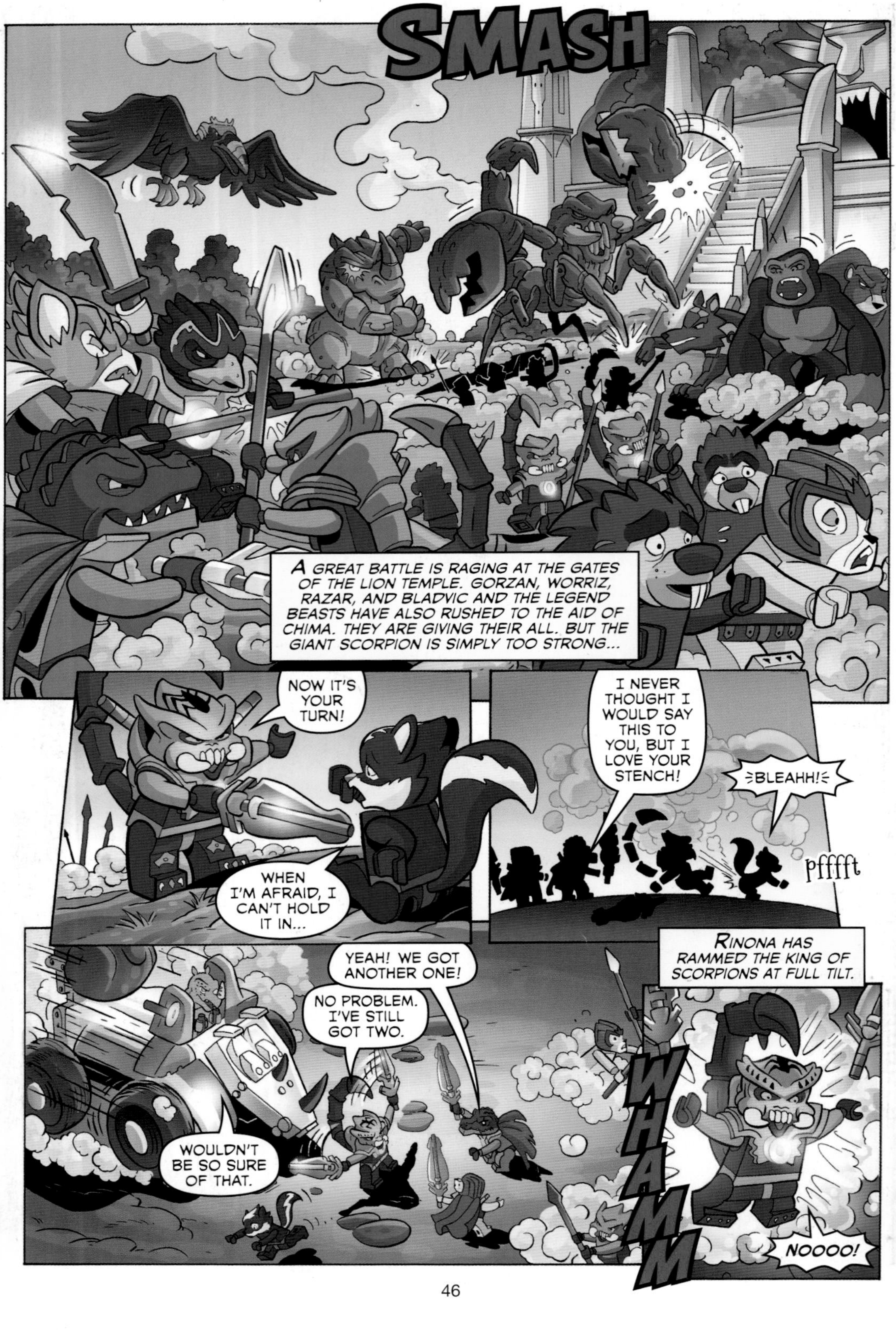
SMASH
A GREAT BATTLE IS RAGING AT THE GATES OF THE LION TEMPLE. GORZAN, WORRIZ, RAZAR, AND BLADVIC AND THE LEGEND BEASTS HAVE ALSO RUSHED TO THE AID OF CHIMA. THEY ARE GIVING THEIR ALL. BUT THE GIANT SCORPION IS SIMPLY TOO STRONG...
NOW IT'S YOUR TURN!
WHEN I'M AFRAID, I CAN'T HOLD IT IN...
I NEVER THOUGHT I WOULD SAY THIS TO YOU, BUT I LOVE YOUR STENCH!
BLEAHH!
pfffft
YEAH! WE GOT ANOTHER ONE!
NO PROBLEM. I'VE STILL GOT TWO.
WOULDN'T BE SO SURE OF THAT.
RINONA HAS RAMMED THE KING OF SCORPIONS AT FULL TILT.
WHAMM
NOOOO!

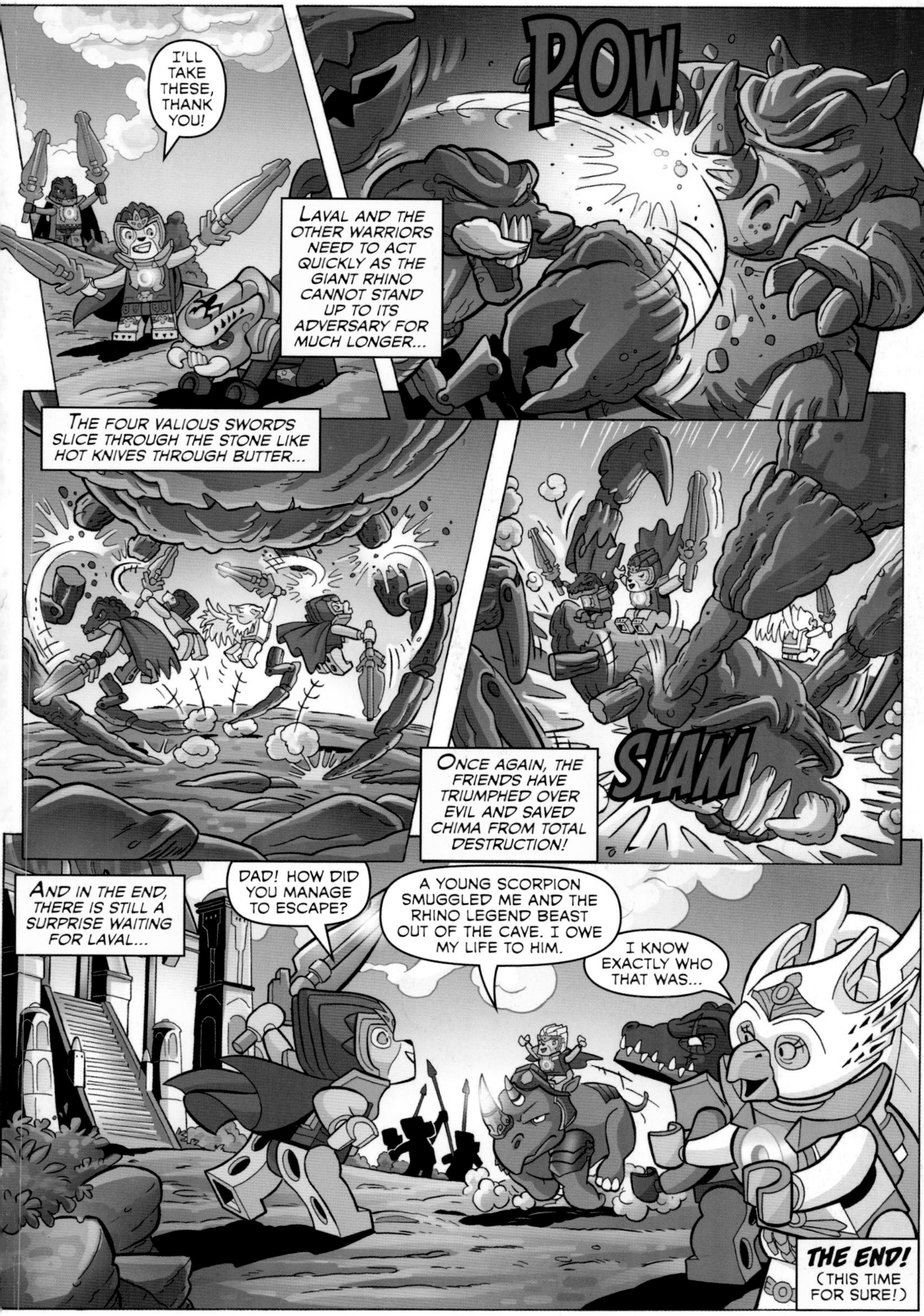
I'LL TAKE THESE, THANK YOU!
POW
LAVAL AND THE OTHER WARRIORS NEED TO ACT QUICKLY AS THE GIANT RHINO CANNOT STAND UP TO ITS ADVERSARY FOR MUCH LONGER...
THE FOUR VALIOUS SWORDS SLICE THROUGH THE STONE LIKE HOT KNIVES THROUGH BUTTER...
SLAM
ONCE AGAIN, THE FRIENDS HAVE TRIUMPHED OVER EVIL AND SAVED CHIMA FROM TOTAL DESTRUCTION!
AND IN THE END, THERE IS STILL A SURPRISE WAITING FOR LAVAL...
DAD! HOW DID YOU MANAGE TO ESCAPE?
A YOUNG SCORPION SMUGGLED ME AND THE RHINO LEGEND BEAST OUT OF THE CAVE. I OWE MY LIFE TO HIM.
I KNOW EXACTLY WHO THAT WAS...
THE END!
(THIS TIME FOR SURE!)

Applied Anthropology:
Readings in the
Uses of the
Science of Man

Edited by
James A. Clifton

Houghton Mifflin Company · Boston
New York · Atlanta · Geneva, Illinois · Dallas · Palo Alto

For my father
A. P. Clifton
Who was a Craftsman

Printed in the U.S.A.

Contents

Foreword

It is commonly assumed that applied anthropology is a novel and recent side development in the science of man. In truth, however, systematic efforts to employ anthropological theories, methods, and findings have always coexisted with the pure or basic variety of anthropological inquiry. Moreover, there is probably no convenient or useful way to disentangle "pure" from "applied" anthropology. What is called basic research, that work not immediately produced from the self-interest of some sponsor, frequently has pragmatic implications, actual or potential. Basic research, if it is good research, has important social consequences whether the anthropologist acts as a responsible, involved participant or not. The essays brought together in this volume all take up one or more of the critical issues in the uses of the science of man. Here anthropologists who have willingly and knowingly assumed roles as active participants in developmental change point up, discuss, and evaluate a variety of these issues — matters such as the ethics of intervention, the influence of the existential setting of anthropological inquiry, the problems of less than detached sponsorship, the limits of the trained spectator's role, and questions of relationships with clients and subjects.

JAMES A. CLIFTON

Introduction

The use of anthropological findings, concepts, and methods to accomplish a desired end is frequently thought to be a recent development in the science of man. Similarly, it is argued that applied (or action) anthropology is neatly separated from pure (or basic research-oriented) anthropology and that the two subfields are contrasted and easily distinguishable with respect to their social relevance, their potential human worth, the rigor of their methods, and their likely contribution to knowledge. Sometimes these two assumptions are fitted together in a plausibly explanatory fashion: a science such as anthropology has to develop and mature for a sufficiently long period for general principles or theories to be formulated and tested before these theories can be usefully applied in some concrete situation so as to bring about a practical result. If this assumption were valid, then of course *applied* anthropology would necessarily *have* to come after the growth of a pure science of anthropology.

Assumptions and convictions of this sort are derived from other beliefs as well as from prevalent institutional and linguistic patterns. One such folk belief is contained in the popular aphorism specifying the difference between "theory" and "practice." From this bit of wisdom we might conjecture that a medical doctor engaged in his practice (or by analogy a social anthropologist working as a community development advisor) is simply applying established scientific principles to bring about desired conditions, when in fact most physicians, directly or indirectly, are simultaneously engaged in diagnosis, treatment, *and* an important variety of research activity called clinical study. This kind of conclusion is buttressed further by the common though inaccurate belief that scientific theory has a finality and durability to it that few scientists themselves would accept. It is also encouraged by the tendency of the structure of our language to force thought about neatly bounded, bipolarized, or dichotomized categories which, simply by naming them, leads to the feeling that the categories differ profoundly in their essential nature.

To contrast applied with basic science has a certain appeal in some academic quarters since to many the two are not only fundamentally different, but they are also ranked in relative worth or prestige. We often find pure research defined as superior to technology or applied disciplines. What is not always evident is that there may be a strong element of self-seeking ego-enhancement involved in such a value judgment. It is often those who wish to view themselves as "pure" scientists who most zealously argue this case. However, in the institutional contexts in which scientists work we can appreciate better the social functions of such invidious distinctions. They consist of useful rationalizations supporting and justifying certain career patterns as against others; they assist the scientist concerned in his competition for scarce resources needed to conduct research; and they can be employed as a useful marker of relative prestige. However, the distinction is not necessarily tenable or useful for an understanding of the varieties of ways in which men create knowledge, the ways in which knowledge is used, or the ways in which application and questing fit together.

Indeed, such a distinction can be entirely misleading, particularly when it is converted into a distorted view of the development of science. The current misperception of that history, in which pure scientific knowledge develops in advance of practical application, simply does not square with the historical record. Daniel S. Greenberg offers this partial summary of that record:

> . . . as often as not, the history of science and technology fails to conform to the pure scientists' tidy model of science as the father of technology. It would be convenient, for example, if a comprehension of thermodynamics had paved the way to the creation of the steam engine, but, if anything, it appears that the steam engine paved the way to a comprehension of thermodynamics — and the inspiration for this effort at comprehension was a desire for a still more efficient steam engine (1967:29).

What is true of other sciences and their applied or technological counterparts is true also of anthropology. The fact is that so long as there has been an anthropology pure, there has been an anthropology applied.

The potential usefulness of anthropological ideas and methods to men of affairs was recognized and publicly stated by such founding fathers of the discipline as E. B. Tylor, Sir John Lubbock, and W. H. Flower (Barnett, 1956:1). The earliest professional anthropological societies of Britain had their origins partly in antislavery and similar ameliorative movements, as Conrad C. Reining makes clear in his essay on early applied anthropology (see Ch. 1). Similarly, in the United States the Women's Anthropological Society of Washington in 1885 called for a firsthand study of problems of poverty and substandard housing and engaged in intervention schemes aimed at improving lower-class housing in the Washington area (Lurie 1966:38–39). Also in the late nineteenth century Alice Fletcher, an early North American ethnologist, worked at securing adoption of a land allotment scheme which was intended to assist in reducing the Omaha tribe's economic distress (Lurie, 1966:48–49).

It should be no surprise that since the days of the founding of anthropology, the creation of anthropological knowledge has proceeded together with efforts to use that knowledge for some worthy purpose. After all, anthropology grew up in an older cultural tradition where the search for knowledge was closely wedded to practical concerns and technological pursuits. Yet the fact that anthropological ideas can be used is a "novel" idea which springs up recurrently in the minds of both anthropologists and potential clients, repeatedly stimulating controversy over a series of issues associated with the ethics of application and intervention into the lives of men. Most of the articles reprinted in this book touch in whole or part on one or more of these issues.

Applied Roles and Activities

The public roles assumed by anthropologists in applied contexts and the associated obligations, duties, and activities engaged in are quite diverse. A brief look at a few of these roles will help illustrate the point that there is no clear, convenient dividing line between pure and applied anthropological activities.

The vast majority of professional anthropologists earn their livelihoods throughout their careers as teachers in colleges and universities. As such they are engaged in a practice which involves the use of their knowledge so as to intervene into the lives of others, a kind of applied anthropology which H. Ian Hogbin has called indirect application, "indirect" because what the student learns is supposed to have an effect on his attitudes and behavior with respect to persons of different cultural heritages (1957:247). Although some would disclaim responsibility for directing the lives of the young, this of course is what education is all about. The inclusion of introductory courses in cultural anthropology in college curricula often is rationalized and justified on the basis that such teaching tends to produce desirable changes in attitude and behavior such as reductions in ethnocentrism and racial prejudice. In the same way, to engage in the scholarly practice of anthropology means to make research findings public. The consequences of this are, at least potentially, an unwitting kind of application, for if the anthropologist does not employ his skills responsibly in practical works, others are certainly likely to do so. At the minimum, then, because of the diffusion of ideas, techniques, and conclusions, all anthropologists are at least indirectly or unwittingly involved in the world of practical affairs.

Outside the university anthropologists have often accepted positions as instructors in special courses and institutes designed to familiarize colonial officials, native administrators, and foreign service personnel with the customs and cultural patterns of the societies where they are to work.

Anthropologists have also served in field settings as "interpreters" of exotic cultures on behalf of policy makers who have little familiarity with or insight into cultural differences. Anthropologists have also organized and participated in regional research institutes and other organizations conceived to obtain fundamental knowledge about little-known societies so that effective colonial policies could be carried out. Anthropologists have also served as expert witnesses before courts where they have explained details of native life and custom so that equitable legal decisions might be rendered.

The assumption by anthropologists of responsibilities within colonial agencies has given rise to the charge that in its formative period anthropology was essentially a tool of colonialism, whether the anthropologist was engaged in patently applied work or was involved in an undirected quest for knowledge. This charge also relates to the form that much "pure" anthropological theory took during this period. The British structural-functional school, for example, was focused largely upon the static elements of social life, being concerned with describing extant customs and traditions. Some anthropologists have concluded recently that in this period anthropology was essentially a defender of the status quo and a conservative force in its own right. This, they feel, clearly violated anthropology's social responsibilities to the peoples of whom it had expert knowledge (Berreman, Gjessing, and Gough; 1968).

Aside from the critical ethical and political issues involved it must be emphasized that such "applied" roles involved much more than the instrumental application of established anthropological principles or communication of knowledge to clients who could then make practical use of the information. There was constant feedback from applied work to the interests of the science proper. In many instances it developed that anthropologists did not have in hand the answers to questions posed by administrators: either they had never systematically raised the questions in the first place (e.g., concerning native educational practices or legal institutions) or the knowledge they had was outdated. Therefore, to provide advice they once again had to undertake research, and such investigations more often than not involved as much of a contribution to basic knowledge as they did to its application. We can conclude that applied missions and questions were directly involved in the development of certain of the newer subfields of anthropology. They provided an important impetus to psychological anthropology, for example, as well as to legal, economic, and political anthropology, while much of the anthropology of socio-economic development stems directly from questions raised by applied anthropologists. Similarly, in an earlier period of the discipline's growth, a great many of the basic ethnographic monographs on the tribal cultures of Africa were financed by government or private parties interested in having more knowledge available (Brokensha, 1966), while the standard reference works on the island cultures of Micronesia for decades were the result of a scientific expedition motivated by German colonial interests early in the century. Even in the use of anthropologists as expert witnesses in court trials, there have been important payoffs for the discipline in findings of fact, the development of new research skills, and the exploitation of data sources little considered previously (see Ch. 16).

Anthropologists have served as researchers, advisors, cultural "interpreters," temporary administrators or executives, intermediaries or go-betweens, and expert witnesses; they have acted in a long-term full-time capacity on the staff of an administrative unit (see Ch. 5), and they have served as temporary consultants to administrative organizations or to several intertwined interest groups (see Chs. 8–11). And they themselves at times have assumed direct power and authority in an organization (see Chs. 6–7). Anthropologists have done all these in a variety of contexts besides the narrow "colonial" setting of the earlier phase of the discipline's development. Very often in such extracolonial settings the unilateral flow of responsibility and authority from policy-making client to anthropologist to a "dependent" population is maintained, but increasingly multilateral relationships are coming into prominence. The unilateral relationship predominated, for example, in the use of anthropologists as community analysts in the detention camps to which Japanese-Americans were relocated early in World War II. A similar relationship holds in the use of anthropologists in industrial or commercial settings where they are employed by corporations to provide advice and information and to make policy recommendations on the corporation's behalf. At first glance, the same one-way relationship would seem to hold true for applied anthropological work in mental hospitals, public health programs, educational settings, in military applications, and in work related to such social problems as poverty, birth control, urbanization, deviant behavior, and economic and technical development. However, to an increasing extent anthropologists are taking into account their responsibilities to all groups involved.

The unilateral flow of authority should not be confused with the separate issue of who stands to benefit from the work of the anthropologist. Very often, because he has been employed by powerful client organizations, it is claimed that few desirable effects accrue to the subjects of the anthropologist's recommendations. In the colonial context, as in the industrial setting, it is easy to assert that applied anthropology benefits the client but not the dependent group. But when a government health institute instructs an anthropologist to investigate cultural factors in the causation of mental disorder or tuberculosis, or when a mining company seeks to reduce its high rate of personal injury accidents with anthropological advice, or when a private foundation finances studies of community reactions to natural disasters, then the accusation of a one-way flow of benefits is not as supportable. Moreover, as was suggested, to an increasing extent applied anthropological programs are patterned on multilateral relationships which consider the interests of many parties. For example, in Africa today it is patently impossible to escape responsible working relationships with the governments of the new nations there as well as with United Nations agencies, regional authorities, international business combines, private foundations, and the local communities involved (Brokensha, 1966:15). Indeed, sound theoretical formulations clearly presume that few intervention schemes have much chance of lasting success without the cooperation of the parties directly involved (Goodenough, 1963). Two of the major "schools" of applied anthropology today — the Research and Development Approach and Action Anthropology — are founded on multilateral relationships and responsibilities as to power, authority, and payoff.

We do not mean to suggest that anthropologists have generally ignored the interests of dependent peoples and subject groups. The standard position of the anthropologist has been as a defender of the weak and oppressed, so much so that applied anthropology has come to be a bad name in many administrative circles. A high official in the United States Trust Territory of the Pacific government, for example, recently commented that if he were offered the choice of three anthropologists or one agronomist he would choose the latter every time. The reason for this is that few anthropologists have hesitated to do battle with administrations over the welfare of dependent populations. As will be clear in the chapters which follow, cultural and social anthropologists share — far more so than any other group of behavioral scientists — a special sense of identification with the subjects of their expert knowledge. This strong empathetic linkage is partly the consequence of the initial alienation from the values of their own society which moves young men and women to undertake intensive, firsthand observation of foreign life-ways; it develops further during long periods of residence in strange social settings; and it is reinforced through the experience of having shared a new and different cultural pattern for a significant period of time. Precisely the same personal qualifications and traits of character which make a successful social anthropologist also predispose him to intense concern with the well-being of his informants and their kind (Berreman, 1968:341–344). It is this identification which motivates some to engage directly in applied work and moves others to resist the work of agencies perceived as interfering with or injuring dependent peoples. Conflicts of several kinds are thereby induced over the issue of subjective overinvolvement with the people being studied and the resulting threat to objectivity of observation and interpretation, over the desirability of promoting or inducing any cultural change, and over the basic issue of the ethics of *using* anthropological skills to manipulate anthropological materials. All of these constitute key issues under debate today.

Issues and Ethics

Many of these critical issues are discussed in the chapters which follow. Can there be an applied anthropology? Do we, in fact, have anything to apply practically? And if we accept that on some level there has always been an applied anthropology in the sense that there have always been some anthropologists willing to use their professional knowledge and skills for practical ends, then we must ask: *Should* there be an applied anthropology?

In the early case of Alice Fletcher and the Omaha tribe we find a situation where intervention was openly sought by the subject people, and where the anthropologist responded on behalf of this group in an effort to develop a program to alleviate their economic plight. The unfortunate truth, however, is that the ideas she brought to bear were seriously defective so that the land-allotment scheme she devised ended in economic disaster. But the fault lay not in the intervention itself but in the failure to learn something from it. This same program of attempting to convert a tribally organized group of buffalo hunters into entrepreneurial farmers in a few scant years was later enshrined in federal law and repeated in case after case, each time ending in catastrophe for the society or community concerned. On the other hand and more recently, the Cornell University-sponsored Vicos Project, emphasizing a research and development approach, has proved to be a many-faceted success. In this case, not only was successful socio-economic development brought about, but a great deal was learned of the how and why of the matter. Here the lessons learned can quickly be fed back into other development programs as well as into general anthropological theory.

The second issue is not whether anthropology can or should be applied, because anthropological findings and ideas are public matters which will be used by someone. The question is, rather, of what controls should be used? In what kinds of working relationships and with what parties? On whose behalf?

Today individual anthropologists are free to undertake any kind of project on behalf of any client for any purpose whatsoever — free of restrictions, limits, and controls by any professional organization. The only operative controls in the profession today are informal ones: the intrapsychic one of conscience and personal values and the informal social sanctions of gossip, shaming, and ridicule. An anthropologist, or anyone who wishes to lay claim to professional qualifications, is free to respond to a recent advertisement issued by the U.S. Navy which seeks a person to evaluate the effects of psychological warfare programs on Viet Cong activists. Similarly, any person is free to accept responsibility for directing poverty program research in the United States, or to commit himself to studying medical doctors "as if" they were a primitive community. The point is not whether these activities are proper roles for an anthropologist to assume, or whether anthropology has the knowledge and techniques for carrying out the work, but that there is no professional organization with the authority to govern the conduct of the discipline. There is no established group that can pass judgment on whether an individual has the requisite skills and training to undertake assigned responsibilities, nor is there a professional organization equipped to approve or limit an individual's acceptance of task responsibilities. The Code of Ethics of the Society for Applied Anthropology, which is reprinted in the concluding pages of this book, is noble in purpose and sound in conception, but it has no teeth. Given the prevailing ethos of extreme individualism which enjoins each anthropologist to do what he himself deems right and proper, the point is not that anthropology will or will not be used, but that it is certain to be misused.

In the absence of clearly stated professional standards of conduct and an institutionalized means of enforcing those standards it should anticipated that an occasional case of pure quackery will appear under the guise of an application of anthropology. The medical doctor project alluded to previously at minimum approaches this classification. Here several individuals promised a medical school they would conduct such a study based upon the stated analogy. They assumed that the basic ideas and methods applicable to the analysis of primitive communities would work in a study of a group of physicians. Needless to say, none of the parties involved had ever actually studied a primitive community, nor were they at all conversant with the actual field techniques used by social anthropologists. Moreover, neither they nor their potential client ever asked whether the physicians constituted a community, or if they were primitive. Similarly, the U.S. Navy's stated need for an anthropologist to conduct what was described as a job of highly technical social psychological research seems to have been based as much on that agency's desperation as upon a soundly reasoned evaluation of the kind of technical expertise required.

Situations of this sort can arise only because charlatanry involves a peculiar collaboration between practitioner and client. The client is not quite certain of what he wants or needs and in this ambiguous situation casts about for the latest quick cure. Unfortunately, there are some persons on the fringes of the profession who are too willing to take advantage of this situation, and this will continue as long as applied anthropology lacks clearly stated standards of professional conduct and a means of enforcing those standards.

Aside from standards and controls, there are a variety of other issues of current interest to the profession. Can the anthropologist, especially the applied anthropologist, be objective? Or does his personal involvement and identification with his subjects inevitably result in distortions of observation and analysis? More importantly, can an anthropologist supported by and dependent upon a client organization avoid making recommendations which are slanted so as to support that organization's goals and programs? This issue strongly reflects the fears of many university-based anthropologists of the pressures of life outside the university. But, as we have seen, even the supposed insulation of the tenured university career itself provides no guarantee that the results of a university scientist's work will not be used by others. At the same time, as Berreman argues, simply to remain aloof and uncommitted is not to be value-free, but, instead, value-committed in a quite unwitting fashion (Berreman, Gjessing, and Gough; 1968:392–393).

A more clearly relevant version of this issue has to do with the appropriate role and the responsibility of the anthropologist in situations demanding application. Should he prescribe only the means to ends stated as desirable by a client? Or should he also attempt to define and secure the acceptance of goals? Whether he works with ends, means, or both, must he restrict himself to short-term and piecemeal changes, or may he legitimately be involved in large-scale, drastic, and even revolutionary modifications of the body politic or activities aimed at sweeping revisions of a society's moral order? Is it true that restricting oneself to limited programs and short-term goals means that one is helping to shore up defective or repressive social systems? Would the anthropologist not be better, wiser, and more responsible if he worked personally and actively with social movements aimed at overthrowing obsolete and dissatisfying power structures? Or, in a much more modest frame, may he only inform, explain, recommend, and perhaps predict on behalf of others, while he himself stands aside, delegating authority and responsibility to an established order?

Selection of the Readings

This collection of articles is designed to introduce the reader to anthropological thinking — past and present — on the uses of anthropology. For this purpose writings were selected according to several criteria. Some discuss the history and scope of the applications of anthropology with regard to geographical range, types of roles assumed, and the scheme of intervention adopted. All these articles bear directly or indirectly upon one or more key issues in the field — technical, methodological, substantive, epistomological, or ethical. Several examine in detail the implications of using anthropology in one particular context, for instance, in technical assistance programs or in medicine. Others discuss one of the three major schools of thought on the proper use of anthropology. In both these sections some issues may only be implicit, for example, the fundamental assumptions on which the intervention scheme is based. In the final section (Part Four) we have included essays which directly confront broad questions and themes involving the use of anthropology in government, the consequences of application for the science proper, the matter of objectivity, and so on.

Suggestions for Supplementary Reading

A standard textbook in applied anthropology is George M. Foster's *Traditional cultures and the impact of technical change* (Harper and Row, New York, 1962). The same author's more recent book *Applied anthropology* (Little, Brown, Boston, 1969) is updated and broader in scope. Edward H. Spicer's *Human problems in technological change* (Russell Sage Foundation, New York, 1952) is an older but still useful casebook, one largely concerned with problems of agricultural development. *Cultural patterns and technical change* edited by Margaret Mead (New American Library, New York, 1955) is a similar casebook, but it is constructed on a different scale insofar as it treats problems of development in more complex societies and along additional dimensions such as nutrition, medicine, maternal care, literacy campaigns, and so on. H. G. Barnett's *Anthropology in administration* (Row, Peterson, Evanston, 1956) wisely surveys the uses of anthropology in native administration. *Health, culture and community,* edited by Benjamin D. Paul (Russell Sage Foundation, New York, 1955) is a standard reference in this specialized field of application. Conrad M. Arensberg and Arthur H. Niehoff's *Introducing social change* (Aldine, Chicago, 1964) encapsulates some anthropological thoughts on the techniques of successfully promoting diffusion and acceptance of innovations, while Neihoff's *A casebook of social change* (Aldine, Chicago, 1964) is an evaluation — using the ideas offered in the former book — of nineteen diverse development projects. Charles J. Erasmus's *Man takes control* (University of Minnesota Press, Minneapolis, 1961) is a sophisticated presentation of a general psychocultural theory of development which is also rich in well-analyzed case materials. *Ethics, politics, and social research,* edited by Gideon Sjoberg, contains fourteen original essays on a variety of issues relevant to the application of anthropology and other behavioral sciences. Finally, Ralph L. Beals's *Politics of social research* (Aldine Publishing Company, Chicago), based upon an impressive survey of the profession and its contemporary problems, one directly commissioned by the American Anthropological Association, is a systematic inquiry into the question of appropriate behavior for anthropologists conducting research that involves government agencies.

The major journal in the field is *Human Organization,* formerly *The Journal of Applied Anthropology.* This journal reflects the strong inter-disciplinary nature of the Society for Applied Anthropology. It contains articles written by industrial psychologists, social psychologists, admin-istrative specialists, and other professionals as often as by anthropologists. Other journals that frequently contain relevant articles are *Economic Development and Cultural Change* and *Practical Anthropology,* the latter being oriented primarily to a missionary audience. Shortly, we should see the emergence of new journals specializing in the rapidly developing fields of the anthropology of education and the anthropology of medicine since professional societies in these areas have been established recently.

The comments above and all the essays included in this text deal with the applications of social and cultural anthropology. Other branches of anthropology have their workers in the applied vineyards as well, notably linguistics and physical anthropology. However, the questions and issues discussed in this collection of readings are rarely raised by linguists or physical anthropologists. Because of this, and for reasons of space, we have included only chapters written by social anthropologists.

. . .

I am indebted to the late Robert Redfield for my first introduction to the key issues of the social uses of anthropology and to Homer G. Barnett for sharing — in lecture, seminar and personal discussion — his broad experience and wisdom in problems having to do with the applications of anthropological ideas and methods. No one could ask for better teachers than these two men. Professor Henry F. Dobyns offered me good advice on the selection of articles on the important research and development approach in the field of applied anthropology. Mr. Bruce Morrison read my introduction and gave me his good judgment on style and exposition and further advice on the selection of readings. Mrs. Barbara Pirtle and Mrs. Eileen Guynes have my thanks for translating crude copy into readable typescript. I am personally grateful to all authors and pub-lishers for their permission to reproduce the articles included in this text. And finally, my thanks to Mr. Robert C. Rooney and Miss Jacqueline Pourciau at Houghton Mifflin for their gentle and invaluable mid-wifery.

C onrad C. Reining's article, the first in Part One, is an illuminating historical survey of the origins of professional anthropological societies. It makes clear the close relationship between theory and practice in the earliest years of the discipline. Bronislaw Malinowski's chapter, theoretically founded on his earlier notions of functionalism, stresses the importance of cultural integration and warns of the dangers of tampering with alien social systems. These ideas were originally addressed to anthropologists, and the article's pejorative antiantiquarianism should be understood in that light. Godfrey Wilson's essay, "Anthropology as a Public Service," describes the conception and establishment of the Rhodes-Livingston Institute of Central African Studies, a research organization devoted to generating knowledge relevant to the needs of colonial regimes. His essay describes the kind of applied anthropology which develops in such a situation. The reader may ask how different the products of the Institute were from undirected basic research.

PART ONE

BEGINNINGS

Sir Apirana Ngata's chapter also evaluates the promise and the problems of applying anthropology in a colonial setting, but he offers quite different opinions and perspectives. This chapter was written by a man who was at once Maori tribal leader, anthropological scholar, and member of the New Zealand House of Representatives. Here we find the kind of wisdom which results from the unusual blend of high level political and administrative experience, participation in two cultures with recognized leadership status in both, and scientific skill and insights. Sir Apirana was by no means an outside technical expert looking inwards upon a tribal culture.

1 ··················

A Lost Period of
Applied Anthropology

CONRAD C. REINING

Research into the history of applied anthropology in the British Empire shows that references to the practical values of anthropology go back to the very beginnings of anthropology and ethnology as recognized fields of study. That the early British anthropological societies were not strictly academic is not so surprising if we realize that they had their origins in the active humanitarian movements of the time, especially the antislavery activities.

After securing the abolition of the slave trade in 1807 and the Emancipation Act of 1833, abolitionists turned their attention to questions affecting the general welfare of the native peoples of the colonial dependencies (Hailey, 1944:5). In 1838 an Aborigines Protection Society was established in London. It was said of the founder, Dr. Thomas

"A Lost Period of Applied Anthropology" by Conrad C. Reining. Reproduced by permission of the American Anthropological Association, from the *American Anthropologist,* vol. 64, 1962, pp. 593–600.

Hodgkin, that he wanted first of all to study the native peoples and to help them only after he had learned how they lived and what they wanted. Early in its history a serious division of opinion developed within the society about the proper methods for protection of aborigines. The faction associated with missionaries wanted to protect the rights of the aborigines by bestowing on them immediately the "privileges" of European civilization, while the more academic faction wanted to study the native races in order to understand them in the process of raising and protecting them. The latter group left the organization and formed the Ethnological Society of London in 1843 (Keith, 1917:14).

In the journal of this society in 1856 appeared a claim to the practical importance of the new subject:

> Ethnology is now generally recognized as having the strongest claims in our attention, not merely as it tends to gratify the curiosity of those who love to look into Nature's works, but also as being of great practical importance, especially in this country, whose numerous colonies and extensive commerce bring it into contact with so many varieties of the human species differing in their physical and moral qualities both from each other and from ourselves (Brodie, 1856:294–95).

The new society was not, however, received quite so categorically by the public. It seems to have been regarded as a rather sentimental negrophile organization with a thin veneer of scientific pretension. A popular journal of the day attacked ethnology for being an inexact and tentative science with little practical value or popular interest. The Ethnological Society was accused of talking for talking's sake and of unduly extending its scope in order to include everything comprehensible (*Pall Mall Gazette,* Jan. 17, 1866).

By 1863 the Ethnological Society was split over the slavery question and over the question of whether man is of one or more than one species. The divergent faction took the name of the Anthropological Society of London. The two organizations ran in competition for about eight years, each marshalling "scientific" evidence to support its claims as to the equality or inequality of man. Practical use was made of anthropological arguments to support philanthropy or to attack vested interests (Myres, 1944:3).

The new society was highly successful from the view of membership. In 1867 it had the impressive total of 706 members, in contrast with the Ethnological Society whose greatest membership was 107 in 1846 (Cunningham, 1908:10–11). This success was the result of popularization of the subject and of frequent discussion in the society's meetings of such topics as religion, politics, and the position of the Negro. Dr. James Hunt, the leading light in the new organization, offered evidence that the Negro was of a different species from the European and, furthermore, that the Negro differed mentally and morally even more than physically from the European. He considered the Negro to be a man, however, and felt that he should be treated as such (Hunt, 1863:3). The attitude held by Dr. Hunt and his followers that Negroes could not be expected to assimilate civilized ways did not prevent them from writing of the "horrors of the slaughter" of the aborigines of Queensland and Tasmania going on at that time (*Popular Magazine of Anthropology*, 1866:6), apparently without realization that their argument about the inequality of races was similar to the justifications used by the white settlers for the "dispersion" of the aborigines.

The interest shown in race matters by the members of the Anthropological Society of London was only part of the considerable discussion they carried on about the practical applications of anthropology, for this was a period of intense interest in such applications. The leaders of the Anthropological Society were concerned that anthropology not be regarded as purely speculative and abstract, and editorially stated that anthropology was "more intimately related than any other branch of science to the sympathies of humanity, and . . . the utilities and requirements of society" (*Anthropological Review*, 1866a:113). In 1866 this society published a *Popular Magazine of Anthropology* containing numerous articles on the value of applied anthropology. The claims ranged from modest speculations to lurid, sweeping statements. On the more modest side were passages such as this:

Anthropology, independently of its scientific interest and importance, may and should become an applied science, aiding in the solution of the painful problems which human society and modern civilization proffer, and tending to the bettering of the conditions of man in the aggregate all over the world.

Or, in speaking of the Queensland aborigine hunts:

Anthropological science, like all sciences, is passionless on the point, but a better knowledge of its deductions and principles would have instilled some feeling of prudence and pity into the murderers, who seem to revel in the unnatural process of extinction (*Popular Magazine of Anthropology*, 1866:6).

This magazine was an experiment in the popularization of the anthropological attitudes and knowledge of the day. It was published as a result of the belief that the diffusion of literature on the subject was calculated to benefit all classes of society and all races of man, and that a more general study of anthropological material would aid in the emancipation of the human mind from preconceived notions. There was an especial claim for anthropology to have the power of assisting all races of man to material prosperity and happiness (1866:1–2). The more extreme hopes are illustrated in this passage:

> Physical anthropology, when applied to practical purposes, must come to every home; the enthusiasm of youth, the fitful despair of advanced age, and the steady glow of a hopeful intellect, steeled for youth to a patience of "the strings and arrows of outrageous fortune" — All these may be diagnosed and classified by the practical anthropologist with great advantage. His diagnosis will thus contribute to a knowledge of race-character, and pave the way to a better future state (1866:97).

Antagonism to the ethnologists, however, brought forth the most far-reaching of the claims for practical anthropology:

> Does ethnology take any heed of the social condition of man? Does ethnology presume to search into causes of epidemics among civilized man? . . . Does the ethnologist consider how to apply the series of facts obtained for the bettering of the domestic condition of the poorer classes of the community — to trace the hidden causes of mental aberration with a view to practical measures for the prevention of lunacy — to investigate race and the affinities of races, so that results may become valuable to social reformers and statesman? I believe almost everyone will agree with me when I say, no! Yet all these things are but a portion, and a comparatively small portion, of the duties of anthropologists (MacKenzie, 1866:67–68).

Dr. Hunt claimed that "there is no science that is destined to confer more practical good on humanity at large than the one which specially investigates the laws regulating our physical nature." He urged that anthropologists should not be "dreaming theorists, but . . . every truth discovered must be for the benefit of humanity at large." He seemed confident that the government must give the same aid to anthropologists that it gave to geologists, since it was not reasonable to care more for the extinct than for the living forms of life. He also considered it to be the duty of the universities to make the science of mankind a special study; he looked forward to the day when all universities would have professors whose sole study would be the philosophy of mankind. While state aid was certain to come, in his opinion, he felt it wise to appeal to private enterprise to assist in carrying out this national work, and considered the establishment of a good and reliable museum to be one of the best ways of arousing interest in anthropology (Hunt, 1863:2–12).

These early anthropologists were filled with confidence in their new science and felt it had limitless potentiality for the betterment of man. They also considered themselves to be able to view man dispassionately on a scientific basis as contrasted with the previous "metaphysical" view. They would admit no subject to be out of bounds to them, making a particular point that no philosophy or religion was exempt from their inquiries (*Anthropological Review*, 1866b:289). At the same time, they were aware of resentment towards anthropology which they attributed mainly to two influential groups which, although they differed widely on many points, agreed in denouncing anthropologists. In fact, much of the opposition to the Anthropological Society was based upon the views of its members on the inequality of races. The first of these opponents was the evangelical religious body which proceeded on the beliefs in the garden of Eden and the flood and that God made all the nations of the earth of one blood. The second group was composed of the political liberals who objected to the notion of inequality of men on the basis of social justice (*Anthropological Review*, 1866a:113–14).

On the continent of Europe there was a reaction against the popular anthropology of the mid-19th century. In 1839 William Edwards had difficulties in forming an organization in Paris similar to the Aborigine Protection Society, because of a ruling against societies having for their object the discussion of social or political questions, even though a Société des Amis des Noirs which had had the purpose of working for the abolition of slavery had been formed in 1788 (Buxton, 1929:781). The difficulty was surmounted by the adoption of a scientific-sounding title for the new organization — the Ethnological Society of Paris (Hunt, 1865:xcvi–xcvii). A police agent attended its meetings, however, to see that it kept within orthodox limits. The Madrid Anthropological Society was suppressed after a short life (Cunningham, 1908:11).

The membership of the Anthropological Society of London fell off after its initial flush, and after severe financial difficulty and the death of its sponsor, Dr. Hunt, it combined again with the Ethnological Society in 1871. The two societies had been battling for a number of years about the proper name for the new discipline. Apparently there was quite a deadlock on this matter in the negotiations for amalgamation, for the firm action of Professor Thomas Henry Huxley was necessary to bring about agreement on the use of the name anthropological for the reconstituted organization (Cunningham, 1908:12).

Although the new Anthropological Institute of Great Britain and Ireland took its name from the old Anthropological Society of London, it took none of the policy. There was a clear change in the interests of British anthropology after the amalgamation of the two factions in 1871. The new organization tended to consolidate its position by quietly gathering information on its area of interest and to expend its efforts in becoming a respectable institution. Not a word about policy appears in its journal, which implies that the society was trying to live down the violent period of the 1860's. However, there was not complete agreement within the organization and some of the former members of the defunct Anthropological Society of London seceded, in the early days of the new Institute, in order to found still another organization: the London Anthropological Society. This society published one volume of memoirs, for 1873–75, in which its president stated that the society had been formed for the study of the science of anthropology in all its branches. He suggested some topics to show the range of interest of the new organization: the causes of the variation in form of the human skull; the extent of prognathism and microcephalism in Europe; hereditary deformities; the difference of the blood corpuscles in various races; human parasites; acclimatization of man; race antagonism; Phoenician colonies; migration and its influence over race characters; the diseases, vices, and crimes of civilization; the doctrines of Malthus and the remedies for poverty; and causes of longevity; Darwinism; music as a race test and the influence of music upon mankind; the effect of diet on the races of man; the physical effects of the adulteration of food and impure air; the effects of premature and over-education; the origin and value of modern spiritualism; the physical effects of superstition; and the origin of human speech (Braunholtz, 1943:3; quoted from Anthropologia, 1873–75:3).

The organization was short-lived and the Anthropological Institute went on with no further radical offshoots. Professor T. H. Huxley has been credited with the establishment of sound guiding principles in the various branches of anthropology; he helped to repress certain elements, such as the persons who, taking advantage of the glamor of the Darwinian theory, talked nonsense in the name of anthropological theory, and he exposed others who saw in the structure of the brain and other parts of the body an impassable gulf between man and the monkey. His steadying influence upon British anthropology was important during this period and his conservative attitude toward anthropology and its applications, as illustrated by this quotation, sounded a new note that was to become the trend in the future:

> Mankind will have one more admonition that the people perish for lack of knowledge. The alleviation of the miseries and the promotion of the welfare of men must be sought by those who will not lose their pains in that diligent, patient, loving study of all the multitudinous aspects of Nature, the results of which constitute exact knowledge or science (Smith, G. E., 1935:200, 204).

For about thirty years after the establishment of the Anthropological Institute, the practical value of anthropology was only rarely mentioned. The efforts of anthropologists were primarily aimed at getting anthropology accepted by the universities. No one had been trained in anthropology, for the early proponents were usually professional men who regarded anthropology as a hobby. In correlation with the emphasis on physical anthropology and the interest in the matter of the races of man, many of the early ethnologists and anthropologists were physicians. At least one of these, Dr. J. C. Prichard, is said to have chosen the medical profession mainly because it gave him opportunities for indulging in his anthropological tastes (Haddon, 1934:105).

The first academic recognition in Great Britain of the new science came when E. B. Tylor was established at Oxford in 1883. Another sign of the acceptance of academic anthropology came in 1884, when a separate section for Anthropology was established in the British Association for the Advancement of Science (Myres, 1931:205).

The interest in applied anthropology was not completely dead, nonetheless, for an occasional reference to it can be found. E. B. Tylor, in the conclusion to his best known work, *Primitive Culture*, stated that ethnography could be used in two ways for the good of mankind: to impress men's minds with a doctrine of development, in light of past progress, and to expose the harmful remains of old culture. In so aiding progress and in removing hindrances, he maintained, the science of culture is essentially a reformer's science (Tylor, 1871:410). Later he wrote, again in the closing paragraphs of a scholarly work, that the study of man and civilization is not only a matter of scientific interest, but enters also into the practical business of life, and that it may guide us to our duty of leaving the world better than we found it (Tylor, 1881:439–40).

Professor W. H. Flower, speaking as President of the Anthropological Institute in 1884, alluded to the practical importance of ethnography to those who rule other peoples. He urged that statesmen should not look upon human nature in the abstract, but should consider the special moral, intellectual, and social capabilities, wants, and aspirations of each particular race with which they have to deal. He pointed out that a knowledge of the special characteristics of native races and their relations to each other has a more practical object than the mere satisfaction of scientific curiosity, that such knowledge is vital to good administration, and may be the basis for the happiness and prosperity of millions of subject peoples (Flower, 1884:493).

Even such vague statements seem to have been rather exceptional, for the general trend from 1870 onward was for the subject of anthropology to become more and more esoteric and to eschew practical applications. Professor J. G. Frazer denied that anthropology had anything to do with the practical problems of statesmen (Smith, E. W., 1934:xiv). He believed his duty was to describe preliterate peoples in order to illuminate the history and evolution of society. He would admit anthropology to be of practical value only in the vague sense that "it might become a powerful instrument to expedite progress if it lays bare certain spots in the foundation on which modern society is built" (Frazer, 1900:xxi–xxii).

The pattern set by Frazer indicates the divergence of academic anthropology from practical considerations. Not only were anthropologists trying to live down the attempted popularization of their subject, but the scope of their interests within the field was such that they did little of interest to the workaday world. Their interest was in the past, their research was centered on the evolution of society. The strong influence of the biological concepts of Darwin as to natural selection and survival of the fittest were adopted to ways of thinking about societies being evolved through a series of stages. This procedure, plus the classical interests of such scholars as Tylor, Frazer, Robertson Smith, and MacLennan, produced numerous volumes on the history of various customs and institutions. Primitive communities were of interest as parallels to hypothetical stages of evolution of human society. Such communities were studied not as total units, but as collections of customs which were analyzed and compared out of their contexts. The resulting material was, nonetheless, of undeniable interest and the quality of the scholarship of these anthropologists furthered the acceptance of anthropology as an academic subject.

We see now that, after the violent period of anthropological controversy and popularization in Great Britain, which was engendered by the crisis in the slavery question during the 1860's, there was a period of quiet reaction and consolidation. The period of the 1860's cannot be said to be of any great or lasting importance for it was forgotten in the period which followed, and it may be called a lost period of applied anthropology. (This impression was heightened by the fact that E. B. Tylor's copy of the popular magazine published by the Anthropological Society of London, which I used in Oxford for this study, had lost its bindings in its 85 years but still had all pages uncut.) And when, about the beginning of the 20th century, there again began to be active British interest in the practical potential of anthropology, no one seems to have been aware of the former intensive interest. In 1903, the President of the Anthropological Institute commented on the need for popular education to show the public the value of anthropology and said that anthropologists had been so engrossed in research or in routine duties that they had not made sufficient effort to draw attention to matters which might appeal to the public (Balfour, 1903:18–21).

The various applications of anthropology have been discovered time and again; the potentiality of anthropology for the betterment of man in general, and native peoples in particular, has been brought up anew from time to time. For instance, in the proposals for the establishment of a School of Applied Anthropology in Great Britain in 1921, we find the remark that "the anthropological point of view should permeate the whole body of the people" and that the lack of this "was the cause of our present troubles" (Peake, 1921:174).

In 1938, Professor B. Malinowski expressed a view on the subject which could be matched with some of the views of the 1860's, though he thought the idea to be a new one, the result of a new trend:

> ... the anthropologist with all his highly vaunted technique of field work, his scientific acumen, and his humanistic outlook, has so far kept aloof from the fierce battle of opinions about the future and the welfare of native races. In the heated arguments between those who want to "keep the native in his place" and those who want to "secure him a place in the sun," the anthropologist has so far taken no active part. Does this mean that knowledge serves merely to blind us to the reality of human interests and vital issues? The science which claims to understand culture and to have the clue to racial problems must not remain silent on the drama of culture conflict and of racial clash.
>
> Anthropology must become an applied science. Every student of scientific history knows that science is born with its applications (Malinowski, 1938:x).

And when we find, for example, in the writings of two American anthropologists in the 1940's, the statement that "humanitarian" anthropology was evolved only in recent years (Chapple and Coon, 1942:4), they appear to be unaware of the ideas expressed in the much earlier period of popular and applied anthropology.

2 ·················

Practical Anthropology

BRONISLAW MALINOWSKI

I am starting from the question: is there any specific task for the Institute so that it shall not duplicate the work of scientific societies or political and educational organizations already existing? The Institute stands in the first place for the practical application of scientific knowledge. It can reach on the one hand various Colonial interests in their practical activities, while at the same time it has at its disposal the knowledge of theoretically trained specialists.

I think that in the very combination of practical and theoretical interests lies the proper task of the Institute. There is a gap between the theoretical concerns of the anthropology of the schools on the one hand, and practical interests on the other. This gap must be bridged over, and in doing this the Institute can make itself very useful.

The practical man is inclined to pooh-pooh, ignore, and even to resent any sort of encroachment of the anthropologist upon his domain. On the other hand it is not always easy to advise the colonial administrator or

"Practical Anthropology" by Bronislaw Malinowski is reprinted from *Africa*, 2:23–38, 1929, by permission of the International African Institute and the author's estate.

missionary just where to find the anthropological information he requires. Now I think that the gap is artificial and of great prejudice to either side. The practical man should be asked to state his needs as regards knowledge on savage law, economics, customs, and institutions; he would then stimulate the scientific anthropologist to a most fruitful line of research and thus receive information without which he often gropes in the dark. The anthropologist, on the other hand, must move towards a direct study of indigenous institutions as they now exist and work. He must also become more concerned in the anthropology of the changing African, and in the anthropology of the contact of white and coloured, of European culture and primitive tribal life. If the Institute becomes a central exchange for practical and theoretical interests, and helps to put them in contact, it will fulfil an important task.

It is then the thesis of this memorandum that there exists an anthropological No-man's-land; that in this are contained studies of primitive economics, primitive jurisprudence, questions of land tenure, of indigenous financial systems and taxation, a correct understanding of the principles of African indigenous education, as well as wider problems of population, hygiene and changing outlook. Scientific knowledge on all these problems is more and more needed by all practical men in the colonies. This knowledge could be supplied by men trained in anthropological methods and possessing the anthropological outlook, provided that they also acquire a direct interest in the practical applications of their work, and a keener sense of present-day realities.

SCIENTIFIC CONTROL OF COLONIAL COOPERATION

By the constitution of the Institute all political issues are eliminated from its activities. This can easily be done by concentrating upon the study of the facts and processes which bear upon the practical problems and leaving to statesmen (and journalists) the final decision of how to apply the results.

Thus the important issue of direct versus indirect rule needs careful study of the various processes by which European influences can reach a native tribe. My own opinion, as that of all competent anthropologists, is that indirect or dependent rule is infinitely preferable. In fact, if we define dependent rule as the control of Natives through the medium of their own organization, it is clear that only dependent rule can succeed. For the government of any race consists rather in implanting in them ideas of right, of law and order, and making them obey such ideas.

The real difference between 'direct rule' and 'indirect or dependent rule' consists in the fact that direct rule assumes that you can create at one go an entirely new order, that you can transform Africans into semicivilized pseudo-European citizens within a few years. Indirect rule, on the other hand, recognizes that no such magical rapid transformation can take place, that in reality all social development is very slow, and that it is infinitely preferable to achieve it by a slow and gradual change coming from within.

A scientific study of facts in this matter would reveal clearly that 'direct rule' means in the last issue forced labour, ruthless taxation, a fixed routine in political matters, the application of a code of laws to an entirely incompatible background. And again as regards education, the formation of African baboos and in general the making of the African into a caricature of the European.

The political indirect rule which was the guiding principle of Lord Lugard's political and financial policy in Africa should be extended to all aspects of culture. Indirect cultural control is the only way of developing economic life, the administration of justice by Native to Natives, the raising of morals and education on indigenous lines, and the development of truly African art, culture, and religion.

But whether we adopt in our practical policy the principle of direct or indirect control, it is clear that a full knowledge of indigenous culture in the special subjects indicated is indispensable. Under indirect or dependent control the white man leaves most of the work to be done by the Natives themselves but still has to supervise it, and if he does not want to be a mere figurehead, or blunderingly to interfere in something which he does not understand, he must know the organization, the ideas and the customs of those under his control. The statesman, on the other hand, who believes in direct control and who wants rapidly to transform a congeries of tribes into a province of his own country, to supersede native customs and law by his civil and criminal codes, needs obviously also to know the material on which he works as well as the mould into which he is trying to press it.

THE NEW BRANCHES OF ANTHROPOLOGICAL INQUIRY

Let us scrutinize some of these subjects which the practical statesman must know if he wants to frame his broad outlines of policy; which the Resident or Commissioner has to understand if he is to administer this policy, which in fact are the real subject matter of the relations between coloured and white in Africa.

The political organization of a native tribe is obviously one of the first things to be known clearly. Now the political organization of an African people may be of an advanced kind, implying a sort of monarchy, with extensive traditions and genealogies, with great ceremonial and ritual, a developed system of finance, military organization, and various judiciary functions. Such native states can be allowed to run on their own lines but they have to be first expurgated and then controlled. Now it is essential to touch as little as possible of the established order, and yet to eliminate all elements which might offend European susceptibilities or be a menace to good relations.[1] Such knowledge obviously ought to be obtained. As a matter of fact in territories such as Nigeria and Uganda, this knowledge had to be actually acquired by the first administrators.

That type of study, however, is really a piece of anthropological field-work for which the trained anthropologist has developed devices and methods which allow him to observe, to write down his observations and to formulate them much more rapidly than a layman can do, exactly as the trained geologist sees details and reads on the face of the earth important geological principles completely hidden from the most intelligent but untrained observer.

What is then the trouble, and why has the anthropologist been little used and of little use? The answer is that, although the methods and technique of anthropological observation are the only ones by which a competent knowledge of primitive social problems can be reached, yet the interests of anthropology have been so far in a slightly different direction. The institution of primitive kingship, for instance, has been studied by the circular route via classical antiquity. Current anthropology has been interested in savage monarchies through the interest which centred around the priestly king of Nemi. The ritual mythological aspect of savage monarchies, the dim quaint superstitions concerning the king's vitality; connexions between this and magical potentialities; these have been studied, and problems of paramount theoretical importance they certainly are. But our information as to the actual way in which primitive politics are worked, the question, what forces underlie the obedience to the king, to his ministers; the mere descriptive and analytical study of what might be called the political constitution of primitive tribes, of these we are largely ignorant. At best such information has been supplied to us as a by-product of the other, the antiquarian study of the institutions, and not through the direct practical or theoretical interest in the mechanism of primitive politics.

THEORY OF PRIMITIVE LAW

One of the subjects which is obviously of primary interest to the practical man is the law of his tribe.

Now in this subject remarkably enough he cannot receive much help from the dominant anthropology of the school because this very subject has been singularly neglected by anthropologists. Those who have studied it produced an extraordinarily unsatisfactory theory which led rather to obscure the issue, to prevent the field workers from seeing the relevant facts, than to enlighten us.

The dominant idea of the continental school of jurisprudence (Bachoften, Post, Bernhöft, Kohler, Durkheim) is that in primitive societies the individual is completely dominated by the group — the herd — the clan — the tribe, and that he obeys the laws and customs of his community with an absolute and passive obedience. Now as modern research is leading us to see, such an assumption is entirely unwarranted. (Cf. for instance the present writer's *Crime and Custom in Savage Society,* 1926.)

First of all we are beginning to see that behind the apparently chaotic welter of savage rules, there can be distinguished certain clear principles, and that the rules themselves can be adequately classified. The savage has his own criminal law, and he has what corresponds to our civil law. He has, that is, a definite system of principles which govern individual or communal rights to land, manufactured objects, or articles of consumption. He has definite, nay at times elaborate, systems of inheritance in goods and of succession in office.

These general principles are deeply connected with the organization of his tribe. This again, far from being a simple subject matter, can only be understood after patient training in the principles of primitive sociology and after some experience in anthropological field work. And here in the study of primitive organization, of kinship, of the family, of the village community, and of the tribe we come to better trodden fields of anthropology.

There is a well defined branch of our learning already in existence which is concerned with such things as 'classificatory' kinship, the organization of the clan and of the local group, and the various problems associated with matrilineal or patrilineal descent. This branch of anthropology is, however, still largely dominated by what might be called sensational or antiquarian interests. It is still very largely concerned with the explanation of customs which appear to us strange, quaint, incomprehensible. The *couvade,* the avoidance of the mother-in-law, the disposal of the after-birth, and the quaint usages associated with the relation between two cousins — all these have received a considerable amount of attention. But the broad and bigger problems of social anthropology are still somewhat in the shadow. We know much more about the so-called anomalous forms of marriage or classificatory exaggerations of kinship than we know about the organization of the family. Take such excellent books as Rattray's on the Ashanti, Smith and Dale on the Baila, E. Junod's on the Thonga, and you will find a strange disproportion between the attention given to the everyday facts of life and the singular, between the treatment of the ordinary and the quaint; the family, for instance, and the more abstruse forms of kinship. Now I maintain that the study, for instance, of how the character of an individual is formed within the family circle at first and then within the local group, and again through a course of initiations later on; the problem, that is, of character formation in the routine of native life-history, is one which can be treated anthropologically and is of primary importance theoretically. So far this problem has been almost completely neglected by anthropologists in theory and observation. I also maintain that the institution of the family is the dominant factor in most social systems, rather than those phantastic kinship anomalies so beloved of the speculatory anthropologist. I have devoted to this contention two volumes so I need not expatiate on it here.[2]

In the study of individual character formation the observer would find also a revelation of the deep-seated moral and legal forces and the various native sanctions which make a law-abiding citizen out of a so-called savage. If anything has been proved by recent anthropological research and colonial practice it is the truth that you cannot with impunity undo or subvert an old system of traditions, of morals or laws and replace it by a ready-made new morality and sense of right; the result invariably will be what might be called 'black bolshevism'.

In all this again it is the changing Native and not an untouched savage whom we would have to study. In fact, the real practice of a modern field worker should become to study the savage as he is, that is, influenced by European culture, and then to eliminate those new influences and reconstruct the pre-European status. I think it will be much sounder, even from the purely scientific point of view, if this process of elimination were not done in a mysterious manner, in the dark so to speak, but if in our field work we collected the full data as they now appear, presented them in this form, and made our reconstruction of the past above board, in the open.[3]

I want to make it quite clear that I am not indiscriminately criticizing old anthropology or trying to revolutionize it. From the very beginning the comparative methods of old anthropology have produced work and special studies of the greatest importance for the practical man. Niebuhr's monograph on Slavery, Steinmetz's work on Primitive Jurisprudence, the above quoted works on savage kinship supply us with excellent material for that new branch of anthropology here advocated. They will have only to be slightly modified, and more observations will have to be collected from the point of view of how institutions function, and not how they 'originated' or 'diffused'.

THE EFFECTIVE STUDY OF PRIMITIVE LANGUAGES

One of the matters in the reorganization of old anthropological point of view which seems to me of primary importance is a closer cooperation between the study of its several aspects which, so far, have been kept in watertight compartments. One of these, the study of primitive languages, seems to me specially important to consider.

There is no doubt at all that a knowledge of the language of his tribe is one of the most essential parts of the equipment of an administrator, a missionary, or a teacher. Now it is clear that when teaching the vocabulary of some African tribe it is quite impossible to translate some of the most important terms into English. All words which cover the native social order, all which express religious beliefs, moral values, or specific technical or ritual proceedings can only be rendered accurately by reference to the social organization of the tribe, their beliefs, practices, education, and economics. The study of a native language must go hand in hand with the study of its culture.

Its grammar cannot even well be taught except with the help of social anthropology. There are grammatical phenomena, as for instance, the classificatory particles of the Bantu languages, and of some Melanesian tongues which cannot be explained except in terms of savage customs and institutions. Again, the sociological differentiations in linguistic usage between the various ranks of society cannot be treated except as part of sociology. The various pronouns of possession in Melanesia, some modifications of verb and noun, are deeply correlated with the practice to which the language is put within its various cultural contacts, and to separate the study of language from the study of culture means merely a waste of time and an amateurishness in most aspects of the work. A close cooperation between linguistic teaching and anthropological training seems to me of the greatest importance in any curriculum prepared for colonial cadets and similar people, and yet unfortunately all the organizations of our universities are completely inadequate from this point of view. The Institute here again could give practical help by embracing the cause of this new effective anthropological method in linguistic teaching.

THE ANTHROPOLOGICAL ISSUES OF LAND TENURE

To take another subject of paramount importance, namely, land tenure in a primitive community. The apportioning of territory must be one of the first tasks of an administrator, and in doing this he has first of all to lay down the broad lines of his policy and then see that they are correctly carried out by his officers.

It is easy to see, however, that even the broad lines of policy are not easily framed unless we start with a scientific knowledge of the subject. Rights of conquest, historical prerogatives, rights stipulated by 'treaties with native chiefs' have been claimed by those interests which demand a maximum of land for European uses. Again, on the other side, those trying to safeguard native interests invoke very often the rights of primitive populations and insist that at least a 'necessary minimum' should be reserved for the Natives. But, whichever point of view is really taken, the whole problem remains a groping in the dark as long as we are not able to ascertain what the necessary minimum for the Natives can be.

Lord Lugard repeatedly insists on the great difficulties in both the theory and practice of dealing with land tenure.

> The absence of any definite sustained policy in regard to land in these dependencies (West Africa) seems to have arisen from the failure to investigate the system of native tenure. The legislators, though desirous of giving due weight to native custom, were not apparently familiar with it, and we find that the various findings relating to land are couched in terms often quite inapplicable to native tenure, and the lease and other instruments are often drawn upon an English model (*The Dual Mandate in British Tropical Africa*, p. 304).

And yet when two Committees between 1908 and 1915, one after the other, were appointed to investigate the subject of land tenure in the whole of West Africa, and collected an immense amount of evidence, the work of the Committees aroused such an upheaval of native public opinion that the reports were never published.[4] We seem therefore to be here between the devil and the deep sea, since ignorance seems to be a complete handicap in dealing with this problem, and yet often ignorance seems to be bliss compared with knowledge which is both difficult to obtain and dangerous to use.

Here I venture to suggest that if the whole question had been investigated, not by a politically appointed committee, but by two or three anthropologists, they would have done the work in far shorter time, with far less expenditure, and would have done it competently and usefully. I have not seen the reports of the West African Committee, but I have seen similar work done in the territory of Papua and the results discussed by administrators, missionaries, and planters. I have found in the first place that wherever I checked the findings of one of these 'practical' men they were essentially erroneous. As Lord Lugard rightly points out in the above quotation, the European lawyer is likely to distort native conditions by forcing them into terminology borrowed from European law. The untrained European, on the other hand, uses such words as 'communism', 'individualism,' 'private property,' 'tribal property' and what not, without giving them the slightest intelligible meaning, or understanding himself what he is talking about.

It is only that anthropologist, who specializes in the study of primitive legal ideas and economic conditions, who is competent to deal with this question. Problems of ownership must always be approached from the point of view of actual use. In dealing with land tenure it is futile to summon, as political committees usually do, a number of witnesses and just ask them simply what is their form of ownership, or, worse, what in their opinion ownership should be. Land tenure among primitive peoples is always very complex, and it is impossible for an untrained person not to be misled into some entirely inadequate translation of native ideas into his own terminology. A number of contradictory statements are invariably obtained by the amateur simply because, as a rule, the land is used by various people and the uses of the land are associated with the native systems of kinship, often a mixture of mother-right or father-right, utterly incomprehensible to the untrained European. And again, Natives will stress at times the more utilitarian aspect of ownership and then bring to the forefront some magical or mythological rights. Even these latter, however, cannot be ignored in practice because the Natives value them extremely, and because a misunderstanding arising out of some injury or insult to a sacred spot or sacred object might give rise to serious trouble. (Cf. for instance The Golden Stool of Ashanti.)

The correct procedure is to draw up a map of the territory, showing the lands which belong to each of the several communities, and the individual plots, into which it is divided. Then instead of inquiring in a wholesale manner into 'ownership' it is necessary to study how each land unit is used, and to find out the details of each of the more or less practical and also all the mystical bonds between a plot of land and the various people who claim some right to that plot.

Such an inquiry would not easily alarm the Native. He would often be not even aware that you are trying to take a survey of land tenure. In the second place such a survey would not only reveal the real legal rights of the individuals, it would also answer the often more important question of how the lands are used and what is the 'indispensable minimum' which must be reserved for them. Finally, since the anthropologist has no vested interest in this question, nor any bias connected with his research, since his aim is and will always be accuracy and fulness of detail, he is the most likely person to give the administrator what is really needed, an entirely unbiased and impartial account of the actual state of affairs.

It is not only between white and coloured interests that there is an issue, but also between the interests of the various Natives, the chief versus the community; the village community versus the clan; the tribe as a whole versus this or that section; and it is impossible to deal adequately and fairly with any of these questions without that impartial cold-blooded passion for sheer accuracy which the anthropologist can provide.

PRIMITIVE ECONOMICS

Land tenure is but one problem of the primitive economic system of the tribe, and if this one problem is so complicated, it is clear that the whole system will not be easy to understand or to handle. In fact the knowledge of what might be called the economic organization of a community is essential in a number of practical problems, such as those associated with improved hygienic conditions, with labour, with education, with the abolition of slavery and forced labour, and last but not least, with taxation.

The substance of serious anthropological work must consist here in the sociological analysis of primitive production and consumption; the types and phases of economic activities; the relations between the economic and the religious aspect, between certain forms of magic even and the practical arts. The facts have to be observed and studied as they now exist and work, and not as a pretext for reconstruction and hypothesis — anthropology should aim at the understanding and explanation of economic processes rather than the establishment of 'origins and stages' or 'diffusions and histories'.

The honest anthropologist will have to confess at once that as subject-matter primitive economics has been neglected both in observation and in theory. Forms of labour and exchange, the way in which the wealth is 'capitalized', that is, pooled or transformed into more permanent values, the psychology of gift and exchange, all these are headings difficult to find in any record of field work or text-book of anthropology.[5]

From the practical point of view questions of labour are in the forefront. Any discussion of this subject should start with a sociological definition of labour. To identify labour with activity in general (as has been done recently in a somewhat unsatisfactory textbook on *Primitive Labour* by L. H. Buxton) is incorrect, for there are various activities, above all, play and games, which are not labour in the economic sense. Not all cultural types of behaviour can be classed as labour.

In the first place labour must be defined in that it achieves something tangible and useful which serves to the satisfaction of man's essential wants. The search for food and its preparation, the procuring of material for housing, clothing, weapons, and direct objects of use constitute the most important types of labour. Even the lowest savages, however, provide certain material goods which are not for direct consumption and really belong to the primitive forms of capital: implements, arrangements for storing and preserving food, traps, hunting weapons and so on. To define the 'savage' as has been done by a recent writer as a man who 'has no means of acquiring more wealth than he can carry about with him, on his person, or on the persons of his family' is misleading. Further, often among the lowest savages there is work devoted to the production of what might be called luxuries, objects of art and monuments of culture, personal ornaments, paintings, rude sculpture, and objects serving for cult and ritual. Labour should be defined as a purposeful form of systematic activity standardized by tradition and devoted to the satisfaction of wants, the making of means of production, the creation of objects of luxury, value, and renown.

This definition, though it sounds very academic and divorced from practical possibilities, allows us at once to draw one or two useful conclusions. We have distinguished labour from other activities by its purpose. The question directly emerges: what is it that in primitive culture drives man to strenuous, prolonged, and often unpleasant effort? The problem of labour can be treated only against the background of the psychological problem of value. What are the effective incentives to effort? In what way are they related to the individual, and how far are they transformed by culture? We see thus, that exactly as it would be useless to investigate land tenure without asking to what uses land is being put, so it is impossible to understand native labour except as part of the problem of their system of values, incentives, and utility. Early forms of labour are obviously correlated with the manner in which economic value comes into existence. The wise entrepreneur and administrator will be interested to know what were the old tribal values and what forms economic ambition took in their area.

To give a concrete example: Among the North-Western tribes of North America most interests centred around the production of certain objects which in a singular and complicated manner satisfied the ambitions and the aesthetic feeling of the owner. The production of these objects forced those people to work intensely and kept them up to a certain pitch of industrial activity. Again, these objects were indispensable to the organization of their family and marriage, of their chieftainship and clan system. A wise system of administration would have got to understand the native economic system and tried gradually perhaps to replace it by new incentives to labour, new values, and new economic wants. The essentially unwarranted act of the Canadian Government, who abolished the institution of the *Potlatch,* has in every respect completely disorganized the life of the Natives, and it has produced most untoward economic consequences.

As we know from all parts of the world, a completely detribalized community, if it is not to die out, is extremely difficult to manage. We have here an example of how an unscientific spirit leads to serious practical errors.

As an offset to this I would like, from personal experience, to mention the case of North-Western Melanesia, where white traders were compelled to reorganize native industries and produce by native labour objects of native value, and through this obtained indirect control over native economic production. (Cf. also Prof. Seligman's article on Applied Anthropology in the *Encyclopaedia Britannica.*)

Forced labour, conscription or voluntary labour contracts, and the difficulties of obtaining sufficient numbers — all these form another type of practical difficulties in the colonies. The chief trouble in all this is to entice the Native or persuade him to keep him satisfied while he works for the white man; and last but not least to prevent the period of work having bad consequences on his health or morale as well as on the temporarily depleted village and home.

In all this the main question again is how to make a man of a different culture satisfied with work. The simplest experience teaches that to everybody work is prima facie unpleasant, but a study of primitive conditions shows that very efficient work can be obtained, and the Natives can be made to work with some degree of real satisfaction if propitious conditions are created for them. And another anthropological generalization teaches that satisfactory conditions of work are obtained only by reproducing those conditions under which the native works within his own culture. In Melanesia I have seen this applied on some plantations. Use was made of such stimuli as competitive displays of the results, or special marks of distinction for industry, or again of rhythm and working songs. Again the arrangement of work in gangs corresponding to indigenous communal labour produced the desired effect, but all such things must never be improvised — an artificial arrangement will never get hold of native imagination. In every community I maintain there are such indigenous means of achieving more intensive labour and greater output, and it is only necessary to study the facts in order to be able to apply efficient incentives. (Cf. here also the interesting work of K. Bücher, *Arbeit und Rhythmus.*)

A great many points could be made on the subject of labour — its incentives, its stimulation, its communal arrangement, its wider organization within the whole tribal system. I should like to add here that on these points as everywhere else the anthropologist doing the work under this new view-point, which the Institute might develop, should not merely try to reconstruct native culture as it existed or exists independently of European influence, but study the social and mental phenomena which Western culture produces in the African.

THE ANTHROPOLOGY OF THE CHANGING NATIVE

A new branch of anthropology must sooner or later be started: the anthropology of the changing Native. Nowadays, when we are intensely interested, through some new anthropological theories, in problems of contact and diffusion, it seems incredible that hardly any exhaustive studies have been undertaken on the question of how European influence is being diffused into native communities. The anthropology of the changing savage would indeed throw an extremely important light upon the theoretical problem of the contact of cultures, transmission of ideas and customs, in short, on the whole problem of diffusion.

This anthropology would obviously be of the highest importance to the practical man in the colonies. Finally, since we are witnessing one of the greatest crises in human history, namely that of the gradual expansion of one form of civilization over the whole world, the recording of that event is an essential duty of those competent to do it. Now it is really the anthropologist, accustomed as he is to deal with the simple mind and to understand simple cultures who ought to study the problem of the westernization of the world. Remarkably enough, however, so far, most contributions on that subject have been made by enthusiasts, while the specialist in his field work still tries to close his eyes to the surrounding reality and reconstructs laboriously a savage who does not exist any more — who, in Melanesia ceased to exist a generation ago, in Africa some two generations ago, and in North America perhaps one hundred years or more. If the Institute succeeds in creating this new branch of anthropology, the study of the diffusion of Western cultures among primitive peoples, and if this is undertaken with as much theoretical zeal and direct interest as the reconstructive study, then the Institute will do a great service to anthropology and to the practical man as well.

To sum up these somewhat diffused considerations; the Institute could fulfil an important practical function: (1) By bridging the gap between theoretical anthropology and its practical applications. (2) It should insist that a series of new or only partially considered subjects should be placed into the forefront of anthropological studies; the problems of population and of a demographic survey of primitive tribes; the study of the social organizations, above all, of its fundamental institutions, the family, marriage, and educational agencies in so far as they mould the character and the social nature of the individual; the somewhat neglected subjects of law, economics and politics as we find them at work in primitive communities; finally, the study of what might be called sociological or cultural linguistics: these are subjects of primary importance which can only be studied anthropologically if they are to be practically useful. (3) The study of all these questions ought to be stimulated from the practical side by linking them, not in a political, but in a merely analytical spirit to such questions as increase or decrease and shifting of populations, direct versus indirect rule, the creation of European schools, the introduction of taxation, and of labour. Only when the practical man becomes aware that he must not flounder and grope in the dark, that he needs anthropological knowledge, can he become useful to the specialist, and in turn make the latter useful to himself. (4) The study of the diffusion of European culture into savage communities, the anthropology of the changing Native must be established as an important branch of work. The anthropologist as he is now is better equipped than any one else to undertake this study, but here again he must enlarge his interests and adapt them to the practical requirements of the man who works with and for the Native. (5) Finally, as regards the directly practical assistance which could be given by the Institute in this matter: (*a*) The work in this modern, as it calls itself, functional School of Anthropology might be encouraged by the Institute. (*b*) The Institute in cooperation with the learned societies and universities could be instrumental in organizing field work on the lines here indicated in Africa. (*c*) The Institute might take in hand the question of anthropological training of colonial cadets, especially the functional anthropology dealing with African communities as they exist today. (*d*) Finally, the Institute could be a general meeting-place or central exchange between the practical and theoretical interests in anthropology.

NOTES

1. An enlightened anthropologist or statesman has to take count of European stupidity and prejudice quite as fully as of those of the African.

2. Cf. my *Family among the Australian Aborigines,* 1913, and *Sex and Repression in Savage Society,* 1927; also my articles s.v. *Kinship and Marriage* in the forthcoming issue of the *Encyclopedia Britannica,* 1929, as well as a book on *Primitive Kinship,* now in preparation.

3. Even in their study of the fully detribalized and yankified Indian, our United States colleagues persistently ignore the Indian as he is and study the Indian-as-he-must-have-been some century or two back.

4. It must, however, be noted that the work of the Committee was brought to an end by the outbreak of war in 1914.

5. Some useful preliminary work on primitive economics has been done, above all in Germany. The names of E. Hahn, H. Schurtz, K. Bücher, R. Thurnwald, and Max Weber will occur at once to the anthropologist. Recently a book has been published in English under the title *Primitive Economics* by R. W. Firth, which fills an important gap, and it is hoped will start a more intensive interest in these problems. This book also contains an excellent bibliography. Cf. also my *Argonauts of the Western Pacific,* 1922, where a native system of exchange has been described, and articles: Primitive Economics (*Economic Journal,* 1921) and Labour and Primitive Economics (*Nature,* 1926).

3

Anthropology as a Public Service

GODFREY WILSON

I. HISTORY OF THE RHODES-LIVINGSTONE INSTITUTE

For many years colonial governments in Africa have made occasional use of the services of trained social anthropologists. Sometimes they have employed them directly as 'Government Anthropologists,' sometimes they have subsidized students in the employ of scientific bodies for particular pieces of research. But it was left for Sir Hubert Young, as Governor of Northern Rhodesia, to set up in 1937 the first institute for systematic sociological research in colonial Africa.

The appeal for support which he drafted in that year was signed by twelve other public men besides himself; and in 1938 the Rhodes-Livingstone Institute of Central African Studies had sufficient funds to begin operations. The new foundation is intended, in the words of the appeal, 'as a contribution to the scientific efforts now being made in various quarters to examine the effect upon native African society of the impact

"Anthropology as a Public Service" by Godfrey Wilson is reprinted from *Africa,* 13:43–60, 1940, by permission of the International African Institute and the author's estate.

of European civilization, by the formation in Africa itself of a centre where the problem of establishing permanent and satisfactory relations between natives and nonnatives — a problem of urgent importance where, as in Northern Rhodesia, mineral resources are being developed in the home of a primitive community — may form the subject of special study.' The name 'Rhodes-Livingstone Institute' is intended to link it in men's minds with the year 1940 — 'the jubilee of the foundation of the two Rhodesias in 1890 by Cecil Rhodes . . . and the centenary of the departure for Africa in 1840 of David Livingstone.' Funds were only asked for three years in the first instance; so that, in 1940, the year of its ceremonial inauguration, the Rhodes-Livingstone Institute might be able to appeal more confidently for funds on the grounds of some initial achievement. Sir Hubert Young left Africa for Trinidad early in 1938 but His Excellency Sir John Maybin, the present Governor of Northern Rhodesia, has continued all the interest of his predecessor in the new venture.

The constitution of the Rhodes-Livingstone Institute deserves consideration by all who are concerned with the right relationship of social science to public affairs. The Institute is not a government department, but an independent body ruled by a board of trustees; while only 52 percent of its funds is derived from government contributions. Its research officers are in no way directly responsible either to any government or for any government policy; and their intellectual freedom is thus safeguarded. On the other hand, the presence of public men on the Board of Trustees[1] ensures that its officers will not waste their time splitting academic hairs but will tackle instead problems of public importance.

Two social anthropologists have now been appointed. I was appointed in May 1938 and Dr. Max Gluckman in September 1939. Each of us is engaged on a separate piece of research. Dr. Gluckman is undertaking an all-around study of the social and political system of the Rozi; while I am attempting a study of the municipal and industrial locations of the Copper Belt and Broken Hill. My own research is only possible because previous work (such as Dr. Audrey Richards' on the Bemba) gives me some knowledge of the tribal backgrounds of these urban populations.

It will be noticed that both pieces of research are within the boundaries of Northern Rhodesia, for at present this territory provides the Rhodes-Livingstone Institute with the bulk of its income; but it is intended, as funds and opportunities permit, to expand both our staff and our sphere of operations. It is our ambition to be, one day, a centre of sociological research for the whole of Rhodesia and British East Africa. Already all the Governments from Southern Rhodesia to Uganda contribute something to our funds, together with the British South Africa Company, the Beit Trust and the great mining companies of the Copper Belt and Broken Hill.[2] And already, as part of our immediate programme, papers are being written on the two tribes in Tanganyika and Nyasaland which my wife and I studied, under the joint auspices of the International Institute of African Languages and Cultures and the Rockefeller Foundation, prior to my appointment here.

Results are being published in a series — the *Rhodes-Livingstone Papers* — to which nonmembers of the Institute staff are also invited to contribute from time to time. Four papers have so far been completed.[3]

Prior to the foundation of the Rhodes-Livingstone Institute, a Museum was founded in Livingstone (in 1934) as a memorial to David Livingstone. This Museum has now been incorporated with the Rhodes-Livingstone Institute and its Curator (Mr. Desmond Clark) also acts as Secretary to the Institute. The Museum has three main sections — ethnological, archaeological, and historical, and our most valued exhibit is the note-book in which Livingstone first sketched the Victoria Falls (on loan from Dr. Hubert Wilson). The Curator's main interest is archaeology, and he has already unearthed many important finds in the Falls gravels and the Mumbwa caves.

Now the foundation of the Rhodes-Livingstone Institute raises the question of the general contribution which social anthropology has to make to the conduct of public affairs, and this we must next consider.

II. THE NATURE AND LIMITS OF APPLIED ANTHROPOLOGY

It is the proper virtue of applied anthropology to be both useful and true, to combine practical relevance with scientific accuracy and detachment. Like all virtues, this is difficult but not impossible of attainment. Its attainment depends upon a thorough-going realization of the limits of scientific method in its application to human affairs and a wholehearted acceptance of those limits.

The social anthropologist[4] cannot, as a scientist, judge of good and evil, but only of objective social fact and its implications; he cannot completely understand any event, but only the matter-of-fact social aspects of it; he cannot predict the future course of events with certainty. Let us take these points in order.

(a) *A Technical Service.* 'What ought we to do about African marriage, chieftainship, beer-drinking in town . . .?' Faced with these questions the social anthropologist must, if he is honest, begin by disappointing his questioners: 'As a scientist I have no answer, for it all depends ultimately upon one's conception of human welfare, and that is a matter not of science but of opinion.' There is no scientific ideal of human welfare; there can be no scientifically authoritative direction of events; the social anthropologist is entitled, as a man, to his own moral and political views

— they are no more and no less worthy of respect than those of any other well-informed citizen — but he is not entitled to pass them off as 'scientific.' The qualities and values of life run like water through the scientific net, which catches only the pebbles of objective fact and the branching twigs of necessary implication.

But if the questions are posed in a different form they can then be usefully answered: 'Can you explain to us the nature of the situations with which we have to deal? What is the exact state of African marriage law at such and such a place at the moment? Why have such and such chiefs apparently lost the respect of their people? Why is it so difficult to enforce the prohibition of private beer-brewing in towns?' — 'Yes, indeed I can! . . .' and the anthropologist will then continue, for several thousand words, to supply his questioners with technical information about the social material which they have to handle.

The conception of 'technical information,' as Malinowski has recently pointed out in *Africa*,[5] is the key to correct relationship between social scientists, on the one hand, and men of affairs, on the other. For human societies, like the earth on which they live, have a hard material reality which cannot be mastered without patient and objective study. It is the scientists' business to undertake that patient and objective study, it is the business of government and industry to make use of their results in fashioning out of the present whatever future they desire.

The scientists must make it their boast that both governments and oppositions can trust them equally because they say nothing that they cannot prove, because they are always pedestrian and never leave the facts. The men of affairs must make it their boast that they allow the scientists perfect freedom in their researches and pay to their results when published the attention which proven fact deserves.

It is not necessary to emphasize in *Africa* our ignorance of the traditional cultures of the African continent. For instance, in the protectorate of Northern Rhodesia, with about 1,400,000 Native inhabitants, over 70 tribes are officially recognized; and of only three or four of them have we any systematic knowledge. Experienced missionaries, compound managers, and administrators all too rarely commit to paper that understanding of African institutions which they have acquired; while the frequent transfers of the latter from station to station often make it impossible for them to acquire very much. And further it is now widely recognized that systematic and detailed knowledge cannot in any case be easily picked up in his spare time by a busy man who has no special training in research; even when he is stationed for years in one spot it is only an exceptionally gifted man who can attain it under such conditions. We do not expect technical veterinary or medical knowledge in a District Commissioner, and we are now realizing that it is just as unreasonable to expect technical sociological knowledge either. The services of trained social anthropologists are essential to the effective development of Africa.

This is true whatever the policies of the governments of Africa, but it is most obviously true in those territories where 'Indirect Rule' is applied. For 'Indirect Rule' demands respect for and deliberate utilization of African institutions. And no one can use to the best effect a material whose properties he only half understands.

Nor is this material stable in form, its properties are changing yearly under the pressure of forces which the governments can only in small part control. And the difficulties of understanding a stable set of social institutions are enormously increased when rapid change is added. Even the social anthropologists themselves have only just ceased their mental flight from the complexities of contemporary change in Africa; for years they took refuge in the relative stability of the remembered past, delicately averting their eyes from their semiliterate, semitrousered informants. They are more robust today — and more useful too.

Bare information is urgently needed: simple and accurate accounts of marriage, chieftainship, economic life, legal procedure and so on, from a hundred changing tribes and compounds. But the social anthropologist has more to offer than bare information, he claims to be able to explain the facts which he describes, and this, as we shall see in a moment, may lead him to a certain technical (but never a political) criticism of policy.

(*b*) *The Implications of Fact.* The facts which the social scientist studies are institutions, ceremonies and commonly expressed opinions: economic, legal, political, and other institutions; ceremonies at birth, marriage, death and so on; popular opinions about this and that. These things he calls 'social facts,' and their special characteristic is that they are common to some group of human beings. Every social fact is a continual recurrence of historical events in a similar form. Take marriage, for instance. All the hundreds of marriages which occur in any one African tribe over a period of five years are found to resemble one another in many ways, they constitute a social fact. And so with work and play, with eating and drinking and with all kinds of human activity — the members of any one community resemble one another in the way they carry them on.

Now the social anthropologist (if he has been trained either by Malinowski, or by Radcliffe-Brown, or by their followers) views every social situation as a whole. The social facts which he finds in it do not, he maintains, just occur at random; each is connected, necessarily connected, with other facts in the same area. The particular forms of marriage, of chieftainship, of economic life, of religious belief and practice in an African tribe, for example, are not separate things, they are inescapably linked together; and if one of them changes then all the others must change too.

Social facts may change, but they can only change together, not one by one. And thus it is that social change exhibits always a flowing and not a staccato movement, continuity is never broken. Because social facts hold together they are none of them free; they determine one another inescapably both in their stability and in their change.

And this means that every social fact can, at any given moment, be explained as the necessary correlate of other social facts: 'It was because some primitive chief,' we can say, 'was believed to be god, and because he had a great many wives and children, and because he was rich and used his wealth in socially approved ways, and because he was a most useful rallying point for tribal defence, that he had such very considerable prestige and power among his people.' Granted the first set of facts the last one necessarily follows, and so we have explained it.

Nor are social changes any less intelligibly linked. For it follows with equal necessity that if the successor of this primitive chief is now no longer believed to be a god, and if he has now fewer wives and children, and if many of the traditional sources of his wealth have now dried up, and if he has now no longer any military functions then, other things being equal, he must have less prestige and power among his people than his primitive predecessor. The conclusion is inescapable. And if the first changes have indeed taken place and if his prestige and power is indeed less than his predecessor's then we have explained why it is so.

But, of course, we may find that, though the first changes have taken place, yet the prestige and power of the chieftainship have not, in fact, appreciably declined. If so, then other things cannot have been equal; changed circumstances must have opened up to the modern chief some new functions and some new sources of wealth. If this were not so, his prestige and power would inevitably have declined.[6]

The only real difficulty in the scientific explanation of social facts and changes lies in their many-sidedness, a very great number of conditions determines each one. There is always the danger of missing some necessary connexion between them and so leaving them bare and unintelligible. And training in social anthropology consists, above all, in learning the kinds of necessary connexion which are to be looked for.

Thus social anthropologists, if they are successful, do not only add to the detailed knowledge of fact at the disposal of responsible public men, they alter the nature of that knowledge and so make it more useful.

Recently, for example, the District Officers responsible for the Nyakyusa in South Tanganyika have had to deal with a knotty problem of land-tenure. Coffee-planting is being encouraged by the Administration and is becoming exceedingly popular. But great difficulties are caused by the

Nyakyusa land laws and by the people's habits of constant movement from village to village. For, when any man who has planted coffee round his house moves away, the site, after reverting temporarily to the joint ownership of the village group, is usually taken over by another man — and then the two men, planter and present occupier, quarrel over the ownership of the coffee trees; while a few years ago, the local chief also would put in a claim to them. In 1935 or 1936 the chiefs of the district, after long and anxious discussion with the District and Agricultural Officers, passed a law that coffee trees should be 'the absolute property' of their planters. But by the beginning of 1938 the new law had proved unworkable; for coffee trees require constant attention and often the absent owners failed to provide it, while the occupiers all protested against the law.

I was in the district at the time and was called into consultation. I was able to describe the general nature of Nyakyusa land law, which is essentially based on the village group, and to show that 'absolute property' in coffee trees was, at present, quite incompatible with it. Further, as the constant movement from place to place was due to the fear of witchcraft, it would certainly continue for many years to come, and no administrative action could prevent it. Only the slow growth of Christianity and modern education could bring any general stability of residence to this district. The claims of planter, present occupier and chief to coffee trees all had some basis in traditional law, which, however, provided no certain guidance on the issue. For coffee trees, with their need of constant attention and the high economic value of their berries, had no exact parallel in the traditional life of the Nyakyusa.

An analysis of the traditional laws of property in bananas, bamboos, and some other trees, however, showed the general lines on which a solution might be found. Bananas, for example, though not very valuable, yet needed constant attention, like coffee. And in their case the law was this: when their planter moved both the bananas and the house-site on which they were planted reverted to the joint ownership of the local village group; while the nearest neighbours looked after the bananas and took their fruit. When a newcomer was given the site, by the village headman with the chief's approval, then the bananas became his individual property, but only so long as he lived there; if he moved they reverted again to the village. This traditional law, it seemed to me, might perhaps be made the basis of the new law of property in coffee trees, with the exception that either a percentage of the crop or some monetary compensation should be allowed to the planter, in view of the relatively great value of coffee, and that, in any case, he be allowed the whole of any crop which ripened within a year of moving. This suggestion was discussed by the District Officer and the chiefs and they agreed to act upon it, with some modifications. When I last heard (February 1939) the final decision of the Central Government was still being awaited.

Now this was a complex situation and no bare statement of fact would have helped the Administration; it was necessary to explain the inescapable connexions between the social organization and the laws of land-tenure and between witchcraft and moving, and so to show the limits within which effective action was possible.

And the truth that all the facts of any social situation are intelligibly, that is necessarily, linked together has a further practical importance, for a policy is itself a social fact. And, though the scientist cannot judge its intrinsic value, he can and must study both its own actual implications and also the relevant implications of the situation to which it is directed. He can never either approve or condemn any policy as such, but he can tell its authors whether or not it is possible of application to given conditions and what its immediate effects will probably be. If it is not possible of application he can point out the conditions which must be changed to make it so.

If, for instance, half the able-bodied men leave a tribal area, in which a primitive subsistence agriculture is practised (Richards, 1939), and go to work in distant industrial towns; and if able-bodied male labour is essential to that subsistence agriculture; then, if other things remain equal, the old men and the sick and the women and the children who are dependent on those able-bodied men must either follow them to town, or import food into the tribal area with money sent back by them, or go hungry. There is, in those conditions, no other possible alternative. If then it were desired to prevent the more mobile part of the general population (i.e. the women and children) from leaving such a tribal area, it would hardly be possible to do so unless very substantial amounts of money were regularly sent or taken back by the industrial workers, and unless that money were largely spent on food. If substantial amounts of money were not sent home and there spent on food, then a drift of a large part of the general population to the towns would be quite inevitable in those conditions. But, of course, the other relevant conditions might be changed; it might be possible so to develop agricultural methods in the tribal area concerned that half the able-bodied men could support the whole of the general population. Or it might be possible for the able-bodied women to learn to perform some, at least, of the traditionally masculine tasks — it would depend on the particular nature of local conditions and, more especially, on the amount of free time which traditionally feminine tasks left the women.

Thus the scientist, once he has mastered the mutual implications of the facts of some social situation, is in a position to give technical, but not political, advice and criticism to the men who have to deal with it. And such continual laying bare of the inevitable mutual implications of social fact is, in the complex conditions of modern Africa, an essential public service.

(c) *The Responsibility of Statesmen.*   But what is all this about *necessary connexions* in the social field? some one will ask. How is it to be squared with the admitted freedom of responsible leaders, whether in government or industry, to choose between policies and to direct events? Do not the claims we have made for social science logically imply that public men are nothing but automata and their actions nothing but the necessary consequences of existing social conditions? — Not at all. We have never suggested that any historical event was wholly determined by social conditions, but only partially, in its social aspects. A government policy, for instance, is, in one aspect, a social fact and inevitably involved in all the matter-of-fact necessities of the existing social situation. But, within the limits of that situation, it is also a series of choices and these choices are real choices, acts of freedom.[7]

The social scientists confine their gaze to the abstract field of matter-of-fact social necessity, but they do not imagine that this field of theirs is all the world there is. All historical events, no doubt, must take place in it, but they are determined by other things besides its nature. We may picture an historical event as a group of people, led by statesmen, walking across the field. Once the group is inside, the social scientists can help it by pointing out the paths and the rabbit holes; but there is nothing in the field to determine the direction of the walk; paths run every way, all of them winding a little and plentifully flanked by rabbit holes. On one side of the field there are a number of gates labelled with the names of the various purposes of man. And it makes all the difference in the world through which gates the group goes out. But the scientists see nothing outside their field and care for nothing but its nature; they can give the group no help as it hesitates which gate to make for; they cannot prevent chance circumstances affecting the decision; when the group goes out they do not know whether it will end up in heaven or in hell. Moreover, the groups which constantly cross the field in different directions are not entirely powerless to alter its topography — it takes time to do so, but it can be done; paths can be changed and rabbit holes stopped. In all this the scientists provide technical assistance only, but continually remapping the field and explaining its nature.

In every historical event, that is to say, there is both necessity and freedom: necessity in the actual social material involved at any one moment — the institutions, ceremonies and beliefs which are the field of action — freedom not only in the chance concatenation of particular circumstances and in the ultimate purpose of the action which is taken there but also in the power, given time and understanding, to modify the social material itself. But with chance, ultimate purposes and politics, as such, the scientists have no concern.

The cat is now out of the bag, but we must forget our previous metaphor if we would see her clearly. A social fact is not an event. When we speak of social facts — institutions, ceremonies, beliefs — we are not speaking of the whole of what happens, but only of its necessary framework; and the scientific explanation of events is always incomplete. A social fact is a general form within the limits of which particular events must, at any given moment, occur, but within those limits chance and human purpose have free play. Nor are the limits themselves unalterable; if chance and human purpose continually place events nearer to one of the limits than the other, then both limits, as it were, will shift in that direction; that is how every change originally occurs. But, as the social facts in any one area form a system which is necessarily connected in all its parts, a change in any one social fact has inevitable repercussions on all the others. A shift of the limits of action in one place means a shift of all the limits everywhere. And it is, above all, because these inevitable repercussions are so difficult to follow and foresee that the services of social scientists are necessary to the public welfare.

This is the crux of the matter: it is both true that every single historical event is necessarily determined in its material form by the social conditions of the time, and that a succession of historical events has power to modify social conditions. Granted a belief in freedom the apparent paradox can be resolved by the analogy of the artist and his material. The necessity in historical events is a material necessity only; social conditions bind the statesman as the nature of bronze or marble binds the sculptor; if he strives against them he is quite helpless, but once he understands and accepts them he can then subdue them to his own purposes.

For an increased technical understanding of the social material involved means an increased freedom of action in public affairs. Many a wise policy has proved abortive in the past because obstructed by social conditions whose relevance to it was hidden from its authors; but once they are clearly understood there are no social conditions which cannot be modified by time and patient effort. Many an apparently wise policy has, in the past, had untoward effects which were in no way foreseen at the moment of its inception; but time and patient research can foresee in detail the probable effects of any given policy.

Firth, for instance, in his studies of Tikopia,[8] a tiny island of twelve hundred inhabitants in the Pacific, has been able to demonstrate that the traditional equilibrium between population and food supply was maintained, among other things, by 'a celibacy in which chastity was not enforced,' by 'a discreet infanticide,' and by war. The younger men were often forbidden by their elders to marry and have children, but no objection was made to infertile intrigues. Married couples with three or four children often practised infanticide. And, as a last resort, when pressure of population on land became too severe, a section of the people was forcibly driven overseas. But now the combined effect of mission teaching, which discourages premarital intercourse and so tends to earlier marriage, and government policy, which forbids both infanticide and war, is upsetting the equilibrium; and there is a very real danger of overpopulation and famine unless something is done in good time to overcome the maladjustment. 'At the present time,' Firth writes, 'there is no acute pressure, nor may there be for another generation; but, if the present rate of increase continues, it will surely come.'

The value of technical sociological information to governments could hardly be more clearly exemplified. Firth has been able to see a danger a generation before it becomes urgent: his careful analysis of causes proves its inevitability, if present conditions remain substantially unaltered; and so the government responsible has both plenty of time to change the conditions and also all the relevant information necessary for doing so effectively. For he then goes on to discuss various alternative ways of avoiding it — agricultural development, migration, the encouragement of birth control — pointing out the difficulties inherent in each. He makes the issues clear for the government's decision, and prevents it being taken unawares by a sudden emergency.

(d) *General Principles.* Hitherto our discussion of social necessities has referred only to those of particular places and times, but an intelligent comparison of the various places and times known to sociology and scientific history[9] leads us inevitably to the formulation of general principles — forms and connexions of fact which obtain at all times and in all places with equal necessity. And we then begin to realize that all the particular facts and all the necessary connexions of particular fact which research lays bare in different areas and periods are but particular instances of such general principles.

Comparative social science is still in its infancy, but there are already a number of propositions which command general assent, the 'marginal' theories of modern economics[10] being an outstanding example. And undoubtedly the most useful contribution which social science can make to the conduct of public affairs is to increase the number of such accepted general truths. For, once they have been understood, they provide guidance to effective action even in those areas where no intensive studies have been carried out. It is not possible for every political action everywhere to be preceded by intensive sociological research; but it is, in principle, quite possible for every political action to be inspired by general sociological understanding.

In this connexion it is important to distinguish clearly between the particular social conditions which can, and the general social principles which cannot be modified by political action. Particular laws and conventions, for example, can be changed, but no society anywhere can possibly continue without some law and some convention. For the existence of law and convention, as such, is necessarily implied in the general nature of human society. And we can go further; we can say, for instance, that it is quite impossible for any law to be enforced in any community unless either it commands the approval of the majority of the responsible members of that community or is backed by the constant pressure of overwhelming central force. This is a necessary implication of the general nature of law. And it does not need any intensive research to see its relevance to such a vexed practical problem, for example, as that of private beer-drinking and brewing by Africans in town.

Now, although there are still relatively few such general principles which can be certainly enunciated, their number is continually increasing. Every good piece of historical research, every good fieldstudy of present social fact is full of hypotheses — formulations of principle which demonstrably fit the particular facts studied and which may possibly be found to fit the whole social field. Such hypotheses cannot be taken as conclusive until they have been checked by careful comparison with the other known facts. But intelligent readers will find them illuminating even in their hypothetical stage.

One such hypothesis was put forward recently by Wagner in the course of a discussion of 'The changing family among the Bantu Kavirondo' of Kenya Colony.[11] He begins with the accepted truism that: 'In a study of social tendencies we must distinguish between dogma and praxis, between the theoretical code of conduct, on the one hand, and the actual conduct, on the other.' And he then goes on to suggest that 'While it is part of human nature that the two will never coincide entirely, *the discrepancy between them increases in periods of rapid change* (my italics). As a rule, actual conduct changes first and becomes only gradually sanctioned by an adjustment of the theoretical code, as new standards of conduct are evolved.' Now this suggestion almost carries its proof in itself, though further research and reflection may possibly lead to a slight reformulation. And it immediately increases our general understanding of the customs of semidetribalized Africans. We begin to see that the legal informality and the apparent carelessness of convention and morality, which characterize them as a group, are inevitable temporary consequences of the rapid change of conditions and standards which we have brought to them. And thus every competent piece of sociological research is useful, not only to those who are responsible for the particular area studied, but to all men of affairs; for it is a contribution to general sociological understanding.

Moreover, within the social field distinct regions can be marked off in which social conditions are broadly similar, and the territories whose governments contribute to the funds of the Rhodes-Livingstone Institute fall within one such area. The great majority of the tribes in Central Africa are Bantu, all were recently primitive in their ways of life, all have now been touched by Christianity, and by European education, enterprise and government; the practical problems which result from European settlement and from agricultural and industrial development are broadly the same everywhere. And so every piece of research in Northern Rhodesia or Tanganyika, or Nyasaland, for example, has a more immediate relevance to the problems of Kenya, Southern Rhodesia, and Uganda than it has to those of Europe or New Guinea or even Nigeria.

It has recently been pointed out by Read,[12] for instance, that one of the most important changes in Nyasaland today is 'the inevitable cleavage between the traditional association of power and resources and the modern divorce of wealth and responsibility.' She shows that, among the Ngoni of Nyasaland, wealth and rank used to be synonymous; while the aristocrats used continually to redistribute their accumulated goods to their inferiors. But now aristocrats are often poor, and the *nouveaux riches* have not the same responsibilities. And this, as we have already partly seen, is true of every tribe in Central Africa.

(e) *Predicting the Future.*   Now as the necessary connexions of social fact are not the whole of history, so the future must always be to some extent unknown. All that scientists can say with particularity about the future is always hypothetical: 'Other things being equal, then such and such a policy will inevitably have such and such results.' But other things may not be equal, indeed they seldom or never are quite equal from one year to the next.

The general principles of society, however, are immutable. And, though we cannot foresee in detail what forms will be assumed by law or convention or economics or marriage or political authority in the Central Africa of the future, yet we know with certainty that in some form these things will always be found; and the more we can prove about them and about their general connexions with one another the more practical relevance will this certainty possess.

Moreover the immediate future is in part determined by the known necessities of present social conditions, and this partial determinism makes it possible to speak of 'scientific probabilities.' At the moment, to take a simple instance, the Government of Northern Rhodesia has decided to increase the salaries paid to its Native Chiefs.[13] And it is quite certain that, were other things to remain equal, this action would do a great deal to increase the present capacity of Native Authorities to fulfil the duties which modern conditions lay upon them. For, as Richards has shown,[14] the ineffectiveness of Native Authorities which is often complained of by District Officers is very largely due to the present poverty of the chiefs. Without the means of entertaining their subordinates and counsellors generously they are helpless.

But we can go further, we can say that it is highly probable that this increase in effectiveness will, in the near future, actually take place; for it is unlikely that other relevant conditions will be much altered. It is obviously very unlikely, for example, that the Government will, while increasing their salaries, take away from the chiefs any of the official powers and backing which they now possess. But the situation a generation hence it is impossible to predict with any assurance.

It is because social change can never in fact be sudden, however sudden it may seem to a superficial observer, but must always grow slowly out of the linked necessities of previous conditions, that some degree of particular prediction is possible. But the more distant the future the less possible it becomes.

III. TIME AND MONEY

Social anthropology costs very little, in money, for each research worker, but a good deal in time when compared with some other sciences. No expensive instruments, laboratories or materials are needed; and the Rhodes-Livingstone Institute, for instance, is able in 1940 to maintain two research workers in the field, together with a Secretary-Curator, a museum, a library and a small staff of clerks and messengers, all for less than three thousand pounds.

But while the Ecological Survey of Northern Rhodesia, to take another fairly inexpensive science, has been able to cover the whole of this territory in two three-year tours, no such wide field can possibly be covered by the present staff of the Rhodes-Livingstone Institute in any similar period. In each small area, whether tribal or urban, a minimum of two years' research is necessary before any results of certain value can be guaranteed; and, if an all-round survey is attempted, the field work and writing-up combined cannot be completed in less than five years.

This lengthy period is inevitably determined by the nature of the material studied. No work can be done anywhere in Central Africa until the local language has been mastered, and that alone takes six months. And then, even if attention is concentrated on one particular aspect of social life alone — say chieftainship, or the economic system, or the laws of marriage — the general nature of the social system must first be grasped; and that takes another year. Moreover, a social anthro-

pologist in Central Africa is inevitably exposed to various infections —
malaria, dysentery and what not — and so loses a certain amount of time
through sickness.

But if it were desired, for instance, to cover the most important tribes
and towns of Rhodesia and British East Africa in a period of twenty years,
a staff of only ten social scientists would be needed, and a total yearly
income of twelve thousand pounds. Such a programme would have an
enormous public value and the expenditure involved would, I think, be
a very small price to pay for it.

If only a third of that income were forthcoming, however, a great deal
could still be done. Three social scientists could be continuously employed and would, in twenty years, be able to undertake a dozen major
pieces of research[15] or, alternatively, thirty studies of particular problems.
Such a programme would add considerably to the detailed knowledge
of fact at the disposal of governments, missionaries, educationalists and
business men. The results obtained would often be found to apply, with
slight modifications only, to neighbouring tribes and urban areas, while
throughout the whole region general sociological understanding would
be greatly increased.

NOTES

1. His Excellency Sir John Maybin, K.C.M.G., Governor of Northern Rhodesia
   (President); the Financial Secretary, Northern Rhodesia; Sir Leopold
   Moore, M.L.C., Northern Rhodesia; the President of the British South
   Africa Company; the Chief of the Federated Caledonian Society of South
   Africa; the Provincial Commissioner, Livingstone; the Mayor of Living-
   stone.

2. Contributors in 1940: Northern Rhodesia Government, British South Africa
   Company, Southern Rhodesia Government, Mufulira Copper Mines,
   Rhokana Corporation, Roan Antelope Copper Mines, Tanganyika Govern-
   ment, Beit Trustees, Kenya Government, Nyasaland Government, Rhodesia
   Broken Hill Development Company, Uganda Government.

3. No. 1. 'The Land Rights of Individuals among the Nyakyusa' by Godfrey
   Wilson; No. 2. 'The Study of African Society' by Godfrey Wilson and
   Monica Hunter; No. 3. 'The Constitution of Ngonde' by Godfrey Wilson;
   No. 4. 'Bemba Marriage' by Audrey I. Richards.

4. '(Social) anthropology', 'sociology' and 'social science' are here used as
   synonymous terms.

5. B. Malinowski, 'The present state of culture contact studies', *Africa*, vol.
   xii, no. 1.

6. For concrete examples cf. Audrey I. Richards, 'Tribal Government in Transition', Supplement to *Journal of the Royal African Society*, October 1935; and Godfrey Wilson, 'The Constitution of Ngonde', *Rhodes-Livingstone Paper No. 3*.

7. I here deliberately step outside the scientific sphere in the interests of simple diction. The social scientist, as such, cannot speak of 'freedom', but only of 'data which are indeterminate within the social field'. He must leave open the question whether these data are really examples of freedom or not; for some philosophers would argue that all such data are determinate in some field or other (e.g. those of psychology, biology, etc.). But, as freedom is probably believed in by most of my readers and as it is a familiar concept to all, it is convenient to make use of it here.

8. Raymond Firth, *We the Tikopia*, Chapter XII: 'A modern population problem.'

9. Scientific history is itself the oldest branch of social science. In method and principle identical, it differs from other social sciences only in its material, which is the past.

10. Economics, which is the specialized study of one particular element of social behaviour, is far more advanced than general sociology.

11. Supplement to *Africa*, vol. xii, no. 1, reprinted as Memorandum xviii.

12. Margaret Read, 'Native Standards of Living and African Culture Change.' Supplement to *Africa*, vol. xi, no. 3, reprinted as Memorandum xvi.

13. Native Affairs Annual Report for 1938. Foreword, paragraph 6.

14. Audrey Richards, *Tribal Government in Transition*.

15. i.e. all-round studies of tribes or urban areas, dealing with economics, marriage, political authority, education, law, religion, in each case.

4

Anthropology and the Government of Native Races in the Pacific

THE HON. SIR APIRANA TURUPA NGATA

Anthropology has been defined as the science of man, considered physically, intellectually and morally, or in his entire nature. As a science dealing with man, the supreme product of nature, it demands tribute from every other branch of science. The scope of this paper is fortunately defined by the relation of the science to the government of native races in the Pacific. Briefly the writer is required to discuss the impact of imported cultures under control of civilized governments on preexisting native polity; and further, it is presumed, to indicate the method whereby the native mind may be influenced to surrender its concepts and to accept the new ideas. It is not possible to cover the question adequately in the time available this evening, but an attempt will be made to deal with the main factors in the problem.

"Anthropology and the Government of Native Races in the Pacific" by the Hon. Sir Apirana Turupa Ngata is reprinted from the *Australasian Journal of Psychology and Philosophy* 6:1–14, 1928, by permission of the publisher.

This paper will be found deficient in those abstract statements and generalizations, that characterize scientific discussions, and to that extent will, it is feared, fall short of the standard of a group interested in psychology and philosophy. The writer, as a Polynesian, accepts without reservation the dictum of students of Maori mentality, that the race had not attained to such a command of ideas and of the language to express them as to have been able to use abstractions and generalizations. Maori literature, such as it is, is characterized, particularly in its poetry, by allusiveness, by its abundant use of concrete illustrations, whence the student may deduce principles and beliefs, and place them in his schemes of classification. The student of the *whakatauki,* or proverbial sayings of the Maori, will note their poverty in those abstractions which distinguish the wise sayings of the Hebrew, the European, or the Hindu. The Maori language abounds in metaphorical expressions; old narratives teem with aphorisms and personifications. The Maori orator delights in allegory. Mr. Elsdon Best has emphasized the mytho-poetic imagery so characteristic of Maori mentality, but deplored the paucity of terms denoting abstractions. It would be well to bear this in mind, when appraising the appeal of European principles, beliefs and standards to the Maori or Polynesian mind and heart; it has too often failed to reach the mark, because of its unfamiliar and foreign apparel.

There is a tendency perhaps in modern science to magnify the importance of terminology; a tendency in ethnographers to work to skeleton charts, such as are outlined in "Notes and Queries on Anthropology," and to measure the quality of their work by the detailed filling of those charts. Much superficial work has been done under this guise. The temptation to make the material observed conform to the principles connoted by the terminology of the charts could not always be resisted. Races under observation are thus often credited with mental and other qualities they never possessed; or more is read into their culture and sociology than the facts warrant. This strain of superficiality is perhaps more apparent in studies of subtropical peoples, where isolation, climate and insufficient communications make the research student impatient of his environment and inclined to rush his "job" to a conclusion. He does not succeed in tuning in to the mentality of the people he has come to study before passing on to other localities, whose survey is planned in the research scheme.

As great a source of inaccuracy and misunderstanding is the mental and, it should be added, the social attitude of the observer. To be thoroughly scientific he must be honest and completely receptive; must not allow preconceived notions to undervalue or overestimate any fact or concept, that may come into view in his observations. The early missionaries were not good observers of the mythology and religious beliefs of the Polynesians. They were prone to measure these by biblical standards or to apply to them a terminology liable to be misunderstood. Shortland in "Traditions and Superstitions of the New Zealanders," speaking of the missionaries, said:

> The missionaries, who from their knowledge of the language, alone had it in their power for many years to converse freely with the native race, seem to have avoided all enquiries on such subjects. They came to teach a religion, and not to learn the principle of superstitions, which, however valuable in matters of ethnological interest, they regarded as having for their author the great enemy of mankind.

> Similar views have probably influenced missionaries in all new countries, for precisely the same course was taken by the early Spanish missionaries at the Philippine Islands, who, we are told, did their utmost 'to extirpate the original memorials of the Natives,' substituting religious compositions of their own, in the hope of supplanting the remains of national and pagan antiquity.

It is said that Maori matter recorded about the middle of last century was not above suspicion, that either the *tohungas* dictating the same, or the scribes who took their notes and extended them, were influenced by the scriptures. The best studies of the moral and religious beliefs of the Maori have been made by men who were not interested in supplanting or converting them to other beliefs; while the best results have been obtained by missionaries, who have accepted the Maori philosophical system as the product of an adult, intellectual, and spiritual nature, and thus entitled to respect, to be put aside by the aboriginal people in view of something better, more satisfying, or less irksome than their former regime.

As prone to err as the early missionaries, were the *pakeha* immigrants, who adopted a pose of superiority, an air of self-sufficiency, that refused to learn aught from a barbarous people or to brook anything but the imposition of their transplanted culture on the barbarians whom they found in prior occupation. Your Association will, I take it, condemn such an attitude as roundly as did the Natives, illustrating as it does your wise saying relative to the blindness of those, who having the capacity to see, will not use that faculty. It should be granted, however, that if the mission of the immigrant culture is complete conquest and destruction, then calculated blindness is the best policy. The aboriginal inhabitants would rank with the indigenous forest and fern, as so many obstructions for the energetic pioneer to remove and replace with imported grasses, and an imported population with its concomitant culture complex. There is no doubt, that most of the errors and misunderstandings have arisen from the intolerance, the narrowness, the prejudice, and intellectual contempt evinced by the European in contact with native races, whether it be in

Polynesia or anywhere else. Such an attitude has too often evoked a corresponding resistance and repugnance, a clash, if it may be so termed, of cultures, the lower being overborne, it is true, together with the people, whose inheritance it was from the ages.

It was not to be expected that in the settlement of New Zealand by the white race there would be, as a preliminary, an ordered and organized study of Maori culture. Colonization, especially of the North Island, was not a deliberate act of a government or of an organization, such as was created in the New Zealand Company or those organizations which settled Canterbury and Otago. An intensive study of the history of the Bay of Islands at the beginning of the nineteenth century by the ethnologist would make an immensely valuable contribution to the problem, which is denoted by the title of this paper. It would be a study of the play of human motives; of the mind of the Maori, actuated by the same motives as have actuated man in all lands and in all ages, now faced with new methods and strange means of satisfying ancient aims and desires; of the mind of the *pakeha* trader and adventurer, be he whaler, flax-merchant, or sailor, breaking new ground indeed for the exercise of his superior knowledge, but repeating a familiar experience — the experience of his forbears in Africa, the Indies, and America; of the mind of the missionary, representing at that time the best elements in the immigrant culture. This mind, however much it was confined and handicapped by the nature of its mission, did seek to probe that of the Native, and did attempt to appraise and register the aboriginal institutions, the social psychology of the Maori people. The "Williams" family, than which no other was more successful in influencing the Maori mind, has left us no connected or extended study of Maori culture at this time. The mastery of the Maori language, evidence by the successive editions of the Maori dictionary by three generations of the family, is sufficient proof that the necessary talent and knowledge were not wanting. Those who had the privilege of knowing the members of the family of the past generations and many of its representatives today can vouch for their intimate knowledge of Maori character and mentality, their great judgment in weighing facts and ideas. It is to be regretted, therefore, that this unique talent has not preserved to us a balanced statement of the factors in the meeting of cultures at the Bay of Islands a century ago.

The missionaries saw the introduction of the most formidable and the most seductively attractive elements of modern civilization, fire-arms, alcohol, and trade. The introduction of the first-named took place at that stage in the history of the Maori people, when all over the North Island tribe warred with tribe and bloody struggles were taking place, which, if civilization, though attended by much evil, had not entered, might have ended in the depopulation of the country. Tribal histories, both published and unwritten, agree that in the third or fourth generation after the *Arawa-Tainui* migration from Eastern Polynesia tribal wars on an extensive scale commenced. Vendettas and reasons therefor accumulated through the generations, until towards the end of the eighteenth century tribal warfare had reached a summit of fury and savagery unparalleled anywhere in the Pacific.

The research student will find ample and highly interesting material in pursuing the effect of the introduction of fire-arms on Native culture. Hongi Hika of infamous memory merely anticipated, what many another war leader might have done, if the whaler and trader had found harbours in other localities as favourable as Whangaroa and the Bay of Islands. The *pu-tawhiti* would have been used as readily and as relentlessly to wipe out old scores. The immigrant culture required, that in regard to its sea-faring vessels they should have ample sheltered anchorage in deep waters, close to provisions, water, and suitable timber, where they might be refitted for further voyages. Contemporary Maori songs abound with references to the new and terrible implement of warfare, which in two generations completely relegated the old weapons to the ceremonial *marae* or the museum. Prescott has related, in a masterly manner, the devastating effects of the Spanish warfare on the ancient civilizations of Mexico and Peru. New Zealand awaits another Prescott to describe in appropriate language the most dramatic effects of the introduction of this element of the culture of Europe.

The historian or ethnologist may contemplate the disintegrating effects of these importations. It would not be possible or necessary to detail them here. But no study would avail which did not emphasize the violence which the three imported factors did to preexisting Native polity. In warfare, it is true, the method of destruction was merely changed and the scale probably increased, though the latter may be doubted. The most serious result, probably was that the possession of fire-arms became the overwhelming motive of the Native mind; his industrial activities were ordered to that end; his control of tribal lands was governed by a new and supreme temptation, so that the new culture appealed to his avarice and desire for vengeance and power.

The gun, alcohol, manufactured clothes and blankets, barter, money, traffic in land — the anthropologist must not neglect to record in the pursuit of his science the part each of these has played in the disintegration of Native cultures in Polynesia, as in other parts of the world.

From this welter of lust and bloodshed the Maori people emerged with terrible scars and unbalanced minds. It should be emphasized that culturally the severest loss was that of the old time sanctions, which fortified custom and their religious system, which supported the *mana* and prestige of the chiefs and priests, round which the communal system evolved. It was at this period that the far-off British Government decided to intervene, and to introduce law and order in a country, where its white subjects had established themselves and required, not only protection, but control in their relations with the aboriginal inhabitants. That remarkable document, the Treaty of Waitangi, was signed nearly two generations after the first serious impact of *pakeha* civilization upon the Maori regime. The student of anthropology will find ample room for speculation as to the mental attitude of the chiefs assembled at Waitangi in February of 1840, and especially as to their conception of the meaning of the terms, "sovereignty," *mana,* "ownership according to Native customs and usages," as Governor Hobson, through Henry Williams, expounded them. Would the Maori tribes have been welded by warfare into a race under a supreme chief and thus evolved, as in some of the Pacific Islands, the institution of Kingship? It is extremely doubtful. The size of the country, the difficulties of transport and the relationships of leading *rangatira* families would have militated against any permanent effective cohesion.

Jurists in successive generations have written tomes to expound the conception of sovereignty. Even now the abstraction is not easy to grasp and comprehend. Fortunately, for the Maori, in New Zealand the British genius had personified abstract sovereignty in the distant King, whom some of the Maori Chiefs had seen in the flesh, with whose successor they or their descendants concluded the Treaty. The nearest approach to an appreciation of the nature and effect of the Treaty was expressed by old Nopera Pana-Kareao, the most powerful chief in the Mangonui and Kaitaia districts, in a speech accounted amongst the finest examples extant of old-time Native oratory:

> I wish you all to love the Governor. We are saved by this. Let everyone say, "Yes," as I do. We have now some one to look up to. My grandfather brought the *Pakehas* to this very spot, and the chiefs agreed with what my grandfather did. He went on board the ship and got trade. He spread it through the land. Let us act right as my ancestors did. What has the Governor done wrong? *The shadow of the land goes to the Queen, but the substance remains with us. We will go to the Governor and get payment for our land as before.*

I have lingered at some length over this famous compact, because of its bearing on the government of the Maoris in this country. We have come to the point where the anthropologist becomes the historian, the jurist, and, in a measure, the psychologist. The attitude of the Maori mind towards the new conceptions of sovereignty, personified by the Queen, Government, as embodied in the Governor and his officials, the ownership of land according to custom and usage as guaranteed by the Treaty, and, finally, towards the abstract idea of legal equality with the representatives of the new culture, is a subject well worth the attention of the ethnologist who sees before his own eyes the actual process of the merging of cultures, the adaptation of one to the pressure of elements in the other, the reaction of the lower upon the higher, and withal the physical, mental, and moral influences generated in the process. In no other land have the circumstances been so favourable for the study. Under no other rule has it been possible to stage such a drama as has been unfolded in New Zealand — the deliberate lifting of a people of lower culture to full equality in political, social, and moral communion with one of the most advanced races in the world.

In every department of material culture the Maori primitive polity could parallel, though on a lower plane, corresponding elements in the new culture. So could every other important branch of the Polynesian race. And in one department or another the new culture met stubborn, conservative elements, that are not yet completely dissolved. I maintain that the function of Government in this country, as applied to the Maori race, has been to discover and appraise these elements, and especially to judge whether in their nature they were detrimental to progress on the lines newly laid down, or worth preserving in a modified form. It is in the disposition shown by legislators, educationists, reformers, churchmen, and all who have had to do with the administration of Maori affairs, to examine sympathetically these elements in the Native culture and to provide for them so that New Zealand may be regarded as the best example of success in the government of a Native race not only in the Pacific, but perhaps in the world.

I wish to refer briefly to some examples to illustrate my contention. In regard to the physical preservation and improvement of the Maori people, reform met with strong and persistent resistance. The disturbance was not apparent in the physical culture of the race. Those of you who have read the observations of Taylor, Thomson, Colenso, Elsdon Best, and others on the manners and customs of the Maori will appreciate that in the economy of their village life, in their customs relating to the treatment of the sick, to the care of children, to their food and clothing, to housing and living conditions, to the disposal of the dead, and to the all-pervading *tapu*, would be found the most conservative elements of Native culture. I must also point out here an element little appreciated in ethnological studies that I have seen, an element that is the fundamental difference between the English conception of the individualistic "home," and the Maori notion of the communal *kainga*. This will be found at the root of all the difficulties of Government of the Native race not only in this country but in other parts of Polynesia.

Where, as in New Zealand, the climate and physical conditions made it one of the most favourable territories on earth for European settlement, it was inevitable that an immigrant white race must establish its culture there and expand in time into a vigorous nation, even at the expense of the culture of the aboriginal inhabitants. Colonization, as planned by Edward Gibbon Wakefield and others, was aimed deliberately at the transplantation of the best elements in English culture to the new land. In the practically virgin areas of Canterbury, Otago, and Southland the scheme met with no checks from a rival Native culture. In the North Island such checks existed and were met. The colonization of the Northern peninsula was a haphazard affair, and afforded a much more interesting study because the cultures found themselves thrown the one against the other without design and, as it were, in the natural, uncontrolled course of ethnic development. In the Wellington Province the Wakefield scheme came into conflict with tribes newly established at Wellington, Otaki, and along the Manawatu Coast, where they had recently succeeded by force of arms in subduing Ngatiira, Muaupoko, and other aboriginal peoples. The newcomers, as colonists themselves and barely established in new *kaingas,* had not perhaps had time to weave associations and traditions round the beaches, the streams, and mountains of the conquered territory. This would probably account for the readiness with which they parted with the conquered lands. It would also account for the ready response of the Ngati-Raukawa, Ngati-Toa, and Ati-Awa, the immigrant tribes, to accept European settlement and culture. With them it is found that the old communal system of land holding and the communal idea of the *kainga* gave way more readily, if not more thoroughly, to the invading conception of individual ownership and privacy in the home. Superficially, they appeared to have become Europeanised more rapidly than any tribes to the north or to the east of them. This was perhaps an accident of history, but the circumstance does give rise to the speculation that, if those who eventually came to control the introduction of European culture to the Maori people had penetrated to the root difficulty, the absence of the idea of "home," and had deliberately swept away communal land-ownership and replaced it with the English conception of a man's home being his castle, the effective adoption of English culture might have taken place much earlier in the history of the Maori race.

To the end of the nineteenth century a policy of drift characterized Government action or inaction in regard to the health of the Maori people. Degeneracy, neglect, infant mortality, the practical abandonment of Maori material and ways of dress and the adoption of European clothing, the removal of the incentive to labour and hard physical exercise — these and other facts have been deplored as contributing to the physical decadence of the race. The old sanctions of *tapu*, priestly control and chiefly *mana* had disappeared or persisted in degenerate forms and practices, and the new culture had not as yet provided effective substitutes, or, if they existed, had not been admitted to full control in the Maori social organization.

It was at this stage that the influence of education on the mind of the new generation of Maoris emerged as a serious factor in the coordination of elements in the disappearing Maori culture with the pervading *pakeha* culture. The emergence of the educated Maori youth and the part it has taken and is still taking in reorganizing Maori culture, if I may still so designate it after it has been battered about by the invading factors, should provide one of the most interesting studies possible for New Zealand psychologists or practical politicians.

The representatives of the Young Maori Movement possessed of the intuitions of their forefathers and having in the schools, at college, and in society acquired some facility in looking through *pakeha* spectacles at racial problems, claimed the privilege of advising the course that legislation and administration should take. They found in the late Sir James Carroll, then Minister of Native Affairs, and a master-psychologist, an elder prepared to indulge the views of the rising generation. The *Maori Council Act*, 1900, resulted. The idea was that a Council composed of representatives of the tribe inhabiting a district should act, *inter alia*, as a Health Committee with power to administer sanitary and kindred regulations in the villages. Model by-laws drafted by the Department were circulated among the various Councils. These were based on the recommendations of the Young Maori reformers. The Councils culled from the draft the by-laws which suited their conditions. In each village a Committee was appointed to administer these. These bodies so effectively broke down the last resistance of old time Maori customs that in 1920 the *Public Health Act*, with European administrators and inspectors, was admitted with very little friction into the everyday life of the Maori people. I may add that recently, when New Zealand assumed the mandate over Western Samoa, the model by-laws prepared for the guidance of the Maori Councils of New Zealand twenty-seven years ago were adopted there with modifications for use in the Samoan Villages.

Most of you have read of our Polynesian customs and practices relating to the dead, of the *tangis* or mourning feasts, of the long lying in state, with the danger, if it was the case of an infectious disease, to the health of others; and, in later days, of the accompanying debauchery and waste. Every reformer had preached against the persistence of these practices as dangerous, wasteful, and degrading, but it was no easy matter to secure improvement. The danger to contacts might have been minimized or removed by embalming and disinfection, but this would have cost too much, and at one time would have been deemed desecration. The altered mental attitude of the people towards these practices was evidenced by the very mild protest made when the Council passed a by-law requiring burial within a limit of three days in the cool weather and of two days in the summer, unless special circumstances demanded speedier interment. This was a small measure of reform on the face of it, but how much of the old culture was surrendered to make way for it, how much adjustment had to be made in the mental attitude?

In the year 1898 it may be said that the *Whare Runanga,* the common meeting house of the village, was still constructed on ancient lines, which as regarded ventilation provided for only the front door and window, both of which remained tightly closed, when the house was not occupied, or at night, when the house was so congested, that you could not stretch yourself out at full length. Doctors, missionaries, schoolteachers had preached ventilation for two generations without appreciable success. To put a hole, much less a window, at the rear end of the meeting house, or on the side walls, was an unheard of thing in Maori land, although our relatives in the warmer islands of the Pacific would have wondered at our ignorance and backwardness in this respect. The educated Maoris once more rose to the occasion with their acquired faculty of seeing with the eyes of both races. This was clearly a case where a concrete illustration of the proposed reform might have far reaching effects. A meeting house on the East Coast was made the first example, two windows being inserted at the rear end thereof. In 1901 the Maori Councils without exception adopted a by-law requiring the proper ventilation not only of meeting houses but of private dwellings as well. Seventeen years later it was possible without straining Maori prejudice to progress as far as the provision of a chimney, a back door, and even an accessory porch over which food might be served direct from the detached cook-house.

These are sufficient, I think, to illustrate in regard to the village life of the present day Maori, how governmental action may adapt itself to the changing mind of a Native race, if that mind is placed under close and honest observation.

So, too, in regard to the ownership and occupation of land. I dealt with this matter at length in an address to a group of students here recently. I showed how New Zealand had pursued for sixty years the policy of individualization of land titles through the Native Land Court, in accordance with the declaration of the Treaty of Waitangi and of the *Native Rights Act,* that Native land titles should be determined according to Native custom and usage. The effect of this process, as conducted through the ordinary machinery of the Native Land Court has been apparently to produce chaos. The policy has been carried to the bitter end, but has apparently failed to secure individualization. Here, again, the Young Maori Movement has taken the situation in hand, for the time had evidently arrived for welding the results of fresh work into useful shape. Consolidation of interests, scattered in almost useless fashion over many counties, was suggested as the solution. It would in one operation aggregate these interests on a valuation basis in one or two compact holdings, and also bring all elements in the title up to date. It has taken sixteen years now to popularize the new system in one district, the East Coast, but it is being adopted elsewhere, and it is hoped that the Government will extend it to all parts of the Dominion.

I am conscious that I have covered the ground very inadequately in this paper so far as New Zealand is concerned. The contention of cultures here has been controlled by the outstanding policy of effective European settlement in a country and a climate eminently favourable to it. Maori culture has been compelled to conform to it, but the adaptation has been vastly facilitated by the education of the Maori people and the development in them of the faculty of seeing from two different angles.

When we leave New Zealand and consider the case of the Cook Group, which came under our direct control in 1900, and the case of Western Samoa, the mandate over which was acquired quite recently, we are brought into touch with two closely related branches of the Polynesian race. Rarotonga and Samoa have this feature in common as distinguished from New Zealand, that it has never been seriously contended that either is suitable for European settlement. In Rarotonga the policy of Government has been largely "Rarotonga for the Rarotongans"; in Samoa it is said, that New Zealand's policy is "Samoa for the Samoans."

British success in New Zealand in administering Maori affairs justified the expectation that her administrators had thoroughly mastered the art of governing Polynesians. This was quite reasonable and has been justified in regard to the Cook Group. The trader element there has caused trouble at intervals, but the complications were never as serious as in New Zealand. The experience of New Zealand has been applied in all departments to Cook Island conditions without difficulty. It should be noted, perhaps, that the Cook Island administration has been more or less associated with the Native Department of New Zealand. The official head of the administration has almost, without a break, been a politician with an expert knowledge of Native Affairs in this country.

I should say something here about the *taihoa* policy so intimately connected with the name of James Carroll. *Taihoa* became a term of opprobrium, synonymous with marking-time, stone-walling, and retrogression. It was thrown at a man who, himself the product of two races, the Irish and the Maori, entered Parliament forty years ago and in his first speech advocated the full equality of the Maori and of the *pakeha* in law. He lived long enough to modify that policy in view of the differences in culture, inequality of experience, training, and standards. He could see as well as, if not better, than any man of his time where advances might be made in legislation and administration. But he could also see that to secure success each reform must be timed psychologically. In resisting the pressure of settlers actuated by their own policies, he earned for the *taihoa* policy public displeasure.

He was followed by Sir William Herries, who presented the contrary policy — the policy of hustle, whether the Maori mind was ready or not to accept his measures. He found in office that the *taihoa* policy was not the creation of his predecessor, but was imposed by the fundamental conditions of the problem to which every Native Minister has to address himself. That policy applied to Rarotonga, administered sympathetically, meant that every element in the immigrant European culture, which, by its substitution for the preexisting usage, fitted the Rarotongan better to live in a world where modern science had brought him into touch with other races and other ideas, was introduced in ordered sequence and to the extent that the Rarotongan was ready to receive and benefit by it. There was no upheaval as in New Zealand, no violent unmooring from old beliefs and sanctions. But a steady pressure is being applied in all directions, whereunder each succeeding generation of Cook Islanders may be influenced to advance gradually from one culture to another, or, as is most likely, to a blending of elements of the old with the new.

A few words on Samoa and I have done. Western Samoa came under New Zealand control in circumstances that are well known to you. One circumstance associated with the Mandate, the fact that it was given by the League of Nations, probably led to the creation of a special Ministry, that of External Affairs. This title had a high imperial sound that seemed appropriate to New Zealand's occupation and conquest of Western Samoa, and to the emanation of her mandate from the conclave of the Nations of the world. New Zealand assumed the mandate with a reputation for expert, tactful, and wise government of two branches of the Polynesian race. She had behind her the experience of a century in this country and of a generation in Rarotonga. She was supposed to have mastered the intricacies of the Polynesian mind. There need then be no fear that in Samoa she would not profit by the lessons so laboriously gathered over four generations.

The case of Samoa is before a special commission, *sub judice*, as the lawyers would say. But one may venture a few remarks without breach of the rule relating to cases under review by legally constituted tribunals.

I can say that in Western Samoa we have not altogether benefited by our New Zealand and Rarotongan experience. Was the creation of a Ministry of External Affairs and its detachment from the Native Department a wise step? The experts of that Department have not been used or consulted. It seemed as if we have ignored the experience whose possession justified an assumption of the mandate.

We have propounded the policy of Samoa for the Samoans, and, as Samoa is not considered suitable for European settlement, this has been easy to formulate, and its pronouncement has given us great satisfaction. In following up our pronouncement of policy we have, I think, shown an over eagerness to prove to the world how competent we are to handle such problems. This may be termed the pardonable pride of the *tohunga*. Here was the opportunity for our ethnologists to survey the social setting of the Samoan race, to appraise the extent to which previous contact with European culture had affected the Native culture and to adapt our New Zealand and Rarotongan experience to the conditions revealed. A *taihoa* policy such as was applied in Rarotonga would have answered well in the years during which we learnt and accumulated data. It was not wise to assume that because we knew the minds of two representative branches of the race, we could forthwith effect easy entry into the mind of the Samoan. Some of our Maori ancestors left islands of the Samoan Group many centuries, perhaps a thousand years, ago. The English, who have not been a century in New Zealand as an organized society, are already resentful of the importation of experts from their homeland to administer departments of State. These would have to acquire what is known as "the colonial view." Our present immigration policy demands that immigrants shall be of the kind most ready to adapt themselves to New Zealand conditions. Was it reasonable, then, to assume that knowledge of Maori culture in New Zealand and the Cook Group would at once enable us to tune in to the Samoan mind, or to appreciate a culture that must in its tropical setting have many local variations?

Our policy is superb in its simplicity; our intentions, their justice and honesty, cannot be questioned by any tribunal in the world. Our methods may be seriously questioned by the anthropologist, whether he be a university professor or the proverbial man in the street. We have probably overestimated the receptivity of the Samoan mind. We have probably not sufficiently appreciated that the social structure of the Samoan people has not been uprooted as was that of the Maori nearly a century ago; that, therefore, it is not as advanced from a *pakeha* standpoint as that of the Maori today. We have much to learn of their customs relating to land tenure. We do not thoroughly understand the status and position of their hereditary chiefs. We have not given ourselves sufficient time to learn about the Samoans from themselves before launching at them those reforms which we think would be for their benefit, because they have proved beneficial to their relatives here and in Rarotonga.

I may conclude by quoting some lines from Lawrence's "Revolt in the Desert," à propos of the blustering tactics of a British general, when a clash appeared imminent between the Arab and British leaders towards the end of the Palestine campaign:

My head was working full speed in these minutes, on our joint behalf, to prevent the fatal first steps by which the unimaginative British, with the best will in the world, usually deprived the acquiescent native of the discipline of responsibility, and created a situation which called for years of agitation and successive reforms and riotings to mend.

In Part Two three major kinds of applied anthropology are examined at length. Homer G. Barnett in "Consultants and Executives" outlines the development and execution of plans for the positioning of staff and district anthropologists within the administrative hierarchy of the government of the United States Trust Territory of the Pacific. Here the role of the anthropologist was that of consultant, intercultural broker and interpreter, and organizer of research projects which — in practice — were determined only partially by the needs of the governing agency. Allan R. Holmberg's two articles on the research and development model for guiding and studying developmental change describe a different role for the anthropologist. In the Vicos setting the scientist-philosopher in fact became the *patrón*-king, assuming a kind and amount of power and responsibility far outreaching that available to the staff anthropologist in Micronesia.

PART TWO

THREE KINDS OF INVOLVEMENT

The third model for the application of anthropology, Action Anthropology, as described and assessed by Tax, Gearing, Peattie, and Piddington, is in some respects very similar to the research and development approach in that it involves both the attempt to promote development and an effort to study the processes of change. Action Anthropology, though, is based on subtly different assumptions. Here intervention involves bringing together diverse interest groups into confrontations, eliciting conscious statements of needs and goals, and adopting an idealized laissez-faire or nondirective mode of relating to all parties. Action Anthropology is still similar to the other approaches in a way which is rarely stated publicly: all three pro-vide a net gain to anthropology in the form of a fund of opportunities for younger anthropologists and students to obtain field research experi-ence. Indeed, often such opportunities are a primary motivation for the anthropologist's accepting responsibilities for the conduct of research, consulting, and development programs on behalf of client organizations.

5

Consultants and Executives

HOMER G. BARNETT

The United States Trust Territory is administered through its principal executive officer, the High Commissioner. He is advised and assisted by a deputy and a staff of departmental officers who are charged with the supervision of certain activities and the implementation of policy respecting them. Those departments most directly concerned with the Micronesians are Education, Public Health, Economics, and Political Affairs. The senior anthropologist for the Territory, whose title is Staff Anthropologist, is for administrative purposes assigned to the Political Affairs Department, a division whose functions are much more diverse than its name implies.

In general and to the extent that it is appropriate, the organizational scheme at headquarters is duplicated in the administrative subdivisions of the Territory. Each group of islands constituting a subdivision is the responsibility of a District Administrator. He is assisted by heads of departments like those at headquarters and by special project managers. The counterpart of the Staff Anthropologist at this level is the District

"Consultants and Executives" from *Anthropology in Administration* by H. G. Barnett (Harper & Row, 1956). Reprinted by permission of the publishers.

Anthropologist. There are five of them, one for each of the districts of Palau, Yap, Truk, Ponape, and the Marshall Islands.[1]

Economic and Political Affairs Officers cooperate closely. In the districts their activities are integrated within one department; at headquarters they have at times come under the directorship of two department heads. Taken together their coverage of native affairs is more comprehensive and less specialized than that of any other administrative unit. They are charged with helping the Micronesians achieve economic self-sufficiency while protecting them against the loss of their lands and resources. In conformance with this broad directive, the departments investigate land claims and land use problems and develop programs for the restoration and resettlement of vacant areas. They are responsible for promoting agriculture and animal husbandry by sponsoring scientific inquiries, by supervising the operation of experimental stations, and by instituting demonstration farms and gardens. They encourage programs for the conservation of animal, vegetable, marine, and mineral resources and propose regulations, legislations, and expenditures to further these programs. They must also safeguard the welfare of laborers through providing opportunities for employment and securing improved working conditions.

The Trust Territory objective of furthering the political development of the Micronesians requires that the director of the Political Affairs Department plan and recommend programs to encourage appropriate forms of local, district, and territorial self-control; review the operation of government with reference to its effects on native culture; study tax programs, budgets, and accounting systems; prepare training schedules for native officials; and disseminate information on the meaning and requirements of self-government.

Finally, the policy of the administration with respect to native culture makes anthropological research an integral part of the responsibilities of the Political Affairs Department. Hence its director initiates surveys and investigations among the Micronesians, keeps other department heads informed of the effects of their programs on native opinion and culture, and advises the High Commissioner on policy and procedure in these matters.

As with any centralized administration, the Director of Political Affairs at headquarters and the District Administrators at the regional centers delegate appropriate aspects of their responsibilities to qualified assistants. With reference to anthropologists this means that questions involving native life are referred to them for advice or investigation. For purposes of maintaining an official record of action taken and to unify and consolidate administrative policy, the Staff Anthropologist formally receives directions from the Political Affairs Officer and through him formally communicates with other department heads and the High Commissioner or his deputy. Both the Staff Anthropologist and the Director of Political Affairs communicate with their district counterparts through the central channel of, and in the name of, the High Commissioner and his field representative, the District Administrator. The activities of the District Anthropologists are in like fashion under the direct supervision of an immediate supervisor who acts on the delegated authority of the District Administrator and the High Commissioner. All official contacts outside the Trust Territory administration are made by the High Commissioner or his deputy.

This system regularizes and regulates all acts having the force of an administrative decision. It does not disallow, and it is not designed to prevent, horizontal and vertical interchanges of ideas through conferences and correspondence between officers of all grades and departments. It presupposes informal as well as unchannelized executive sessions involving all appropriate personnel. Organized as it is on a staff plan, it does preclude the designation of functional groups; hence there is no anthropological unit, just as there is no integrated educational division or branch comprising all teachers in the employ of the administration. At the same time, private exchanges, preparatory discussions, and other negotiations which do not commit the administration take place freely between headquarters and district officers. Particularly important to members of the organization with specialized training is the fact that discussions of technical matters take place directly between those best qualified to deal with them. Official sanction for such activities is required only insofar as they bind the administration to some action. The anthropologists confer and correspond freely among themselves and with others within this limitation.

In most general terms, then, the Staff Anthropologist's duties are, either directly or indirectly, to organize and conduct research in the field and to maintain professional relations with outside specialists interested in research in the Territory. The District Anthropologist engages in research and reports to his District Administrator on the latter's authorization or on the request of the High Commissioner. His special obligation is to know the native language and customs of his district. The Staff Anthropologist's responsibilities in this respect are more generalized since they cover the Territory as a whole. Both specialists are regarded as technical experts, and as such they are expected to function as impartial intermediaries between the administration and the Micronesians. Neither has executive status, and the value of both lies in their objectivity and in their abstention from policy determination and implementation. As experts on Micronesian attitudes and behaviors, they are expected to devise and recommend techniques to accomplish the objectives settled upon by the administration. In short, they are responsible for means, not ends.

This understanding of the government anthropologist's role in the Trust Territory administration has been arrived at only recently. It is recognized as an experiment designed to cut through the tangle of con-- flicting opinions and incompatible assumptions reviewed in the last chapter and to eliminate weaknesses which inhere in most of the approaches sketched in Chapter 1 (see Barnett, 1956). The plan was not put into effect all at once or entirely on a speculative basis. It was shaped out of an already existing design for anthropological consultants in the Territory, and it emerged in clear and official form only after a tentative and unofficial introduction of its main features.

BACKGROUND

Anthropological research as a function of government got its start in the Trust Territory as a sequel to the Coordinated Investigation of Micronesian Anthropology (CIMA), a project which was sponsored by the Pacific Science Board. As has been noted, the United States Navy requested the United States Commercial Company's economic survey of the Territory in 1946 and in so doing recognized the importance of including anthropologists on the investigating team. Its experience with anthropology predated that decision.

In 1943 the Office of Naval Intelligence, jointly with the Military Government Section of Naval Operations, contracted with Yale University for the services of a research unit to process information on Micronesia. This unit, which was directed by an anthropologist, translated foreign-language sources and compiled a file of data classified by area and topic. Later that year and during 1944 another unit associated with the Naval School of Military Government at Columbia University, which was directed by the same anthropologist, organized this material and prepared the "Civil Affairs Handbooks" on the Marshall, Caroline, and Marianas Islands to which reference has been made above.

With postwar CIMA the emphasis was upon the human aspect of the Navy's administrative responsibility in the area, and consequently there was a decided emphasis upon ethnological research. A significant feature of this program was its allowance for fundamental research. The major objective was practical knowledge; but it was appreciated that the practical is not synonymous with the superficial. In the memorandum on the investigation which established the basis for an agreement between the Navy Department and the National Academy of Sciences as contracting parties, it was stated that the methods to be employed by the investigators were those of the anthropological sciences. To be included were the methods of ethnology, which yield systematic knowledge of native technology, economy, religion, social life, and political organization; those of linguistics, which produce phonetic, phonemic, lexical, and grammatical analyses of local dialects; those of human geography, which reveal the man-land relationships; and those of physical anthropology, which attend to the anatomical and physiological characteristics of the population. The practical implications of each subject area were also indicated. Thus, it was noted that ethnological particulars were relevant to problems of local administration; that linguistic analysis should provide a foundation for systems of orthography, dictionaries, grammars, and textbooks in the vernaculars; that a geographical survey was pertinent to problems of land tenure and land use; and that the proposed projects in physical anthropology were significant for a public health program. Nevertheless, it was understood by both the naval authorities and the participants that scientific considerations and not administrative expediencies came first. The final reports of participants bear witness to the recognition of this principle. None were designed on request and most only indirectly engaged administrative problems (Pacific Science Board, 1950:13–15).

The CIMA ended in March of 1948. It was followed immediately by another project called Scientific Investigation in Micronesia (SIM), which was likewise sponsored by the Pacific Science Board and made possible by a grant from the Office of Naval Research through its Geography Branch. Its participants have included specialists in botany, forestry, geology, geography, hydrology, marine and vertebrate ecology, as well as anthropology:

> The principal activity under this [SIM] program has been the Coral Atoll Project, which is largely in the field of basic research and involves essentially an ecological approach to the study of environmental factors affecting life on coral atolls. The project involves three activities — field work conducted according to a uniform plan by teams of selected scientists on sample atolls in different climatic and cultural areas of the Pacific; assembling and correlating known information, particularly from literature on the environment and economics of inhabitants of coral atolls; and program planning, advice and evaluation of the results of research being conducted under the previous two mentioned activities by an advisory committee of scientific specialists in fields represented in the Coral Atoll Project (Pacific Science Board, 1951:22).

In 1951 a research team worked on the wet atoll of Arno in the Marshalls; in 1952 another group went to the dry atoll of Onotoa in the Gilberts; in 1952 Raroia in the Tuamotus was added for comparative purposes; and in 1953 Ifalik in the Western Carolines was studied. In each case anthropologists have been included in the field parties. The results of the investigations continue to appear in a series called the "Atoll Research Bulletin."[2] In addition to this project, others under the same auspices bearing upon Micronesian anthropology have been conducted in nutrition, linguistics, child training, ethnology, and archeology.

Inasmuch as the Navy relinquished control of the Trust Territory in 1951, the work of SIM is a reflection of administrative responsibility only until that date. It is to be noted, however, that the present administration is in full accord with its objectives and has offered all possible assistance in promoting them. Moreover, mention of the program is pertinent to the present discussion since it witnesses the Navy's recognition of the value of basic research in the field of human relations, a conviction which was clearly expressed in the instance of CIMA. The official directives and memoranda which preceded and accompanied that investigation were sympathetic to it and called for all reasonable assistance to the participants. Island Government officers in Washington, Guam, and at the Military Government (later Civil Administration) units on the island bases manifested a genuine and a personal interest in the project. This interest was enhanced at the field level by the fact that by mid-1947, when civil regulations became effective, many of the officers comprising the administrative units were graduates of the School of Naval Administration at Stanford University. It was not surprising that at the conclusion of CIMA the authorities accepted a further proposal of the Pacific Science Board and agreed to employ anthropologists selected on advice of the Board as regular research specialists and consultants.

At first, in 1948, the Navy planned to appoint anthropologists to the staffs of the Civil Administration units in Palau, Truk, and the Marshalls. Due to budgetary and other difficulties, it was not possible to inaugurate the plan as envisaged until 1950. At that time it was expanded to include other units. Meanwhile, a start was made with the appointment of three civilians, who moved directly from their CIMA projects, and one naval officer, likewise a professional anthropologist, who was recalled to active service to become a staff advisor to the Deputy High Commissioner. During the same period another anthropologist, who was in Saipan working on a SIM project, acted as part-time advisor to the Civil Administrator for the northern Marianas.

During 1950 Anthropological Field Consultants were attached to units in Palau, Yap, Truk, Ponape, and the Marshalls; and the Staff Anthropologist was assigned to the Chief Administrator at Field Headquarters on Truk. During that year another anthropologist served as Internal Affairs Officer with the Truk unit, and the SIM anthropologist continued to act as advisor on Saipan. Field Consultants were permitted to reserve one-third of their time for research of their choice. The rest of their time was taken up by directed duties either of an administrative or research character.

Although officially entitled to reserve their own research time even at cost to other requirements, in practice it often happened that administrative demands made it necessary to postpone the allowance indefinitely.

In addition to these ethnologists the administration also appointed a linguist to serve on the headquarters staff. This move was made on the recommendation of the Educational Advisory Committee referred to on page 28 (Barnett, 1956). The selection of an appointee was conditioned by the requirement that he have an interest in applying his linguistic skills to educational problems of the Territory. There was at first some question as to whether he should be associated administratively with the Staff Anthropologist within the Political Affairs Department. Eventually he was assigned to the Education Director but maintained a close working relationship with anthropologists in the field and at headquarters. The urgent need to develop standardized orthographies to record the several languages of the Territory and to follow them up with the preparation of reading material made this assignment especially fitting.

There was no model for the anthropological positions or for the duties allocated to their incumbents. Undoubtedly, the anthropologists concerned, and some of the administrative officials as well, were familiar with work that had been done in applied anthropology and were to some extent conversant with other experiments involving anthropologists in government. While this knowledge had its effects, it did not result in the adoption of a system tried elsewhere. If anything, there was a rejection of what was known of other attempts, or certain aspects of them. In any event, the most important determinants were not anthropological theories and practice elsewhere; they were the requirements of the situation and the history of anthropological work in the Territory. Those circumstances dictated the key relationships of the anthropological advisors to the administrative system. Beyond that, their roles took shape gradually and tentatively under the play of events.

It was necessary, of course, to outline the anthropologists' duties from the start; but within the general terms of these directives there was room for interpretation and modification according to need. For Civil Service positions such definitions of function are embodied in "job descriptions." These statements accompany requests for new positions, and they serve as charters and guides for both the administration and future incumbents. By early 1951 plans were under way to convert the Staff Anthropologist's position to civilian status, and this meant creating it as far as Civil Service was concerned. At that time a job description was prepared which stated that the Staff Anthropologist:

(1) Receives administrative direction from the Director of Internal Affairs, usually consisting of orientation in problems or program objectives

of the Department with explanations of policies, organizational relationships, and governing procedures. Independently determines methods, techniques, research areas, and specific problems for study.

(2) Plans research projects in the various fields of anthropology to achieve the program objectives of the Department. This involves the interpretation of scientific data and field reports to isolate problems and conditions for study; the determination of approach and methodology to be employed; the establishment of contacts and relationships necessary to the successful execution of projects; the evaluation of results and consequences to be expected from pursuing alternative courses of action; the securing of clearance for specific anthropological studies; the promotion of working relationships with indigenous organizations and the devising of means for overcoming linguistic barriers to the execution of projects; the monitoring of projects by keeping advised of new developments, suggesting changes of emphasis on lines of research, or changing methodology completely in the light of time, funds, facilities, and resources available.

(3) Performs anthropological research which results in significant generalizations relative to the complex biological and cultural relationships of the indigenes, the impact of exploiting or governing races, the cultural patterns of development to be expected under existing conditions or under modifications of the social milieu. Integrates findings from the fields of ethnology, archaeology, linguistics, and physical anthropology to develop principles, concepts, and conclusions regarding racial history and culture or the interaction of racial elements. Attempts to isolate and determine the relative emphasis to be given to environmental and geographical conditions as well as biological factors. On the basis of findings and conclusions recommends practical measures to achieve given program objectives.

(4) In cooperation with District Administrators and with the assistance of District Civil Affairs Officers and Anthropological Field Consultants, investigates and reports on political and social aspects of the administration and recommends to the Director of Internal Affairs the formulation of policy regarding such matters. Cooperates with the Public Defender and the Legal Department in the resolution of legal problems pertaining to law and order in the Territory. In cooperation with agricultural and economic development specialists, continuously evaluates the potentials of public lands in relation to population groups or to the community as a whole to the end that the High Commissioner may be kept informed on the availability of usable land and the needs therefor. Inspects and evaluates recommendations of District Civil Affairs Officers for the establishment of conservation areas, public monuments, and preserves. Directs through Civil Affairs Officers in each District the development of district and municipal political institutions and the conduct of liaison and mediatory operations on problems arising between government and local leaders.

The job description of the Anthropological Field Consultant, who was to become District Anthropologist under the civilian regime, differed only in that its terms of reference were more restricted and specific. It gave administrative supervsion to the District Internal Affairs Officer and made the anthropologist responsible to him in the same general areas and in the same way as is set forth in the preceding description, but it contained specific assignments answering to district needs. Thus, the Field Consultant was to promote "good working relations with indigenous organizations, exercising a knowledge of native language to overcome linguistic barriers . . . interpreting official regulations, orders, and programs from English to native tongues, and serving as an interpreter between native and administrative officials in court or at official gatherings." His duties also included the making of field trips to outlying villages within his district.

Most of the Field Consultant's directed research was focused on problems of district importance only, even though such problems were the concern of the administration as a whole and the investigation of them might be requested by headquarters. A field team survey of the social and economic conditions among the inhabitants of Woleai Atoll in late 1950 provides an illustration.

Woleai, which lies about midway between Truk and Palau, is a mere dot in the Pacific — one and three-fourths square miles of land in twenty-three islets rimming a lagoon of about eleven square miles — with a population of less than four hundred. It was far from the administrative center of the Palau District to which it belonged; and this fact, together with its small population, led to its neglect during the immediate postwar years. Under this handicap the islanders were attempting to recover from the damage inflicted on their lands by direct war action. With the beginning of hostilities in the Pacific, the Japanese began construction of an airstrip on the largest island. The people were ordered to evacuate, and while the men were conscripted for labor the women uprooted their taro and replanted it on other islands. Coconut and breadfruit trees were cut down to make room for the airfield and for Japanese troops. When the Americans began to attack the Japanese installations, there was further destruction and necessity for removal to more remote spots. Eventually about three hundred natives took themselves by canoe to Ifalik Atoll. At the end of the war they began to return to Woleai in parties of ten and twenty at a time. They found their main island almost completely denuded of coconut and breadfruit trees and too hot to endure. In addition, nearly half of their taro swamp area had been filled in with coral and concrete. They were therefore confronted with the double problem of procuring food and rehabilitating their land. The first problem was met for about six months by their using abandoned food stores and the produce remaining in gardens planted by the Japanese. In the meantime, taro and coconuts were brought from other islands and, where possible, replanted.

The general character of the hardships of the Woleai people was known to the administration; details were necessary before an assistance program could be planned. A survey team was requested to conduct an investigation and to make recommendations for action.

The purpose of the anthropological part of the survey was to explore the social, economic, political, religious, and educational conditions on the island and to determine the inhabitants' needs for assistance in their struggle for readjustment. In his report the Anthropological Field Consultant reviewed the history of developments leading up to existing conditions and summarized the results of his inquiry into each aspect of the situation noted above. He found that

> . . . their common experiences, especially in the last ten years, and the very sensible and realistic collective actions taken by the islanders in solving their common problems of food production and distribution have given the community a high degree of integration. . . . [They] have voiced on several occasions that they are "hungry." They understandably do not have as much as they would like to eat, but no one can say they are facing starvation. . . . The most pressing need in Woleai, in the writer's opinion, is a cash income, which was fairly sufficient in Japanese times and is now almost completely lacking. . . . This lack assumes greater proportions when . . . [it is realized] that elsewhere islanders are still able to produce copra and procure a few supplementary goods.

After specifying relief measures which should be adopted, the report concluded:

> In brief, it is recommended that the cash economy of these islands be aided, but only by utilization of what the natives themselves can produce, and that their food situation be alleviated by the introduction of plants which they can raise themselves. Any handout of canned goods and rice, which they obviously will not be able to afford for many years to come, would only hinder their adjustment to more permanent future conditions; and furthermore, the American administration would only be risking the possibility of more cries for food from other islands in this area.

Another example of a Field Consultant's assignment to meet a district problem may be mentioned briefly. When it was decided to reactivate phosphate mining on Angaur in the Palaus (see p. 72), it became necessary to know the clan affiliations of each of the 350 inhabitants of the island. This came about as a consequence of an agreement with them whereby they were to be paid royalties on the processed mineral, not individually, but by clans, some of the latter to receive a greater proportion of the proceeds than others because of their land being destroyed by the operation. The royalties were to be placed in a Permanent Trust Fund, and withdrawals from it by landholders and their heirs were arranged on a plan which would provide income long after the mining ceased. Inasmuch as the Angaurese insisted upon payments being made in accordance with clan membership, it was necessary to determine what the affiliation was in each individual instance. It was also necessary to investigate cases of adopted membership and other irregularities as well as to determine lines of succession to clan leadership and land proprietorship.

The Palau Field Consultant was sent to Angaur for the detailed inquiry. His report included genealogical charts which showed the kinship connections of all members of the community along with historical data bearing upon these connections. This document now constitutes an official record by which "the administration ensures an equitable distribution of the phosphate royalty benefits, one that accords with the expressed wishes of the natives and with their social structure" (Drucker, 1951:310).

Many administrative questions demanding anthropological answers applied equally to all districts and so necessitated parallel inquiries by all Field Consultants. In every district of the Trust Territory, as in other areas where indigenous peoples have been displaced by outsiders, problems involving land ownership and use have been troublesome from the beginning of American control. The difficulty of restoring lands to their owners was doubly complicated in this instance, for the Germans and the Japanese imposed property laws which conflicted in essential respects with the native system and to some extent with each other. With the arrival of the Americans, the question of a land policy inevitably obtruded, and their lack of information on which to base a policy to satisfy claims and requests for reoccupancy thwarted their desire for an early restoration of the normal economy of the areas. It also forestalled planning on other fronts which had to be grounded on economic stability. It was felt that only a time-consuming investigation of land rights under native custom and under previous governmental commitments would justify the adoption of a policy and permit the desired action. Consequently, all Field Consultants were urged to apply themselves to the inquiry to the extent that their other duties would permit. By July, 1951, most of them had submitted final or preliminary reports on the problem as they saw it in their districts.

The nature of the reports may be indicated by the prefatory remarks of their authors. The Introduction to "Contemporary Ponapean Land Tenure" stated that:

> This report is an attempt to collect information on contemporary Ponapean land tenure which will be of use to the courts and land claims officials in determining the legal status of disputed land, and to the administration in setting up a program which will give the Ponapeans sufficient

land of their own for a secure livelihood and in evaluating any land law or programs which may be proposed by the recently constituted Ponape Provisional Congress or other native groups. . . .

Many anthropologists, economists, and experts in the administration of dependent peoples have emphasized the importance of a just and workable system of land tenure to the security, prosperity, and peace of a society. The ideal land tenure system is not the same for all societies. It will vary depending on the type of use which is made of the land and on the working social and political organization of the society. Whatever the system, it should ensure that the land is used directly or indirectly for the common welfare, and that any concentration of rights over land in the hands of a limited number of individuals is in some way balanced by corresponding responsibilities to future generations and the rest of society.

As is shown in the body of this report, there are definite and critical problems concerning land tenure on Ponape in at least two respects: (1) the freeing of land in the public domain, at present in use and needed for use by natives, making it secure in native possession, and (2) the development of a clear, flexible, and workable code defining rights of various people in land, and the procedure of inheritance and other transfer.

In his Introduction to "Yapese Land Ownership and Inheritance Customs," another Field Consultant wrote:

The following study was instigated as an adjunct to a recent census of all lands owned by persons of Dalipebinau District, Yap. Underlying this land census was the desire to set up, on the basis of experiment, a more systematic method of recording property ownership, which could at the same time give the administration some idea of the total amount of various kinds of productive land available at the present time. Such an effort seemed advisable in view of certain deficiencies of the present land registry. . . .

It was also felt desirable at this time, for reasons of future economic planning, to have some reasonably accurate estimate of the ratio of total available productive lands to the amount in actual use during the present year. In addition to the above-mentioned special lands, a count of gardens and coconut trees was made, the latter in view of the present importance of copra as the dominant cash crop of the area.

Lastly, an attempt was made in the Dalipebinau experimental census to estimate the maximal population size of the area, presumably in late pre-foreign times. This was done in order to evaluate the "carrying capacity" of Yap at some remote future date, assuming population increases with a continuance of present subsistence techniques. The writer feels that it is possible to make such a population reconstruction with relative accuracy by counting house platforms.

Some land reports contained policy recommendations, some not. The Ponapean Consultant suggested revisions in current practices at appropriate junctures in his discussion and appended a section on "Some Policy Considerations and Recommendations." In that section he advocated precautionary measures against ownership fragmentation, sales and mort-gages, and large-scale immigration to Ponape. He also proposed that certain government-held lands be returned to native use and suggested that some of the questions raised in the report be brought gradually before the Ponapean Congress for discussion.

Under civil administration the legal code of the Territory was made to apply to all occupants of it, whether they were Micronesians or Americans. This at once created certain difficulties, since it was felt that criminal law should reflect American morality while not violating the announced inten-tion of the administration to not interfere with native custom beyond the requirements of maintaining peace and decency. The law of the land was embodied in so-called Interim Regulations which, pending constitu-tional legislation, were promulgated by the High Commissioner. Some of their provisions had been lifted rather directly from American state statutes and, as became increasingly evident in court cases, certain of them were so foreign to Micronesian life and ideology that the wisdom of en-forcing them was called into question by the Chief Justice and others entrusted with law enforcement. Most dubious were those regulations defining sex offenses. In order to provide a basis for reviewing their ap-plicability, Field Consultants were asked to prepare reports on the legal aspects of indigenous sex customs in their districts.

The Truk report on this matter, like most of the others, proposed certain revisions of the law, some on the basis of principle, some because of their inapplicability.[3] The first part set forth some generalized differences in American and Trukese attitudes toward sex:

> An American, in approaching consideration of the sexual customs of any other people, must bear in mind that his own American culture lies near the extreme in explicit statement of rigid morals in the sexual sphere. . . . Just as the Trukese do not subscribe to such strict definitions of morality as do Americans, so their reaction to breaches of the sexual code which they do recognize is not nearly as violent as is the case with us. . . .

Then each relevant section of the Interim Regulations was considered with reference to Trukese concept and custom. Finally, the report con-cluded, in part:

> It will be noted that while it is recommended that certain provisions be omitted from the Criminal Code, and certainly some rephrasing would be advisable to eliminate such ambiguous terms as "defiled," "unnatural," "carnal," and the like, the most consistent and important recommendation throughout is that maximum sentences (except perhaps for "abduction of a female") be reduced to six months. As outlined at the outset, this brings

the sentences for sex crimes down to a realistic level from the Trukese standpoint, and, more important, makes the native Community Court the court of first instance in these cases which are so deeply enmeshed in the local social and cultural context. Only a person in the defendant's own community can judge properly the gravity and implications of his act. . . .

The Staff Anthropologist was largely responsible for initiating investigations, both local and Territory-wide. In any event, he undertook to coordinate the work of the Field Consultants. He also engaged in research himself. For example, he, in company with a conservation expert, made a special study on Angaur in the fall of 1949 preliminary to the opening of negotiations on the renewal of phosphate mining there. In years past, the Germans had uncovered the deposits and mined them in a small way. The Japanese continued the operation on a greatly expanded and intensified scale. At the end of the war the need for fertilizer by the Japanese and the willingness of the United States government to assist them in their rehabilitation efforts led to a request by the Supreme Commander for Allied Powers (SCAP) that the Japanese government be permitted to resume the mining under military surveillance and control. It was indicated that if this could be arranged everyone would benefit — the Angaurese, the Japanese, and indirectly the American taxpayer. The Trust Territory administration was receptive to the proposal, but only on condition that the Angaurese would not ultimately suffer in consequence. Its apprehension arose from the fact that the best agricultural lands of the Angaurese lay over or adjacent to the area of the richest deposit and from its fear that further excavation might breach the subterranean walls that prevented salt water from flooding the fresh-water lens. It was for reassurance on the doubts raised by these prospects that the Staff Anthropologist and the conservationist were dispatched to Angaur in 1949. They were to ascertain the agricultural potential of the island, study the land use pattern of the people, and estimate the consequences if mining were to be resumed. Their recommendations were against the proposal. SCAP, however, pressed for a conference between its representatives, those of the Trust Territory, and those of the Angaurese on the basis of a geological analysis made by its own personnel, whose studies gave evidence that no damage would result from the mining operations as contemplated. This was the only issue at the conference; no one questioned that Angaurese welfare should be safeguarded even at cost to the Japanese. The SCAP proposal was accepted, and an agreement was drawn up after a committee of hydrologists had reported that the island water supply could be protected by certain precautions and after the Trust Territory had stipulated that one agriculturally valuable area be exempt from mining (Drucker, 1951:309–10).

A much more difficult assignment was given to the Staff Anthropologist in February of 1950. It was prompted by the succession of misfortunes which befell the Bikini people following their evacuation from their traditional homeland. They had been removed to Rongerik in March, 1946, but there they experienced near-starvation due to a combination of unforeseen circumstances. From Rongerik they were taken to Kwajalein as a temporary shift until a new home could be found for them. After another disappointment due to their not being able to go to Ujelang, which was preempted for the Eniwetok evacuees, little choice was left to them except Kili, a wave-swept island without the protection and re-sources of an encircling lagoon, to which their economy was adapted. The climate and the vegetation of Kili also differed considerably from that of Bikini. They were transported to Kili in November, 1948, after advance preparations for their housing and other facilities had been arranged by the Navy (Mason, 1950). They were unable to adjust to Kili, and the field-trip services could not meet their needs for help. The latter circum-stance derived chiefly from the fact that landing difficulties were such that field ships could not approach the island on schedule or handle cargo over the reef. While the administrative and public health functions of field trips were accomplished, little copra was taken on board, and only inade-quate provisions and few trade goods were set on shore between the summer of 1949 and the spring of 1950. At that time the High Commis-sioner considered that an investigation was imperative. Accordingly, the Staff Anthropologist was sent to the island and stayed there for five weeks (Drucker, 1951:310–311).

The Kili study represented "an application of an anthropological ap-proach and field techniques to a current administrative problem." The report upon it is one of the most comprehensive analyses of a single problem in the High Commissioner's files. It included observations on the physiographic structure of the island, its water supply, its vegetation, and its food resources and their utilization. The complex attitudes of the people were presented in the light of their recent history; their efforts at adjustment were also analyzed. The report ended with a section on recommendations premised on the understanding that the ex-Bikinians were to remain on Kili. It proposed an assignment of title to Kili and compensation for the loss of Bikini, the inauguration of an educational and assistance program in agricultural expansion, the extension of credit for trade goods, the purchase of a boat, and the establishment of a small colony on nearby Jaluit Atoll as a base of operations for outside contacts.

The Staff Anthropologist sometimes formulated projects on the basis of information requested from the field. One such project was an educational program for the Woleai people. The Field Consultant's previous report disclosed that school facilities on that atoll were inadequate to the demand. Students had to come long distances, and sometimes weather did not permit them to commute. Children and adults alike had a great desire to learn English, American songs, and American sports. The two teachers then available were not well trained and received no pay; they wanted more education for the prestige which it brought. The chiefs of the islands were interested in having young men educated to intrepret for them and represent them in their dealings with the Americans. The Field Consultant suggested that it would be an important contribution to rapport with the administration if candidates selected by the chiefs could be given intensive training at the school on Truk.

Adopting this suggestion, the Staff Anthropologist recommended that a special program be devised whereby one or two young men would be selected by their communities for training as teachers and interpreters. The training was to have a practical emphasis and include instruction in English, personal and public health, simple arithmetic, American systems of reckoning in money, weights, and measures, and the elements of navigation. The course was projected for six months on Truk, at the end of which time the boys were to be returned to their islands to act as teachers and intermediaries between their people and administrative field parties.

DEFINITION

The Department of the Interior formally took control of the Territory in July, 1951. The replacement of naval personnel by civilians had been proceeding by gradual steps since the early part of the year. All of the Field Consultants were civilians, and they continued at their posts after the transfer, the only change being that one was added for the Saipan District, where none had been employed under the naval administration. The Staff Anthropologist was new, as were most of the other headquarters personnel. As in all similar instances, the mass replacement was significant, since it induced a phase of adjustment and led to an examination — and in some cases to a reformulation — of means and ends in the headquarters office.

After a few months at his desk, the Staff Anthropologist was sent on an extended tour of the six districts of Saipan, Yap, Palau, Truk, Ponape, and the Marshalls. The object was not only to acquaint him with the area and its operations, but also to organize the work of the field anthropologists and to define in a tentative way the nature of their duties. In each district, conferences were held with the District Administrator, the Internal Affairs Officer, and the Anthropological Field Consultant, during which the question of their interrelationships was discussed. In each instance the acceptable interpretation was that, ideally at least, the anthropologist should be regarded as a technical specialist and not as an administrative officer. More specifically, this meant that the anthropologist was to serve as a vehicle of communication between the Micronesians and the administration and that he was not to make or execute policy. In other words, he was to accept directives and refer action decisions to the Internal Affairs Officer or the District Administrator; he was to confine his efforts to sociological analyses which would enable these officers to arrive at their decisions or to take into account the consequences of their past actions for future determinations. It was also agreed that the designation of the anthropologist as a "consultant" carried undesirable implications of a detached expert waiting to be called on as occasion arose and that the less presumptive title of District Anthropologist was preferable.

It is perhaps unnecessary to say that the plan had the approval of those members of the headquarters staff most directly concerned with the activities of the field anthropologists; namely, the High Commissioner, his deputy, and his Political Affairs Officer. It was also understood by them that their relationships with the Staff Anthropologist were to be ordered on the same plan as that suggested for the districts, with his duties being restricted to the sociological analyses of means and results and with responsibility for decisions on action, purposes, ends, and policies being left to them.

This plan was on trial for approximately a year without a formal seal of approval. During that time it appeared to work satisfactorily when and where circumstances permitted it to operate. There were, however, some uncertainties about its official status, some failures to appreciate its ramifications in practice, and a questionable number of necessitous deviations from the ideal which it envisaged. At headquarters it was believed that the situation could be improved by a statement of clarification. Therefore, the following memorandum on the functions of District Anthropologists was sent to all District Administrators in August, 1952:

> The lack of a comprehensive definition of the functions of anthropologists employed in the Trust Territory has given rise to some uncertainty regarding the activities in which they might be properly and profitably employed. The High Commissioner considers that a clarification of the situation with respect to District Anthropologists will be helpful to all concerned. Accordingly, the following statement of objectives has been formulated for the guidance of District Administrators and District Anthropologists. It attempts to set forth propositions which have acquired validity as a result of administrative experience during the past year and to make explicit certain working relationships which until now have been only loosely defined.
>
> (1) Since anthropologists are concerned with collecting information about, and maintaining an intimate knowledge of, the indigenous cultures

of the area, they should be in a position to contribute to effective administration in three principal ways; namely, by:

(*a*) Advising on the implementation of departmental projects and on the solution of problems arising from such implementation. The anthropologist, by reason of his personal contacts and knowledge of local customs, value systems, and attitudes, should be able to make a reasonably accurate estimate of prospects for the success of a proposed program. He may also contribute substantially to the realization of a project by preparing the way for its acceptance by the people for whose benefit it is designed. Examples would be the interpretation of American legal terminology and concepts, collaboration in developing education programs, the encouragement of favorable attitudes toward new economic enterprises, and an analysis of attitudes toward native medical practitioners trained by the government.

(*b*) Evaluating the success of particular departmental programs. The worth of the anthropologist's contribution in this area would stem from his background of continued observations rather than from specific investigations, although the latter approach might also be undertaken by him. In general, he should be in an especially favorable position to evaluate program results simply because of his familiarity with them as an intimate and trained observer of village life. In this capacity his observations on the consequences of health-improvement projects, labor policies, educational methods, legislative measures, and judicial procedures can afford an invaluable complement to official checks and surveys.

(*c*) Independently formulating and implementing researches of theoretical interest to the anthropological profession and/or of practical importance to the Administration. The Territory is rich in research possibilities of both descriptions and of combinations of the two. Among the examples which might be cited are: a comparative study of the adaptations of displaced populations in the area, an analysis of Yapese conservatism, a record of the development of religious and political factionalism, and a survey of the incidence and characteristics of ethnic prejudices within the native population.

Lest this aspect of the anthropologist's activities appear to be too far removed from the purposes for which he is employed, it should be pointed out that it is the only means by which he can advance his knowledge of the people about whom he is called upon for information. Only through continuously engaging in research can he justify his position as a technician with the training and experience to warrant his offering reliable and up-to-date information. A familiarity with existing information is seldom enough to satisfy this requirement. Conditions, and native reactions to them, change so continuously that it is essential for the anthropologist to constantly carry on investigations of this nature.

(2) It is essential that insofar as District Anthropologists are concerned, administrative and technical services be kept separate. This means that

the anthropologist should be regarded as a source of information relative to native culture and not as an administrative officer who makes or enforces policy. He has the obligation to collect, in a reliable and systematic way, information that is useful to the administrator. This obligation cannot be adequately met if he assumes, or is called upon to assume, the role of an agent of control or enforcement. Apart from the question of job training, there is the important fact that the anthropologist must maintain, insofar as possible in the eyes of the people, a neutral position with respect to administration policy and action. Anything which tends to identify him as a government official invested with the power to impress his ideas detracts by so much from his usefulness as a source of unbiased information, because it jeopardizes confidential relationships with his informants and frequently involves him in factional struggles.

For these reasons, the employment of the anthropologist in such capacities as that of a government spokesman, or a court investigator, or an internal affairs officer is to be discouraged. It is recognized that personnel shortages may require some deviation from this policy; but should it become necessary to temporarily assign the anthropologist to an administrative position, every effort should be made to relieve him of the necessity of personally taking actions that could prejudice his neutral position in the eyes of the community with which he works.

(3) In line with the observations contained in the last section, it is desirable that the District Anthropologist be accorded the freedom and the facilities to interview informants under the most favorable conditions. It is to be expected that at times information will be given him in confidence. Allowance should be made for this in local housing and office arrangements whenever possible. In any event, the anthropologist should be given, and make the most of, every opportunity to carry on investigations away from the administrative center. The information that is available to him around the district office is obviously limited in scope and character; and while it is valuable, it cannot substitute for investigations of customs and problems in their native setting. Only by maintaining continuous contacts with the local population at the village level is it possible to gain the optimum in the confidence of the people, establish a foundation for evaluating popular reactions, and keep in touch with new developments against the background of their growth.

Visits to outlying villages need not be prolonged or projected on such an exhaustive schedule as to interfere with the anthropologist's usefulness to the administration or with his convenience in maintaining a household at a district center. Within the framework of the indicated emphasis upon investigations beyond administration centers, a weighing of all the relevant factors in the local situation is in order.

(4) With reference to the information relayed by District Anthropologists, certain safeguards are essential to maintain its usefulness. It is evident that the anthropologist's familiarity with, and his acceptance by, the people of his district gives him knowledge that is otherwise unobtain-

able by outsiders. It is also apparent that his obligation to assist the administration and his need to cultivate the sources of his intimate knowledge may prove at times to be embarrassing. From both an ethical and a practical standpoint, he is obligated to preserve confidences. Consequently, certain allowances must be made for this requirement if the anthropologist is to continue to function effectively. While in any particular case the necessity of preserving confidences will reduce the amount of information that can be used, in the long run this safeguard is certain to pay off.

(5) The foregoing summary is based upon the premise that District Anthropologists have a background of training in collecting information which should be utilized to full advantage by the administration and that this can be done only by recognizing their professional qualifications and by making provisions for an adjustment of these qualifications to administrative needs. This definition of functions and relationships, together with the reasons given for their determination, is offered, not with the thought that the anthropologist should be treated differently from other personnel, but rather to increase his value to the administration and hence to achieve a more efficient utilization of his skills. It is believed that this will be of value to the anthropologist and the District Administrator.

A short time after this document was issued, a meeting of all Trust Territory anthropologists was held in Koror, Palau Islands. The conference was suggested by the Deputy High Commissioner, who consistently appreciated the efforts and the requirements of this group of specialists. In addition to the seven participants, several observers were invited to join the conference at appropriate times, and they were asked to contribute their views on questions which concerned their own activities.

One purpose of the meeting was to acquaint the District Anthropologists with each other and with problems in districts other than their own. In the past they had been isolated from each other through a lack of personal acquaintanceship and an ignorance of problems and conditions beyond the limited perspective of their own districts. The lack of communication between them was considered to be undesirable, both professionally and personally. A related purpose of the meeting was to provide as many of the anthropologists as possible with an opportunity to observe conditions in unfamiliar parts of the Territory. It was anticipated that the Palauan situation would be instructive. The extent to which acculturation had proceeded in Koror and the variety of administrative problems presented by it offered an illustration of the sort of change which might occur in other parts of the Territory with a multiplication and an intensification of outside influences.

The foregoing objectives were incidental to the conference proper. The agenda of the meeting was concerned with an assessment of anthropological interests and aims in the Trust Territory. The items brought up for consideration were: (1) a review of the recent work of each anthropologist, (2) an evaluation of the past year's work in the light of the anthropologist's conception of his job, (3) plans for future work, and (4) discussion of topical questions.

The review of the past year's activities was accomplished by asking each anthropologist to give a verbal summary of his duties. It was indicated that it would be helpful if each statement were organized in terms of routine assignments, special assignments, cooperation with other departments, and self-initiated research. In summary, the following observations appeared to be justified:

(1) Except for two districts, routine assignments (that is, day-by-day, month-by-month duties) consumed the greater portion of the anthropologist's working day.

(2) In most instances, the routine assignments were administrative rather than technical in nature.

(3) The majority of special assignments (projects with a definite beginning and end) had been initiated by the High Commissioner's Office rather than at the district level.

(4) Well-established working relations with other departments had been practically confined to Education and to Public Works; and usually the cooperation was with one or the other of these departments rather than with both. Less definite but tending to become more firm in most districts was a mutually helpful liaison between the anthropologist and the Judicial Department.

(5) Self-initiated research projects on local problems had occupied a minimum of time during the working day of the anthropologist except in two districts; and with these exceptions, they were carried on during off-hours and at odd times when the anthropologist could fit them in.

The next item on the agenda was a discussion of the place of anthropology in the administration of the Trust Territory and a definition of its objectives as conceived by the anthropologists themselves. The then recently issued statement on the "Functions of District Anthropologists" (see above) was used as a point of departure, its declarations being considered with reference to the descriptions of actual duties just concluded. The assumptions upon which the statement of functions rested were made explicit: namely, that for a democratic government such as the one the administration represented it was essential to have knowledge of the attitudes of the people governed, and that anthropologists were singularly qualified to get this information. Then the consequences of these premises were analyzed.

There were no significant differences of opinion regarding the statement of functions or about its value to the anthropologist as an exposition of his position and as an aid in furthering his technical usefulness to the administration. It was suggested that the Staff Anthropologist prepare a brief article on the conference for the *Micronesian Monthly* (an administrative publication for internal distribution), the article to contain a statement for the layman on the meaning of anthropology in the context of administration.

Several particulars were brought up under the heading of "Plans for Future Work." The Chairman expressed his concern over the lack of professional contacts among the six District Anthropologists and suggested several means of improving their communication with each other as well as means of establishing contacts with external sources of information pertinent to their work. In this connection, (1) the District Anthropologists were urged to correspond with each other concerning their local problems; (2) subscription funds for professional journals for each district were proposed; (3) it was suggested that the Staff Anthropologist explore the possibility of supplying each district with relevant ethnographic materials and duplicates of reports, such as those on land tenure, which had so far been sent from the districts only to the Commissioner's office; (4) it was suggested that each District Anthropologist maintain a file of basic anthropological data for his area, such deposits serving to eliminate duplication of research by others.

To further promote the usefulness of anthropology in the future, emphasis was placed upon the importance of developing rapport with departments outside Internal Affairs. It was recognized that to a large extent this possibility was dependent upon the personalities of the individuals involved; but it was also brought out that past failures to cooperate derived partially from the lack of understanding of what the anthropologist was willing and able to do to bridge the gap between native and American thinking. It was also recognized that, in the main, it was necessarily the function of the Staff Anthropologist to prepare the way for the interdepartmental effectiveness of the District Anthropologist. The hope was expressed that certain tentative moves in the direction of cooperation might be systematized and given recognition at the appropriate level. In particular, it was suggested that "the Staff Anthropologist and the Chief Justice record their concurrence on the value of anthropological research in promoting the ends of justice among the native populations of the Territory."

The writing of monthly reports was suggested as a means of (1) improving the usefulness of the District Anthropologist to the District Administrator and (2) keeping a headquarters check on anthropological activities in the field. Under the existing system it was often difficult to distinguish the work of the District Anthropologist from that of the District Internal Affairs Officer. For the benefit of both the District Administrator and the Staff Anthropologist, it was therefore recommended that the District Anthropologist submit a separate report of his activities to the Internal Affairs Officer and that this resume accompany the monthly District Administrator's report sent to the High Commissioner.

As a final item under the heading of future planning, each District Anthropologist was asked to submit notes on a research program of practical importance to the administration of his district. With all the proposals in the hands of the Staff Anthropologist, it was contemplated that a research program for each district could be formulated and acknowledged as a part of the District Anthropologist's duties.

The development of the anthropologist's role as an intermediary and a two-way consultant was premised on the view that he must demonstrate ways in which his services could be used rather than argue that they should be. This requirement was essential to the establishment of a relationship of mutual confidence with executive officers who, with few exceptions, had no knowledge of the subject and were inclined to think of the anthropologist as an unnecessary frill. It was not to be hoped that these men would be impressed by statements of general principles or by the kind of argument for the utility of the science advanced by anthropologists among themselves. It was even less likely that anthropologists would be welcomed as district team members on order by superior authority. Their knowledge could be made available and their duties described, but their acceptance would depend upon the definition of their usefulness by their fellow workers. In short, District Administrators and department heads must ask for help, not have it forced on them.

An illustration of the procedure is provided by the previously mentioned suggestion made at the Koror conference that "the Staff Anthropologist and the Chief Justice record their concurrence on the value of anthropological research in promoting the ends of justice among the native population of the Territory." This resolution grew out of a background of many tentative collaborative attempts by judicial officers and anthropologists. There was no question that legal officers acknowledged the need for help, for they had repeatedly asked for it; but there was uncertainty on both sides about how far the anthropologist should go in assisting the courts and about his relationships with judges, prosecutors, police officers, and the attorney (Public Defender) appointed to secure the civil rights of any defendant in a legal action. It appeared to everyone that the time had come to define this area of cooperation beyond the reference to it in the earlier general memorandum on the functions of District Anthropologists.

After an exchange of correspondence between the Staff Anthropologist and the Chief Justice, the latter's recommendations were issued to all

District Administrators by the High Commissioner with the request that anthropologists be advised of them and, as circumstances permitted, be encouraged to cooperate as suggested. In this document the Chief Justice stated that he and his associates were grateful for any assistance in achieving the ends of justice. The more formal and public the assistance, the better, from the court's viewpoint; but it was most important that, to be helpful, the advice of an anthropologist be candid and honestly reflect his views.

The Justice then suggested that anthropologists be encouraged to (1) appear as "friends of the court" in cases in the High Court involving questions of customary law, particularly those involving land law; (2) make a substantial part of their time available to the Public Defender to advise him on local customs and practices which might help to justify or excuse the conduct of the accused; (3) assist in a general dissemination of knowledge of the law, particularly as it might apply to problems noted by court officials; (4) keep in touch with court proceedings in their respective districts and advise the High Court judges informally of any apparent injustices, unnecessary irritations, or methods by which the courts might improve the administration of justice, particularly in such matters as suspended sentences and rehabilitation; and (5) send to the High Court judges copies of any of their unclassified reports and recommendations for change dealing with social or legal conditions in their respective districts. It was further suggested by the Chief Justice that each District Administrator be encouraged to report to the High Commissioner instances in which he disagreed with his anthropologist on matters of major importance and to forward a full explanation of the issue, his own views, and a full copy of any report the anthropologist wished to submit.

This procedure, it was hoped, would tend to set a precedent for the anthropologist's relations with other departments. It was formalized and put on record for this purpose as well as to give official sanction for the cooperation it proposed. It was fully appreciated that it could amount to nothing more than an available model. Other department heads would have to find merit in it as they saw fit and accept or reject the implied suggestion of its general adoption.

NOTES

1. Until recently there was a sixth, assigned to the Saipan District.
2. Issued by the Pacific Science Board of the National Academy of Sciences through its National Research Council.
3. This report was actually prepared by the Internal Affairs Officer who had just finished a CIMA project in the Truk area.

6

The Research and Development
Approach to the Study
of Change

ALLAN R. HOLMBERG

What I have to say on the question of values in action stems largely from a rather deep and personal involvement with this question for the past five years. In 1952, quite by design, although unexpectedly and suddenly, I found myself in the delicate position of having assumed the role of *patrón* (in the name of Cornell University) of a Peruvian *hacienda*, called Vicos, for a period of five years, for the purpose of conducting a research and development program on the modernization process.

"The Research and Development Approach to the Study of Change" by Allan R. Holmberg is reprinted from *Human Organization* 17:12–16, 1958, by permission of the publisher and the author's estate.

As you can readily imagine, such action on my part clearly shook (or perhaps I should say shocked) the Board of Trustees — to say nothing of the some 2,000 residents of the *hacienda* and no few of my anthropological colleagues — to the extent, I might add, that had events subsequently taken other turns than they eventually did, I would probably not be writing this and would be much more in disgrace as an anthropologist and human being than I presently am. Moreover, had I known then what I now know, I am not so sure that I would be willing to repeat the experience, even though it has been one of the most rewarding ones of my whole professional career. My doubts lie not so much with the fruitfulness or legitimacy of the research and development, as contrasted with the strictly research, approach to the study of the social process but more with the wear and tear that it might cause to the inadequately financed or inadequately staffed anthropologist or other behavioral scientist who is brash enough to attempt to apply it, especially in a foreign area. On this point I shall have more to say later. For the moment, suffice it to say that having recently retired — again quite by design — from playing the dual role of God and anthropologist (the status of Vicos has recently changed from a dependent to an independent community) and having again assumed the role of a plain anthropologist, I find the change in status a highly comforting one. Nevertheless, on the basis of the past five years of experience at Vicos, I remain convinced that the interventionist or action approach to the dynamics of culture, applied with proper restraint, may in the long run provide considerable payoff in terms both of more rational policy and better science. My concern here, therefore, will be with some of the reasons why I believe this to be the case. What, then, are some of the implications — the advantages and disadvantages, the gains and losses — of the application of the research *and* development approach to the study of change, both from a value and scientific point of view?

II

On the question of values — in the ethical sense — I really have little to say, more than to state my stand. No one — professional or layman — can scientifically justify intervention into the lives of other people, whether they be of his own kind or of a different breed. However, by its very nature, the social process is an influencing process among individuals and social groups, one upon which the very existence of society depends. It is no less a necessary condition for the study of social life. Even the most "pure" anthropologist imaginable, conducting his research with "complete" detachment and objectivity, cannot avoid influencing his subjects of study or in turn of being influenced by them. In some instances,

I believe, this has led to very salutory effects, both on anthropologists and their informants. Certainly the science of anthropology has been greatly enriched by these informants who were influenced by anthropologists to become anthropologists, even though it may be more questionable, perhaps, that native cultures have been correspondingly enriched by those anthropologists who were influenced by their informants to go native. While this may seem beside the point, I simply want to emphasize the fact that influence and consequently the values which motivate that influence are always part of the process of human interaction and while they can be studied by science, their validation must rest on other grounds.

This does not mean that any anthropologist — pure or applied — can manipulate his subjects without restraint. Some code of ethics must govern his behavior, as the Society for Applied Anthropology long ago recognized. In the case of Vicos, however, where power was held by us, this became an especially delicate issue because having assumed the role of *patrones* we expected and were expected to intervene in the lives of the people. It was at this point that the question of values entered and it was at this point that it was very necessary to take a value stand. What then was this stand?

I long ago made the decision for myself, which is shared by a great many people and communities of the world, that the best kind of a community in which to live is one that is, to quote Aldous Huxley, "just, peaceable, morally and intellectually progressive" and made up of "responsible men and women." To my way of thinking, and I am by no means unique in this view, the best way of approaching this Utopian state of affairs is to pursue as a goal the realization of basic human dignity to which every individual is entitled. And by basic human dignity I mean a very simple thing: a wide rather than a narrow sharing of what I regard as positive human values, some expression of which, as Professor Harold Lasswell (no date) has so clearly shown, is found in every society and towards a wider sharing of which, if I interpret Professor Robert Redfield (1953) correctly, the broader course of civilization itself has been moving for a considerable period of time.

For lack of better terms of my own to express the meaning I wish to convey, let me again refer to Lasswell who speaks of the following categories of value: power, wealth, enlightenment, respect, well being, skill, affection, and rectitude. The wide sharing of such values among members of the Vicos community was essentially the overall basic value position and policy goal to which we subscribed. In other words, everyone, if he so desired, should at least have the right and the opportunity, if not the responsibility, to participate in the decision-making process in the community, to enjoy a fair share of its wealth, to pursue a desire for knowledge, to be esteemed by his fellowmen, to develop talents to the best of his ability, to be relatively free from physical and mental disease, to enjoy the affection of others, and to command respect for his private life. While no such value stand, of course, can ever be validated by science we and a surprising number of Vicosinos, as I have said elsewhere, and, as revealed by a baseline study, believed them "to be good and desirable ends (Holmberg, 1955).

Movement towards such goals, of course, rests on a couple of fundamental assumptions (or better, expectations) in which I happen to have a very strong faith: (1) that human traits are such that progress can be made towards the realization of human dignity and (2) that the natural order (physical nature) is such that with greater knowledge and skill, human beings can turn it progressively to the service of social goals.[1]

In stating this overall value position, I have not meant to suggest that movement towards these goals can occur only through a single set of institutional practices. Like most anthropologists I subscribe to the doctrine of the relativity of culture and I firmly believe that people have the right of self-determination, as long as they respect that right in others. From the very beginning at Vicos we recognized this principle. In short, we used our power to share power to a point where we no longer hold power, which is just as matters should be.

Before leaving these value and policy matters let me simply cite a few of the developmental changes that have come about as a result of the application of the research *and* development approach to change at Vicos:

(1) *Organization.*

1952. Vicos had an *hacienda*-type organization. Outside renters not only had free use of *hacienda peones* for labor and personal services, but also of their animals and tools. Power was concentrated in the hands of *patrón.*

1957. *Hacienda* system and free services have been abolished; new system of community organization now in march is based on shared interests and local control.

(2) *Land Ownership.*

1952. No title to land, although Vicosinos had tried on numerous occasions to purchase the land on which they had been living as *peones* for 400 years.

1957. Based on reports of development by the Cornell-Peru Project, the Institute of Indigenous Affairs asked the Peruvian Government to expropriate Vicos in favor of its indigenous population. This expropriation has now taken place.

(3) *Local Authority.*

1952. Under the *hacienda*-type organization there were no responsible secular authorities within the community.

<u>1957</u>. The Vicosinos have organized a board of their own delegates elected from each of 6 zones of the *hacienda*. They have the legal responsibility for the direction of community affairs.

(4) *Income*.

<u>1952</u>. The indigenous community of Vicos had no source of income of its own.

<u>1957</u>. Former *hacienda* lands are now farmed for the public good, providing a steady income for the payment of lands and the development of public service.

(5) *Education*.

<u>1952</u>. In the aspect of education Vicos had a very small school, with one teacher, 10–15 students.

<u>1957</u>. Vicos now possesses the most modern school in the whole region, recently made a *nucleo escolar*, with a capacity of 400 students. There are now 9 teachers and about 200 students, many of whom have had five years of continuity in school.

(6) *Production*.

<u>1952</u>. Low economic production — each *hectare* of potato land produced a value of only $100.

<u>1957</u>. Each *hectare* of potato land is now producing a value of $400–$600.

(7) *Health Facilities*.

<u>1952</u>. There were no modern health facilities.

<u>1957</u>. A modern health center has been built by the Vicosinos and a neighboring community; a clinic is held twice a week and a public health program is underway.

Most of the cost of these developments have been borne by members of the community themselves.

As a final development outcome I should perhaps mention that the Cornell-Peru Project has had considerable impact outside of the area of Vicos. When originally undertaken there was not a single project of its kind in Peru. At the present time, the Institute of Indigenous Affairs is directing five programs of a similar nature in other areas of the country. And attached to all are Peruvian anthropologists, many of them trained in part at Vicos.

But more important have been the effects on the outside produced by the Vicosinos themselves. Word of their freedom has got around. Let me cite but one example. Recently an *hacienda* community, in conditions similar to those obtaining at Vicos in 1952, sent a commission to Vicos for advice. Their *hacienda*, a public one as Vicos has been, was about to be rented at public auction for a period of ten years and they were desirous of freeing themselves from service to a *patrón*. One of the ways in which this can be done is for the residents of an *hacienda* to rent it directly from the government themselves. But in the case of this community sufficient funds were not immediately available.

The Vicosinos sent a return commission to *Huascarán,* a fictitious name for the community under discussion. On the recommendation of this commission the community of Vicos, which had funds in the bank, lent the community of Huascarán sufficient money to rent their *hacienda* directly from the government, thus freeing them from service to a *patrón.* More than that when the commission from Vicos first went to Huascarán they noticed that the Huascarinos planted their fields by somewhat antiquated methods and suggested more modern methods of agriculture which were originally introduced into Vicos by the Cornell-Peru Project. These are the kind of developmental effects that give the applied anthropologist an occasion for joy.

III

Now what of the scientific implications of the research and development approach to the study of change?[2] Here again I take a positive view, particularly in a situation like Vicos, where it was possible to work in a complete cultural context, where it was possible to specify social goals for almost all aspects of culture, and where it was possible for the anthropologist to maintain some control over the interventions and variables involved. In such an environment, hypotheses can be tested by comparing actual goal achievement with predicted goal achievement.

Actually in the natural sciences, research and development are inseparable. It is even common to join them in one formal project as is the case in many technologically advanced industries, in government, and in private institutions. But whether formally joined or not, scientific discovery is sooner or later inevitably put to the test of success or failure through the application of research results in engineering and technology. In other words, a great strength of, if not a necessary condition for, natural science is feedback through development.

Anthropology, like other behavioral sciences, profits little from such corrective feedback. In part this is because it is not systematically employed in social decision-making, as let us say, physics is employed in missile or building construction. But even if it is employed the results are either not fed back to the anthropologist or they are fed back too slowly to facilitate rapid scientific advance. Moreover, research and development work in behavioral science are seldom joined, even though they were to some extent in Vicos, for the systematic exploitation of their reciprocal benefits, as they are in the research and development laboratories of the natural sciences. To get the feedback necessary for rapid advance in a behavioral science like anthropology, policy is needed, even if policy does not need science.

The connection between research and development in anthropology and other behavioral sciences is probably even closer than it is in the natural sciences. In science, as everyone knows, every generalization is both an insight and a prediction, even though its explicit statement is usually cast in one form or another. Now when a generalization on behavior is communicated to people who are also its subjects, it may alter the knowledge and preferences of these people and also their behavior. Thus a scientific generalization on behavior, by altering behavior, appears to falsify or obsolesce itself. This is called "pliancy factor" by my philosophical colleague at Cornell, Max Black.

In general this complication has been viewed as a cross that the behavioral scientist must bear. Actually, a generalization about behavior is not falsified when predictions based upon it are made obsolete when the subject to whom it is made known prefers to modify himself rather than to conform to an earlier prediction. It is simply that the possibility of modification of behavior must be taken into account and turned to scientific advantage. In the continuous interplay between scientific generalization and goal-seeking behavior, the insight-feedback of a scientific generalization can be employed both for goal revision and as empirical data for research. This is one of the great advantages of the research and development approach. Perhaps an example will illustrate what I mean.

One of the developmental goals of the Vicos program was to bring decision-making bodies of the community up to a level of competence at which we, the *patrones*, could be dispensed with but without the community's falling victim to its most predatory members as has sometimes been the case. Thus, arrangements had to be made for group survival and stability and, through controlling the complexity of the problems dealt with and by other devices, the groups gradually brought to their highest level of competence. This required that hypotheses be formulated and acted upon — hypotheses concerning the requirements of viability and competence of groups. Once acted upon the hypotheses were tested by their results. Hence each successive developmental step was a step in the isolation of another variable for research.

Concretely, both development and research interests merge in following the consequences of such successive steps as the following, at least some of which were taken for one group of potential decision-makers at Vicos (1) the group was asked for advice in the settlement of land disputes; (2) it was invested with prestige by calling public attention to its role; (3) the group was given the opportunity to settle land disputes; (4) the group was provided, through skilled observers, the feedback of an understandable analysis of its performance; (5) the *patrón* was withdrawn from the group meeting, reserving only the right to veto under certain conditions; (6) the jurisdiction of the group was enlarged with gradually decreasing veto.

While this detail is much abbreviated, it suggests how research on the developmental steps provides an opportunity for the dogged pursuit of whatever variables one wishes to isolate. Every insight into the variables can be put to a test; and, where predictions are disappointed, a reformulation of the hypothesis can be followed by a further test until predictions are no longer disappointed. By no means will all the unknowns of human behavior become unveiled, but development requires correct insights, hypotheses, and analytic models. It compels their never-ending revision until they pass the test of application.

The essence of the connection between research and development in this illustration is that each developmental intervention — say, introducing legal principles by which land disputes might be resolved — is both a necessary step towards reaching community goals and in the research sense a method of varying the group situation to isolate another variable in group dynamics — in this instance isolating the effect of introducing formal principles against which individual cases are to be judged. It is precisely because of feedback to the researcher from the development application that research needs development just as much as development needs research.

Whatever the particular example, the story is much the same. The researcher is compelled to follow through, to keep on trying for the refinement of an hypothesis or model that will stand the test of application. If, for example, he wants to know what is necessary to break down prejudice between Indians and Mestizos, his research is not terminated when he has tested one popular hypothesis and found it invalid, because his developmental objectives require that he try a whole series of interventions until prejudice begins to decline.

In the case of Vicos, attempts were made in collaboration with several colleagues[3] to lay out about 130 specific possible lines of research and development, each matched to a specific developmental goal such as the diversification of agriculture, the development of community leadership, the reduction of social distance between Indians and Mestizos, the increase of educational opportunities for both children and adults, etc. Wherever possible an attempt was made to make fairly precise statements about the goals in question. To lay out the various possibilities in order subsequently to develop a strategy of research and development, each line of possible intervention was represented in a semi-diagrammatic way by a column on a very large bulletin or map board taking up the walls of a room. The diagram below represents how 3″ x 5″ cards were used to lay out visually the research and development sequences, subject to constant revision as research and development continues:

An ideological goal or end point

A corresponding institutional goal or end point

Program plans for probes, pretests, interventions, and appraisals

Present ideological situation with respect to above goals summarized

Present institutional situation with respect to above goals summarized

Record of past interventions

Base line ideological situation

Base line institutional situation

At the top of the column is posted for some end-point date the particular goal in question to be reached. At the bottom of the column are posted the counterpart institutional and ideological situations found at the base line period before interventions. Above them are summarized any interventions so far made, and above them the present institutional and ideological situation with respect to this one line of development. The remainder of the column is given over to a proposed schedule of probes, pretests, interventions, and appraisals.

By utilizing such a method, interventions are not likely to be hit or miss and their developmental and research gains can be fully appreciated. Scheduling them requires the careful appraisal of the facts describing the existing situation and trends, probes of readiness of the community to take the proposed step, pretests of interventions on a small scale, then the intervention itself and subsequent appraisal, which in turn becomes the first step in a still further intervention. Hence in diagrammatic terms, the upper part of the column, including the goals themselves, is constantly undergoing revision on the basis of the growing lower part of the column representing past experience.

To illustrate the distinctiveness of research, where the whole life of the community is available for study, as it was to a considerable extent in Vicos, it may be helpful to visualize a great many columns such as have just been described, set side by side. The interrelationships among these columns can hardly go unnoticed, and it becomes both possible and necessary to consider these interrelationships in devising a research and development strategy.

One more thing should be said about this contextual mapping in a research and development approach to change. It makes possible, for *development,* an economy of intervention. For example, one way in which to reduce social inequality between Mestizos and Indians is to schedule public functions in Vicos attractive enough to draw neighboring Mestizos in and then conduct these functions in such a way as to break down the traditional acceptance of segregation. One can conceive of an experiment along this line that might test the hypothesis that prejudice between Indians and Mestizos will be reduced by contact under conditions of social equality.

Now with reference to quite a different goal of reducing communal binges, movies are an effective competitor with alcohol because the Vicosinos prefer to be sober when watching a movie. Movies are also an obvious method for adult education, including literacy. Finally, the importation and showing of films may become the nucleus of a small-scale experiment in Indian entrepreneurship. Hence a variety of lines of desirable research and development converge on a movie program for Vicos. Actually such an experiment is now underway at Vicos and a skillful plan for introducing movies into the community may turn out to be a strategically sound intervention because many birds may be killed with one small stone.

I have now said enough to indicate what I believe some of the value and scientific implications of the research and development approach to the study of change to be. Most of what I have said is positive and I have not suggested that this approach be applied to the exclusion of others. My greatest doubts about it, on the basis of my experience at Vicos, stem from the unlikelihood of mobilizing sufficient funds and personnel to do a research and development job well. It is a man's job that a boy cannot be sent to do. I hope that the powers supporting research will soon take cognizance of this fact.

NOTES

1. These statements were originally formulated by a work group at the Center for Advanced Study in the Behavioral Sciences. Members of this group were John Kennedy, Harold Lasswell, Charles Lindblom, and myself.
2. Much of the material here has been revised from an unpublished document prepared by Harold Lasswell, Charles Lindblom, John Kennedy, and myself, entitled "Experimental Research in the Behavioral Sciences and Regional Development." In a sense they should be regarded as joint authors of this section.
3. See Note 2.

7 ....

The Changing Values and Institutions of Vicos in the Context of National Development

ALLAN R. HOLMBERG

More than fifty percent of the world's population is peasantry, the large majority of whom are living in the so-called underdeveloped countries or newly emerging nations under natural conditions and social structures that have denied them effective participation in the modernization process. In the context of a modern state, this peasantry plays little or no role in the decision-making process; its members enjoy little access to wealth; they live under conditions of social disrespect; a large majority of them are illiterate, unenlightened, and lacking in modern skills; many

"The Changing Values and Institutions of Vicos in the Context of National Development" by Allan R. Holmberg is reprinted from the *American Behavioral Scientist*, Volume VIII, No. 7 (March, 1965), pages 3–8, by permission of the Publisher, Sage Publications, Inc.

are victims of ill health and disease. Characteristic of this sector of the world's population is a deep devotion to magico-religious practice as a means of mitigating the castigations of a harsh and cruel world over which it has little or no control. Such, in fact, were the conditions of life on the *Hacienda Vicos* (Vasquez, 1952), a community which is the subject of this paper and those to follow (see Holmberg, 1965).

Operating on the assumption that these conditions of human indignity are not only anachronistic in the modern world but are also a great threat to public and civic order everywhere, Cornell University, in 1952 — in collaboration with the Peruvian Indianist Institute — embarked on an experimental program of induced technical and social change which was focused on the problem of transforming one of Peru's most unproductive, highly dependent manor systems into a productive, independent, self-governing community adapted to the reality of the modern Peruvian state (Holmberg, 1960).

Up until January, 1952, Vicos was a manor or large estate, situated in a relatively small intermontane valley of Peru, about 250 miles north of the capital city of Lima. Ranging in altitude from about 9,000 to 20,000 feet, Vicos embraced an area of about 40,000 acres[1] and had an enumerated population of 1,703 monolingual Quechua-speaking Indians (Allers, 1964) who had been bound to the land as serfs or peons since early colonial times.

Vicos was a public manor, a type not uncommon in Peru. Title to such properties is frequently held by Public Benefit or Charity Societies which rent them out to the highest bidder at public auction for periods ranging from 5 to 10 years. Each such manor has particular lands, usually the most fertile bottom lands, reserved for commercial exploitation by the successful renter who utilizes, virtually free of charge for several days of each week, the serf-bound labor force, usually one adult member of every family, to cultivate his crops. The rent from the property paid to the Public Benefit Society is supposed to be used for charitable purposes, such as the support of hospitals and other welfare activities, although this is not always the case. Under the contractual arrangements between the renter and the Public Benefit Society (and sometimes the indigenous population) the former is legally but not always functionally bound to supply, in return for the labor tax paid by his serfs, plots of land (usually upland) of sufficient size to support the family of each inscribed peon.

Manors like Vicos are socially organized along similar lines. At the head of the hierarchy stands the renter or *patron,* frequently absentee, who is always an outsider and non-Indian or Mestizo. He is the maximum authority within the system and all power to indulge or deprive is concentrated in his hands. Under his direction, if absentee, is an administrator, also an outsider and Mestizo, who is responsible to the renter for conducting and managing the day-to-day agricultural or grazing operations of the property. Depending on the size of the manor, the administrator may employ from one to several Mestizo foremen who are responsible for the supervision of the labor force. They report directly to the administrator on such matters as the number of absentee members of the labor force, and the condition of the crops regarding such factors as irrigation, fertilization, and harvest.

Below and apart from this small non-Indian power elite stands the Indian society of peons, the members of which are bound to a soil they do not own and on which they have little security of tenure. The direct link between the labor force and the administration is generally through a number of Indian straw bosses, appointed by the *patron* and responsible for the direct supervision of the labor force in the fields. Each straw boss or *Mayoral,* as he was known at Vicos, had under his direction a certain number of *peones* from a particular geographic area of the manor. In 1952 there were eight straw bosses at Vicos, with a total labor force of about 380 men. In addition to the labor tax paid by the Indian community, its members were obligated to supply other free services to the manor such as those of cooks, grooms, swineherds, watchmen, and servants. The whole system is maintained by the application of sanctions ranging from brute force to the impounding of peon property.

In matters not associated directly with manor operations the Indian community of Vicos was organized along separate and traditional lines. The principal indigenous decision-making body consisted of a politico-religious hierarchy of some seventeen officials known as *Varas* or *Varayoc* (Vasquez, 1964) so named from the custom of carrying a wooden staff as a badge of office. The major functions of this body included the settling of disputes over land and animals in the Indian community, the supervision of publc works such as the repair of bridges and the community church, the regulation of marriage patterns, and the celebration of religious festivals. The leading official in this hierarchy was the *Alcalde* or mayor who assumed office, after many years of service to the community, by a kind of elective system and who occupied it for only one year. The *Varayoc* were the principal representatives of the Indian community to the outside world.

In 1952 all Vicosinos were virtual subsistence farmers, occupying plots of land ranging in size from less than one-half to about five acres. The principal crops raised were maize, potatoes and other Andean root crops, wheat, barley, rye, broad beans, and quinoa. In addition, most families grazed some livestock (cattle, sheep, goats, and swine) and all families raised small animals like guinea pigs and chickens as a way of supplementing their diets and their incomes. After thousands of years of use and inadequate care, however, the land had lost its fertility, seeds had degenerated, and the principal crops and animals were stunted and diseased. Per capita output was thus at a very low level, although the exact figure is not known.

In (Collazos *et al.*, 1954); most were victims of a host of endemic diseases. Studies in parasitology (Payne *et al.*, 1956) demonstrated that 80 percent of the population was infected with harmful parasites, and epidemics of such diseases as measles and whooping cough had been frequent over the years. There were, to be sure, native curers employing magico-religious practices and ineffectual herbal remedies to cope with these well-being problems but it can be said that the community had little or no access to modern medicine. The goal of the traditional Vicosino was simply to survive as long as he possibly could, knowing full well that he might be a victim of fate at any moment.

The principal avenue for gaining respect in traditional Vicos society was to grow old and to participate in the politico-religious hierarchy, the top positions of which could be occupied only after many years of faithful service to the community. Wealth was also a source of gaining prestige and recognition but it could not be amassed in any quantity, by native standards, until one's elders had died or until an individual himself had lived frugally and worked very hard for many years. In other words, the principal role to which high rank was attached was that of a hard working, muscle-bound virtual subsistence farmer who placed little or no value on other occupations or skills. Consequently there was just no place for a rebellious or symbolically creative individual in traditional Vicos society. The manor system was, of course, in large part responsible for this. It needed few skills beyond brawn and enlightenment could not be tolerated, because the more informed the population, the more it might become a threat to the traditional manor system. Records show (C. Barnett, 1960) that all protest movements at Vicos had been pretty much squelched by a coalition of the landlords, the clergy, and the police. As a result, over a period of several hundred years the community had remained in static equilibrium and was completely out of step with anything that was occurring in the modern world. The rule at Vicos was conformity to the status quo. It pervaded all institutions and dominated the social process. The peon was subservient to the overlord; the child, to the parents; and both were beaten into submission. Even the supernatural forces were punishing, and the burdens one bore were suffered as naturally ordained by powers beyond one's control.

INTERVENTION FROM WITHOUT

The Cornell Peru Project intervened in this context in 1952 in the role of *patron*. Through a partly fortuitous circumstance — the industrial firm which was renting Vicos on a ten year lease that still had five years to run went bankrupt — we were able to sublease the property and its serfs for a five year period. For a couple of years prior to this time, however, the Peruvian anthropologist, Dr. Mario Vazquez, had conducted a very detailed study of this manor as a social system, as part of a larger comparative study of modernization of peasant societies that the Department of Anthropology at Cornell was conducting in several areas of the world. Thus when the opportunity to rent the *hacienda* arose, we seized upon it to conduct our own experiment in modernization. In its negotiations prior to renting the *hacienda,* Cornell received full support of the Peruvian Government through its Institute of Indigenous Affairs, a semi-autonomous agency of the Ministry of Labor and Indigenous Affairs. In December, 1951, a formal Memorandum of Agreement was drawn up between Cornell and the Institute of Indigenous Affairs, and the Cornell Peru Project became a reality at Vicos on January 1, 1952.

Several months prior to assuming the responsibilities of the power role at Vicos, a plan of operations was drawn up (Holmberg, 1952) which was focused on the promotion of human dignity rather than indignity and the formation of institutions at Vicos which would allow for a wide rather than a narrow shaping and sharing of values for all the participants in the social process. The principal goals of this plan thus became the devolution of power to the community, the production and broad sharing of greater wealth, the introduction and diffusion of new and modern skills, the promotion of health and well being, the enlargement of the status and role structure, and the formation of a modern system of enlightenment through schools and other media. It was hoped that by focusing on institutions specialized to these values as independent variables this would also have some modernizing effect on the more dependent variables, namely, the institutions specialized to affection (family and kinship) and rectitude (religion and ethics), which are sensitive areas of culture in which it is generally more hazardous to intervene directly.

In designing our program and a method of strategic intervention, we were very much aware of two, among many, guiding principles stemming from anthropological research: First, innovations are most likely to be accepted in those aspects of culture in which people themselves feel the greatest deprivations; and second, an integrated or contextual approach to value-institutional development is usually more lasting and less conflict-producing than a piecemeal one. Consequently, we established our operational priorities on the basis of the first principle but tried to optimize change in all areas at the same time, realizing, of course, that with scarce resources, all values could not be maximized concurrently. Perhaps, a few examples will best illustrate our use of the method of strategic intervention.

Our first entry into more than a research role at Vicos coincided with a failure of the potato harvest of both the *patron* and the serf community due to a blight which had attacked the crop. The poor of the community were literally starving, and even the rich were feeling the pinch. Complaints about the theft of animals and food were rife. At the same time, previous study of the manor had enlightened us about the major gripes of the serfs against the traditional system. These turned out not to be such things as the major commitment of each head of household to contribute one peon to the labor force for three days of each week, but the obligation of the Indian households to supply the extra, free services to the manor previously mentioned. Since we were in a position of power, it was relatively easy to abolish these services. A decision was made to do so, and volunteers were hired to perform these jobs for pay. Thus an immediate positive reinforcement was supplied to the community in our power relationship with it.

An added incentive to collaborate with the new administration resulted from the fact that we as *patrones* reimbursed the serfs for labor which they had performed under the previous administration but for which they had not been paid for approximately three years. Under the traditional system, each peon was entitled to about three cents per week for the work performed under the labor tax. In some Peruvian manors this is paid in the form of coca leaves, which most adult males chew, but at Vicos it was supposed to have been paid in cash. By deducting the back pay from the cost of the transfer of the manor to our control, we fulfilled earlier commitments, with the money of the previous administration, and received the credit for it. Through such small but immediately reinforcing interventions, a solid base for positive relations with members of the community was first established. In this regard, of course, we were greatly aided by Dr. Vazquez, who had previously spent almost two years in the community, living with an Indian family, and who personally knew, and was trusted by almost every one of its members.

INCREASING AGRICULTURAL PRODUCTIVITY

As mentioned above, one of the most immediate and urgent tasks at Vicos was to do something about its failing economy which, in reality, meant increasing its agricultural productivity. Manors like Vicos are never productive because the renter during his period of tenure puts as little as possible into the operation and exploits the property for as much as he possibly can. The serfs, on the other hand, make no improvements on their lands, or other capital investments, because they, too, have no security of tenure. As a consequence, most such manors are in a very bad state of repair.

Since the Cornell Peru Project possessed funds only for research and not for capital development, the wealth base had to be enlarged by other capital means. It was decided, in consultation with Indian leaders, who were early informed about the goals of the Project, that no major changes would be initiated immediately in the day-to-day operations of the manor. We even retained the former Mestizo administrator, a close friend of the Project Director and Field Director, who agreed to reorient his goals to those of the Project.

The principal resources available to the Project were the labor of the Indian community and the lands which had been formerly farmed by the overlord. By employing this labor to farm these lands by modern methods (the introduction of fertilizer, good seed, pesticides, proper row spacing, etc.), and by growing marketable food crops, capital was accumulated for enlarging the wealth base. Returns from these lands, instead of being removed from the community, as was the case under the traditional system, were plowed back into the experiment to foment further progress towards our goals. Profits from the Project's share of the land were not only employed further to improve agricultural productivity but also to construct health and educational facilities, to develop a wider range of skills among the Indian population, and to reconstruct what had been a completely abandoned administrative center of operations. At the same time, new techniques of potato production and other food crops, first demonstrated on Project lands, were introduced to the Indian households which, within a couple of years, gave a sharp boost to the Indian economy. In short, by 1957 when Cornell's lease on the land expired, a fairly solid economic underpinning for the whole operation had been established, and the goal of considerably enlarging the wealth base had been accomplished.

DEVOLUTION OF POWER

From the very first day of operations, we initiated the process of power devolution. It was decided that it would be impossible to work with the traditional *Varas* as a leadership group, because they were so occupied during their terms of office with religious matters that they would have no time to spend on secular affairs. On the other hand, the former straw bosses, all old and respected men, had had a great deal of direct experience in conducting the affairs of the manor for the *patron*. It was decided not to bypass this group even though we knew that its members had enjoyed the greatest indulgences under the traditional system and, being old, would be less likely to be innovative than younger men. Under prevailing conditions, however, this seemed to be the best alternative to pursue. As it turned out, it proved to be an effective transitional expedient. Gradually, as success was achieved in the economic field, it became possible to replace (by appointment) the retiring members of this body with younger men more committed to the goals of modernization. For instance, men finishing their military service, an obligation we encouraged them to fulfill, returned home with at least an exposure to other values and institutions in Peruvian society. In pre-Cornell days such returning veterans were forced back in the traditional mold within a few days time, with no opportunity to give expression to any newly found values they may have acquired. Insofar as possible, we tried to incorporate people of this kind into decision-making bodies and tried to provide them opportunities to practice whatever new skills they had acquired. In the first five years of the Project, not only did age composition of the governing body completely change, but decision-making and other skills had developed to a point where responsibility for running the affairs of the community was largely in indigenous hands. A complete transfer of power took place in 1957, when a council of 10 delegates, and an equal number of subdelegates, was elected to assume responsibility for community affairs. This council, elected annually, has performed this function ever since.

In the area of well-being it was much more difficult to devise a strategy of intervention that would show immediate and dramatic pay-off. This is a value area, to be sure, in which great deprivation was felt at Vicos, but it is also one in which the cooperation of all participants in the community was necessary in order to make any appreciable impact on it. The major well-being problems at Vicos, even today, stem from public health conditions. All individuals are deeply concerned about their personal well-being but are unwilling to forego other value indulgences to make this a reality for the community as a whole. Nor were the resources available to do so at the time the Project began.

A variety of attempts was made to tackle the most urgent health problems. In collaboration with the Peruvian Ministry of Health and Social Welfare, a mobile clinic was started at Vicos, which made at least one visit to the community each week. Support for this effort came from the community itself in the form of the construction of a small sanitary post at which the sick could be treated. It was hoped to staff this clinic through the Public Health services of Peru, but all attempts to do so were frustrated by lack of budget and responsibly trained personnel. In Peru, such services seldom extend into rural areas because the preferred values of the medical profession are, as almost everywhere, associated with city life. Consequently, no major public health effort was launched and the community's state of well-being has shown little net gain. What gains have been made stem principally from improved nutrition, but as enlightenment about the germ theory of disease diffuses and the results of modern medicine are clearly demonstrated, through the application of public health measures that take native beliefs into account, we expect a sharp rise in the well-being status of the community to follow.

OPTIMIZING GOALS

Strategies for optimizing Project goals for the respect, affection, and rectitude values, first rested heavily on the examples set by Project personnel. From the very beginning, for example, an equality of salutation was introduced in all dealings with the Vicosinos; they were invited to sit down at the tables with us; there was no segregation allowed at public affairs; Project personnel lived in Indian houses. At the same time, we attempted to protect the constitutional rights of Vicosinos, which had been previously flagrantly violated by the Mestizo world. Abuses by Mestizo authorities and army recruiters were no longer tolerated. The draft status of all Vicosinos was regularized; they were encouraged to fulfill their legal obligations to the nation. While not directly intervening in the family, or tampering with religious practice, the indirect effect of optimizing other values on the respect position of the community soon became evident. As Vicosinos mastered modern techniques of potato production, for example, they were approached by their Mestizo compatriots in the surrounding area, seeking advice as to how to improve their crops.

Even the rectitude patterns at Vicos began to change. When we first took control of the manor, rates of theft were extremely high. Every peon farmer, as his crops were maturing, had to keep watchmen in his fields at night. As the Indian economy rose and starvation was eliminated, this practice disappeared completely. Even the parish priest became an enthusiastic supporter of the Project. His services were more in demand, to say nothing of their being much better paid.

A strategy of promoting enlightenment at Vicos was initiated through the adaptation of a traditional manor institution to goals and values of the Project. In most Andean manors run along the lines of Vicos, the peons, after completing their three days labor, must report to the manor house where they receive their work orders for the following week. This session of all peons, straw bosses, and the *patron* is known as the *mando*. We devised a strategy of meeting the day before the *mando* with the *mayorales* or decision-making body and utilizing the *mando* to communicate and discuss the decisions taken. Since heads of all households were present, the *mando* provided an excellent forum for the communication of news, the discussion of plans, progress towards goals, etc.

A long-run strategy of enlightenment rested on the founding of an educational institution at Vicos that could provide continuity for Project goals, training of leadership dedicated to the process of modernization, and the formation of a wide range of skills. Through collaboration with the Peruvian Ministry of Education and the Vicos community itself, this became a possibility. Within the period of Cornell's tenure, levels of enlightenment and skill rose sharply and their effects have been substantial throughout the society.

TRANSFER OF TITLE

In 1957, at the time Cornell's lease in Vicos expired, the Project made a recommendation to the Peruvian Government, through its Institute of Indigenous Affairs, to expropriate the property from the holders of the title, the Public Benefit Society of Huaraz, in favor of its indigenous inhabitants. By this time we felt that a fairly solid value institutional base, with the goals of modernization that we had originally formulated, had been established in the community. The Peruvian Government acted upon the recommendation and issued a decree of expropriation.

It was at this point that the experiment became especially significant, both in the local area and throughout the nation, for national development. Prior to this time, although considerable favorable national publicity had been given to the Project, little attention had been paid to it by the local power elite, except in terms of thinking that the benefits of the developments that had taken place would eventually revert to the title holders. It was inconceivable in the local area that such a property might be sold back to its indigenous inhabitants. Consequently, local power elites immediately threw every possible legal block in the way of the title reverting to the Indian community. They set a price on the property that would have been impossible for the Indian community ever to pay; members of the Project were charged with being agents of the communist world; the Vicosinos were accused of being pawns of American capitalism; Peruvian workers in the field were regarded as spies of the American government. Even such a "progressive" organization as the Rotary Club of Huaraz roundly denounced the Project, accusing its field director of being an agent of communism.

Fortunately, the Project had strong support in the intellectual community of the capital and among many of Peru's agencies of government. The codirector of the Project and President of the Indigenous Institute of Peru (also an internationally recognized scholar in high altitude biology), Dr. Carlos Monge M., was tireless in his effort to see justice done to the Vicosinos. But even his efforts did not bear fruit until almost five years had passed. The reason for this was that not only were the legal blocks of the resistance formidable, but the central government of Peru at this time was an elite government, which, while giving great lip service to the cause of the Vicosinos, was reluctant to take action in their favor. It is a matter of record that many high officials of government were themselves *hacen-*

dados, hesitant to alter the status quo. Consequently, they were able to delay final settlement.

Meanwhile the Vicosinos, now renting the manor directly, were reluctant to develop Vicos because of the danger of their not being able to enjoy the fruits of their labor. While agricultural production rose through the stimulation of a loan from the Agricultural Bank of Peru, other capital investments were not made because of the fear that the price of the property would rise with every investment made. Finally, through pressure exerted by the President of the Institute of Indigenous Affairs and U.S. government officials in Peru, an agreement was reached between the Public Benefit Society and the Vicos community for the direct sale of the property to the Vicosinos at a price and on terms that they could realistically pay. Thus, after a five year wait following the devolution of power, the community actually became independent in July, 1962. Since that time Cornell has played largely a research, advisory, and consultant role, although the Peruvian National Plan of Integration of the Indigenous Populations has had an official government program of development at Vicos since Cornell relinquished control in 1957.

RESULTS

What can be said in a general way about results of the Vicos experience so far? In the first place, if one criterion of a modern democratic society is a parity of power and other values among individuals, then vast gains have been made at Vicos during the past decade. Starting from the base of a highly restrictive social system in which almost all power and other value positions were ascribed and very narrowly shared, the Vicosinos have gradually changed that social system for a much more open one in which all value positions can be more widely shared and they can be attained through achievement. This in itself is no mean accomplishment, particularly since it was done by peaceful and persuasive means.

In the second place, the position of the Vicos community itself, vis-a-vis the immediately surrounding area and the nation as a whole, has undergone a profound change. Starting at the bottom of the heap, and employing a strategy of wealth production for the market place and enlightenment for its people, the community of Vicos has climbed to a position of power and respect that can no longer be ignored by the Mestizo world. This is clearly indexed by the large number of equality relationships which now exist at Vicos (and in intercommunity relationships between Vicos and the world outside), where none existed before.

Finally, of what significance is Vicos in the context of national development? Peru is a country with a high degree of unevenness in its development. The highly productive agricultural coast, with off-shore fishing grounds that are among the richest in the world, is moving ahead at a modern and rapid pace. In contrast, the overpopulated sierra, containing major concentrations of indigenous populations, many of whom live under a medieval type agricultural organization, such as exists at Vicos, is lagging far behind. The major lesson of Vicos, for Peru as a whole, is that its serf and suppressed peasant populations, once freed and given encouragement, technical assistance and learning, can pull themselves up by their own bootstraps and become productive citizens of the nation. It is encouraging to see that the present Peruvian Government is taking steps in the right direction. Its programs of land reform and Cooperation Popular may go a long way towards a more peaceful and rapid development of the country as a whole.

NOTES

1. Earlier publications on Vicos estimated acreage as much smaller. This figure is correct, based on accurate measurements made by Mr. Gary Vescelius.

8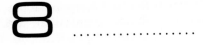

The Fox Project

SOL TAX

Picture a piece of land on the Iowa River in Central Iowa. Some of it is bottomland that floods over. Some of it is wooded hillside. Some is useful for farming. For the past 100 years this has been the home of a growing community of American Indians who call themselves Mesquakies. They are commonly known as Fox Indians. After the Blackhawk War they were removed from Illinois and Iowa to Kansas. They defied the government, however, and in 1857 a few of them sought and received permission from the state of Iowa to buy 80 acres of land on which to settle. The 80 acres have grown to 3300. The population has grown to some 600 persons who think of this settlement as home even though many work and live in the towns and the cities of the white world — which in the meantime has surrounded their land and their lives.

There have been a hundred years of peace — of peaceful coexistence. Time enough for the Indians and their neighbors to take one another quite

"The Fox Project" by Sol Tax is reprinted from *Human Organization* 17:17–19, 1958, by permission of the author and the publisher.

for granted — time enough for Indians and whites in daily contact to become unaware each of the other. With some help from government and with a great deal of official interference, the Indians have maintained their own community, their language, their religion, their peculiar family interrelations, their Mesquakie values. Successful hunters turned unsuccessful farmers; an independent tribal state with its proud chiefs and law became the dependent pawn of a confused government bureaucracy — everything was changed; the Indians would not be unfaithful to the only "right" they could accept. Thus when I first visited the settlement in 1932 and 1934, to study the social organization, I suppose that they had achieved a kind of adjustment to the surrounding white world. I came away then with the impression that they were remarkably well-organized in terms of Indian forms, even taking account of an old factional split. Needless to say, they were poor; but in the depth of the depression of '32 and '34 so was everybody. They seemed to be a going concern in terms of their ancient culture. This was surprising, to me, since I would have expected that a small community of the only Indians in a large and populated state would after 75 years have become pretty much like others in Iowa. But they had maintained not only their identity and pride in their own history, but also a large core of their traditional culture. Few of the Indians spoke English; fewer still were Christians in spite of two missions that seemed well-established.

In the summer of 1948, mainly to provide opportunity for field training, the University of Chicago sent six students to this settlement to study various problems according to their interest. The depression had turned into the New Deal and WPA and CCC and other projects in which the Indians participated. The Mesquakie had organized under the Indian Reorganization Act of the Collier regime. Then in the great war many Indians had fought, and returned veterans were having difficulty readjusting to life in the Indian settlement. We therefore expected many changes from 1934 to 1948.

It turned out that the community had increased in size from about 400 to 600; more people were graduating from high school; more people were working successfully in a greater variety of occupations in more communities in Iowa. But the community was as distinctive as before, and perhaps as proud. If there was a great difference it was that the Indians felt a greater sense of problem; they wanted their local security, but they also wanted things from the world.

Or perhaps anthropology had changed with the depression and the war and we noticed the problems more than I had earlier. In any event, this field party in 1948, became concerned less with the traditional aspects of the culture than with the ways in which the community and the people were dealing — or not dealing — with their internal factionalism and with their relations to whites. The field workers began to try to understand in this local setting the processes of acculturation, adjustment, community organization. The problems of the Indians were accepted as problems for study. And instead of observing from the outside we began to do what every physician does — learn while helping.

Just for the historical record, let me emphasize that when the six students came to the Indians in 1948 nobody had in mind a role for them other than that of anthropologist. On my first visit to them they asked me if they could not try to help the Indians solve their problems. I have never decided why I said yes; surely I had not thought through the consequences; but with the word the project was launched. Back in Chicago I wrote them a letter rationalizing what I called "participant interference." All of our justification has come after the fact. Indeed, the theory and practice have grown up together. The phrase action anthropology dates from a session at the last annual meeting of the AAA held in Chicago just six years ago. We knew no precedent for what we were trying to do in combining research and action; it did not seem to us we were exactly applying science. So, as Allan Holmberg and James Spillius (working in Tikopia in 1952–53) did independently, we coined a new term.

After we were fairly underway in understanding the problems of the Mesquakie community, we began of course to look at other Indians and have ranged widely and, in at least one other case, also deeply. We have reason now to believe that our diagnosis of the problems of the Mesquakies applies to many other Indians, and our answers to the problems may also be generally useful. With respect to the Fox themselves, we see a configuration of interrelations too complicated for this short presentation. This is an hypothesis we test. In a general way we now understand the ways in which the Indians will and will not change.

II

The two irreducible conditions of community-wide change are that the new behavior does not require either (1) a loss of Fox identity, or (2) a violation of Fox moral beliefs. One takes for granted also that the change is practicably possible — that the new behavior required is understandable and feasible, and that there is some reason, from the point of view of the Indians, to make it. Given these two general limitations, *we suppose any change is possible.*

It is the object of our action to free the Indians to make the changes that they wish and which would appear from our hypothesis to be in their interest. We want to break into the circle at any point, and actually we have been attacking at several. Most simply, we have been telling everyone we can just what I am saying here: that neither assimilation nor its opposite are inevitable; that Indians can maintain their identity as Indians while making such changes as will not violate their own values but are still sufficient to make them self-sustaining. We say further, that one necessary condition is a continuation for as long as needed of the small amount of money provided by the Federal Government for Indian education and health. But preaching is also accompanied by other activities. We attempt to interest politicians in the idea of some financial arrangement that will guarantee the maintenance of the school and clinic, but on a basis where the Indians will make their own decisions concerning their education and health so that the whites see that they are capable of running their own affairs. We have also embarked on two specific programs both closely tied to our general diagnosis: One is a scholarship program to bring young Indians into the professions, so that they can enter the white economy at levels other than as laborers and artisans. The second is to help the Indians to develop a cooperative industry to produce and sell Indian crafts. Perhaps the greatest end served by these is removing obstacles that keep Indians from relating to functional white organizations and interest groups. Such new relations are desired by the Indians and need not require that they change either their identification as Indians or their moral values. Needless to say, we look forward to an occasion when we can describe these programs in detail, perhaps with a report of the results achieved. Suffice it to say now that the scholarship program was received enthusiastically by the Indian community to the remarkable end that all or nearly all Indians in high school now take it for granted that they will seek higher education. We think this is partly because we succeeded in separating the question of remaining or not remaining an Indian from the question of how a person makes his living.

The results that we hope for from the crafts program are much more far-reaching. If we are successful, we will have helped the Fox Indians to adopt patterns for relating to the larger society that will at once break down the functional isolation that exists and also establish patterns for constructive internal community organizations. Again, if we are successful we believe it will be because the new institutions neither imply social death nor violate basic Fox values, at the same time they do permit new identification with prestigeful white occupation groups and new service relations among Indians.

III

If you ask me what are the values that are involved in our interference, I must say — looking back now — that they are three in number:

First, there is the value of truth. We are anthropologists in the tradition of science and scholarship. Nothing would embarrass us more than to see that we have been blinded to verifiable fact by any other values or emotions. We believe that truth and knowledge are more constructive in the long run than falsehood and superstition. We want to remain anthropologists and not become propagandists; we would rather be right according to canons of evidence than win a practical point. But also we feel impelled to trumpet our truth against whatever falsehoods we find, whether they are deliberate or psychological or mythological. This would be a duty to science and truth, even if the fate of communities of men were not involved. But as some myths are part of the problem of American Indians it is also a duty to humanity and to outraged justice. Our action anthropology thus gets a moral and even missionary tinge that is perhaps more important for some of us than for others.

Second, we feel most strongly the value of freedom, as it is classically expressed and limited. Freedom in our context usually means freedom for individuals to choose the group with which to identify and freedom for a community to choose its way of life. We would also be embarrassed if it were shown that we are, for example, encouraging Indians to remain Indians, rather than to become something else, or trying to preserve Indian cultures, when the Indians involved would choose otherwise. All we want in our action programs is to provide, if we can, genuine alternatives from which the people involved can freely choose — and to be ourselves as little restrictive as is humanly possible. It follows, however, that we must try to remove restrictions imposed by others on the alternatives open to Indians and on their freedom to choose among them. We avoid imposing our values upon the Indians, but we do not mean to leave a vacuum for other outsiders to fill. Our program is positive, not negative; it is a program of action, not inaction; but it is also a program of probing, listening, learning, giving in.

Such a program requires that we remove ourselves as much as possible from a position of power, or undue influence. We know that knowledge is power, and we try hard to reject the power that knowledge gives us. Perhaps this seems contrary to the functioning of applied science? We realize that we have knowledge that our Indian friends do not have, and we hope to use it for their good. But to impose our choices on the assumption that "we know better than they do what is good for them" not only restricts their freedom, but is likely to turn out to be empirically wrong. The point is that what is best for them involves what they want to be. Operationally this is knowable only by observing which alternatives they actually choose, and we defeat ourselves to the degree that we choose for them. Hence we find ourselves always discovering and not applying knowledge.

So our value of freedom is partly an ethic and partly a way of learning the truth. At least we see no contradiction between our first two values.

A *third* value — or is it a principle of operation? — is a kind of Law of Parsimony which tells us not to settle questions of values unless they concern us. This in a way is a value to end for us the problem of values. In the beginning of our Fox program, having decided to interfere for some good purpose, we were beset with value problems. Some of us were for and some of us were against the assimilation of the Indians; what a marvelously happy moment it was when we realized that this was not a judgment or decision *we* needed to make. It was a decision for the people concerned, not for us. Bluntly, it was none of our business. This not only freed us, but the particular instance was the beginning of the philosophy of our action program. As I look back now I see that this has been our general solution to value problems. When it became necessary to decide which of conflicting values to choose, we eventually found ourselves not deciding at all, and finding some way around it. Perhaps it is time now to set this down systematically as an operating value.

People are always asking us whether we think cannibals have a right to self-determination. With respect to cannibalism, would we not have to impose some value of our own? Now, I neither eat human flesh, nor like the thought of being eaten; I am as revolted as others in our culture by the whole idea. I have no notion what I would do if I found myself involved in an action program on a cannibal isle; I can only think of jokes to say. If I attempt to answer seriously I am beset with all the value contradictions involved in so-called cultural relativism. But whatever my personal position on this, *it has no significant bearing on what we should do tomorrow to help the Fox Indians* develop more constructive relationships within their community, or with other Iowans.

IV

I do not want to be interpreted now as anti-philosophical; problems of values are intellectually and personally important to all of us, and to anthropology. We need to discuss them. The only question at issue is the degree to which they need to be resolved before action can be taken. Clearly the answer depends upon the actor, the problem, and the alternatives open. It must be different for every case. The general rule that we have found useful is therefore only a limiting principle. It is that which, I understand, underlies the operations of the Supreme Court of the United States. The Court will not decide constitutional questions in the abstract, but insists that a *case* be at issue; and even then it tries to decide the case on technicalities if possible, and avoid as long as possible deciding the general issues.

I take it this is wise and necessary because in human life issues arise only when there are no good easy answers, and the decision becomes a choice of evils. By definition, it is good to postpone doing something bad.

In the same way, and generally for the same reason, we, too, avoid making decisions when (1) (as in the instance of Indian assimilation) they are not clearly ours to make, and when (2) (as in the instance of cannibalism) they can be postponed. This is a general rule of action for us, to be followed — like all our rules — as well as humanly possible. But I mention it here only in the context of the problem of values itself, to the point that this rule of parsimony puts a limitation on our liability for value judgments as they relate to our programs of action.

An issue that has lately arisen among us, for example, is whether we put freedom or self-determination as a higher value. What we ask, if a community wants to remain dependent? The book by O. Mannoni recently translated into English as *Prospero and Caliban* (1956) argues that Melagasy communities resist being given independence, and the question arises: Does self-determination include the right to determine not to be self-determining; and if so, are we still for it? Or do we rather force freedom on a community? These questions seem critical only because some people think that American Indians have become dependent in this sense, and that an umbilical cord tying them to the Government must be cut. Our procedure in the face of this is first of all to forget about Madagascar — we don't know if what Mannoni says is or is not true; we have no way of finding out, by methods which satisfy us, except by going there and working with a community in an experiment with freedom, and second to re-examine the factual situation of American Indians to be sure of our conclusion that American Indian communities can operate independently under given conditions that they help choose. The result is that we analyze the *conditions* of independence. This is our answer to the question for purposes of action; we find we do not need to settle the hypothetical problem of the general issue, and need no longer be diverted from our task. Thus new data, new alternatives, new value issues give rise to new problems for analysis and study — but the problems are settled in the concrete instances where we operate even though left unsettled forever in the abstract.

I would say the same thing about the problem repeatedly suggested here — whether science sets values, or whether we can scientifically justify our interference. I would simply postpone the general question and worry about the alternatives open to us for action tomorrow, and the consequences of each for ourselves, for the Indians and the general society and for science or for the profession of anthropology. I only hope that we are able to behave responsibly at each point of decision.

Maybe that is why we call this Action Anthropology.

9

The Strategy of the Fox Project

FRED GEARING

We will be acting in the Fox community and in surrounding white Iowa communities in the coming years. Our plan of action derives from a hypothesis about the nature of the Fox problem. We see that problem as residing in the relations between the Fox and their neighbors. We think the Fox and nearby whites have slipped into a vicious circle.

The total activities of the Fox project in the coming three or four years will be a refinement and test of that hypothesis.

I will first characterize that vicious circle. Then I will outline the strategy in our coming attempts to break into that circle and change its nature.

You will find on page 114 a schematic diagram of the vicious circle. It will probably help if you follow that diagram.

I enter the vicious circle, in this description, from the left. You see a circle reading: Fox self-organization and a square reading: Whites believe

ct is

"The Strategy of the Fox Project" by Fred Gearing is reprinted from Fred Gearing, R. McC. Netting, and L. R. Peattie, *Documentary History of the Fox Project: 1949–1959*, pp. 294–300, Department of Anthropology, University of Chicago, 1960, by permission of the author and the Department of Anthropology, University of Chicago.

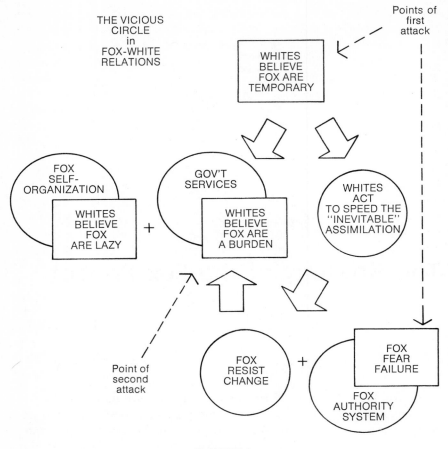

FIGURE 1

Fox are lazy. Items in circles refer to behavioral phenomena (or inferences from them); items in squares refer to more purely mental or verbal
phenomena — ideas and attitudes. Where the two overlap as in this instance, the meaning is that the idea springs, in important degree, from the
behavior. So, I begin with a behavioral item, the Fox self-organization,
and a belief item, Whites believe Fox are lazy.

Deep-seated psychological differences between Indians and non-Indian
Americans have been suggested by scores of students. Most often the
difference has been characterized by the terms shame and guilt. Our
strong impression is to accept the contrast. We descriptively characterize
it in terms of self-organization. In terms of self-organization, Anglo-
Americans seem to adopt as they mature a personal, ideal self. That self

is a more or less consistent collection of virtues. The life careers of white men are, ideally, a ceaseless effort to make the real self coincide with that ideal self. Restated in terms of ethos, a — perhaps the — primary ethical principle of Anglo-American society is virtue. In spite of individual and class variation, and in spite of the doubtlessly true reports of decreasing inner-directedness, and in spite, even, of variation within the Fox community, contrast with the Fox is striking. The Fox individual does not seem to create such an ideal self; he does not see himself as *becoming* at all; he is. Restated in terms of ethos, the primary ethical principle of the Fox is harmony.

The effects of that contrast are great. White individuals, if psychologically healthy and not self-consciously marginal, can engage in a sustained effort in a single direction over a long period of time, and — here is the crux — they can do so more or less independent of their group. In contrast, a Fox is guided almost exclusively by his moment-to-moment relations with others; he bridles under long-term, rigid work schedules; he becomes listless in situations requiring isolated self-direction.

Whites who know Fox Indians almost invariably interpret the contrasting work patterns as laziness, and unreliability. And, omitting perhaps the value judgment bound up in that English word, it *is* laziness. (But conversely, of course, the Fox look at white men and say they are aggressive and selfish.)

When white men make the judgment that the Fox are lazy, that is devastating enough to the relations between the groups. (In white society it seems to be far worse to be lazy than stupid, for instance.) But the effects of that judgment are compounded by the added fact that — moving now to the right on the diagram — the Fox are seen as a burden on honest, hard working taxpayers. The federal government does finance two services in the Fox community — education and, minimally, health. Most whites exaggerate the facts considerably and see the Fox as living off some sort of dole. The idea of lazy people living off of taxpayers' money is something less than tolerable to Iowa farmers when they think of it, which is fairly often.

Because the situation is intolerable, there is a strong disposition to see it so temporary. America has had the experience of the melting pot. (You will see that I am now arguing the connection to the second element of the vicious circle on your diagrams.) But America also has a tradition of cultural pluralism. There is a very wealthy colony of German pietists less than 100 miles from the Fox — the Amanas, who made freezers until they sold the name for a fabulous sum. Iowans do not feel that that German colony is temporary, or that it should be. But an Iowan simply does not entertain the idea that the Fox are here for more than, as they put it, another generation.

Once the idea is intrenched, that the Fox are temporary, important actions follow (the third element in the circle). If there is an inevitable process of assimilation under way, then, if one is to do anything, he will attempt to speed the process. Whenever debates arise as to what to do, argument is over whether to spend money in order to create opportunities for the Fox to move upward, or whether to quit spending anything at all and thereby force them to move upward. And, of course, Fox individuals are evaluated according to how far along that imagined line of progress they seem to have individually traveled.

The Fox live in very close contact with the neighboring whites and they are in intimate contact with the government. So the effects of that continual pressure from whites are great. The effects are a marked degree of resistance to change. (I have now moved to the lower right hand corner of the diagram.)

On one level, that Fox resistance to change reflects a positive evaluation of a life. But it is much more. It reflects a sense of threat. The Fox value their school and wish not to lose it and wish not to have it merged with schools in nearby towns. They want their lands to remain in protected status. They are instantly opposed to any suggested changes — in their school system, in their trust status, in the jurisdiction of their law and order. They oppose the idea of change, irrespective of the substantive details which never really get discussed. They do this because they fear failure — generically.

They fear failure because they have often failed. They have often failed because white society demands, in effect, that the Fox do things the white way. And there are basic structural reasons why the Fox simply cannot. The Fox *can* undertake the tasks — they run a pow wow each year which clears several thousand dollars and involves the coordinated efforts of at least 200 persons. But they must do it their own way.

Those basic structural reasons are the Fox authority system. In Fox social organization, authority roles are all but nonexistent. As Miss Furey has said, the Fox cannot effectively choose a course of action except in the absence of all overt opposition.

Fox tribal government under the Indian Reorganization Act is based on majority rule. Majority rule means that majorities exercise authority over minorities. It doesn't work. White men have gotten the Fox started on cooperative handicraft production and sale, based on majority rule. That didn't work. The pow wow organization has, on paper, a host of grand-sounding, authoritative positions such as president, treasurer, etc. But the organization actually functions the Fox way — by leisurely discussion until overt opposition disappears. That works.

On the whole, white-initiated activities have been organized in a hierarchical arrangement of authority and the Fox have failed. Failing repeatedly and having mixed feelings about what the white man calls progress in the first place, the Fox have settled down to a grand strategy of holding the line. Having set on that course, they tend, through time, to become more of a financial burden. So the beginning of the vicious circle is rejoined.

Turn now to what we plan to do about it. The word attack connotes much more aggressiveness than we are likely to exhibit. But in the upper right hand corner on your diagrams you read: points of first attack. We have the hope that something can be done by simple verbal communication — education. Education is the first attack.

One prong on the diagram points to the white belief that the Fox are temporary. This historical record makes a pretty good case, we think, that one cannot assume the Fox, or any Indian group, is *inevitably* temporary. We hope that, if we say that often enough and to enough of the right people, it will have detectable effect. Further, some of those people can be affected by pointing out the undesirable results on the Fox when white men act *as if* the Fox are temporary.

But, according to the vicious circle, white men believe the Fox are temporary because, in part, they believe the Fox are lazy and are a burden. I will return to the Fox burden later. What to do about the belief in Fox laziness? We intend to do nothing directly. Rather, by talking about certain other facets of Fox life, we hope to reduce white man's preoccupation with that laziness. We imagine that it would be futile to tell almost any white man that laziness is only culture. After all, we white men hold that work is a virtue; and faith in that is extremely basic in the operations of white society. But there are other areas of Fox life which are now understood and positively valued by the neighbors of the Fox. And there are still other facets of Fox life which, though now misunderstood by whites, could come to be understood and positively valued with relative ease, we think. Iowans say, for example, that the Fox are poor farmers. We think Iowans could be interested in learning that the Fox aren't farmers at all.

In short, we have our focus on the white belief that the Fox are temporary and want to correct that. In order to do so, we will try to draw the attention of whites away from the highly resistant belief that the Fox are lazy and toward more easily valued aspects of Fox life.

Now, turning to the second prong of this first attack, we will attempt, again by verbal communication, to reduce the Fox fear of failure. Some success has already been recorded when we have experimentally talked to Fox individuals about so-called failures in terms of their authority system. Almost invariably the failures occurred because some Fox wasn't authoritarian; he wasn't authoritarian because it would have been indecent to be. The Fox value those patterns of authority highly; they usually combine them with other things under the term, freedom. In one recorded instance, we had written something about the authority patterns, and a Fox had read the article and he came to us quite excited about it. It was apparent that the Fox individual had made the logical connection between that valued freedom and past failures he had experienced. This, no doubt, for the first time; and quite obviously, to his great relief.

To the degree that such understanding becomes general and internalized, the Fox should be better off. That understanding will help relieve their anxieties about past failure and help them to better select future undertakings. It should *help* restore their self-confidence.

The Fox will best come to understand their own social structure through contrasting it with that of white society. We plan such activities as an informal adult education program as alluded to by Mr. Marlin. This would be in the Fox community and would cover the history of their relations with the federal government. The subject is of intense interest to them. In examining with them such things as particular treaties, there will be ample opportunity to attempt to explain Fox and white behavior in terms of culture and social organization. This may be the first time an adult education course on civics has been attempted in an Indian community.

In these first, verbal, attempts to break into the vicious circle, we expect uneven results. The Fox will probably learn more about whites (and about themselves) than whites will learn about the Fox. Fox interest is more pressing. However, the very failure of whites to understand should present further opportunities to demonstrate to the Fox the nature of white society.

One footnote before turning to the second point of attack. I should not leave the impression that all the learning is going from us to them. We expect to learn much more than we now know about both societies by the very act of discussing the contrasts between them.

The second point of attack will begin soon after the first and continue concurrently with it as shown on the diagram, the main focus here, is on the fact and fiction of the Fox burden. We intend in this second approach to restructure certain situations so as to create learning experiences. In some instances, the new situations will be designed to demonstrate facts about Fox or white behavior. In others, situations which are threatening will be altered if possible so as to create a better atmosphere for learning.

As an example of creative situations which demonstrate facts, we tried, with some success, a small experiment in cooperative farming. The experiment demonstrated to the participants (including us) some facts about cooperative endeavor under the Fox authority system. I spent many hard hours in a hot Iowa corn field and I cannot discover any subconscious sabotage on my part. But I would mislead if I did not admit to some

THE STRATEGY OF THE FOX PROJECT

secret pleasure in the low level of economic success of the project. The lack of economic success confirmed an important hypothesis — and confirmed it as much for the participating Fox as for us. In the future, in regard to such situations which demonstrate facts, we plan to encourage undertakings which seem workable ones, and assist in the implementations when asked. So much for situations which will demonstrate facts.

The threatening situations have more pervasive effects. And more hinges on our hopes to alter them. The matter of government health and education services are especially damaging as they stand today. It is unlikely that the Fox will have sufficient tribal income in the foreseeable future to pay for those services. The federal government's withdrawal policy has created great anxiety among both the Fox and nearby Iowans. The Fox fear they will lose the services. The Iowans fear the costs will be shifted to them. Furthermore, you will recall the important effects, in the vicious circle, of the white man's picture of the Fox as a burden. We think that the fact of government subsidy could be altered in a way which would remove those bad effects. The threat of withdrawal to both Fox and Iowans, and the picture of the Fox as a burden could be greatly altered by establishing a permanent tribal fund large enough to pay the costs of those services from income from the fund. We are willing, if and when the Fox are ready, to undertake political action with them to the end of getting such a fund appropriated by Congress. The odds are clearly not great. We do not rule out the possibility of Fox self-sufficiency without such a fund but the prospects are very remote.

In summary, we have hopes of breaking into the vicious circle and, through trying, of reaching a more adequate and precise analysis of the relations between the Fox and their neighbors. We will undertake two sets of actions in the attempt. Through education, we will try to alter certain ideas; our focus is primarily on the white belief that the Fox are temporary and the Fox fear of failure. Through changing situations, we will attempt to assist the learning processes; our focus here is primarily on Fox financial dependence.

You perhaps have noticed that throughout we have left the resistant white beliefs, such as the idea that the Fox are lazy, alone. We do not intend to come directly to grips with them. It is felt that one or both of two things will happen to them, assuming a degree of success in our other efforts: Some will become less important and some less true. As for the ideas about Fox laziness, we count more on the first. The idea will be less important because it will be no longer joined with the idea of the Fox being a burden.

A key index of success will turn on how much we are able to increase Fox self-confidence. That self-confidence and its most basic element — the greater Fox understanding of Fox and white behavior — should make it possible for the Fox to adjust their own behavior sufficiently to cope with the white world, especially in the economic sphere. By adjusting we mean self-conscious actions — acting — doing things deliberately for desired ends. It is clear that this sort of change differs radically from the basic change that would be required of whites — to recognize that work is not an absolute virtue. It is clear, too, that the changes we expect of the Fox are not the sort of basic changes that are generally thought of when one speaks of acculturation.

10

The Failure of the Means-Ends
Scheme in Action Anthropology

LISA REDFIELD PEATTIE

What I am going to say amounts to a general methodological comment
on the strategy which Fred Gearing has outlined. I do not plan to discuss any part of this program. Instead, I want to call attention to a
characteristic of the program as a whole, one which seems to me rather
different from a good deal of applied anthropology. This is a difference
not so much in what we do, as in how we have come to think and talk
about what we do and plan. I hesitate to sound as if I were talking
philosophy — that is not my field — but I think that this difference can
be stated most clearly as follows: We have come to talk about social
action in ways which lie outside the usual means-ends scheme which our
culture prescribes as usual for this subject.

"The Failure of the Means-Ends Scheme in Action Anthropology" by Lisa Redfield
Peattie is reprinted from Fred Gearing, R. McC. Netting, and L. R. Peattie,
Documentary History of the Fox Project: 1948–1959, pp. 300–304, Department
of Anthropology, University of Chicago, 1960, by permission of the author and the
Department of Anthropology, University of Chicago.

This difference was first suggested to me in a paper on our Fox project by a philosopher, Paul Diesing. In this paper, Diesing distinguishes two sorts of planning which are applied to social processes. The first type of planning sharply distinguishes ends and means. In Diesing's words, it "consists of first deciding what one wants to do, and then finding out how to do it." This is evidently the classic type of applied science, including social science; writings on the application of science to solving social problems generally presuppose some such scheme. "Applied anthropology," as generally discussed, also follows this means-ends scheme. The anthropologist here sees himself as a kind of social technician. He takes some goal, perhaps one set for him by an administrative agency, occasionally one which he sets for himself, and discovers means to bring it about. His analogue is the technician of the physical sciences. Just as the electrical engineer reports to his company on how to build a certain kind of switchboard and estimates the cost of building it, so the applied anthropologist may report to an administrator the most effective way of getting a cattle-raising tribe to reduce their cattle herds, and on the social costs of making the change. So in the early days of the Fox project we talked about means to get the Fox to farm more efficiently. This way of thinking, which sharply distinguishes the "end" to be achieved from the "means" to it, is familiar to all of us.

However, it is not the only possible way to think about planning and social action. In fact, our "action anthropology" enterprise tends to follow lines something like an alternative scheme put forward by Diesing in his paper on the Fox project. Diesing speaks of this scheme as one in which "neither ends nor means are regarded as given at the start, but both are determined in a single inquiry, each by reference to the other." The action anthropologist is not so much involved in the application of theory to determine means to a given end as he is in "the development and clarification of goals and the compromising of conflicting ends and values." The action anthropologist, with his coordinate activities of action and research, thus becomes involved in a three-fold process. Our action research among the Fox is the process by which we discover the facts — those relevant to action and to the setting of goals for the Fox community, as well as those relevant to general scientific hypotheses. It is secondly, and at the same time, the process by which we and the Fox together set and clarify the goals of the action program. Thirdly, and simultaneously, it is itself the action which is to help bring about those goals. In this three-fold process, ends and means can no longer be distinguished from each other.

When the action anthropologist states his goals or "ends" they tend to be open-ended objectives like growths in understanding, clarification of values, and the like, rather than fixed goals like the quotas in a five-year plan. They are not properly speaking "ends" at all, for they can never be said to have been reached. They are more properly modes of valuing — modes of valuing all stages in a continuous and infinite process.

This scheme, which deals with a continuous process of discovery and action and valuing, rather than with ends and means, is by no means unique to action anthropology. Readers of John Dewey's *Theory of Valuation* will recognize that it has a respectable status in American philosophy. In practice, it has an interesting analogue in psychotherapy, in which the process of discovering the nature of the patient's illness is at the same time a process of curing that illness, and a process of redefining what the patient wishes to become — in other words, what the "ends" of the process are in the particular case. But although the parallel to psychotherapeutic practice is particularly clear, I suspect that it is not unique. In fact, it seems likely that much more social planning follows the model I have described than one would suspect from writing on the subject of applied social science. But however much all of us may in practice fail to keep our "ends" and "means" separate, this is not the model which we usually follow in our thought.

I think there are a number of reasons why even in America, the home of pragmatic philosophy, discussions of applied social science usually follow the traditional means-ends scheme rather than the Deweyan form which the Fox project has come to adopt. In the first place, our group's way of thinking runs counter to a general technological bias of our culture. We Americans like to conceive of action on the model of the machine, action directed as efficiently as possible to a clearly-defined purpose. In the social sciences, such action is less clearly possible than it is in physics or mechanics. But we social scientists tend to hope that it is possible, even to act as if it were possible when we are not sure that it is, hoping against hope as it were; such seems to be the entry to respectable status among the family of sciences and applied sciences. Secondly, the whole structure of our language and thought presupposes a scheme where one acts and the other is acted upon the technician, the action anthropologist acts on society, on people. Thirdly, to the extent that only one agent is acting to determine ends, a definitive setting of goals, and the control necessary to achieve set goals, is made more possible. This situation is approached when the anthropologist works for an administrative agency with a good deal of power — for example, a colonial government. Historically, this has been the classic type of situation in which the applied anthropologist has been found, and the discussions of applied anthropology tend to reflect this circumstance.

Finally, a real difficulty of our "Deweyan" way of planning is that it carries with it a need for new methods of evaluation. In the traditional means-ends scheme, the mode of evaluation is clear. Have you done what you set out to do? But we reserve the right, in fact, assert the obligation, to modify our particular objectives (e.g., setting up a clinic) at all stages of the action process. Thus the simple test of determining whether the plan has been "fulfilled" can be applied only to small, even trivial steps in the action process. As for our more general and permanent objectives, such as increasing the areas of mutual understanding between Indians and whites, these are so general that they are hard to give operational definition; in any case, they are practically infinite in character, so that no matter how much has been accomplished it could always be argued that more could and should have been. But evaluation is clearly necessary. In fact, since our way of working conceives of every stage of our action as both means and end, we must evaluate each stage as well as the whole process; nothing can be treated as a mere utility, a means. Methods for doing this kind of evaluating with any rigor have yet to be devised. Again it is interesting to compare our problems with those of psychotherapy. The psychotherapeutic "cure" is unique to each case, and the therapist may not know what it is until the end of the therapy. How much and what kinds of change may be considered success? I note that the therapists have not answered this group of questions very effectively either.

In view of all these difficulties, the obvious question is: Why have we adopted this philosophically interesting but otherwise slippery and complicated way of looking at our activities? This question has to be answered first historically. Such changes in ways of thinking are rarely made by logical decision at one point in time; certainly this was not. We came to think in this way, and made the change before we knew that we were making it; then we saw that we had come to think in a new way. So our conceptualization has a history first, rather than a logical reason. But the history has its own logic of functional utility. The change came about because the new way of thinking was more useful to us.

In the first place, we have in general had a role in which we were discussing with, rather than acting on, people. In contrast to the traditional role of the applied anthropologist, as adviser to some administrative body, in our Fox project we had no power position whatsoever; we could only counsel with both Indians and administrators, and neither was under any compulsion to accept our counsel as having weight. It would have been futile for the action anthropologists to set long-term goals and programs if only because they would have no way of causing these to be executed. As they could affect the actions of the Indians or of the administrators only by education, discussion, persuasion which necessarily must proceed step by step, their operations were necessarily of a step by step character. They placed more emphasis on the clarification of goals and on mutual understanding, than on rapid program towards some set objective. The Fox progress thus became one of "interacting-with" rather than "acting-on" people. And this way of acting, developed historically, has now become for the project a method of choice; we would now act in this way even if there was no need in the circumstances of our action.

In the early days of the Fox project there was a good deal of discussion among the anthropologists as to whether the ultimate goal of "assimilation" or of "nonassimilation" would be most desirable as the ultimate end for a program in that community. No agreement was ever reached on this point. But at the same time the anthropologists did agree on two other points: that certain forms of action would be helpful, regardless of decision on this ultimate choice, and that the action should in general take the form of increasing the areas of free choice available to the Indians, and of helping the Indians understand better the choices available. The general outcome was a program which might be styled a kind of nondirective counselling for a community.

Further, I note that one reason for our use of Deweyan ends-means scheme is that as a group we tend to be sceptical about the degree of positive predictive knowledge and control available to us from social science. The setting of ends in the traditional mode of operations supposes that at least sometime pretty early in your program you know enough of what your goals mean and what our means involve in the way of further consequences so that you can set a long-range plan and act according to it. We of course make such predictive judgments at all stages of our operations. But we tend not to trust them too much, we would rather not have too much at stake on our "scientific" predictions.

Finally, and I think most importantly, this treatment of means and ends in our own work has also kept pace with a change in our view of Fox culture which has clearly represented a healthy development. In the first months of our work in the Fox community we were struck by a gap which appeared to exist between the goals of individual Fox Indians in the material sphere — such things as better housing, cars — and the cultural means available for their realization — in other words the means for making a living, and the social machinery of corporate action. This led us to think of culture as a system of means and ends: the means, technology, social organization, and so on: the ends such material items as food and clothing and such nonmaterial ones as "a sense of being respected." For some purposes, this is a useful scheme. But if you try to work within a culture it gets you into difficulties, and as we tried to work with the Fox we were led to abandon it. For a culture cannot be so neatly separated into means and ends — not even our own which believes in the separateness of means and ends, and probably less so in most other cultures. Technology and social organization are not merely means; they are valued, and therefore also ends. As we came to have a view of Fox culture which saw all the parts as valued and as therefore both means and ends we came more to drop the ends-means distinction in our own work; correspondingly, as our own work lost the distinction we came less and less to see it as a useful axis for an analysis of Fox culture.

It is not true of course that in our program we have abandoned the ends-means distinction altogether. We often find it possible to separate out one part of our action program, and to conceive of it in the traditional means-ends form. Thus we have separated out the problem of providing better dental care for the Fox, and sought means to get it. Now would we argue against the traditional means-ends scheme in general. It is only that we have come to find our way of thinking more useful in an action program which tries to work as we do within a complex social situation. It has a kind of "fit" to the pattern of causality in such a social situation, in which all the parts are equally causing and being affected by the others. It has a "fit" to a view of culture in which all parts are both means and ends to the participants. So despite the difficulties, we find that on the whole this is the way we find it more congenial to think — because it is knowledge and control, because it helps in thinking of culture as a valued whole, rather than as a system of separated parts.

11 ....

Action Anthropology

1. ANTHROPOLOGY AND PRACTICAL PROBLEMS

Attempts have been made to apply anthropology to practical problems of human welfare in a variety of situations — consider for example the widely differing types of contribution which have been made by such anthropologists as G. G. Brown, John Embree, and Edwin Smith. In this paper I shall confine myself to what is the most common and the most important type of situation — that in which a non-European group of alien culture or differing subculture is affected by administrative policies deriving from governments which form part of Euro-American culture. Such situations would include colonial administrations in Africa or Melanesia, the problems of the Maori of New Zealand and those of Amerindian groups such as the one which will be described later.

The relations between anthropologists and administrators in such situations have been ably summarised by Homer Barnett, who reaches an

"Action Anthropology" by Ralph Piddington is reprinted from the *Journal of the Polynesian Society* 69:199–213, 1960, by permission of the author and the Polynesian Society.

unpalatable but correct conclusion when he writes: "No matter how tactfully it is phrased, the truth is that anthropologists and administrators do not, on the whole, get along well together" (Barnett, 1956:49). He points out, moreover, that in spite of the numerous projects for collaboration between anthropologists and administrators, the number of anthropologists engaged in such projects at any one time has not been impressive. The effect of anthropology on administration has probably lain more in the dissemination among administrators of an understanding of broad general principles than in giving them concrete advice on *ad hoc* practical problems, though the contribution in this field has been far from negligible.

The relative failure of anthropology as an applied science, in the ordinary sense of the term, has been due to a variety of factors, among which the following may be mentioned: The expense of long and thorough investigations of particular situations without which the advice of the anthropologist (even if he were willing to give it) would usually be worthless; the consequent delay in taking decisions which to the administrator may be matters of immediate urgency; occasional examples of misguided judgment by anthropologists which attract more attention than they would in such fields as medicine or meteorology; the stereotype in the public mind of the anthropologist as a student of "bizarre, dead and primitive humanity" (Barnett, 1956:56), as a conservative antiquarian yearning for a romanticised picture of a primitive Golden Age; and the tendency of some administrators to regard the anthropologist's activities as a threat to their authority or positions either by bringing to light administrative errors or by usurping their functions.

But the most significant obstacle to effective collaboration is inherent in the present situation and can never, I believe, be wholly eliminated. I refer to the essential difference betwen anthropologists and administrators not in regard to what they think but in regard to what they say and do, in other words the roles which are assigned to them by our culture. It is largely a matter of social personality, in Radcliffe-Brown's sense, not one of individual personality involving merely subjective attitudes and evaluations. The anthropologist is a scientist and like all scientists he is expected to have a deep interest in his subject matter; this usually extends to some measure of personal affection for non-Europeans as individuals and esteem for at least some features of their ways of life. As holder of a university appointment or research grant the anthropologist is free to say publicly what he thinks — to criticise governments, administrators, missionaries, and economic interests. He may regard this freedom of speech as a responsibility as well as a right and if so he is perfectly free to become a whipping boy for the *Pacific Islands Monthly*.

Contrast the position of the administrator. He is the servant of a government which, whether blatantly or not, is in the last analysis concerned with vote-catching. He must carry out a policy which has been conceived within the framework of Euro-American institutions and values and which is rarely inspired by a profound knowledge of alien cultures, let alone a sensitive appreciation of the significance of non-European values. And he must be forever conscious of a variety of individuals and pressure groups whom his actions may offend, ranging from the local trader or missionary through the public press of his own country to world-wide agencies of the United Nations. All these and many others must be placated so that, whatever he may think, he must act and speak (so far as he speaks at all) as though non-European values and aspirations were of secondary importance compared with those of the dominant European-type culture. The inherent differences between anthropologists and administrators, let me repeat, lie in the field of speech and action and not necessarily in that of belief and sympathy. Many administrators have as sensitive an appreciation of non-European cultures as the average anthropologist. And some anthropologists, particularly when they think of economic development and material progress, are sometimes as culture-bound in their own way as any bigoted missionary of the old school.

The dilemma, then, is this: It is admitted by all but the most impractical of practical men that anthropology can be of value in dealing with problems of human welfare. Yet because of the institutional framework within which he must operate, the anthropologist can in fact make only minimal and sporadic contributions to the solution of such problems.

Owing largely to this dilemma, anthropologists are sharply divided among themselves as to what role they should play in human affairs. Some hold that they should retire to an ivory tower and divorce themselves from practical issues which they cannot effectively influence and which, some believe, distract attention from fundamental research problems. Still others hold that the anthropologist should concern himself with practical problems, but only as a fact-finder. He should aim to provide the administrator with facts relevant to the carrying out of a given policy, but should play no part in the formulation or criticism of policy itself. He should refrain from advocating decisions which are necessarily based largely on his own value judgments. A third school of thought holds that the anthropologist is the person most intimately aware of the human problems, both general and particular, which are involved. He should therefore shamelessly make pronouncements on administrative policies and should provide facts relevant to the carrying out of policies which he approves.

The first of these views, being essentially negative, can be dismissed as irrelevant to our problem. The second school of thought represents a point of view which is widely held in relation to other social sciences besides anthropology — what might be called the schizoid interpretation of the role of the social scientist. According to this view the social scientist should keep his value judgments rigidly distinct from his scientific work. When not on duty as a scientist he may indulge himself in the human luxury of value judgments, but when he is carrying out research or speaking of practical issues his mind should be as free from emotion or sentiment as that of a biologist studying newts. Actually, of course, all significant social science research involves value judgements if only in the selection of hypotheses for testing and methods of research (Garigue, 1958:17). The third view is attractive and would work well if non-European peoples were governed by a benevolent dictatorship of anthropologists. But because of the characteristics of administrative institutions, mentioned previously, it is not likely to achieve widespread effectiveness. The administrator may be willing to accept help in doing his job but he is not prepared to be told what his job is or ought to be.

2. THE FOX PROJECT IN ACTION ANTHROPOLOGY

A fourth approach to practical problems has been termed "action anthropology". It was developed in the course of a project of Sol Tax and his associates of the University of Chicago among the Fox Indians at Tama, Iowa. The work at Tama started in 1948 as a field training situation for research workers, that is as a project in "pure" science. As the work advanced, the research workers became interested in the human problems of the Fox and were attracted to them as people. From this arose a desire to help in the resolution of their practical difficulties, and the formulation of a policy and a set of techniques designed to achieve this.

The Fox (also called Mesquakie) came originally from Wisconsin. With the westward expansion of white population during the nineteenth century they moved to Illinois, Iowa, and subsequently to a reservation in Kansas. Being a woodland people, they did not like the treeless plains of Kansas where they felt their land rights to be insecure. By selling their horses they were able to purchase land near Tama in southern Iowa in 1854. Their present settlement of about 3,000 acres thus differs from the ordinary Indian reservation allocated by Government, though it has a school administered by the Bureau of Indian Affairs, which also supplies minimal medical services. The soil of the settlement is poor and the working men commute to Tama and other neighbouring towns where they are largely employed in unskilled occupations. The standard of living is consequently low. At present there are about five to six hundred Fox living in the settlement.

The religious life of the Iowa Fox provides a paradigm of their adjustment to contemporary American civilization. Some are Christians but most of them, including nominal Christians, adhere either to a modified version of traditional Fox totemic religion or to one of two adjustment cults borrowed from other Indian groups. One of these is the widespread peyote cult (Sol Tax in Eggan, 1955:262–268).

The Fox, like many other Indians, want to make their religious life something essentially their own and essentially Indian. This feeling is reflected in a contemporary myth which tells of a Chippewa reincarnation of Christ: "About eighteen years ago the daughter of an old Chippewa couple, who lived off in the woods by themselves, became pregnant. The mother, knowing that her daughter had had no chance to see boys, accused the father of making the girl pregnant. When the baby was born, she raised an axe to kill the (as she thought) incestuous child. At this moment the child spoke, saying, 'I was born to the whites across the sea and they killed me; are you going to kill me too?'. Raising His hands He showed her the stigmata on them." This boy will soon become a religious leader of the Indians, as his Predecessor did for the white man (Gearing, Netting, and Peattie, 1960:56–57).

The social logic behind the refusal simply to accept the white man's religion in its entirety is revealed in another item of contemporary Indian folklore: "Once there was an Indian who became a Christian. He became a very good Christian; he went to church, and he didn't smoke or drink, and he was good to everyone. He was a very good man. Then he died. First he went to the Indian hereafter, but they wouldn't take him because he was a Christian. Then he went to heaven, but they wouldn't let him in because he was an Indian. Then he went to Hell but they wouldn't admit him there either, because he was so good. So he came alive again, and he went to the Buffalo Dance and the other dances and he taught his children to do the same thing."

The action anthropologists were, of course, keenly interested in race relations at Tama. Their interpretation of the socio-economic position of the Fox *vis à vis* the surrounding white population is summarised in a diagram prepared by Fred Gearing which is reproduced in modified form in Figure 2.

In this diagram, items in circles refer to behavioural phenomena, or inferences from them; items in squares refer to ideas and attitudes. Where the two overlap, the meaning is that the ideas and attitudes spring from the behavioural phenomena. Thus, starting at the left hand side of the circle, we have first a set of behavioural phenomena characterised as "Fox self-organization," that is the system of drives and motives which go to make up the self of an individual in relation to the outside world. The training of white Americans, like that of most people in Western civilizations, tends to develop in each individual a conception of a perfected, ideal self consisting of a more or less clearly defined collection of virtues. According to our value system the life careers of all individuals are, or

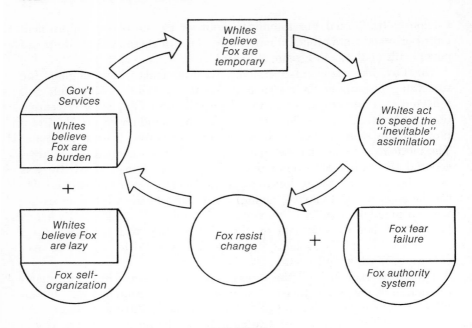

FIGURE 2

ought to be, marked by a constant effort to make the real self, reflected in actual behaviour, coincide with the ideal self — "above all else to thine own self be true. . . ." The Fox, however, do not seem to construct such an ideal self but to accept themselves as they are. They tend to be motivated by external rather than internal moral sanctions — the desire for public approval, the fear of condemnation, material considerations, magico-religious sanctions, and others familiar to anthropologists.

The effects of that contrast are great. White individuals, if psychologically healthy and not self-consciously marginal, can engage in a sustained effort in a single direction over a long period of time, and — here is the crux — they can do so more or less independent of their group. In contrast, a Fox is guided almost exclusively by his moment-to-moment relations with others; he bridles under long-term, rigid work schedules; he becomes listless in situations requiring isolated self-direction (Gearing in Gearing, Netting, and Peattie, 1960:295–297). (See Chapter 9, p. 115.)

The popular white interpretation of this situation is, understandably, that the Fox are unreliable and lazy. Laziness reflects a lack of what is regarded as one of the most essential virtues in a civilization geared to progress and material achievement. And for the whites the situation is aggravated by the educational and medical services provided for the Fox by Government. These are seen as an intolerable burden upon hard-working Iowan taxpayers. And — since an intolerable situation cannot continue indefinitely — there arises, as we move clockwise round the vicious circle, the belief that the Fox are temporary, that sooner or later they will abandon their distinctive characteristics and so cease to be a burden. This in turn leads to attempts to speed the "inevitable" assimilation, particularly by withdrawing the special educational facilities which the Fox enjoy and by urging them to take decisions which will bring them into line with white American ways and institutions. In fact, such decisions are not taken, for two reasons: Firstly because the Fox, like most cultural minorities, value their way of life and resent any threat, real or imagined, to it; and secondly because they fear failure.

> They fear failure because they have often failed. They have often failed because white society demands, in effect, that the Fox do things the white way. And there are basic structural reasons why the Fox simply cannot. The Fox *can* undertake the tasks — they run a pow pow each year which clears several thousands dollars and involves the coordinated efforts of at least 200 persons. But they must do it their own way.
>
> [The] basic structural reasons are the Fox authority system. In Fox social organization, authority roles are all but nonexistent. . . . The Fox cannot effectively choose a course of action except in the absence of all overt opposition.
>
> Fox tribal government under the Indian Reorganization Act is based on majority rule. Majority rule means that majorities exercise authority over minorities. It doesn't work. White men have gotten the Fox started on co-operative handicraft production and sale, based on majority rule. That didn't work. The pow pow organization has, on paper, a host of grand-sounding, authoritative positions such as president, treasurer, etc. But the organization actually functions the Fox way — by leisurely discussion until overt opposition disappears. That works. (See Chapter 9, p. 116.)

The Fox have failed, then, in white-initiated ventures because these have been organised along white lines and are not adapted to the Fox way of life. "Failing repeatedly and having mixed feelings about what the white man calls progress in the first place, the Fox have settled down to a grand strategy of holding the line. Having set on that course, they tend, through time, to become more of a financial burden. So the beginning of the vicious circle is rejoined (Gearing in Gearing, Netting, and Peattie, 1960:295–297).

The main attempts which were made by the action anthropologists to break this vicious circle were twofold: Firstly, informal "adult education" work among whites through pamphlets, newspaper articles, personal contacts, and correspondence with the Bureau of Indian Affairs; and secondly, measures intended to help the Fox to help themselves. The first was designed to enable the whites to appreciate the social realities underlying the difficulties of the Fox. It includes a simple charter for policy making: Any policy which is to be of value must work. It will not work unless it is accepted by the Fox. Therefore no policy which is not acceptable to the Fox can be of value.

This adumbrates the most significant distinction between action anthropology and applied anthropology as ordinarily conceived. It emphasises the right of Fox self-determination or, as Sol Tax bluntly puts it, the freedom to make mistakes. The Fox are faced with the need of making decisions relevant to their future. The function of the anthropologist is not to impose his own decisions, much less those of administrators and other whites. His function is to act as a catalyst, to help clarify issues for the Fox and to make available to them possibilities of choice which may not have occurred to them, or which might not have been available to them apart from the programme of action anthropology. In the light of such clarification, any decision reached by the Fox is by definition the right decision. Any lines of action, including those which appeal to the action anthropologist, must be rejected if they are not acceptable to the Fox. And this policy works in practice. Thus factionalism in Fox society has rendered abortive many attempts by whites to improve their condition.[1] Yet factionalism is hardly significant when the Fox are dealing with their own problems in their own ways. An example is the annual pow pow, previously mentioned, which is at the same time an exciting social occasion and an economic mechanism for extracting money from tourists. The organisation of this event is usually smooth and efficient, with few difficulties arising from factionalism; nor have the action anthropologists found factionalism a serious obstacle to their programme.

The effects of this programme are exemplified in the Tama crafts project. The anthropologists discovered a young Fox called Charles Pushetonequa who had high artistic ability. He had left the Fox community for a while and received some training in art. But he preferred to sacrifice his artistic aspirations in an alien community and to return to Tama to take up unskilled employment. The Fox, with the assistance of the action anthropologists, organized a small group which, with Indian style designs drawn by Pushetonequa, produces highly ornamental and original ceramic tiles and greeting cards. The project has been a commercial success and its effects have been threefold: Firstly it has added to the self-esteem of the Fox, has made them feel that they can operate effectively within the American economy, and has added substantially to their income. Secondly it has made the whites aware that the Fox are capable of taking practical steps to help themselves and so has modified the stereotype of them as a burden; last, but by no means least, it has provided Charles Pushetonequa with a career in which he can realise his artistic aspirations without losing his identity as a member of the Fox community.

The same sort of effects have been produced by the action anthropologists' project in higher education. Using funds contributed by various institutions and individuals, they arranged for a number of young Fox graduating from High School to proceed to institutions of higher education — something unprecedented in the history of the Fox. As had been anticipated, the success of this scheme has been moderate but significant, its failures being largely due to the difficulty experienced by the Fox in adapting themselves to the unfamiliar environment of American universities and colleges. But the academic successes of the scheme in its initial phases are not a reliable index of its value, for it has achieved two important collateral effects: Firstly it has inculcated in the minds of Fox youth the idea that higher education is a goal which should be sought. Practically all Fox graduating from High School since the inception of the scheme have taken part in it, and one of the few who did not do so was at pains to apologise to the field director because personal circumstances made it impossible for him to participate. Secondly the project is providing the Fox with a number of young people who, whether academically successful or not, will be in a position to act as mediators between them and the wider American culture which they so imperfectly understand.[2]

Returning to the philosophical basis of action anthropology, it should be noted that it is not an "applied" science in the sense of being divorced from "pure" research. On the contrary, as we have seen, it emerged in a context of pure research and holds the pursuit of this to be an aspect of the work complementary to the practical programme. Neither is given priority, and they are not mutually incompatible. As increasing knowledge enlightens action, so the social changes produced in action provide new data on the nature of Fox society and shed new light on its fundamental characteristics through the process which has been called "learning through action".

As a scientific discipline action anthropology is clinical rather than predictive. It does not aim to apply general anthropological principles directly to a body of observational data existing at any one time so as to produce a "blueprint" for the future of the Fox. Instead, by picking up a series of cues (in the light of general principles, of course) it allows concrete plans for action to emerge progressively from the ongoing processes of social change among the Fox.

An incident described by Sol Tax illustrates two important principles which have been mentioned in connection with action anthropology: Firstly that, far from being inconsistent with "pure" research, action anthropology from its very nature provides new opportunities in this field;[3] and secondly that the action anthropologist must be ready to abandon willingly and graciously any of his proposals for action which do not meet with ready acceptance by the community. As regards the first of these Tax writes: "I suppose that everything we learn in anthropology we learn from experience — things that happen — events. One special thing about action is that it greatly increases the frequency of events of which the anthropologist is aware. It is not, however, only the frequency that increases. The quality changes; the quality of the events for the anthropologist is quite different because they are important to him."

The incident described by Tax occurred in the summer of 1956 when the Native American Church — an institutionalised pan-Indian development of the peyote cult — held its national convention at Tama. Sol Tax was invited to attend, and it occurred to him that it would be a good idea to make a documentary film of the whole proceedings, including the peyote ceremony itself. The object of this was to impress upon white people (some of whom contemplated restrictive action against the Church) that the convention was that of a legitimate church and that far from being an orgiastic ritual, the peyote ceremony is sober and highly sacred in character. After meeting many practical difficulties, Tax arranged for a moviemaker, sound truck, crew, and supplies to assemble at Tama and in due course put his proposal to the convention. Some members spoke for it and some against. Their dilemma was this: It was clear to all that white objections to the Church would be minimised if it could be shown to be the expression of a genuine and serious religious faith and if peyote could be revealed as the sacrament they felt it to be. But there was a fatal objection to filming the ceremony itself. Not only would the ritual inevitably be disturbed by technical activities, but they simply could not envisage themselves engaged in the very personal and sacred activity of prayer in front of a camera. During the discussion the issue became plain to all, including the anthropologist: Whether to defile a single ritual to save the Church. Finally the president of the convention said that if others wished to have a film made he had no objections, but he begged to be excused from the ceremony. Tax continues:

> Of course this ended the movie, and the sense of the meeting was clear. It was over, and then the realization seemed to come over the Indians that I must be hurt; for all my good and unselfish intentions, and high hopes, and hard work my reward . . . was a clear rebuff. They had suffered through their dilemma, and had made the painful choice that should have relieved their tension. But they realized now that their peace with themselves had been bought at our expense, and they began speeches painfully to make amends.

They were wrong, of course. As their decision was being made I understood that what I had proposed was akin to asking a man to deliver his wife to a lecherous creditor to save the family from ruin. Now, therefore, I arose to speak, and could with genuine sincerity apologize for having brought so painful an issue to them. I had meant to be a friend, but had hurt them. I agreed with their decision. I would be a poor friend indeed if I resented their deciding an issue for their own good.

Relief was great; the euphoria was instantly restored; and it was evident then and in the days that followed that they were more genuinely grateful to me than any Indians have ever been to me for any material or moral help, and felt closer rapport with me (Tax in Gearing, Netting, and Peattie, 1960:304–306).

The approach to practical problems embodied in action anthropology is undoubtedly attractive to most anthropologists, resolving as it does many of the ethical and scientific problems with which they are faced. But there are circumstances which must for many years limit its general application. In the first place it calls for complete independence from Government control, and therefore from Government finance. Secondly, specific kinds of action (such as the higher education project) may call for funds on a scale not usually available to the anthropologist. Thirdly, as originally conceived, it might not apply in communities, for example some groups of Australian aborigines, where the original culture has almost completely disintegrated and where "community goals" might be well-nigh impossible to define. The fact that the Fox have successfully maintained their "Foxness" accounts in large measure for the success of the Chicago project among them. Fourthly, as Sol Tax admits, action anthropology would be difficult to apply in situations where there exists a fundamental clash between the economic interests of different ethnic groups — in Kenya, for example. And, finally, it is difficult to see how it could be consistently applied in situations where the indigenous culture includes features which are morally repugnant to Euro-American standards, such as cannibalism, infanticide, or human sacrifice. It should however be pointed out that such instances are comparatively rare today.

3. ACTION ANTHROPOLOGY IN THE PACIFIC

The limitations as well as the potentialities of action anthropology, as outlined in the preceding paragraphs, must be borne in mind when we consider its application in the Pacific area. It is unlikely that any formal programme, comparable with that carried out at Tama, will be possible in this part of the world in the immediate future. Yet the general principles underlying action anthropology should constantly be stressed because they have potential applications in particular situations.

Such a situation arose when Raymond Firth, accompanied by his associate James Spillius, revisited Tikopia in 1952. The object of the visit was to restudy the community in order to assess the changes which had occurred since Firth carried out his original field work in 1928–9. But the anthropologists found themselves faced with a critical situation which called for action going beyond the limited field of pure research. A disastrous hurricane and drought had drastically reduced food supplies and finally produced famine conditions. In 1928–9 Firth had refrained from advising the Tikopia on their practical problems, which were in no way acute at that time. But in 1952

> the hurricane and threat of famine on the one hand and our possession of radio-telephonic communication on the other, made it almost impossible for us to hold aloof from the decisions of the Tikopia on practical problems. We reported to the Government on the situation, as it developed. We reported the intentions of the Government and transmitted the questions of Government to the Tikopia. This involved two things: it meant deciding on the most effective channel of communication and reply, in particular deciding on what subjects Tikopia should be asked for views to be transmitted to Government. It also meant assisting the Tikopia to put their point of view in terms most easily understood by Government. There was also a further development. When the Government decided to send relief supplies of food, they also decided that in the absence of a fully established local administrative system, we must supervise the distribution. This involved an active intervention in Tikopia affairs, which needs no justification by ordinary humanitarian standards, and is fully defensible on purely scientific grounds inasmuch as, without it, the continuance of our work would have been impossible. Such intervention was continued and extended by Spillius after I left, when the lessening of public order through widespread theft of food supplies seemed for a while to have imperilled the stability of Tikopia society, and when the Tikopia eagerly sought guidance on Government policy and actions. But for the most part our role was that of prime consultants or social catalysts. We helped the Tikopia to explore the possibilities of a situation and decide for themselves what was best to be done in the light of the fuller knowledge we could give them. In the last resort, as Spillius has pointed out, even when the food situation was most desperate, and social order seemed most in danger, *it was the Tikopia who eventually decided what should be done and carried out their decisions* (Firth, 1959:27; italics Piddington's).

The last sentence underlines the vital distinction between the principles underlying action anthropology and those of applied anthropology as ordinarily understood. The latter could have been employed quite easily and effectively in the Tikopia situation, in fact it is probable that no anthropologist has ever been in a better position than was Firth to draw up a "blueprint" for action. He was thoroughly familiar with the socio-economic system of the Tikopia, which had not changed basically since 1929. He could easily have tried to persuade them what to do, and have influenced the Government to implement his policy by administrative action. It is possible that, in terms of material welfare, this might have produced even more beneficial results than were actually attained. But it is certain that relations with the Tikopia would not have been so satisfactory; that they might well have been driven to resist suggestions because these were put in mandatory form and were backed by the authority of Government; and that the principle of self-determination would have been violated by quasi-dictatorial methods, however well-intentioned and potentially beneficial.

Firth repudiates the suggestion that the work done in connection with the practical problems of the Tikopia amounted to a programme in action anthropology[3] (Firth, 1959:28). And, since the project was not planned and executed with the dual and complementary goals of learning and action in mind, he is correct in doing so. But the results achieved by Firth and Spillius illustrate how, under appropriate circumstances, the principles of action anthropology can fruitfully be employed to promote the human welfare of a community without doing violence to their values and aspirations.[4]

It must be emphasised, however, that the situation on Tikopia was singularly propitious for the kind of work done. The community was small and closely integrated; contacts with Europeans and with the external world were minimal; the stringency of the needs of the Tikopia under famine conditions made them receptive to suggestions which might mitigate their sufferings and the urgency of the situation was not conducive to seemingly interminable discussion and procrastination; finally, and most important of all, the indigenous culture was still vigorous enough to allow new adaptations to emerge from it by the process which I have called emergent development (Piddington, 1957:Ch. XIX). In highly detribalised parts of the Pacific (Rarotonga, for example) this would not be true. But it must be remembered that imponderable though significant phases of indigenous culture (such as implicit values and patterns of interpersonal relationships) have a way of surviving unnoticed by European observers who are apt to be overimpressed by such obvious processes of acculturation as the adoption of European dress and other artefacts, the introduction of a money economy and religious conversion. In Samoa, again, though much of the indigenous culture still flourishes, the problems are vastly more complex than in Tikopia. But it can safely be predicted that, under complete political independence, action anthropology is the only kind of anthropology with a practical orientation which has any chance of achieving results in Samoa.

In Fiji the problems are also complex and are rendered more difficult by the numerical predominance of Indians over Fijians. But here too the action anthropologist may have something to say. He explicitly repudiates the idea of social blueprints, and by implication reserves the right to ask questions about the blueprints of others. In Fiji, such questions badly need asking.

Consider, for example, the most recent, most comprehensive and most scholarly summary yet published on the economic problems of the Fijian people. (Spate, 1959). In offering certain criticisms of sections of this report, we must at the outset draw attention to its terms of reference: "I was not asked to *describe* the social organisation of the Fijians; I was asked 'to consider how far it may be a limiting factor in their economic activity'" (Spate, 1959:101). The author's terms of reference might quite as well have read: "To consider how far actual and potential lines of economic development threaten to deprive Fijians of the nonmaterial satisfactions inherent in their traditional social organisation".[5] This would have been a much more difficult task and would have taken infinitely longer to accomplish. But if carried out with the scientific thoroughness and objectivity shown by Spate, it would almost certainly have led to a different analysis of the situation, particularly as regards the sections of Chapter II dealing with rank and kinship. As regards the former, Spate writes as though the major pristine functions of chieftainship (leadership in war and the settlement of land disputes) were the only ones; and as they are no longer discharged, he implies that the rank system is obsolete. Yet practically any system which is based on ascribed status has at least two advantages over one based on achieved status (though these advantages may, of course, be outweighed by disadvantages): Firstly a form of psychological security; psychologically, it is probably more healthy to believe that one is a serf once and for all than to be constantly worried as to whether one is effectively keeping up with the Joneses.[6] Secondly, a hereditary system usually provides educational mechanisms which tend to produce in those destined to succeed both the skills and the moral sentiments appropriate to leadership. Thus we read of an eminently successful economic venture organised by a traditional *mataqali* leader whose three sons "are already groomed for their allotted roles" (Spate, 1959:86). In particular cases such grooming may or may not be effective; but if it is, it is likely to produce more effective leadership than that of an upward mobile person of lower status.

Again, in considering the traditional Fijian kinship organisation, Spate points out that this did take care of the sick, the old, and the orphaned though today it cannot provide such benefits as proper medical care and higher education. But do such purely utilitarian prestations exhaust the satisfactions provided by non-European kinship systems? Most anthropologists would answer in the negative. It is not merely a matter of material advantages provided and practical services rendered. An important point is how, by whom, and in what spirit this is done, of the essentially personal character of kinship prestations in closely knit kinship systems. Thus in modern society, with its degenerate[7] kinship organisation, many old people are relegated to geriatric wards in hospitals not because they need medical care but because nobody is interested in looking after them. No doubt they have in hospital, in material terms, treatment as good as or better than they would receive from loving relatives. But clearly this does not tell the whole story.

The balance sheet of satisfactions and frustrations — material, social, and psychological — which kinship produces is of course a matter for empirical investigation in any given society. But such investigation cannot be based merely on verbal statements in brief interviews carried out through an interpreter but must include a thorough study of kinship behaviour and attitudes. Spate includes kinship among the "burden of obligations" of which Fijians complain. Presumably informants were speaking of their own obligations. They might have been asked whether, when exercising their rights, they thought of themselves as imposing a burden on others. In any social system, individuals are apt to take different views of a given prestation according to whether they are discharging an obligation or claiming a right.

Spate's overall picture of the tensions, anxieties, and conflicts existing in modern Fijian society is convincing and illuminating. But these phenomena exist in all underdeveloped non-European societies which value features of their traditional culture yet long for the material benefits and social advantages of more fortunate segments of the population. There are certainly plenty of them at Tama (Furey in Gearing, Netting, and Peattie, 1960:292–293). They are a necessary and painful part of the process of emergent development whereby such peoples modify, more or less successfully, their traditional ways to meet new material conditions. Adherence to such ways is not merely a matter of obstinate, irrational conservatism. It results from the very real satisfactions which they provide. To imply, as Spate does, that material advancement is the preeminently significant criterion by which social welfare should be measured is to beg the question. But that is the fault of the Fijian Government for begging it in the first place.

There is, then, plenty of room for action anthropology in Fiji to help the Fijian people to make up their minds as to how their problems should be solved, rather than accepting prefabricated answers in terms of material advancement alone. But, so far as the Pacific is concerned, it is probably New Zealand which offers the most promising field, because well-informed Maori leaders already see fairly clearly the main outlines of the problems involved and are solving them neither by blind adherence to tradition nor by passive acquiescence in total assimilation to the Pakeha way of life. This has led to the development of a number of new institutions which are partly derived from modified forms of traditional Maori culture and partly from European practices and beliefs, likewise modified (Metge, 1959 and 1960). This happy, though by no means Utopian, state of affairs has been produced largely by the efforts of people whom Schwimmer calls "mediators," belonging to both ethnic groups (Schwimmer, 1958). The reader will at once perceive certain similarities between Schwimmer's mediators and action anthropologists. Yet there are also important differences. The motive of pure research is not an essential feature of the mediator's work. "He may be a teacher, clergyman, doctor, public servant or social worker or simply a special person to whom the community has become attached" (Schwimmer, 1958:335). Persons in each of the categories specified have a particular goal in relation to members of the community, who must be taught, evangelised, cured and so on. This means that most mediators necessarily enter the community with certain preconceived (though not necessarily incorrect) ideas as to what is good for it; the mediator "has to win acceptance first for himself, then for his ideas" though "the effect of his work is that the community of its own free will accepts certain innovations which are already features of the dominant culture" (Schwimmer 1958:335, 337). This sounds like the "blueprint" idea of applied anthropology as ordinarily understood, the idea of imposing on the community, however gently and solicitously, a programme of action which is not primarily of its own making. This is not to denigrate the work of mediators but merely to suggest that, even though they may have no anthropological training, they might well bear in mind the more objective, more passive, approach of action anthropology.

In the application of action anthropology in New Zealand and in the Pacific generally there are of course many difficulties, some of which have been mentioned at the end of Section 2. But these difficulties should not blind us to the very real value and practical importance of the principles on which action anthropology is founded. In most cases these principles can be only imperfectly realised in practice. But they provide a valuable orientation for all anthropologists, administrators and others concerned with the rights and aspirations of ethnic groups whom historical events have placed in a culturally subordinate position.

NOTES

1. For example: "In 1944 the Government drafted an ambitious, laudable ten-year improvement plan for the Fox settlement. They proposed paving the roads, doubling the land area, establishing a retail store, and raising

the economic level generally by practicable means. These were projects that almost all the Fox would like to see in effect. The Government embarked upon a mild promotion campaign, but only with Tribal Council members. The Council voted it down. For the Council, with the support of only a section of the community, is afraid to act and is virtually immobilized. And, of course, acceptance by the Council without community support would not be enough for implementation of such an undertaking as the Government put forward" (Furey in Gearing, Netting, and Peattie, 1960: 292).

2. New Zealand readers may note here an interesting, though by no means exact, parallel with the Maori situation. Young Maoris are increasingly achieving success in secondary and higher education. But there is a regrettable tendency in both academic and official circles to evaluate this success in purely scholastic terms. As everyone familiar with the careers of Maori students knows, their actual and potential social contribution to progressive development in New Zealand society is only very inadequately measured by examinations passed and degrees conferred.

3. Cf. Spillius 1957:119–121. Spillius employs the term "operational research" for what corresponds broadly to action anthropology. The appropriateness of the term chosen by Spillius might perhaps be questioned since, according to common usage, all research is operational.

4. The later phases of the Tikopia project (after Firth left the island) illustrate very well some of the difficulties with which the action anthropologist may be faced (Spillus, 1957).

5. Other questions should of course be asked as well.

6. This of course does not imply that these two alternatives represent the only possibilities in the organisation of a status system.

7. This epithet does not apply to all kinship systems in modern societies. That of French Canada, for example, has preserved to a remarkable degree its function of providing material and psychological security for the individual (Garigue, 1956).

Part Three contains a small group of articles that discuss particular uses to which anthropology has been put. Jules Henry's essay on "Attitude Organization in Elementary School Classrooms" says nothing overtly about the application of anthropology, yet it is an example of what that scholar calls "passionate ethnography," research conducted by a scientist who is fully and wholeheartedly involved in the consequences of his work. Henry thus has opted for the position of empathetic commitment to reform and change. Both Erasmus and Schaedel discuss various aspects of anthropological involvement in overseas technical assistance programs. Since World War II this has been perhaps *the* area which has occupied the attentions of applied anthropologists most. Erasmus and Schaedel point out some of the contributions to general theory which result from this sort of involvement and experience.

PART THREE

SOME VARIETIES OF APPLICATION

Like Schaedel, Cara E. Richards in her article on anthropology and medicine ("Cooperation Between Anthropologist and Medical Personnel") discusses some of the problems that arise when anthropologists, with their own brand of epistimocentrism, come into contact with other types of professional personnel, each with its own distinctive disciplinary biases and blindnesses. Finally, Nancy Oestreich Lurie in "Anthropology and Indian Claims Litigation" points to the initial difficulties of thinking of the expert witness's role as being part of applied anthropology at all. She goes on to examine the ramifications and implications of this kind of practical activity for anthropology.

12

Attitude Organization in
Elementary School Classrooms

JULES HENRY

The word *organization* in this paper is used to stand for order and determinateness as distinguished from disorder and randomness. The emotions and attitudes of prepubertal children in our culture are not, on the whole, directed toward generalized social goals, but focused rather on the peer group and parents. From the point of view of an observer who has in mind the larger social goals, like the maintenance of stable economic relations, common front against the enemy, maintenance of positive attitudes toward popular national symbols, and so on, the emotions and attitudes of prepubertal children in our culture may be viewed as lacking order. The adult, on the other hand, is supposed to have so organized his tendencies to respond to the environment that his emotions, attitudes, and activities subserve over-all social goals. While it is true

"Attitude Organization in Elementary School Classrooms" by Jules Henry is reprinted from the *American Journal of Orthopsychiatry* 27:117–133, 1957. Copyright, the American Orthopsychiatric Association, Inc. Reproduced by permission.

that attitudes and feelings are bent toward social goals even from earliest infancy (Henry and Boggs, 1952), many institutions combine to organize these attitudes and feelings so that ultimately a social steady state will be maintained. The elementary school classroom in our culture is one of the most powerful instruments in this effort, for it does not merely sustain attitudes that have been created in the home, but reinforces some, de-emphasizes others, and makes its own contribution. In this way it pre-pares the conditions for and contributes toward the ultimate organization of peer- and parent-directed attitudes into a dynamically interrelated attitudinal structure supportive of the culture.

This organizing process is comparable to, though not identical with, the *re*organization of attitudes and resources that takes place as a society shifts from a peacetime to a wartime footing. During a period of peace in our society, adult hostility and competitiveness may be aimed at overcoming competition in business or social mobility, while love and cooperation are directed toward family and friends, and toward achieving specific social and economic ends *within* the society. With the coming of war the instru-ments of government seek to direct hostility and competitiveness toward the enemy, while love and cooperation are directed toward the armed forces, civilian instruments of war (price controls, rationing, civilian of-ficials, etc.), and national symbols. From the point of view of an observer *within the war machine,* the civilian attitudes at first seem random and unorganized. He wants to change them so that from *his point of view* they will seem organized. The situation is similar, though not identical, with respect to the child: to an observer inside the head of even some psychotic children, attitudes and behavior may seem organized. But to the observer on the outside, whose focus is on social goals, the child seems *un-* or *dis-*organized. The prime effort of the adult world is *to make child attitudes look organized to adults.* The emphasis in this paper is on the description of the process of organizing child attitudes as it can be observed in some middle-class urban American classrooms.

THE WITCH-HUNT SYNDROME

One of the most striking characteristics of American culture since the settlement has been the phenomenon of intragroup aggression, which finds its pathological purity of expression in witch hunts (Starkey 1949). It comes as a frightening surprise to democratic people to find themselves suddenly in terror of their neighbors; to discover that they are surrounded by persons who carry tales about others while confessing evil of them-selves; to perceive a sheeplike docility settling over those whom they considered strong and autonomous. The *witch-hunt syndrome* therefore, as constituting one of the key tragedies of democracy, is selected for the elucidation of the organization of attitudes in our culture. In this witch's brew *destructive criticism* of others is the toad's horns; *docility* the body of the worm; *feelings of vulnerability* the chicken heart; *fear of internal (intragroup) hostility* the snake's fang; *confession of evil deeds* the locust's leg; and *boredom and emptiness* the dead man's eye. The witch-hunt syndrome is thus stated to be a dynamically interrelated system of feelings and actions made up of destructive criticism of others, docility, feelings of vulnerability, fear of internal aggression, confession of evil deeds, and boredom.

The witch-hunt syndrome in full panoply was observed in but one of the dozen classrooms in four schools studied in the research which I discuss here. Thus it seems a relatively rare phenomenon. But the question I set myself to answer is, How could it occur at all? What are the attitudes, present in the children, that were organized by this teacher into the syndrome? How could she do it? With what materials did she work? She did not create out of nothing the attitudes she manipulated in her "Vigilance Club" in this fourth-grade classroom in a middle-class American community. She had to have something to start with. The argument of this paper will be that the feelings and tendencies to action which this teacher organized into the witch-hunt syndrome in her class are present in an *un*organized state in other classrooms. Given a certain type of teacher, he or she will be able to develop into a highly specialized, tightly integrated system in his classroom those attitudes which are present in differently organized state in the children in all classrooms. Let us now look at a meeting of the Vigilance Club.

(1) In the extreme back of the room is a desk called the "isolation ward." A child has been placed there for disciplinary reasons. The Vigilance Club of the class is holding a meeting. . . . Officers are elected by the group. The purpose of the club is to teach children to be better citizens. The order of procedure is as follows: the president . . . bangs her gavel on the desk and . . . says, "The meeting of the Vigilance Club will come to order." Each child then takes from his or her desk a booklet whose title is *All About Me* . . . and places it on top of his desk. The vice-president calls the name of a child, gets the child's booklet, and places it on the teacher's desk. The president then calls on the child and asks, "———, have you been a good citizen this week?" The president says, "Name some of the good things you have done," and the child tries to recall some, like opening doors for people, running errands, etc. Next the president asks the class if it remembers any good things the child has done. Each point is written in the child's booklet by the teacher. The president then . . . says to the child, "Name the bad things you have done. . . ." The child reports the wrongs he has committed during the week, and the class is asked to contribute information about his behavior. This too is written in the booklet by the teacher, who also reprimands the

student, registers horror, scolds, etc. . . . When one child reports a misdemeanor of another the teacher asks for witnesses, and numerous children sometimes volunteer. . . . The child in the "isolation ward" reported some good deeds he had done; the children reported some more, and the isolated child was told he would soon be released. . . . [During this meeting some children showed obvious pleasure in confessing undesirable behavior. One child, by volunteering only good things of the students, seemed to be using the situation to overcome what seemed to the observer to be her unpopularity with the class.][1]

Before analyzing this protocol for the attitudes present in it, it will be well to look at some events that occurred in this classroom on another day.

(2) During the game of "spelling baseball" a child raised her hand and reported that Alice and John had been talking to each other. This occurred when neither child was "at bat." The teacher asked Alice if this was so, and she replied that it was, but John denied having spoken to Alice. The teacher said that John must have listened to Alice, but he denied this too. Then the teacher asked whether there had been any witnesses, and many hands were raised. Some witnesses were seated on the far side of the room, and hence could not have seen Alice and John from their location in the room. All those testifying had "seen" Alice talking, but denied John's guilt. Alice was sent to the "bull pen," which meant that she had to sit on the floor behind the teacher's desk, and could no longer participate in the game. . . .

(3) Mary raised her hand and said, "It hurts me to say this. I really wish I didn't have to do it, but I saw Linda talking." Linda was Mary's own teammate, had just spelled a word correctly, and had gone to first base. The teacher asked Linda if she had talked, and Linda said, "No, I just drew something in the air with my finger. . . ." She was sent to the "bull pen."

In these examples we see intragroup aggression; docility of the children in conforming, with no murmur of protest, to the teacher's wishes; and confession of "evil." In such a situation children develop feelings of vulnerability and fear of detection. Let us now look for these phenomena in classrooms presided over by teachers who seem to represent the more normal American type, in comfortable, middle-class, white communities: teachers who are conscientious and reasonably gentle, but creatures of their culture, and humanly weak. We begin not with internal aggression as expressed in spying and talebearing, but with the milder, though closely related phenomenon of carping, destructive criticism. While this occurs throughout the sample, I give here examples only from a fifth-grade classroom in the same school system.

(4) Bill has given a report on tarantulas. As usual the teacher waits for volunteers to comment on the child's report.

Mike: The talk was well illustrated, well prepared. . . .

Bob: Bill had a piece of paper [for his notes], and teacher said he should have them on cards. . . .

Bill says he could not get any cards.

Teacher says that he should tear the paper next time if he has no cards.

Bob: He held the paper behind him. If he had had to look at it, it wouldn't have looked very nice.

(5) Betty reports on Theodore Roosevelt.

A child comments that it was very good but she looked at her notes too much.

Teacher remarks that Betty had so *much* information.

Bob: She said "calvary" [instead of "cavalry"].

(6) Charlie reads a story he made up himself: "The Unknown Guest." One dark, dreary night . . . on a hill a house stood. This house was forbidden territory for Bill and Joe, but they were going in anyway. The door creaked, squealed, slammed. A voice warned them to go home. Spider webs, dirty furniture . . . Bill wanted to go home. They went upstairs. A stair cracked. They entered a room. A voice said they might as well stay and find out now; and their father came out. He laughed and they laughed, but they never forgot their adventure together.

Teacher: Are there any words that give you the mood of the story? . . .

Lucy: He could have made the sentences a little better. . . .

Teacher: Let's come back to Lucy's comment. What about his sentences?

Gert: They were too short. . . .

Charlie and Jeanne are having a discussion about the position of the word "stood."

Teacher: Wait a minute, some people are forgetting their manners. . . .

Jeff: About the room: the boys went up the stairs and one "cracked"; then they were in the room. Did they fall through the stairs or what?

Teacher suggests Charlie make that a little clearer.

Lucy: If he fell through the step. . . .

Teacher: We still haven't decided about the short sentences. Perhaps they make the story more spooky and mysterious.

Gwynne: I wish he had read with more expression instead of all at one time.

Rachel: Not enough expression.

Teacher: Charlie, they want a little more expression from you. I guess we've given you enough suggestions for one time. (Charlie does not raise his head, which is bent over his desk as if studying a paper.) Charlie! I guess we've given you enough suggestions for one time, Charlie, haven't we? (Charlie half raises his head, seems to assent grudgingly.)

The striking thing about these examples is that the teacher supports the children in their carping criticism of their fellows. Her performance in this is not, however, consistent; but even where, as in Example 6, she seems at one point to try to set herself against the tide of destruction, by calling attention to the possible artistry in Charlie's short sentences, she ends up supporting the class against him, and Charlie becomes upset. Thus teacher, by rewarding the children's tendencies to carp, reinforces them. Teachers, however, are able to make their own contributions to this tendency. The single example given below will serve as illustration:

(7) Joan reads us a poem she has written about Helen Keller . . . which concludes with the couplet:

"Helen Keller as a woman was very great;
She is really a credit to the United States."

Teacher (amusedly): Is "states" supposed to rhyme with "great"?
When Joan murmurs that it is, the teacher says, "We'll call it poetic license."

From time to time one can see a teacher vigorously oppose tendencies in the children to tear each other to pieces. The following example is from the sixth grade:

(8) The Parent-Teachers Association is sponsoring a school frolic, and the children have been asked to write jingles for the publicity. For many of the children the experience of writing a jingle seems painful. They are restless, bite their pencils, squirm around in their seats, speak to their neighbors, and from time to time pop up with questions like, "Does it have to rhyme, Mr. Smith?" . . . At last Mr. Smith says, "All right, let's read some of the jingles now." Child after child says he "couldn't get one"; but some have succeeded. One girl has written a very long jingle, *obviously the best in the class.* However, instead of using Friday as the frolic day she used Tuesday, and several protests were heard from the children. Mr. Smith defended her. "Well, so she made a mistake. But you are too prone to criticize. If *you* could only do so well!"

It will be observed that all the examples are taken from circumstances in which the child's self-system is most intensely involved; where his own poetry or prose is in question, or where he has worked hard to synthesize material into a report. It is precisely at the points where the ego is most exposed that the attack is most telling. The numerous instances in the sample, where the teachers, by a word of praise or a pat on the head, play a supportive role, indicate their awareness of the vulnerability of the children. Meanwhile, as I have pointed out, the teachers often fall into the trap of triggering or supporting destructive impulses in the children.
The carping criticism of one's peers is a form of intragroup aggression,

which can be quite threatening and destructive. Talebearing, however, countenanced by some teachers more than by others, can be an overwhelming threat to autonomy. While telling on others can be organized into the patrol-monitor complex (prestige through controlling and telling), useful perhaps in maintaining order in large school populations, its operation within the classroom may have serious consequences. Let us look at a couple of examples:

(9) Second grade. As teacher asked the children to clear their desks one boy raised his hand, and when called on said, "Jimmy just walked by and socked me on the head."
Teacher: Is this true?
Jimmy: He hit me first.
Teacher: Why don't you both take seats up here (in front of the room). I'm not sure people like you belong in the second grade.

(10) Sixth grade special class for bright students.
The children are working on their special nature study projects. Joseph passes where Ralph is working. Ralph (to teacher): Joseph is writing too much on his birds.
Teacher: Joseph, you should write only a few things.

In our sample, telling on other children in the classroom is infrequent outside the class in which the Vigilance Club was formed. Destructive criticism is the preferred mode of attack in most other classrooms. The ease with which tendencies to attack peers can be organized into telling on others, however, is illustrated by the monitor-patrol complex, and by the Vigilance Club (Example 3).

COMPETITION

Competition is an important element in the witch-hunt syndrome. Since witch hunts involve so often obtaining the attention and approval of some powerful central figure, the examples of competitiveness that I shall cite illustrate how approval and attention seeking occur as the child attempts to beat out his peers for the nod of the teacher. It would be easy to cite examples from the protocols of the merciless laughter of children at the failures or gaucheries of their classmates. I am interested, however, more in showing the all-pervading character of the phenomenon of competition, *even in its mildest forms.* The first example is from a fourth-grade music lesson:

(11) The children are singing songs of Ireland and her neighbors from the book *Songs of Many Lands.* . . . Teacher plays on piano while children sing. . . . While children are singing some of them hunt in the

index, find a song belonging to one of the four countries, and raise their hands before the previous song is finished in order that they may be called on to name the next song. . . .

Here singing is subordinated, in the child, to the competitive wish to have the song he has hunted up in the index chosen by the teacher. It is merely a question of who gets to the next song in the index first, gets his hand up fast, and is called on by the teacher.

The following examples also illustrate the fact that almost any situation set by the teacher can be the occasion for release of competitive impulses:

> (12) The observer enters the fifth-grade classroom.
> Teacher: Which one of you nice polite boys would like to take [observer's] coat and hang it up? (Observer notes: From the waving hands it would seem that all would like to claim the title.)
> Teacher chooses one child . . . who takes observer's coat. . . .
> Teacher: Now children, who will tell [observer] what we have been doing?
> Usual forest of hands . . . and a girl is chosen to tell. . . .
> Teacher conducted the arithmetic lesson mostly by asking, "Who would like to tell . . . the answer to the next problem?"
> This question was usually followed by the appearance of a large and *agitated* forest of hands; apparently *much competition to answer.*

Thus the teacher is a powerful agent in reinforcing competition.

It has already been pointed out that carping criticism helps to settle in the child a feeling of vulnerability and threat. In this connection it is significant that *the failure of one child is repeatedly the occasion for the success of another.* I give one illustration below from the same class as the one from which I have taken Example 12.

> (13) Boris had trouble reducing 12/16 to lowest terms, and could get only as far as 6/8. Much excitement. Teacher asked him quietly [note how basically decent this teacher is] if that was as far as he could reduce it. She suggested he "think." Much heaving up and down from the other children, all frantic to correct him. Boris pretty unhappy. Teacher, patient, quiet, ignoring others, and concentrating with look and voice on Boris. She says, "Is there a bigger number than 2 you can divide into the two parts of the fraction?" After a minute or two she becomes more urgent. No response from Boris. She then turns to the class and says, "Well, who can tell Boris what the number is?" Forest of hands. Teacher calls, Peggy. Peggy gives 4 to be divided into 12/16, numerator and denominator.

Where Boris has failed Peggy has been triumphant; *Boris's failure has made it possible for Peggy to succeed.*

This example and also Example 6 are ones in which the discomfort of the child was *visible,* and such instances may be multiplied. They illustrate how vulnerable the children feel in the presence of the attacks of the peer group in the classroom. But since these are children who face the world with serious anxiety to begin with, the classroom situation sustains it. Let us look at some stories created by these very children, and read by them to their classmates. We have already seen one, Example 6, Charlie's story of "The Unknown Guest." Here are *all* the stories read to their classmates by these children during an observation period.

(14) *a* Charlotte's story: "Mistaken Identity." One day last year my family and I went to the hospital to visit somebody. When we were coming out and were walking along my father hit me. I came up behind him to hit him back, but just as I was about to do it I looked back and he was behind me! I was going to hit the wrong person!

b Tommy's story: "The Day Our House Was Robbed." [Observer has recorded this in the third person.] He was coming home from school one afternoon. He knew his Mom was away that afternoon. He started to go in the side door, but decided, he doesn't know why, to go round the back. He found the door open, went into the kitchen, looked into the front room where he saw a thief. Tommy "froze stiff" (chuckle of appreciation from the class), ran out, shouted, "Stop thief" as the man ran out after him. He went to a neighbor, rang the bell, called his mother at the store. The cops came, asked questions, but the man had gotten away with $99 and his mother's watch. If he had gone in the side door he would not have had a chance to see the man. Changing to the back door "may have saved my life." [Teacher's only remarks about this story were: 1) instead of having said "froze stiff," Tommy should have said, "froze stiff as something"; 2) he should have left out the word "then" in one place; 3) he could have made the story clearer; 4) he changed from the past to the present tense.]

c Polly's story: "Custard the Lion." Custard the Lion was the most timid animal in Animal Town. The doctors couldn't cure him. Then they found a new medicine. It had strange effects, but Custard wanted to try it. When he did he felt very queer. (Child gives details of queer feeling.) But he soon realized he wasn't afraid of anything. [Teacher's first remark: "You didn't let us hear the last sentence."]

d Dan's story: "The Boy Hero." Bill wanted to be a fireman, so he went to the firehouse. The Chief was telling him to go home when the bell clanged. While the Chief was getting into the engine, he didn't see that Bill was getting on too. (Class or teacher picks up flaw in sentence and it is reread correctly.) The Chief said O.K. as long as Bill was aboard, "But you're not to get into no mischief." (Class choruses, "Any. . . .") Everyone was out of the fire except a little girl and her doll. The firemen cannot figure out what to do, but Bill, seeing a tree near the house, climbs it over the protests of the firemen. He misses the girl on his first try, but gets her on the second. While sliding down the tree she slips and almost falls, but grabs Bill's pants, and they make it to safety. . . . [Children's remarks center on position of "clang, clang, clang" in the story. Teacher talks about how to use direct quotations, which, it seems, Dan had not used properly.]

e Bertha's story: Title not recorded. The story is about Jim who was walking home past the Smith's house one night and heard a scream. Penny Smith came out and said there was a robber in the house. When the cops came they found a parrot flying around in there, and Penny's parents told her to shut the parrot up before she read mystery stories again. [This story was followed by much carping criticism, which was terminated by the teacher's telling Bertha to change the story to suit the class.]

These stories contain elements of anxiety and even of terror. As each child finishes, the carping criticism of students and teacher then reminds him of his vulnerability. As the child sends out his cloud of fear, it returns with the leaden rain of hostility.

DOCILITY

It comes as a somewhat shocking surprise, perhaps, to middle-class parents, to find their children described as "docile." Yet we have already seen the perfection of docility in the Vigilance Club, and we shall presently see its manifold forms in more normal classrooms.

(15) First grade. The children are to act out a story called "Pig Brother," which is about an untidy boy. The teacher is telling the story. One boy said he did not like the story, so the teacher said he could leave if he did not wish to hear it again, but the boy did not leave.

(16) In gym the children began to tumble, but there was much restless activity in the lines, so the teacher had all the children run around the room until they were somewhat exhausted before she continued the tumbling.

(17) Second grade.
The children have been shown movies of birds. The first film ended with a picture of a baby bluebird.
Teacher: Did the last bird ever look as if he would be blue?
The children did not seem to understand the "slant" of the question, and answered somewhat hesitantly, yes.
Teacher: I think he looked more like a robin, didn't he?
Children, in chorus: Yes.

Item 17 is one of a large number of instances, distributed throughout all grades, in which the children exhibit their docility largely through giving the teacher what he wants. Thus in the elementary schools of the middle class the children get an intensive eight-year-long training in hunting for the right signals and giving the teacher the response wanted. The rest of the examples of docility document this assertion.

(18) Fourth grade.

a An art lesson.

Teacher holds up a picture.

Teacher: Isn't Bob getting a nice effect of moss and trees?

Ecstatic Ohs and Ahs from the children. . . .

The art lesson is over.

Teacher: How many enjoyed this?

Many hands go up.

Teacher: How many learned something?

Quite a number of hands come down.

Teacher: How many will do better next time?

Many hands go up.

b Children have just finished reading the story "The Sun Moon and Stars Clock."

Teacher: What was the highest point of interest — the climax?

The children tell what they think it is. Teacher is aiming to get from them what *she* considers the point of climax, but the children seem to give everything else but.

Bobby: When they capture the thieves.

Teacher: How many agree with Bobby?

Hands, hands.

(19) Fifth grade.

This is a lesson on "healthy thoughts," for which the children have a special book depicting, with appropriate illustrations, specific conflictful incidents among children. The teacher is supposed to discuss each incident with the children in order to help them understand how to handle their emotions.

One of the pictures is as follows: A sibling *pair* is illustrated by *three* boys : (1) One has received a ball. (2) One is imagined to react with displeasure. (3) One is imagined to react benignly and philosophically, saying, "My brother couldn't help being given the football; we'll use it together."

Teacher: Do you believe it's easier to deal with your thoughts if you own up to them, Betty?

Betty: Yes it is, if you're not cross and angry.

Teacher: Have you any experience like this in the book, Alice?

Alice tells how her brother was given a watch and she envied him and wanted one too; but her mother said she wasn't to have one until she was fifteen, but now she has one anyway.

Teacher: How could you have helped — could you have changed your thinking? How could you have handled it? What could you do with mean feelings?

Alice seems stymied. Hems and haws.

Teacher: What did Susie (a character in the book) do?

Alice: She talked to her mother.

Teacher: If you talk to someone you often then feel that "it was foolish of me to feel that way. . . ."

Tommy: He had an experience like that, he says. His cousin was given a bike and he envied it. But he wasn't "ugly" about it. He asked if he might ride it, and his cousin let him, and then, "I got one myself; and I wasn't mean, or ugly or jealous."

Before continuing it will be well to note that since the teacher does not say Alice was wrong the children assume she was right and so copy her answer.

Two boys, the dialogue team, now come to the front of the class and dramatize the football incident.

Teacher (to the class): Which boy do you think handled the problem in a better way?

Rupert: Billy did, because he didn't get angry. . . . It was better to play together than to do nothing with the football.

Teacher: That's a good answer, Rupert. Has anything similar happened to you, Joan?

Joan can think of nothing.

Sylvester: I had an experience. My brother got a hat with his initials on it because he belongs to a fraternity, and I wanted one like it and couldn't have one; and his was too big for me to wear, and it ended up that I asked him if he could get me some letters with my initials, and he did.

Betty: My girl friend got a bike that was 26-inch, and mine was only 24, and I asked my sister what I should do. Then my girl friend came over and was real nice about it, and let me ride it.

Teacher approves of this, and says, Didn't it end up that they both had fun without unhappiness?

Here we note that the teacher herself has gone astray, for on the one hand her aim is to get instances from the children in which they have been yielding, and capable of resolving their own jealousy, etc.; yet, in the instance given by Betty, it was not Betty who yielded, but her friend. The child immediately following Betty imitated her since Betty had been praised by the teacher:

Matilde: My girl friend got a 26–inch bike and mine was only 24; but she only let me ride it once a month. But for my birthday my mother's getting me a new one, probably (proudly) a 28. (Many children rush in with the information that 28 doesn't exist.) Matilde replies that she'll probably have to raise the seat then, for she's too big for a 26.

As we go on with this lesson, we shall continue to see how the children's need for substitute gratification and their inability to accept frustration are the real issues, which even prevent them from getting the teacher's point. We shall see how, in spite of the teacher's driving insistence on her point, the children continue to inject their conflicts into the lesson, while at the same time they gropingly try to find a way to gratify the teacher. *They cannot give the "right" answers because of their conflicts; teacher cannot handle their conflicts, even perceive them, because her underlying need is to be gratified by the children!* The lesson goes on:

> Teacher: I notice that some of you are only happy when you get your own way. You're not thinking this through, and I want you to. Think of an experience when you didn't get what you want. Think it through.
> Charlie: His ma was going to the movies and he wanted to go with her, and she wouldn't let him; and she went off to the movies, and he was mad; but then he went outside and there were some kids playing baseball, so he played baseball.
> Teacher: But suppose you hadn't gotten to play baseball? You would have felt hurt, because you didn't get what you wanted. We can't help feeling hurt when we are disappointed. What could you have done; how could you have handled it?
> Charlie: So I can't go to the movies, so I can't play baseball, so I'll do something around the house.
> Teacher: Now you're beginning to think! It takes courage to take disappointments. (Turning to the class) What did we learn? The helpful way . . .
> Class: is the healthy way!

Before entering the final section of this paper, we need to ask: Why are these children, whose fantasies contain so many hostile elements, so docile in the classroom; and why do they struggle so hard to gratify the teacher and try in so many ways to bring themselves to her attention (the "forest of hands")? We might, of course, start with the idea of the teacher as a parent figure, and the children as siblings competing for the teacher's favor. We could refer to the unresolved dependency needs of children of this age, which make them seek support in the teacher, who manipulates this seeking and their sibling rivalry to pit the children against each other. Other important factors, however, that are inherent in the classroom situation itself, and particularly in middle-class classrooms, ought to be taken into consideration. We have observed the children's tendency to destructively criticize each other, and the teachers' often unwitting repeated reinforcement of this tendency. We have taken note of the anxiety in the children as illustrated by the stories they tell, and observed that these very stories are subjected to a carping criticism, whose ultimate consequence would be anything but alleviation of that anxiety. Hence the classroom is a place in which the child's underlying anxiety may be heightened. In an effort to alleviate this he seeks the approval of the teacher, by giving right answers and by doing what teacher wants him to do under most circumstances. Finally, we cannot omit the teacher's need to be gratified by the attention-hungry behavior of the children.

A word is necessary about these classrooms as middle class. The novel

Blackboard Jungle (Hunter, 1954) describes schoolroom behavior of lower-class children. There we see the children *against the teacher,* as representative of the lower class. But in the classes I have described we see the *children against each other,* with the teacher abetting the process. Thus, as the teacher in the middle-class schools directs the hostility of the children toward one another and away from himself, he reinforces the competitive dynamics within the middle class itself. The teacher in lower-class schools, on the other hand, appears to become the organizing stimulus for behavior that integrates the lower class, as the children unite in expressing their hostility to the teacher.

CONFESSION

The Vigilance Club would have been impossible without confession, and the children's pleasure in confession. But, as with the other parts of the syndrome, confessing occurs in other classrooms also; it can be elicited when the proper conditions are present, and the children can be seen to enjoy it — to vie with one another in confessing. Let us follow the lesson on "healthy thoughts" a little further. We will see how confession occurs as the children seek to give teacher *precisely* what she wants.

> (20.) Teacher asks if anyone else has had experiences like that [of two children who have just recited], where they were mean and angry.
> Dick: He has a friend he plays baseball with, and sometimes they fight; but they get together again in a few minutes and apologize.

In this first example we note one of the important aspects of the confession element in the syndrome: the culprit must have given up his evil ways, and now be free of impurities.

> In response to Dick's story, teacher says: You handled it just right. Now let's hear about someone who had a similar experience and didn't handle it just right.
> Tom: His little brother asked for the loan of his knife, but it was lost, and he got angry with his little brother for asking. [This knife story follows a sequence of several stories about knives told by other children. The exuberance of knife stories following immediately on the teacher's approval of the first one suggests that some of them are made to order and served up piping hot for teacher's gratification.]
> Teacher: Now Tom, could you have worked it out any differently? (Observer notes that Tom seems to enjoy this confession; certainly he is not abashed or ashamed.)
> Tom: Later he asked me if he could help me find it. He found it in a wastebasket, and then I let him borrow it.
> Harry: Sometimes I get angry when my friends are waiting for me and . . . (observer missed some of this) and my little sister asked if she could borrow my auto-racing set, and I hit her once or twice. (Class laughs.)

Here we see another factor so important to the flourishing of the syndrome: the audience gets pleasure through the confessor's telling about deeds the audience wishes to commit: who among Harry's listeners would not like to have hit his sister, or anyone, "once or twice"?

The teacher then goes on: What would you do now — would you hit her?

Harry: Now, I'd probably get mad at first, but let her have it later.

Thus Harry has mended his ways — in teacher-directed fantasy at least — and returned to the fold.

So far we have had confession of mean and angry thoughts and violence. We shall now see confession to unacceptable fear. In all cases the teacher says what type of confession she wishes to hear, and what the resolution should be of the unacceptable behavior; and the children vie with one another to tell commensurable tales, as they derive pleasure from the total situation — through approval of the teacher, expression of their own real or fantasied deviations, and the delight of their peers. In these situations the pleasure of the peer group is seen to derive not so much from the "happy ending" the children give their stories but rather from the content of the story itself. It is interesting that no carping criticism appears; rather the entire situation is a jolly one. It seems that within unspoken limits the children permit one another to boast of "evil" behavior because of the deep pleasure obtained from hearing it. Thus impulse expression becomes a device for role maintenance in the classroom.

The lesson proceeds:

Two children enact a little skit in which they have to go to the principal to ask him something. One of them is afraid of the principal, the other is not. The moral is that the principal is the children's friend, and that one should not be shy.

Gertrude: Well, anyway, the principal isn't a lion, he's your friend; he's not going to kill you.

Teacher: That's right, the principal is a friend, he says hello and good morning to you. . . . Have you ever felt shy?

Meriam: The first year I sold Girl Scout cookies I didn't know how to approach people; and the first house I went to I didn't know the lady; and I stuttered and stammered, and didn't sell any cookies. By the second house I had thought it all out before I rang the bell, and I sold two boxes. (Triumphantly.)

Teacher: It helps to have self-confidence.

Ben now tells a story, with a happy ending, of being afraid of a principal. Then Paul tells a story, amid gales of laughter, about his being scared on a roller coaster. By this time there is so much excitement among the children that the teacher says: Wait a minute — manners!

John: He was scared to go on the Whip-the-Whirl (scornful laughter from the class); but after he went he liked it so much that he went eight times in a row. (This is well received.)

Many hands go up. Teacher waits. . . .

Michael: He was at Pleasure Park on the ferris wheel (scornful Aw from the class) and a girl kept rocking it, and I started to get green (roar of laughter).

Teacher: Now we'll have to stop.

Certain phenomena not emphasized before appear in this section. Confession is used by the authoritative figure, the teacher, to strengthen attachment to significant but potentially terrifying figures like school principals, and to polish up cultural shibboleths like "self-confidence." For the child storytellers confession becomes an opportunity for bathing in the emotional currents of the peer group, as the child stimulates the group's approval through presentation of group standards, and awakens group pleasure as the peer group responds to its own anxiety about weakness, and experiences resolution of the anxiety through the happy ending. With a perfect instinct for what is right, each child provides catharsis for his peers. By presenting himself as weak, he enables his peers to identify with him; and then, as he overcomes his weakness, he enables his companions too to feel strong.

What this lesson on healthy thoughts may have accomplished by way of creating a permanent reservoir of "healthy thoughts" is difficult to say, but that it helped create solidarity among the students, and between them and the teacher is clear from the fact that when she suddenly shifted ground to say, "Do you think you are wide enough awake for a contest in subtraction of fractions?" the children responded with a unanimous roar of "Yes," as if she had asked them whether they were ready for cookies and ice cream!

Thus in this lesson, in which all have participated more with their *unconscious* than with their conscious emotions, solidarity has been achieved. Teacher thought she was teaching the children to have healthy thoughts, but she was showing them how to gratify her. The children sensed this and struggled to gratify her, while they sought acceptance by their peers also. The essential difference between this teacher and the one who perpetrated the Vigilance Club is that though the latter tended to demolish solidarity among the children while placing the teacher in supreme command, the lesson on healthy thoughts tended to a dubious solidarity among all. *Both teachers organize some of the same elements in the children, but into different configurations, of total feeling and behavior.*

BOREDOM

It seems unnecessary to document the fact that children become bored in class, for much of modern thinking and curriculum arrangement is aimed at eliminating it. The shifts at 15-minute intervals from one subject to the next in the elementary school classrooms is one example of this effort. Boredom, which means emotional and intellectual separation from the environment, is an insupportable agony, particularly if the emotional vacuum created by such separation is not filled by gratifying fantasies, or if it is filled by terrifying ones. To fill this vacuum people in our culture will throw themselves into a great variety of even relatively ungratifying activities. Since in this situation, bored children attack almost any novel classroom activity with initial vigor, the witch-hunt syndrome or any modification thereof helps to overcome boredom: better to hunt than be bored. In a full and satisfying life there is no place for witch hunts. The school system that can provide a rich program for children has no need of Vigilance Clubs, nor even of lessons on "healthy thoughts."

DISCUSSION AND CONCLUSIONS

In this paper I have used suggestions from communications theory in an effort to order the data obtained from direct observation of elementary school classrooms. Information, the central concept of communications theory, refers to measurable differences in states of organization. In human behavior, as seen in the classroom under discussion, we observe *qualitative shifts in state*, for *different teachers organize the same underlying emotional characteristics of the children to achieve different organizations of the emotions.* One teacher so organizes the children's emotions as to accomplish an intensification of the fear of intragroup aggression, while she turns the children's hostility toward one another. A different teacher may organize the emotions of the children so that a euphoria in which students and teacher are bathed in a wave of emotional gratification is achieved. The great skill in being a teacher would seem to be, therefore, a *learned* capacity to keep shifting states of order intelligently as the work demands. This does not mean the traditional classroom order, where you can hear a pin drop, but rather the kind of order in which the *emotions of the children are caught up and organized toward the achievement of a specific goal.* It is not necessary, perhaps, that even the most prominent emotions of the children, like competitiveness, for example, form part of the organized whole. Yet, on the other hand, it is difficult to see how, in the present state of our culture, competitiveness can be overlooked. It would seem, perhaps, that the important outcome to avoid is that the competitiveness should become destructive of peers, while reinforcing dependence on the teacher.

The phenomenon I have labeled "docility" occurs because of the absolute dependence for survival of the children on the teacher. That is to say success in school depends absolutely on the teacher, and self-respect, as a function of the opinion of others, in the home or among peers, is in part a function of success or failure in school. In these circumstances the child's capacity to respond automatically to the signals he gets from the teacher is bound to acquire somewhat the appearance of instinctive behavior. Although it occurs at a much higher level of integration than instinct, the child hunts for the proper signals from the teacher, and the child's responses take on instinctual quality. They *must;* otherwise, like the nestling who does not open its mouth when the mother arrives with a worm, he will never eat the ambrosia of teacher's approval, so necessary to his survival. In this situation both children and teacher easily become the instruments of their own unconscious processes, as they, like Joseph and his brethren, fall on each other's necks in a shared ecstasy of exuberant dependence. Teacher and pupil will have gratified each other, but it remains an open question whether the children will have learned what the curriculum committee planned.

We see in the organization of the components of the witch-hunt syndrome an important phase in the formation of American national character, for tendencies to docility, competitiveness, confession, intragroup aggression, and feelings of vulnerability the children may bring with them to school, are reinforced in the classroom. This means that independence and courage to challenge are observably played *down* in these classrooms. It means, on the other hand, that tendencies to own up rather than to conceal are reinforced — a development which, in proper hands, might become a useful educational instrument. It means, further, that while many teachers do stress helping others they may inadvertently develop in the children the precise opposite, and thus undermine children's feelings of security. One could come from a very secure and accepting family and yet have one's feelings of security and acceptance threatened in these classrooms. On the other hand, what seems most in evidence from the stories they make up is that the children come to school with feelings of vulnerability which are intensified in the classroom.

Meanwhile we should try to understand that all the teachers in the sample were probably trying to be good teachers,[2] and all the children were trying to be good pupils. Their unconscious needs, however, naturally dominated their behavior. The teacher who organized the Vigilance Club probably thought she was teaching her children to be upright and honest, and to perform good deeds, but her unconscious tendencies caused these worthy inclinations to seek the wrong expression. All teachers need conformity in the classroom in order that the children shall absorb a respectable amount of academic knowledge. But the teacher's (often unconscious) need for acceptance by the children, and her fear (sometimes unconscious) of her inability to control free discussion, compel her to push the children into uncritical docility at times, while they seek her approval.

The creation of stories, and their discussion by the class, are accepted principles of progressive education. But the teacher's own (at times unconscious) need to carp and criticize gets in the way of her adequately developing the creative and supportive possibilities in her charges. Thus these are not "bad," "vicious," or "stupid" teachers, but human beings, who express in their classroom behavior the very weaknesses parents display in their dealings with their children. The solution to the problem of the contradiction between the requirements of a democratic education on the one hand, and the teachers' unconscious needs on the other, is not to carp at teachers, and thus repeat the schoolroom process, but to give them some insight into how they project their personal problems into the classroom situation.

NOTES

1. In order to prevent identification of teachers and children, the names of my student observers are not used.
2. I am indebted to B. Bettelheim for this suggestion.

13 ·················

An Anthropologist Views Technical Assistance

CHARLES J. ERASMUS[1]

This paper is concerned with conscious attempts to direct or to accelerate culture change, and is based largely on personal observations in several Latin American countries. It does not pertain specifically to the work of any one agency or to technical assistance programs directed only by agencies and governments foreign to the countries concerned. Many if not most of the examples used are drawn from cases where local governments have attempted to introduce change within their own countries. The purpose of the author is to synthesize these observations into a discussion of the patterns of resistance and acceptance demonstrated by the peoples of "underdeveloped" areas in the face of directed attempts to change their ways and to point out the implications of these patterns for the successful and economical operation of technical assistance programs.

"An Anthropologist Views Technical Assistance" by Charles J. Erasmus is reprinted from *Scientific Monthly (Science)* 78:147–158, March, 1954, by permission of the author and publisher.

EMPIRICISM

Introduced changes that bear clear and immediate proof of their effectiveness and desirability usually achieve a more rapid and widespread acceptance than changes of long-term benefit or changes in which the relationship between the new technic and its purported results is not easily grasped on the basis of casual observation. In agriculture, for example, the introduction of improved plant varieties (higher yielding or more disease-resistant) which result in a greater profit to the farmer has repeatedly resulted in spectacular success stories in many of the Latin American countries, and with a variety of cash crops. A foreign agency in one country developed an improved hybrid corn through local genetic selection. The first year that samples were distributed to farmers, the yield was so much higher than normal that the agency was deluged with requests for seed at the next planting time. In fact, the demand was so great that private enterprise quickly became interested in taking over the job of seed multiplication. In contrast, attempts to introduce soil conservation practices frequently encounter considerable difficulty. Practices that do not bear clear and demonstrable proof of their efficacy in a short period of time usually do not diffuse well on their own, with the result that their diffusion may often be no greater than the range of the agronomist's personal contacts.

The spectacular nature of certain introduced agricultural practices may vary considerably, however, with local environmental conditions. In arid badlands, as those found in some parts of Arizona, for example, where rainfall is confined to one brief season in the form of intense downpours, soil conservation practices may demonstrate remarkable benefits within a very short period. Dobyns shows us how eagerly such practices may be accepted under these conditions, in his case study of a conservation experiment among Papago Indians (H. F. Dobyns in Spicer, 1952:209).

In the tropical lowlands of one Andean country, improved varieties of mosaic-resistant sugar cane have all but replaced the "criollo" varieties since their introduction some ten years ago. The newer varieties demonstrated their usefulness so successfully in the form of higher yields and greater profits that they diffused from one farm to another with a minimum of extension support and promotion. In only two or three small valleys have the older criollo varieties persisted and in these cases because mosaic disease was never a problem, apparently as a result of certain prevailing dry winds. Here the farmers see no advantage to the newer varieties and prefer their criollo in the belief that it is easier to refine.

In public health programs, spectacular curative measures seem to take precedence over preventive ones in the rapidity with which they are accepted. Yaws campaigns carried on by the Institute of Inter-American

Affairs, in collaboration with the governments of Colombia and Ecuador, have quickly and successfully overcome the initial resistance of the coastal Negro groups, among which the disease is endemic, and these campaigns are profoundly altering the folk beliefs and the fatalistic attitude formerly surrounding this disease. Even native curers now admit that modern medicine is more effective in the treatment of yaws than their own herbal and magical treatments (Erasmus, 1952b). On the side of preventive medicine, however, the story in most countries is quite different. For example, the symptoms of intestinal infection in a young child may be diagnosed as "evil eye" by rural populations. In order for these people to be convinced that boiling their polluted drinking water will prevent the symptoms we attribute to intestinal infection, they must be able to observe some measurable decrease in the incidence of the symptoms as a result of the preventive technic. Owing to the conditions under which they live and their failure to understand the reasons behind the new device, intestinal infection may take place through other media, and consequently no relationship between the two is empirically established.

In the case of crops, naturalistic explanations are usually and understandably given to insect plagues while ailments due to microorganisms are sometimes attributed to supernatural causes for which magical preventive measures may be employed. However, when a commercial fungicide, which effectively protects one man's crop against the supernatural maladies that afflict his neighbor's is introduced into a rural farming area, an empirically measurable relationship is established between the preventive device and the malady. Even though the farmers may not fully accept and understand the modern explanation nor completely abandon their former beliefs, they quickly adopt the fungicide (if they can afford it).

From these examples we begin to see that the people of the so-called underdeveloped areas do not reason very differently from those of areas considered more advanced. Unaccustomed or unable to read, they lack the one great avenue by which more sophisticated populations avail themselves of a broader range of experience (including laboratory and statistical analyses) than would be possible if they were limited to the range of their own casual observations. The reasoning processes of both groups, however, are largely empirical and rest primarily on a frequency interpretation of events. Thus, in the case of a preventive measure for plant diseases or a remedial campaign for an easily distinguishable endemic disease such as yaws, the great number of individual cases plus conditions involving fewer variables permits a frequency interpretation in their favor within the limits of casual observation, whereas conditions involving a preventive measure for intestinal infections in a family of two or three children may not. Therefore, where a new practice can demonstrate its relationship to the improvements in such a fashion that a frequency interpretation is possible within the limits of casual observation, it has a much greater chance for rapid acceptance among the populations of underdeveloped areas.

Very often the nature of an innovation will depend upon proper follow-through by the innovator. In most of Latin America, new technics must be adapted to conditions on which few reliable data are available. Under such circumstances, an unknown factor, which would have been known and allowed for in the United States, will upset the results in such a way that the new practice fails to make what might have been a spectacular demonstration. In one country, a U.S. technician who was attempting to introduce the practice of broadbase terracing had no data available regarding maximum rainfall and soil conditions to guide him in calculating slope and channel capacity. By diligently checking his first experimental terraces under rainfall conditions, he corrected all errors before any damages might occur. As a result of this careful follow-through and sense of obligation to the farmers, not a single terrace failed when the area was later subjected to a heavy rain of flood proportions. In fact, the erosive action of the storm on adjoining nonterraced fields was such as to make the terracing demonstrations more valuable.

NEED

The needs felt by the people, as distinguished from those felt by the innovators, constitute one of the most important factors pertaining to the acceptability of an innovation in any particular case. If the people fail to feel or to recognize the need for an innovation, it may prove impossible to introduce it on a voluntary basis.

Several of these examples, pertaining to the introduction of new agricultural practices, involved not only the factor of their empirical verification at the level of casual observation but also appealed to a profit motive. An improved crop variety, which results in a higher yield or a greater margin of profit, appeals to the profit motivation and the desire for greater purchasing power when the improved variety is a cash crop. When it is not a cash crop, the story may be different. From a study by Apodaca of the introduction of hybrid corn into a community of Spanish American farmers in New Mexico, we can see how motives other than those of greater profit may affect the outcome when the crop to be improved is not being grown for market (A. Apodaca in Spicer, 1952:35). Within two years after the introduction of the hybrid, three-fourths of the community had adopted it. But after four years, all but three farmers had reverted to planting their original variety. The hybrid had doubled production per acre; the farmers had met with no technical difficulties in planting it, and the seed were readily obtainable. However, the corn was raised by the community only for its own consumption. As these people eat their corn largely in the form of tortillas (unleavened corn cakes), an important mainstay in their diet, and since the new hybrid did not yield tortillas of the same color, texture, and taste as their own corn, they reverted to their older variety. These reasons were more important to them than was the quantity produced. Apodaca notes the fact, however, that the hybrid was dropped with considerable reluctance by the farmers because of its much greater yield. They had empirically verified the fact that the hybrid was an improvement over the old in one sense, but not in the prime sense which pertained to their particular needs and values. This illustrates what can happen when an improvement that would normally have high appeal under cash-cropping conditions is introduced into a subsistence-oriented cropping pattern.

Let us now turn to examples where subsistence-oriented agricultural improvements are introduced into a cash economy situation. Several years ago the ministry of agriculture in a South American republic sponsored a program to introduce the planting of soybeans in many rural areas. Today, the only place where this crop is planted on any scale is near a city where it is manufactured into vegetable oil. The object of this program was to induce the rural population to improve their diet. Soybeans, considered more nutritious, were to be produced solely for family consumption. The farmers not only found the new food distasteful but discovered that no one cared to buy it, and the movement quickly collapsed. In this case the appeal was made to a better health rather than a greater profit motive, but for the farmers the improvement was not empirically verifiable. Symptoms of malnutrition are often confused or combined with symptoms having other etiologies according to modern classifications of disease and are ascribed to supernatural and other causes which bear little or no resemblance to the medical explanations of the innovators. Therefore, in such cases no feeling of need for a new practice may arise to offset the disagreeableness of changing long-established food habits.

In numerous countries attempts have been made to induce rural populations to cultivate vegetable gardens for home consumption. In all cases observed this, too, usually fails after the program has terminated, if the farmer has found no market for the new product in the meantime. Vegetable crops generally enter an area close to cities and towns, or along reliable communication routes leading to them, where the market is greater. Once farmers grow vegetable crops for profit, they invariably consume some. In one Latin American mestizo community where a health program had enjoyed some degree of success in introducing family vegetable gardens, several farmers said that the best way to pacify government programs was to go along with them and do as one was told; eventually the program would terminate, and then they would abandon the nuisance of vegetable gardens without creating any disturbance.

In another Latin American republic, a government-sponsored agency, designed to look after the welfare of farmers growing a cash export crop of importance to the national economy, instituted a program of aiding farmers to build new homes and improve farm structures that were necessary for properly processing the crop. The agency found that it received many more requests for the processing structures than for the homes, although the cost of both types of units was being borne largely by the agency. The farmers were required to pay a small percentage of the total construction costs, and a majority of them preferred to invest in the labor-saving devices. Frequently the field men of the program scolded the farmers for thinking only of their own convenience and never of the cramped and unsanitary quarters of their families. Again we find an example where the needs felt by the people were not entirely in accord with those felt by the innovators. Farmers accustomed to living under housing conditions which the innovators considered undesirable did not necessarily share this view. The processing structures, however, were already known to the farmers who were aware of their labor-saving advantages. The theory underlying the housing program was that more sanitary living conditions would result in more able-bodied farmers and in higher production. But a majority of the new houses rapidly returned to the same state as those they had replaced, a further indication that the needs felt by the innovators were not generally perceived by the farmers. New houses built on farms located along main highways or near population centers showed better maintenance than those that had to be reached by mule-back. Apparently, greater contact with external influences and the cultural environment of the innovators created a sense of need similar to that felt by the innovators.

Let us turn next to an instance of rapid change independent of any superimposed direction. Near two large cities along a semitropical coast, dairy farming recently has come into greater prominence because of the increasing market for milk. Large and poorly managed haciendas, formerly devoted to the pasturing of beef cattle, are breaking up into smaller and more efficiently operated dairy farms. The dairy farmers on their own initiative have improved dairy strains and have adopted improved feeding practices and silage. Some farmers have learned to keep daily records of the milk production of each cow, and on the basis of these records to practice selective breeding of their best producers. These dairymen are sensitive to new technics and knowledge. The local economy already has created an urgent need for new ideas, with the added promise of a high degree of acceptance. Diffusion of ideas from the most advanced to the least advanced farms is proceeding at a rapid rate.

We can see that when the objective of technical assistance is to increase production in an underdeveloped area, it is easier to realize among people who participate in a cash economy. Rural people who are cash-cropping for national or international markets frequently tend to specialize. More attention is usually given to a particular crop, such as coffee, sugar cane, wheat, or potatoes. The local group often forfeits a great deal of its self-sufficiency in the process of specialization and consequently grows more accustomed to purchasing specialized products of other areas. An increasing tendency to purchase products external to the area is in turn usually accompanied by an increase in the number of new products and ideas entering the area, and the number of new needs thereby created. This type of situation seems to be more conducive and sensitive to change. Needs created by the process of specialization and the desire for increased production and profit actually seem the easiest for technicians from another culture or subculture to meet. The solution is often largely technical, fewer cultural barriers to a common understanding are presented, and the perception and feeling of needs are more easily shared by the innovators and the people.

However, when change is being attempted in a field not directly related to increased production in a cash economy, in other words not directly in terms of profits, the difficulties increase. In the field of public health, for example, the innovator may consider it highly desirable to introduce basic disease prevention measures into an underdeveloped area. But the folk still subscribe to an age-old system of beliefs about the cause, prevention, and treatment of disease, a system so different that the preventive measures of the innovator were meaningless. Lacking an understanding of the modern concepts of the etiology of disease and consequently the reasons for modern methods of prevention, they may feel no need to adopt the prescribed changes. Thus, despite the fact that they feel a general need for assistance in combating the ailments common among them, they may fail to perceive the need for the specific measures proposed and may actively resist them.

COOPERATION

Until now this paper has purposely been limited to examples of changes whose acceptance and diffusion are largely an individual matter. As has been seen in the case of spectacular innovations such as improved plant varieties, this type of change frequently spreads with phenomenal rapidity from one individual to another with very little outside stimulus. However, some changes may require group or community adoption, a circumstance that can greatly increase the operational difficulties of introducing them. Not only must the need for the change or changes be perceived by the entire group or a large majority simultaneously, but the members of the group must cooperate for the given end.

Holmberg provides us with an excellent example of an assistance project which depended upon collective acceptance and which failed even though it was concerned with a need already felt by the people (A. R. Holmberg in Spicer, 1952:113). In a community in the Viru Valley of Peru, villagers had petitioned the Peruvian government for aid in obtaining well water to supplement their river supply during periods of shortage in the dry season. A permanent and reliable water supply was important to these people for household and for irrigation and production needs. Although a well was successfully dug, the entire project failed because the technicians did not consult with leaders of local opinion or seek to involve the people. Antagonisms based on local social and political conditions became so great that it was necessary to withdraw the project.

Throughout one Andean country an attempt was made to establish farmer committees, by means of which it was planned to bring about agricultural improvements. In only one small mountain sector did the movement have success, and here only among farmers who until a few years before had been living in indigenous communities. Accustomed to a measure of independent local government in the past, they were organized with very little effort. Obviously, then, the failure of this program must have been due in part to the organizing technics, for the few successful cases were the result of highly favorable local circumstances.

It would seem that in many parts of Latin America there is a tendency to consider rural populations as more cooperative than they really are, or at least to take their cooperation for granted. However, in Latin America today many of the age-old customs promoting cohesion and cooperation in rural society are being or have been replaced by social relationships of a more impersonal and individualistic nature. Such replaced customs would include the mutual aid and assistance patterns involved, for example, in reciprocal farm labor and the ceremonial kinship obligations of godparenthood. Apparently the economic aspects of such mutual assistance customs were functional in a subsistence-oriented rural economy, where the peasants cropped largely for family and local consumption. As roads increased the possibilities of marketing farm surpluses over larger areas, farmers began to specialize and came to be more dependent on other regions and countries for marketing their products and for the food and goods no longer produced on their own farms. Thus, the interdependencies existing between members of the local group in daily contact were gradually superseded by national and international interdependencies between peoples who never met. When the economic interdependencies between members of the local group were superseded by larger and more impersonal ones, the cooperative functions of older customs were unnecessary. The rural peasantry became more individualistic and less dependent on their daily contacts.

Actually, it may be fairly argued that the rural populations of Latin America are becoming more competitive than collective. Perhaps one of the clearest illustrations of this may be found in 4-H club work. Results are usually better when the young people work separate plots in competition than when they work the same land together in such a way that they cannot compare their work. Similarly, when earnings of club members are pooled for the purchase of livestock or tools used in common, the results are usually poorer than when each individual has the right to the fruits of his own labor. In such instances we can see how the profit motive coincides with individualistic and competitive tendencies.

When a technical assistance project in a certain country attempted to contour level rice fields across ownership boundaries in order to facilitate irrigation flooding in a pilot area, it was faced with the problem of obtaining the permission and collaboration of all the small landowners within the area. However, the technicians neglected to unite the various landowners concerned, to explain the project to them, and to seek their cooperative support. The project was carried out as if it were a type of change which could be effected on an individual or family basis. One farmer was induced to permit the contouring, then another, and so on. Because of the severe land fragmentation problem, the owners of neighboring plots were not necessarily neighbors insofar as the residence patterns were concerned. Even when a farmer and several of the friends who lived near him were convinced of the benefits of contouring, their plots within the area were found to be widely separated. As planting time approached, the project officials felt obliged to rush the job through, and so began contouring the individual and widely separated plots as functionally separate units. As the work progressed, other landowners began signing up. Eventually, nearly all gave permission to contour their land and agreed to pay the costs. But the sequence of requests was such that practically all contouring had to be done within, rather than across, ownership boundaries. Inasmuch as nearly all the farmers eventually collaborated, there is reason to believe that with the proper inducement they could have been encouraged to do so before the work began. As a result, one of the major objectives of the project, to contour according to the topography rather than ownership boundaries, was lost.

INDUCEMENT

The problem of inducement, as we shall use the word here, refers to the task of overcoming popular resistance to a proposed change for any of the reasons discussed so far. Even in the case of new technics or traits which demonstrate their effectiveness in a spectacular fashion, there is still the initial problem of bringing them to the attention of the public. If the problem is one of introducing an improved plant variety, some farmer or farmers must be persuaded to try it. If these initial experiments result in a much greater yield, the new variety usually sells itself. Generally, farmers are suspicious of government authorities and prefer to let someone else try the new technic before they adopt it. If a well-known neighbor obtains satisfactory results, others will often rush to follow his example. Demonstration farms are not so readily copied, as the farmers are not sure what additional advantages beyond their own means may have biased the results. When a large brewery in a certain country found that the home production of barley was insufficient to supply its needs, it hired agronomists to stimulate production in new areas. The agronomists circulated through the highland regions, promised farmers a good price for barley, gave instructions for planting, and provided seed. The first year very few farmers in a given area tried the new plant on a very modest scale. However, by the third or fourth year, after all had been convinced that the agronomist would keep his word about the price and that the plant would give profitable yields, barley had become one of the important crops.

Where the advantages of a new technic or trait are long term in nature or difficult to demonstrate empirically, long-term methods of introduction through formal education should seriously be considered. Extension work with adolescents through 4-H clubs and the like frequently demonstrates that it is easier to instill new habits among individuals who do not have to unlearn old habits. Furthermore, young people usually find it easier to substitute the prestige of the specialist for the prestige of tradition (Erasmus, 1952a). Even when introducing nonspectacular innovations on a long-term basis through formal educational procedures, it will usually be necessary to take popular beliefs and practices into account so that persons may perceive a relationship between the needs they feel and the remedies proposed. In Quito, Ecuador, tests were given to school children who had been receiving formal lectures in health education, including the use of visual aid technics for some two years. Results showed that the period of instruction had made little or no impression. Whereas modern explanations of the etiology of disease and its prevention were now familiar to the children, they were largely related to modern disease terminologies that had no meaning to them. The symptoms of those diseases were still being classified according to a folk system which included such causes as fright, evil eye, malevolent air, and witchcraft. According to the school children, these folk illnesses could not be caused by modern etiologies, could not be prevented by modern means, and could not be cured by medical doctors. In collaboration with the educators, attempted changes in the methods of instruction were made so as to allow the children to discuss their folk beliefs freely in class. During the discussions the educators attempted to show the children, without deriding their beliefs, that the symptoms they ascribed to fright, evil eye, and the like were the symptoms of the very diseases that the educators had been talking about for the past two years. They also tried to disassociate folk symptoms from folk etiologies and practices and to link them to modern methods of treatment and prevention. Retesting after the lectures gave very different results. Written tests, of course, do not necessarily indicate a change of habits, but these certainly indicated that for the first time the children were cognizant of a relationship between the measures and explanations of the educators and their own maladies. This illustrates the necessity of thoroughly understanding the local culture of a people, in cases where it is difficult for them to perceive the needs felt by the technicians under the ordinary limitations of casual empiricism. Ironically enough, salesmen for patent medicine concerns frequently give very careful consideration to folk beliefs in order to adapt the advertising of their products to the local concepts of disease.

In some cases people can be induced to accept new technics and changes, which they find difficult to accept, by linking them or making them conditional to other changes or services more desirable to them. For example, in anticipation of an irrigation project that they know will materially benefit them, farmers may be more willing to satisfy government wishes concerning secondary improvements which they would ordinarily resist. In the example of the contour leveling of rice fields, it seems very possible that one of the principal mistakes of the program was in failing to obtain commitments by the farmers for the leveling before the irrigation project was completed. As the farmers had already been provided with irrigation water, the inducement value of the irrigation project had been lost.

Similarly, where public health centers give attention to curative as well as preventive measures, their rapport with the public as well as their influence in implementing changes in disease prevention habits is noticeably greater. At a charity maternity hospital in Quito, those new practices, in conflict with popular beliefs but with which mothers had to conform in order to receive treatment at the hospital, were found to be having an important and permanent influence in altering their beliefs. In agriculture, the distribution of seeds and tools at cost may offer a decisive inducement to adopt recommended new cultivation practices. Where farmers can see no need for a program objective, it may be possible to alter the emphasis of the objective so as to enhance its appeal. In one Haitian valley, agronomists were able to effect measures of soil conservation by appealing to a local interest in coffee planting and by helping the farmers to start seed beds of coffee and shade trees for transplanting to hillside plots.

Where joint and cooperative action on the part of a community is necessary for the success of a project, considerable attention must be given to involving the people in the activity at an early stage. The leaders of opinion in the community must be discovered and consulted first. Whenever possible, the community should be made to feel that it has participated in the planning of the program. When cooperative programs are simply dropped upon the peoples of underdeveloped areas from some high planning echelon within their government, without any explanation and without any consideration for local opinions, the programs are very likely to fail either partially or totally.

In any technical assistance program one of the most important and most variable aspects of the problem of inducement involves the factor of person to person relationships. Much has been expounded on this subject, but the desideratum usually consists of little more than a consideration for the beliefs and customs of other peoples and a sincere attempt to understand them. Yet understanding can be no greater than allowed by the amount of personal contact and the ability to communicate.

A most effective foreign technician was a U.S. soils scientist attached to an agricultural research station in an Andean country. Good-natured and affable, he set out at once to make a friend of every member of the staff. Within his special field he led the local technicians to adopt several new research procedures, and saw several research projects of considerable importance well under way. Yet he never allowed his name to be attached to any project. He encouraged the local man most interested in the plan to initiate it, carry it through, and take the credit, while he played the part of a counsellor who continued to make suggestions but never gave an order. Three nights a week on his own time he held classes in English because he had discovered that many local technicians wanted to learn the language and that he made friends by helping them.

COMPLEXITY

Frequently a change which seems desirable to the innovator may depend upon so many other secondary accompanying changes that its introduction is difficult. Perishable food products, such as fresh vegetables and fish, are most easily exploited near markets where transportation to markets is reliable, inexpensive, and rapid, or where storage and processing facilities have been developed. Successful adoption of improved livestock may depend upon many correlative changes in husbandry practices. The latter in turn may depend upon the farmer's financial ability to provide better feed and care.

Failure to recognize the factor of complexity is one of the most serious problems in technical assistance work, partly because there are no established principles of diagnosis which can be applied to every case. Oftentimes the standard of living may be so low that the innovator's heart goes out to the evidences of suffering which seems unnecessary to him from his different cultural or subcultural viewpoint. Let us take for example country "X," whose density of population and infant mortality rate are among the highest in the world and whose per capita production is among the lowest. Is the first job of technical assistance to save lives and reduce the immediate evidences of human suffering, or is it to help the country itself to solve its health problems? The answer to this question depends on who provides the funds to build the public health centers, the water purification systems, and the public hospitals, and to educate the doctors and nurses. If the innovators provide these funds, the effort may involve much more than technical assistance; it may involve heavy financial assistance. As a result the population may increase more rapidly than ever, and with it all the existing economic and political stresses may be aggravated. However, if the innovators are concentrating on purely technical assistance, they may endeavor to help country "X" raise per capita production to a point where the country can pay for its own secondary improvements as it feels the need for them. In short, this would mean that technical assistance in country "X" might be aimed first at increasing productivity in agriculture and industry, while assigning the high infant mortality rate to a secondary position on its list of problems.

This extreme case is used simply as an example and does not mean that technical assistance in public health should be relegated to a secondary position in all countries desiring technical aid. In some countries productivity per capita is much higher than in others and public health services for the population are already well established. In such cases, technical assistance for making these services more efficient is readily grasped and utilized and effects of the technical assistance are far more permanent and far reaching. U.S. public health technicians in one small country have played an important role in a malaria campaign to clean up a wide coastal zone that was formerly poorly exploited. Roads are now being cut through the jungles, exploitation of forest products is intensifying, and new settlers are entering the area to establish banana and other plantations. Thus an entire nation has been benefited by these public health workers.

A price-support program for cotton was adopted in one country in order to induce greater home production for local textile industries. Within a period of three years agricultural changes in some areas have been almost revolutionary. On flat coastal plains to the east, land that was formerly yielding a very low rate of income per acre from an extensive type of beef-cattle ranching is rapidly changing into a zone of mechanized agriculture. Cotton has become white gold. Not only have many farmers rushed to exploit the new opportunities with mechanized farm equipment, but they have adopted new farming technics such as the use of fertilizers, insecticides, and crop dusting. This example is not used to justify price-support programs, but it does show how increased profits facilitate the adoption of new practices. They do not make such change automatic, however, for the same factors of need and empiricism still apply. Many farmers started planting cotton without heeding advice to use insecticides. They suffered serious crop damages the first year and saw the difference between their yields and those where insecticides were used, and then they adopted the practice the second year. Nor did cotton planting itself become generally adopted until a few enterprising farmers had made a handsome profit.

In situations of extreme land fragmentation where farmers must supplement their agricultural earnings by means of other endeavors, it is usually extremely difficult to initiate changes in farming practices. A higher yielding plant variety may be readily adopted, but many other innovations are difficult to introduce on uneconomical farm units. However, a desire to help impoverished farmers may lead administrators and technicians to attempt the introduction of improvements of a subsistence nature which require little or no capital expenditure. Programs may thereby develop with the purpose of introducing the household manufacture of family clothes, home gardening of all food necessities, home food-preservation practices, and inexpensive animal varieties such as rabbits as a source of meat for the family. All such devices are aimed at making farm families more self-sufficient and less specialized, a process contrary to the usual economic trends. Social welfare programs of this type seem to require more extension personnel and promotional activity than those designed to bring production-increasing technics to farmers who have the financial means to exploit them.

In one South American country where soil erosion has become extremely severe, U.S. soil conservation experts found that practically no remedial steps were being taken. In some areas, erosion had reached a point where only such drastic measures as complete reforestation would suffice. In others, the erosion problem was complicated by absentee land-ownership patterns or the exploitation of uneconomical farm units. However, by selecting an area of medium-sized mechanized farms personally administered by resident owners, the technicians were very successful in introducing many new soil conservation practices with a minimum of promotional activity. Farmers responded readily, were quick to recognize the benefits of the new measures, and found them easy to carry out at their level of operations. As a result of the impetus given to soil conservation by the successes in this area, the government created a special soil conservation division, within its ministry of agriculture, to attend to the erosion problems of the country as a whole.

In one sense, the areas of worst erosion in a country might be thought of as presenting the greatest need for correction, or the poorest farmers as the ones most in need of improved agricultural practices. Frequently, however, the persons most in need, in the judgment of the innovator, may be those who feel the need the least. For this reason it may often be more expedient and practical to work where the need, from the innovator's standpoint, is less acute but where there is greater willingness on the part of the people to make the change. The interest shown by the people themselves is more often a better index to their ability to successfully adopt a given change than the judgment of the innovator.

ECONOMIC FEASIBILITY

Any technical assistance project will cost money, the expense of this assistance being in proportion to the number of man-hours necessary to complete it successfully. It would be quite logical to suppose that, given unlimited financial and human resources, a technical assistance program could effect any change desired. However, no technical assistance project has such unlimited funds; therefore, in any decision concerning the selection of projects, their feasibility with respect to budgetary limitations must be taken into account.

From observations of technical assistance projects, the kinds of innovations which would seem to be most inexpensive are those which require the least man-hours for strictly promotional purposes. Such innovations include those from which benefits are easily verifiable through casual observation, which are accepted and diffused on an individual basis, which meet a strong need already felt by the people (of particular appeal to a profit motive), and those which are in sequence with local development (not too complex). However, certain circumstances may justify considerable promotional activity. For example, in the case of projects requiring cooperative acceptance and action on the part of the people, the necessary groundwork must be done to involve them in the activities, or the time and money spent in the purely technological aspects may be lost. In such cases the two deciding factors are the amount of money being invested in the technological aspects, and the need which the people feel. In the case of an expensive irrigation project, about which the people are highly enthusiastic and for which their cooperation is requisite, the extension work necessary to iron out local social and operational problems for the maximum success of the project should be considered a functional requirement. However, where considerable money is to be spent on a project in which the cooperation of the people is essential but for which they do not even feel a need, the project should be reexamined to see if it fits into the local sequence of development. If a project is very inexpensive but would require costly promotional work to secure the necessary cooperation from the people, the project should be reexamined to see if the ends really justify the means. It frequently happens, for example, that innovators like to initiate projects which require cooperative action from the people because they consider the encouraging of cooperation and community spirit as good and worthy projects in themselves.

The principal consideration in questions of economic feasibility is that of the needs felt by the people. When the people do not feel a need for the innovations proposed, promotional activity necessarily must be increased. Fortunately, actual situations are usually neither all negative nor all positive; differences exist in degree, and some persons within the same group or area are more receptive than others. In the case of soil conservation, for example, some farmers with better farm equipment, more capital, and a long-term outlook can be shown the benefits of soil conservation with relatively little difficulty, while neighbors with more modest resources continue to take a skeptical view. However, when a nucleus for change can be permanently established, even though the prospects of diffusing the change outside that nucleus in the immediate future are poor, the long-term gains may justify the modest beginning. Eventually others may come to recognize the benefits of an innovation at a time when conditions make it easier for them to adopt it or to appreciate its advantages. Thus, rather than spend time and money to promote the adoption of an innovation among people who cannot perceive its desirability, it may prove more expedient to establish it among strategically located nuclei or groups who can.

Another long-term alternative to costly promotional activity to establish a sense of need for new measures is that, already mentioned, of appealing to the younger members of the society through existing educational institutions. A few strategic lectures to groups of teachers, as well as assistance to them in the form of educational aids and printed matter, can often have a widespread, long-term effect.

The most unfavorable conditions for introducing innovations are frequently presented by such marginal peoples as Indian groups who more than anything else may simply wish to be left alone. The effort involved in introducing changes among them will be particularly great when their economy is still subsistence-oriented. Their conception of needs may be so different from that of the innovators that the two groups may find it very difficult to establish a common meeting ground for mutual understanding.

In general, the absorption of marginal peoples and cultures into the national sphere seems to follow most rapidly upon their further involvement in the national cash economy. In many cases it may prove more expedient to develop areas bordering on marginal groups in such a way as to draw them more closely into the national economy than to attempt to superimpose an extraneous need system directly upon them. While living in a Mayo Indian *comunidad* in southern Sonora, Mexico, during 1948, the writer had an opportunity to note the effects produced on an indigenous community by the rapid development of bordering areas. The development of irrigation and a more intensive machine agriculture to the north was creating more job opportunities and prosperity. Not only were members of the *comunidad* going north more frequently to work as seasonal agricultural labor, but they were returning with new ideas, needs, and wants. In fact, a growing nucleus was advocating division of the communal land as a means by which wealthy farmers could gain access to much of the virgin land and extend irrigation into the area. Thus it was hoped that a more intensive and profitable type of agriculture would be possible for all.

A similar situation was encountered at the plantation of an American fruit company in a Latin American republic. The manager of the plantation told how the labor turnover the first year or two was over 90 percent. Individuals worked until pay day and then went on a drinking spree, or worked only until they had earned enough to buy something they had specifically wanted. However, as new laborers kept replacing the old, some of them would inevitably join the nucleus of steady workers. These valued the permanent income, the clean and comfortable company housing, the superior company school for their children, and the company medical treatment. Within a few years the plantation had a permanent resident labor force. The company showed an interest in the upkeep and attractiveness of the workers' housing and helped them landscape gardens around their homes; thus a model community had been formed that was influencing the entire area. Workers in neighboring locally managed plantations were beginning to demand the same treatment, as they perceived a need for it themselves.

Not everyone can be induced to share the values and needs of the innovators at once but, by working first with those who already share them, the changes may eventually have far-reaching results without the unnecessary expense of promotional methods. In short, action programs among those who already feel a need for an innovation would seem to be more effective and less expensive in the long run than promotional programs for those who must first be inspired to feel the need.

One of the greatest weaknesses in most technical assistance programs is the failure to recognize the indispensable part played by research in increasing their economic feasibility. In this respect, government might conceivably learn from business. One writer on the subject of business management has said that any company that lacks an organized program of research will eventually find itself out of business (Trundle, 1948). Two major forms of business research, market and engineering studies, might be paralleled by technical assistance agencies to their advantage. Market studies could be designed to get all the pertinent facts about the people to be changed, including their needs and wants, their ability to absorb a given innovation, and their previous reactions to similar programs in the past. Engineering studies might include research in any number of technical fields, as well as comparative research in the methods and results of other agencies in other parts of the world, and the continued self-evaluation by the agency of its own programs to perfect the least expensive and most effective means of realizing its objectives. However, in government assistance programs, research can probably be realized best through an organization pattern that recognizes the difference between staff and line functions. Government reporting is prone to be a line function originating with operations personnel, who execute it with a bias toward justifying the further existence of their programs. By avoiding the disclosure of mistakes in specific operations, short-term benefits may accrue which on a long-term basis prevent the self-evaluation and self-correction necessary to avoid those seriously damaging setbacks that result from the accumulation of hidden errors.

NOTES

1. The author is indebted to A. W. Patterson, Point Four Director in Chile, at whose suggestion this article was written.

14 ⋯⋯⋯⋯⋯⋯⋯

Anthropology in AID Overseas Missions: Its Practical and Theoretical Potential

RICHARD P. SCHAEDEL

The purpose of this paper is to present briefly an anthropologist's point of view of the practical work accomplished by the anthropologist in ICA missions overseas and to indicate some of the theoretical potential that can be exploited in this type of work. What follows is largely based upon the writer's experience with ICA programs in Latin America both as an outside observer and as a participant.

At the outset of ICA and predecessor agency's operations in Latin America some twenty years ago there was a wide divergence of interest between the ICA mission personnel overseas and the anthropologists who

"Anthropology in AID Overseas Missions: Its Practical and Theoretical Potential" by Richard P. Schaedel is reprinted from *Human Organization* 23:190–192, 1964, by permission of the author and publisher.

were doing research or teaching in the same country. There may have been more of an awareness of common interests between anthropologist-consultants in Washington and ICA than in the overseas mission, but it did not reach down to the mission level. This divergence consisted largely in the type of objective the ICA mission had as compared with that of the research anthropologist. The United States Operations Mission had as its immediate goal to plan and implement a program of measures for economic and social development in countries which were assumed to be underdeveloped. The anthropologists were concerned with studying the culture from any variety of special problem angles, but generally did not preoccupy themselves with the application of their knowledge to a pre-defined program of economic and social progress. While the USOM operated largely with government agencies in the host country, the anthropologists tended to avoid them, seeking out academic colleagues and generally staying clear of any government involvement lest such affiliation should mar the degree of rapprochement they might be able to secure among the groups they were interested in studying. The divergence of interests was further accentuated by the stereotypes that each group formed of the other. Since at the outset many of the ICA personnel were drawn from the ranks of county extension agents, rural education specialists, farm machinery experts, etc., the highly trained anthropologist tended to look with a certain amount of disdain on his compatriots who were charged with a responsibility which he certainly felt to be much greater than he would care to accept. To put it crudely he looked upon most ICA personnel as good-natured but ethnocentric "folks" getting highly overpaid for being "do gooders." The ICA group for its part had only the vaguest idea of the scope and variety of the anthropological research. They conceived of anthropologists as an exotic group of characters who either liked to go out and sleep in tents and study the sex life of the Indians or else concerned themselves with digging up bones; in any case the products of their investigation had little if any practical value.

Nonetheless the continued coexistence of the ICA mission, growing over the years to include a number of nonrural, professionally trained specialists, and the American anthropologist-researcher or visiting professor eventually produced a gradual awareness of common interests and a willingness to examine each other's point of view. The ICA group came to appreciate the potential application of the anthropologist's research and observations, largely because of the difficulties they encountered in trying to change the host country's culture. The anthropologist began to become more convinced that his ICA compatriots were going to try to modify the host country's culture whether he liked it or not, and that perhaps some effort at providing them with a general understanding of the social complexities involved would be worthwhile. A point has finally been reached where an ICA overseas mission often comprehends the need for an anthropologist on its staff. While there is still much anxiety over the unknown consequences of employing an anthropologist, there is general consensus in many missions that he should be able to perform a useful role. The usefulness of anthropologists to ICA missions overseas has been summarized in published articles (Kelly, 1959; Gladwin, 1960) and has been discussed by Mr. Miniclier. Now I should like to present objectively a brief picture of the limitations under which the anthropologist works and briefly to review the chores to which he is customarily assigned; that is, what I call the practical potential. This incidentally corresponds to the shabbier side of the anthropologist's role as viewed from the standpoint of his academically based colleague.

Most important of the limitations within which the anthropologist works are the ICA (and for that matter the State Department) policy, both as defined in Washington and by the mission. However much we feel that a series of measures being carried out in a host country may be more harmful than beneficial, once the policy is established we are no longer free to criticize it. This does not mean that we cannot make every effort when channels are open to communicate our opinions and seek thereby to modify the policy, but it does mean a limitation on the outspoken expression which our academic colleagues are at liberty to exercise.

Secondly, carrying out field work through a governmental administration is much more complicated, time-consuming and frustrating than doing the same operation under a research grant. To illustrate I need only mention such phenomena as clearances, administrative officers, memoranda, travel vouchers in triplicate, and you will rapidly conjure up an image of what I mean.

Thirdly, we are subject to the limitations of a given mission program. Programming is a constant process in ICA which provides the guidelines for the mission's activities and is subject to frequent modifications because of adjustments to allocations requested and granted from Washington. In order to function effectively in an overseas mission, the anthropologist has to adjust himself to the program or the program to him. This is a time-consuming process of memorandum drafting and personal negotiations, particularly in missions where there is little awareness of the possible uses of anthropology.

Finally, there is the problem of adjustment to other ICA personnel, administrative and technical. It is seldom possible for the anthropologist to "free-lance" it. He is usually expected to be available to all the technicians for help on social problems, and in many cases he depends upon the other technicians for carrying out his own work. Since most technicians have not had previous experience working with anthropologists, some effort must be spent in establishing a satisfactory interpersonal relationship, followed by careful insinuations as to the sort of work the anthropologist has in mind or the sort of suggestions he has to offer. While this experience, as I hope to bring out later, has its positive aspects, it should be recognized as a type of limitation which our academic colleagues do not have to undergo.

Within these limitations the anthropologist usually finds himself dedicated to one of four major categories of activities: program evaluation, planning, operations support, or community development. He may even find himself involved in all four or any combination thereof. In the role of program evaluator, he investigates the various activities of the mission, assesses them in terms of their adaptability and effectiveness on the host country, makes recommendations for changes. While his talents qualify him particularly well for this role, since he of all of the mission specialists is trained to look for a balanced interrelationship and a pace in the planned operations in accord with the local culture, it is rarely that the mission chief is willing to give him more than consultative responsibility. Planning offers the anthropologist perhaps the greatest independence. He is assigned a specific goal and asked to come up with a plan that will be in keeping with the host country's human potential. In so doing he carries out a certain amount of independent research that is not only applicable to the plan but that can be generally valuable in providing needed information on unstudied areas of the local culture. Operations support is a sort of "trouble shooting" job that involves on-call service to the mission's technicians who are operating programs and who have run into difficulties of a social nature, or who would like to have additional assistance in getting the program accepted more readily by the recipient community. While this chore is a challenge to the anthropologist's dexterity in handling diverse situations adroitly, it also harbors dangerous snags. He is sometimes called in as the doctor who is summoned belatedly to cure the patient who has been given up for dead. Anthropologists are also used to administer what is known as community development programs, actually programs in applied anthropolgy. This subject is dealt with abundantly in the literature[1] and will be discussed in other papers.

Whatever adjustment he makes to the above chores, and this will largely depend upon his temperament, the anthropologist in ICA overseas missions has an opportunity to pursue his own theoretical interests as he moves from country to country that would only be available to the academically based anthropologist over a much longer time span. While the main categories of these theoretical interests will be largely in the field of applied anthropology and cultural dynamics, they may include many others, such as primitive economics, folk medicine, and enthnobotany. For the purposes of illustration I have made a threefold division of the types of theoretical inquiry to which ICA experience particularly lends itself.

The first category is largely dependent upon the particular interests of the anthropologist who may profit by on-the-job interdisciplinary exchange.[2] In the field of primitive economics the anthropologist with ICA overseas is usually favored by the expert advice of an agricultural economist and a horticulturist, and frequently by one or more of the following: an entomologist, a soil chemist, a livestock specialist, or a forester. A comparative study of productivity between two peasant cultures with a number of ecological constants could be carried out with this type of interprofessional interchange. Its results could be further enhanced by utilizing the capabilities of nutritionists and other public health advisers in establishing comparable physiological limitations.

The degree of utilization that a given society makes of its natural resources, given a certain basic technology, is presumably an index of cultural vigor, ingenuity, efficiency, or whatever concept one cares to employ. Establishment of such indices in the field can be greatly facilitated by the assistance of some of the cadre of ICA technicians. Many of the hypotheses that the field anthropologist can propose about this or that resource or technique, which he feels from his limited experience should produce better results, can be resolved in consultation with the expert or by having the item in question demonstrated. This problem is particularly real to me at the moment in Haiti where concern about underutilization of resources has assumed polemical dimensions (see Aristide, 1958–1959).

Since practically all operations of ICA involve changing the host country's culture, the experience of an anthropologist in observing these cases is unique. He can study the reactions of the recipient community and individuals as well as the roles of the innovators or agents in a dynamic setting. He can witness the same kind of innovation that was successful in one culture fail in another, weighing the variables of the agency, the institutional constellation that accompanied the process, and the values of the recipient culture. Case studies like this range in dimension from the introduction of traction-plowing by mules on a single farm to an entire regional program of imposed change from subsistence agriculture to production for export. I should like to suggest that a legitimate theoretical objective of assembling these case studies in the world-wide ICA culture laboratory might be the establishment of what might be termed a scale of the thresholds of receptivity.

My final point has to do with the contribution anthropologists can make to economic growth theory especially in these days when it is playing such an influential role in government. Rostov's hypothesis of the five stages of economic development (Rostov, 1960) has had considerable impact in government circles and has been favorably received by anthropologists. Of the societies in these five stages, I would like to confine my remarks to those classified as traditionalist and transitional.

The traditionalist group, as Dalton and Bohannan note (1961), are rather cavalierly dismissed by Rostov at the outset. It is clear nevertheless that there are a number of traditionalist societies (by Rostov's own criteria), constituting independent nations today, which are included in our foreign aid programs. Thus, not only for empirical but for theoretical reasons, it would be desirable to extend the analysis of the traditionalist societies and to attempt to understand the process and rhythm of change from the traditionalist to transitional stage. Clearly, this is a field for the anthropologist's contribution, particularly anthropologists who are likely to be serving in one or both type societies.

Concerning the transitional societies, Rostov makes the point that they are undergoing a basic institutional change prior to takeoff, characterized by centralization, a shifting of the elite, and nationalism. He puts most underdeveloped countries in this stage. However brilliant the generalization, there is considerable danger in underplaying the significant differences between groups of societies sharing radically different cultural traditions as well as between individual societies. Here again there is a need to give the theory greater depth and specificity. Rostov implies that one can conceive and even deal on the same time scale with a variety of elites as though they all represented the same tendency. It should be clear that the sequence of changes within the transitional stage as well as the different types of elite constellations require further definition before the process can be sufficiently well understood to be applied in policy.

The anthropologist overseas is in an ideal position to provide such definition and clarification. Because of the immediacy of the need for a profound consistent and correct basis for foreign policy to underdeveloped countries, I consider contributions in this area of theory to be the most challenging and urgent we can make.

NOTES

1. See particularly the *Community Development Review*.
2. For a good discussion of the potential and problems of "on-the-job" interdisciplinary exchange, see Council on Social Work Education, *Interprofessional Training Goals for Technical Assistance Personnel Abroad*, Ithaca, New York, 1959.

15 ....

Cooperation Between Anthropologist and Medical Personnel

CARA E. RICHARDS

The annals of applied anthropology are full of reports on situations where behavioral science knowledge and skills have not been used. It is a pleasure, therefore, to report on a situation in which members of the medical and anthropological professions work actively together, pooling their abilities and information to accomplish their task more effectively.

The project where these desirable circumstances prevail is the Navajo-Cornell Field Health Project at Many Farms, Arizona. This project was initiated on July 1, 1955 by an agreement between the Cornell University

"Cooperation Between Anthropologist and Medical Personnel" by Cara E. Richards is reprinted from *Human Organization* 19:64–67, 1960, by permission of the author and publisher.

Medical College and the United States Public Health Service which had just taken over responsibility for the health of Indians on reservations. The major objectives of the project were:

(1) To define the proper concerns of a health program among a people such as the Navajo Indians.

(2) To find ways to adapt modern medicine for delivery in an acceptable form across formidable cultural and linguistic barriers without compromising essential medical standards in the process.

(3) To study insofar as possible, the consequences of this innovation in terms of the community.

(4) To determine whether information important with respect to environment and disease in our present-day society can be obtained from the study of a people who are emerging from a relatively primitive culture into one more closely approximating that of present-day rural United States.[1]

Anthropology has been part of the project from its beginning. Dr. John Adair has worked closely with physicians Dr. Walsh McDermott and Dr. Kurt Deuschle in setting up the project, and he continues as principal anthropologist. The project thus has a history of cooperation in the planning stage and in the initial implementation. Cooperation with anthropologists has been and still is considered an essential part of the project.

The purpose of this paper is to give some details on day-to-day experiences in cooperation and to examine some of the factors involved in the development of that relationship.

My role was considerably structured before I came to the project. Informally, my predecessor as resident anthropologist had created certain role expectations by his behavior. Formally, my work was intended to contribute to further understanding of two medical problems, diarrhea and heart disease. I was to make an intensive study of between five and ten families, paying particular attention to their diet, sanitation, and activity pattern.

As my research progressed, I discussed data with the doctor most concerned with the problem to which the data were best related. This made it possible to refine problems further, to decide what avenues of research most needed to be pursued, etc. For example, on routine checking of translation, I found that Navajos have only one word for cooking fat, which is translated "lard." Thus research based on statements from Navajos that they use "lard" for cooking may be suspect unless the researcher has made sure just what item "lard" actually refers to in each specific case. From discussions with the doctor, I learned that in connection with the effect of diet on heart disease, the difference between lard and an hydrogenated vegetable oil is considerable. From the finding that "lard" did not necessarily mean lard, we were able to focus our research more sharply in this area.

In addition to this fairly clearly defined role, I was expected to help in various social science aspects of the project. This part of the role was left rather undefined, since no one could predict in advance exactly in what way and at what time I might be useful. On occasions my advice was asked on how to present a delicate question to a family. On other occasions, because of my less formal relationships, I was told about attitudes, fears, etc., concerning health that the people had not mentioned to other clinic personnel. This sometimes led to improved medical service to the individual.

An anthropologist can often make use of casual information that happens to come his way. In other situations, his contribution comes from information deliberately collected as well as from his specialized knowledge.

What everyone on the project calls "congenital hip" — a malformation of the pelvic joint which results in limping — occurs with considerable frequency among the Navajo population: a frequency between 500 and 1,000 times greater than in Anglo populations. For some time medical personnel have been interested in getting Navajos with this condition into clinics or hospitals for treatment, but there has been stiff resistance. Surgery has been performed on a number of children in the clinic area without success. This has tended to make people reluctant to cooperate with medical personnel in finding and treating new cases by hospitalization. At Many Farms we have recently been studying congenital malformations more intensively. Part of the study is genealogical, part purely medical (i.e., diagnosis and treatment), and part is concerned with resistance of the population to treatment. All three phases have involved discussion and exchange of ideas among staff members. In this paper I intend to discuss only one aspect — the resistance to treatment.

I have asked most of my informants what they thought caused "congenital hip" and how they felt or how they thought other Navajos felt about attempts to cure or remedy the condition. Answers seem to indicate that resistance to treatment centers on the idea of surgery, which is not surprising in view of the lack of success surgery has had on children in the area. Treatment that can be carried on at home, however, without any painful operations (i.e., by mechanical leg-spreaders, special diapering techniques, etc.,) apparently does not arouse so much resistance. In addition, Navajos in general are apparently not convinced that "congenital hip" is worth all the trouble. If an individual is not in pain and can function effectively (as "congenital hip" victims usually can) there appears to be no compulsion to persuade them to endure considerable discomfort to change the situation. "Congenital hip" is a good example of differing cultural values. It is a public health problem in the eyes of medical personnel. It is not one in the eyes of Navajos. Apparently Navajos would rather have a person who limps but functions effectively than one who walks more smoothly but cannot climb, crouch, or squat (most Navajos homes still do not have chairs, but doctors operate in terms of a chair-culture).

The anthropological findings concerning attitudes toward "congenital hip" have been turned over to the project medical personnel. This case of cooperation has no clear-cut ending inasmuch as a program of medical service which would lead to diagnosis and earlier correction of the malady had not been put into operation by the time the writer left the project. Basic genetic research is now under way in an attempt to understand inheritance patterns of the disease.

FACTORS IN COOPERATION

As the above cases illustrate, cooperation is possible and effective between disciplines. Since so many instances of uncooperative behavior exist, a major problem is how to bring the much desired cooperation into being.

Many problems faced in attempts to develop cooperation within an interdisciplinary team can be traced to the fact that people accustomed to operating in a fairly autonomous fashion are forced to function in the context of an organization. The problems involved in getting people in any organization to work well together are certainly not unknown to the readers of this paper. Interdisciplinary cooperation is merely a special instance of the general case. Some of the solutions to general organization problems which have been found can be applied to interdisciplinary team research as well.

A special problem faced by the social scientist in interdisciplinary research is how to keep professional identity and still contribute to the general research. The temptation either to retreat to an ivory tower of pure theory or to become a technician like a laboratory assistant is difficult to resist. Yet it is necessary to find a balance between the two because neither extreme contributes to effective cooperation. Studying kinship terminology may be interesting to an anthropologist but it is difficult to see how such knowledge will be of assistance to the medical practitioner. On the other hand, persuading families or individuals to do something the doctor wants may assist the medical practitioner, but turns the anthropologist into a rather high-priced messenger boy.

An anthropologist faces another problem which is peculiar to interdisciplinary research. Medical personnel are part of the field situation and must be considered as such. As in all field situations, the anthropologist seeks acceptance and must build rapport. Ordinarily the anthropologist achieves rapport on a personal basis. He is friendly and people like him. They want to help him. In a situation where cooperation between professional groups is important, however, mere popularity is not sufficient. An anthropologist must also build respect for his professional competence and judgment. The usual research population would not know what an anthropologist was if he told them, and would not much care if they did know. An anthropologist may be able to do a perfectly good job (or even a better one) if the people regard him as a slightly subnormal but pleasant child who has to have the simplest rudiments of normal living explained. This is most definitely *not* the case when dealing with members of other professions.

In creating respect for his professional judgment, the anthropologist cannot rely on techniques he uses to gain respect from other anthropologists. His colleagues make their judgments on the basis of criteria with which he and they are completely familiar. Members of other professions, however, are no more familiar with the anthropologist's standards of judgment than he is with theirs. The criteria they use, therefore, are the same ones used by most members of our culture in judging the ability of another person, that is: do his statements "make sense"; is his reasoning logical; are his predictions generally accurate; is he apparently truthful; does he exaggerate or dramatize, etc.? Most of these criteria are fairly obvious to anyone familiar with our culture.

An anthropologist must not try to influence decisions on the grounds that he is an "authority" since that is not likely to impress members of another profession. He should admit ignorance and uncertainty and not try to pose as infallible. He must admit the possibility that he could be wrong. For example, the writer has been told that on occasions in the past, anthropologists have told physicians that Navajo women were very modest about the area of their bodies below the waist (which is correct) and that therefore pelvic examinations could not be performed. Such predictions proved to be inaccurate because they did not take into account the ability of Navajo women to adjust to practical requirements of a new situation. Anthropologists are likely to make such statements when relying on ethnographic data gathered with description or historical reconstruction rather than culture change in mind. Ideal patterns reported in ethnographies must be carefully weighed for applicability in the contact situation.

A fair statement of probability is extremely important because medical personnel have the responsibility for the welfare of their patients. This is a serious responsibility which the anthropologist does not share. It is very easy for an anthropologist to be glib and assured, but if he is wrong, and the medical personnel follow his advice, serious consequences may result. Subsequently, medical personnel may lose all confidence in the anthropologist. It is much wiser to state as clearly as possible what is almost certain, which is probable, and what is only a possibility. Then the medical personnel can weigh anthropological advice against medical necessity and make their own decisions. An anthropologist may be a better judge of the emotional reaction of a patient and his relatives to certain situations and medical procedures, but he is not competent to judge the medical necessity. Since the responsibility is the medical doctor's, the decision should also be his. The function of an anthropologist is to provide the doctor with the necessary relevant information so his decision can be based on the best possible knowledge of all known factors in the situation.

The anthropologist must try to keep communication lines open. This may require a great deal of effort in a busy research situation, but can be a very important factor. One time I spoke to an informant about her new grandchild, born about a month earlier, and commented that she must be pleased with him. Unfortunately, the child had been taken to the hospital a day or so before, and had died that very day. I was unaware of this because no one in the clinic told me. Rather than expect the clinic people to interrupt their busy routine and check up for me, I made it a point to examine clinic records before I went out to visit an informant after that.

Feedback from anthropologist to medical personnel and vice versa is essential to effective cooperation. In another instance, I reported to the medical officer in charge that one of my informants was quite disturbed because he feared he had a brain tumor. I had encouraged the man to come to the clinic. When he did, the doctor went to great lengths to convince him that he did not have a brain tumor. The doctor informed me what he had done. The next time I went to see the family, I was able to ask specific questions about the treatment, and was able to report the family's satisfaction to the doctor. This case improved my rapport, the clinic's position with the family, and the doctor's morale.

An anthropologist must be practical and remember that medical personnel have certain goals they wish to reach. If he does not approve of these goals, he should not accept the position of working with the team. Once he has accepted the position, he has committed himself either to helping the medical personnel attain their goals, or else to modifying their goals slightly so they can realistically be attained. He is not justified in obstructing the medical personnel, nor in trying to force them to abandon any of their goals entirely.

An anthropologist must always remember that medical personnel operate in terms of a subculture and are apt to be as disturbed as anyone else when basic tenets of their subculture are challenged. The anthropologist must be willing to learn. Many things medical personnel do seem unnecessary and even foolish to nonmedical people. The anthropologist must find out if there is a valid medical reason behind an action or if it is really only part of "tradition" which can be discarded or changed if necessary. To find out function or lack of it in specific cases, it is necessary to treat medical personnel as informants and extract information from them because they take their bases for various behaviors and assumptions for granted and do not always realize that their reasoning is by no means obvious to others. The best example of this occurred in connection with clinic policy of not permitting area patients to have their babies in the clinic. Women on the point of delivering would even be sent to nearby *hogans* to have their babies instead of being delivered in the clinic. This procedure seemed highly arbitrary and even cruel to the area patients, and to some of the project personnel. Questioning to try to find out the rationale behind the prohibition took approximately the following course:

> Anth.: Why can't women have their babies in the clinic?
> Dr.: Because we don't have the equipment.
> Anth.: Why can't you get some equipment?
> Dr.: Because we don't have any room ("obviously" was conveyed by the tone of voice although not actually spoken).
> Anth.: I don't understand. We have four examining rooms, a lab, an emergency surgery room, plus others. I thought there were plenty of rooms.

It was this question that finally brought forth the medical reason for not allowing babies to be born in the clinic. It had been so obvious to the medical personnel that they never explained it. None of the available rooms could be made sterile for a delivery. All were open to other rooms in the clinic since the partitions did not reach the ceiling. People with various diseases passed by and moved about in the rooms all day long. The dangerous "staph" organisms were undoubtedly present, and there was no sure way to protect mother or baby from them. Because of this, the medical personnel felt even *hogans* (where few or no outsiders were present) were preferable to delivery in the clinic. The risks of infection that were run by any mother delivering in the clinic appalled them, and they quite rightly refused to accept patients for delivery under the circumstances. Once this full explanation was made, nonmedical and subprofessional members of the staff appreciated the situation and were no longer so ambivalent in regard to the prohibition.

The anthropologist must also be prepared to give detailed explanations for his actions and assumptions since his reasoning is often as obscure to medical personnel as theirs is to him. It is not necessary, however, to try to win acceptance of anthropological abstractions. It is usually sufficient simply to demonstrate the practicality of certain information. For example, it is usually difficult to convince any nonanthropologist that it is desirable to collect information about clans. Medical personnel will, however, readily appreciate the importance of determining the unit of infection for the study of the spread of epidemics — and to determine the unit of infection, social relationships, including clans, must be studied. In other words, explanations "make sense" when placed in the context of the culture of the individual.

Another factor contributing to good or poor cooperation is one which "everyone knows," yet which is frequently ignored in actually establishing a team. It is essential to pick the right personnel. Rigid individuals — people who cannot accept authority, specific job requirements, criticism, questioning of their opinions, rapid adjustments to changing situations — will have difficulty in cross-disciplinary research and probably in any kind of team research. People who do best in interdisciplinary research are open-minded, flexible, tolerant of other views, and willing to learn. On the other hand, if administration is one of the functions of a position, then a certain amount of firmness and decision is necessary.

A by-product of successful cooperation on this project and probably similar projects as well, is that medical personnel have become increasingly convinced of the importance of understanding the culture of patients and in our cases are turning more and more to Navajos themselves for answers to various questions. While this is a healthy sign, it must be watched, since it can easily be overdone. Project members may grow to rely on the word of one or two informants, and as anthropologists have learned by sad experience, one individual may not be at all typical of his culture. In addition, a native informant is apt to be less aware of some things in his own culture than the social scientist is. One of the Navajo staff told me to leave avocados off a list of food items because "Navajos never eat those things." He was quite startled when I told him the item was listed because on one of my visits to a *hogan* I had observed two Navajos eating avocados. They told me they ate avocados every now and then — their uncle liked them a lot.

In a team situation the anthropologist generally plays a major role in building rapport. That is probably inevitable. An anthropologist is almost never in a position of authority over members of other professions so they are seldom required to justify their position to the anthropologist. Instead it is usually up to him to explain why he is in favor of or opposed to some procedure. In the case of medical personnel, they *know* their value in the field of medicine and public health. They do not know how useful a behavioral scientist may be. It is up to the anthropologist to demonstrate his value. He must not expect to be accepted on the mere assertion that he is useful.

SUMMARY

There are several pitfalls to beware of in team research, and several precepts to follow to increase chances of successful cooperation.

There is the danger of the behavioral scientist becoming a technician or the reverse — of losing touch with reality. There is the problem of academic personnel working in a type of organization with more rigid requirements than social scientists are usually accustomed to. There is the possibility that the behavioral scientist will lose the respect of his colleagues by being too positive in his statements and therefore being wrong too often. Communication between one professional group and the other may collapse, causing frustrating misunderstanding and mistakes. There is the danger that members of the other profession will be "converted" to behavioral science techniques, and like many new converts overdo the new things they have learned — such as using "native" informants.

Of the positive steps necessary to increase chances for good cooperation, the first, chronologically at least, is to choose the best personnel — flexible persons, willing to learn. Next, the anthropologist should consider the other profession as part of the situation under study with all the cautions in dealing with people of another culture which that implies. The anthropologist should win acceptance on a professional basis, however, as well as as a person. A third step is for the anthropologist to keep the goals of the project firmly in mind, and make his contributions to attain these goals as practical as possible. The fourth step is to avoid the pitfalls mentioned in the above paragraph, if possible.

The advantages of successful cooperation are apparent to everyone. The experience of the Many Farms project makes it clear that with care such cooperation can be attained even in the comparatively difficult situation of interdisciplinary research.

NOTES

1. This material was taken from the Navajo-Cornell Field Health Research Project Progress Report covering the period April 1, 1957–March 1, 1959, which was prepared by Dr. Kurt Deuschle, Associate Project Director, and Dr. Hugh Fulmer, Assistant Project Director.

16

Anthropology and Indian Claims Litigation: Problems, Opportunities, and Recommendations

NANCY OESTREICH LURIE

Ethnology used in connection with Indian claims is sometimes referred to as a form of applied anthropology. However, to those actively engaged in claims research, it is apparent that the ordinary scope of the term, applied anthropology, must be broadened considerably to encompass such endeavors as testifying before a legal body in the capacity of an ethnological expert. More likely a new dimension of anthropology is developing, but whatever terminology is adopted, it is important to recognize the

"Anthropology and Indian Claims Litigation: Problems, Opportunities, and Recommendations" by Nancy Oestreich Lurie is reprinted from *Ethnohistory* 2:357–375, 1955, by permission of the author and publisher.

unique character of the work and to take stock of various implications that transcend the Indian Claims Commission Act.

For example, the applied anthropologist is called upon to further certain courses of action in a culturally effective manner, which may include the introduction of western medical practices, the raising of economic standards, or the rehabilitation of people in new areas. He may even contribute to the setting of policies in regard to the initial feasibility of making given changes. In contrast to the applied anthropologist the ethnologist concerned in Indian claims neither sets policies nor expedites those already provided. He is merely consulted for his expert and impartial opinion concerning facts of a cultural or historical nature as these are required to test the validity of various claims put forth by the Indians themselves. In his role as an objective scientist, he has no intellectual stake in the outcome or in actions taken on the basis of his information.

It has been pointed out that the plaintiff and defendant in Anglo-American law may each present expert witnesses, and in the course of the current litigation there have appeared discrepancies between the data provided by experts testifying as witnesses for the Government and those testifying as witnesses for the Indians. The reasons for these differences may be traced to several sources, and it is well to consider their significance to the discipline at large rather than as simply entrenched personal divergencies of interpretation. Such matters have in times past been the stimuli for professional feuds. However, on careful examination, the difficulties of an ethnological nature arising out of Indian claims may provide for an expansion of our knowledge generally and for the better communication of our ideas.

It may be noted first that in some instances the lawyers for one side have argued against the qualifications of the witness for the opposition to speak as an expert. When this matter is brought to the attention of those ethnologists not involved in claims work, there is a tendency to mention summarily the status of fellow in the American Anthropological Association as an automatic and exclusive device available to attorneys to test the qualifications of a given expert. Yet, some nonprofessional people with first-hand knowledge of many years' standing regarding given groups may be better able to speak of these societies than ethnologists making brief surveys at the present time. The distinctions between enthusiastic amateurs, over-grown Eagle Scouts, Sunday relic collectors, professional novices and knowledgeable nonprofessionals are fine indeed. We cannot ignore the problem nor look for easy solutions as long as such a variety of witnessing is classified as ethnological and gives promise of continuing for some time to come. By complacency, we may eventually risk the plague of opportunist, of which psychology and psychiatry have barely rid themselves since becoming "popular." When a plethora of Hollywood films suddenly are devoted to alleged anthropological subjects and when other media of mass entertainment from comic strips to radio and television programs introduce anthropological characters, we must face the reality that anthropology, like psychology, is a household word. Thus, it does not seem an unduly alarmist notion to point out the need to our own protection while at the same time taking careful note that worthwhile contributions have been made to the discipline of ethnology by people who are not acknowledged experts in the field generally. If this type of work continues, which seems a reasonable surmise, the duty of designating experts' qualifications and ethnological data as such ought not to be the result of solely legal disputation.

We may note that ethnological testimony and ethnographic data are already recognized by legal people as separate categories to a certain extent. Attorneys concerned in Indian claims have taken depositions in the field from tribesmen and their White neighbors in the hope of discovering various facts. They might also ask to reproduce the ethnologists' raw field notes as evidence and not bother to retain ethnologists as witnesses. However, the increasing reliance on ethnologists as investigators and witnesses is indicative of the realization that such persons are specially trained to collect cultural data in an impartial manner and to draw valid conclusions from myriad scattered facts. That the techniques and results of ethnological field work among Indians who are "interested parties" in their own cases seem to carry greater weight than first-hand depositions from those same Indians argues for the need to make explicit in testimony the now somewhat obscure, albeit appreciated, characteristics of professional ethnology.

This problem is intimately related to a second source of disagreement: differences of opinion between equally recognized and unquestioned authorities. Such disagreements, of course, are the essence of scientific advancement, but they should occur in the nominally objective atmosphere of professional meetings and journals where an exchange of ideas between protagonists and others interested in similar problems may be impartially reviewed by people in a position to judge the validity of the arguments. A court of law, which is the basic form of the Indian Claims Commission, is not intended nor able to discern the technical merits of highly complex, academic differences of opinion. Yet, in practice this is precisely what is being required of the Commissioners. Several suggestions have been made to overcome the difficulty. It has been proposed that advisors be available to the Commissioners to aid in assessing experts' qualifications as well as to explain the underlying complications of their data. In fact, the Indian Claims Commission Act provides for an Investigative Division to submit data to the Commissioners and to make documents and other pertinent materials available to attorneys defending the government or representing tribal clients. This provision has never been effectively utilized, but if sufficient need were felt for it, possibly such an Investigative Division could be established and its scope extended to technical analysis of evidence presented in hearings. Thus, where a more extended background of ethnological knowledge and theory were required for complete understanding of different interpretations, they could be provided.

Another possible aid to understanding lies in agreement on the part of the Commission and all parties concerned to allow the two or more experts to discuss their data as fellow scientists before formal legal procedure on a case begins. Certainly much time could be saved which is now devoted to repetition of data by plaintiff and defendant. In one case, for example, after an expert had presented all of his information and expressed his opinions, he later conceded to the greater accuracy of the statements of a witness for the opposition who happened to have done extensive field work with the tribe in question, but who had never published any of his field data. Their existence was virtually unknown to anyone but himself until his testimony was presented. It is possible that many disputes might be as easily resolved were the experts able to discuss their information together as fellow scientists rather than as antagonists pitted against one another.

There is the inescapable fact that legal procedure being what it is, each attorney is going to make the best case out of the information provided by his expert and attempt to weaken the testimony of the opposition. Most ethnologists have expressed pleasure at the sincere efforts by the attorneys with whom they are associated to use their data as honestly as it is in their power to do so. The situation remains, nevertheless, that an ethnologist answering questions propounded from a legal point of view is at a disadvantage in comparison to expressing his opinions as he would among other professionals or for the benefit of laymen where the salient points and organization of the material are of his own choosing.

However, because the law is flexible to some extent, even this obstacle may be overcome if we consider closely another source of ostensible arrangement between witnesses who are unquestionably qualified to speak as experts. This relates to the recency and lack of precedents both in the law and in ethnology regarding the use of ethnological information for legal purposes. Were experts permitted to discuss their data together, they still might not be in perfect agreement, but the reasons for their differences might be made more clear and the utility and meaning of their data enhanced when certain hidden sources of discrepancies were thus revealed. These may be considered in respect to two related problems.

First, ethnologists have a unique approach to the world of man and should not be expected to discard this outlook but should make it explicit when nonethnologists require their services. Second, the legal instrument under which the ethnologist testifies may be inadequately propounded for the use of social scientific data.

In regard to the first problem, ethnological testimony cannot be like that of "exact scientists" such as physicists who can give precise mathematical reasons for the collapse of a bridge. Even a physician is on fairly uncontrovertible ground when he expresses his opinion on a death certificate as to the cause of a patient's demise. Neither are ethnologists like historians who work primarily within the scope of written records. In the case of Indian claims the documents stem from Euro-American sources, were produced from the standpoint of those cultures, and are read and analyzed by people oriented in Euro-American historical traditions. Ethnology is probably closest to psychology in that the subjects involved are so intimately related to the matters in question and it is their unwitting testimony which is strained through and refined by the expert witness. Yet, ethnologists do not define normality in terms of social adequacy in our own culture as even the most objective psychologist must do ultimately in commitment cases. Finally, ethnologists are not lawyers who see loss and restitution if not justice *per se,* largely in economic terms.

Thus, when asked if a given tribe used and occupied certain lands, the ethnologist answers yes or no, but not in terms of mathematical surveys, nor as the physician or biologist might refer to minimal nutritional necessities for existence. The ethnologist, like the historian may cite old documents, and indeed has developed a greater appreciation for such records, thanks to work in Indian claims. But the ethnologist is still far more complete and secure in the use of oral tradition, first-hand observation, and the peculiar checks of his own profession on the accuracy of such data. The ethnologist's opinion as to land use and occupancy may have psychological connotations, but of a somewhat more distinctive nature than ordinarily encountered in the law; the practicing psychologist would be apt to make quite a different interpretation of land use where an area in question is claimed as a place inhabited by spirits and valued as a good location to have visions. Finally, when asked by a lawyer about use and occupancy, the ethnologist speaks of shared lands, shared rights, formalized exchanges of hospitality and the like in a manner to confuse the mind geared to Anglo-American concepts of common-law. Briefly, the ethnologist considers various practices as valid as any accepted as the basis of common-law in culture, but which may be at variance with existing legal precedents.

Occasional recognition and attempts to reconcile the ethnologist's basic assumptions with standard legal procedures have resulted in such necessarily labored analogies on the part of lawyers as saying that Indian tribes used and occupied uninhabited lands in the sense that the people of the

United States use and occupy deserts and national parks. An example even more painful to the ethnologist is the attempt to equate remote areas used in the vision quest with "shrines" or sacred nondwelling places in our culture. These approaches toward greater understanding do not make clear that the working hypotheses of ethnology are relativistic in nature and tend to assess values, property and loss in terms of the specific culture in question rather than to attempt to justify them in terms of roughly comparable situations in our own culture. Furthermore, the ethnologist would run short of analogies in this type of approach.

Apart from any later generalizations, the implicit methodological procedure of ethnography is to recognize certain broad categories of cultural facts, within which there are many and even mutually exclusive examples. Marriage — socially sanctioned mating — is such a category and includes among its sundry valid illustrations polygyny and monogamy. When an ethnologist testifies, this type of assumption is not always clearly stated nor is it tacitly understood by the nonethnologist, as we so frequently realize is the case in conversations with laymen generally. Yet these very basic assumptions are of particular concern in Indian claims since interest is in specific tribes and in the facts of their existence. Such simple ethnological facts, apart from any finely spun theories and hypotheses of culture generally, require careful definition when the ethnologist must communicate them to laymen.

It may be that one ethnologist, dealing with attorneys as people familiar with the values of our own society, endeavors to answer questions as these are best understood by the questioner. Such a witness is being as scientifically aware and tolerant of cultural biases as another ethnologist who speaks from the viewpoint of social science without taking into account that he is not addressing fellow scientists. If no precedents have been established to indicate how an ethnologist testifies, the occurrence of opposite interpretations of the same data is understandable. Thus, some differences in testimony which would seem to reflect the greater accuracy of scientific impartiality of one witness compared to another, are simply questions of communication among ethnologists and between ethnologists and laymen.

Whether the profession as a whole would want to establish procedural preferences in this type of work or whether each ethnologist is to resolve the problem for himself, it behooves us to be aware of the difficulties that can arise as a result of incomplete communication of the ethnological *modus operandi*. The matter of designating whereof an expert witness speaks has had to be dealt with by many professions and occupations in turn when their services became of increasing value in legal situations. The law itself has attempted to provide definitions of what constitutes an expert witness, and it has not been a simple feat. Before satisfactory designations were achieved there arose as a result of conflicting testimony the cynical superlatives: "liars, damn liars, and expert witnesses." Since lawyers are still chary of even "exact scientists" as witnesses, our developmental difficulties need not be attributed solely to the complacent complaint of social science as the eternal voice crying in the wilderness of cultural intolerance and social misunderstanding.

One of the difficulties of which the ethnologist must be especially aware is that lawyers think in terms of precedents while ethnologists think in terms of cultural generalizations. Thus, the ethnologist may see his concepts of land ownership as derived from one society interpreted as firm precedents in another case. For instance, extreme and explicit boundary-consciousness in one tribe may not be repeated in another. Superficially it appears that in the latter case the evidence of use, occupancy and extent of range is not as "strong" as in the former case. In the mapping of tribal territories, the data are of equal validity to the ethnologist whether his informants are conscious of how far they extended their operations or whether the information lies buried in their unconscious behavior. In fact, he makes the same observations of behavior, even if his informants speak of tribal varieties of metes and bounds, simply to check on the accuracy of their seemingly definitive awareness. To the ethnologist, this is simply a common matter that the field worker must be constantly alert to the distinctions between so-called ideal and real behavior, but unless he makes this explicit he may find a different legal construction placed on verbal reification of ideal behavior than he might be inclined to place on it himself.

A further illustration that social scientific assumptions as part of ethnological technique require exposition is seen in the second problem under discussion, namely, the appropriateness of the legal instrument under which the ethnologist testifies. The Indian Claims Commission Act, with its broad jurisdictional provisions, might be construed as permitting any type of pertinent testimony in its application. However, a careful analysis of the Act reveals that it was based on motives of humanitarian justice but ethnological naivete. It may be observed that the situation could be much worse, and that the shortcomings derive largely from the unusual and virtually unprecedented nature of the Act, as well as the unexpectedly great reliance on ethnological data in the cases heard. Nonetheless, it stands as a warning that the profession in the future ought not leave such matters almost exclusively in the hands of lobbyists and legislators of commendable intent, but little social scientific training. Nor should we disregard such legislation when it is in the offing as something with which only applied anthropology may eventually be involved. It is instructive to consider the language of the Act in certain particulars. It begins by stating that it is concerned with claims "on behalf of any Indian tribe, band, or other identifiable group of American Indians residing within the territorial limits of the United States or Alaska." The framers of the Act did attempt to simplify the problem of identity to the following extent as shown in Section 10:

> Any claim within the provisions of this Act may be presented to the Commission by any member of an Indian tribe, band, or other identifiable group of Indians as the representative of all of its members; but wherever any tribal organization exists, recognized by the Secretary of the Interior as having authority to represent such tribe, band, or group, such organization shall be accorded the exclusive privilege of representing such Indians.

What this means in effect is that where an organization exists, the tribe, band, or group is automatically identifiable. However, the implicit feature of identifiability rests on an historical foundation; that the group, however defined, be identified continuously from the time of the origin of the claim to the present day. This is reasonable, of course, but unintentional confusion is presented to the ethnologist when the identity of today rests on formal organization influenced by administrative policies of the government, while ethnographic identification rests in the past on primarily native concepts. In regard to relating living claimants to their ancestral groups, cultures and territories, the term "since time immemorial" is of such frequent reiteration that it is something of a surprise to discover that it is nowhere stated explicitly in the Indian Claims Commission Act, but that factors of time and title may be variously construed.

Thus, it may be noted that some tribes which were sole native occupants of given lands at the time they were appropriated or purchased were relatively recent interlopers who drove out the original inhabitants in the course of moving ahead of the pressure of the White frontier. Although claims are brought by Indians against the government and not by one tribe against another, such situations allow of alternative interpretations of ownership, whether based on use and occupancy or original title insofar as this may be traced back. Some tribes extended their range of activities and changed their social organization in response to the introduction of horses and guns; others exploited increasing amounts of territory as a function of the hunting requirements of the fur trade. Yet other groups at the time of the loss of their lands were small remnants of once large populations, due to epidemics of smallpox and other diseases. While they and their neighbors might be clearly aware of the area considered their own, they obviously were not using or occupying it in their customary manner. In fact, the early treaty makers used this as an argument that the Indians could sell their lands because they no longer needed them, and then added the tautological inducement to accept a reservation of limited size so that with proper medical care they could be restored to their former grandeur.

In some cases where tribes signed treaties setting forth the areas claimed by them, difficulties arose because most such areas were unsurveyed at the time; misunderstandings between Indians and Whites developed through the use of interpreters; and some tribes ceded the land of other tribes or were unaware that part of their lands were not included in the territorial descriptions. Matters of this nature may all be grounds for claims. The divergencies between treaty descriptions and ethnological mapping point up sharply the problems of time and identifiability. The ethnologist must be able to state with certainty the period of time to which his map applies for it to have value in legal proceedings. Where the government never even recognized Indian occupation of lands by treaty, the ethnologist is concerned with establishing where these Indians lived, when the land was actually appropriated, and whether or not the group existed as an identifiable entity at the time the land was taken.

To date, the cases have varied in these details with both archeological data and historical documents brought in to provide a full picture of various claims. Too few decisions have been handed down to discern any legal pattern in regard to these matters except that the Commissioners have tended to express the greatest interest in clear statements concerning land use and occupancy at the time land was actually ceded or lost rather than since time immemorial. The ethnologist is obliged to present his data in chronological sequences and let the decisions occur as they may.

The language of the Act is particularly confusing to the ethnologist, in regard to identifiability, not only in terms of time but in reference to societies. Disregarding the word group as a legal device providing the broadest possible jurisdiction for the definition of the petitioner, and turning to the words tribe and band, it is obvious that any given ethnologist uses these terms with multiple connotations. Not infrequently the terms are used synonymously. Therefore, a tribe may be so defined because it consists of several bands which gathered into increasing political and social unity. Or, a given tribe may be made up of bands which were once one unit, but for various reasons developed into several groups still maintaining a sense of over-all identity and greater or lesser coordination of activity. Finally, a tribe may be a single local group. A band may be defined as one of many local groups within a larger entity designated a tribe, or several such groups may be considered a band having more in common with each other than with similar assemblages of local groups, all of which considered themselves part of a larger whole. Thus, what may be called a band is actually an unrepresentative fragment of a larger tribe in one case; or a tribe may be a vague aggregation of many bands each of which occupied its own territory, and, as to identifiability, might each make a separate claim.

It is understandable that confusion arises when the Commissioners and lawyers are faced with such alternatives within definitions of given terms, in the course of hearing varied types of cases. Nor is the situation simplified for the ethnologist who sometimes must testify within the framework of existing definitions that may be legally expedient but do violence to basic ethnological concepts of the internal criteria that distinguish social groups from miscellaneous aggregations of people. The "Chippewa Nation" and "The Indians of California" represent two extremes in regard to accord and lack of accord respectively between the law and ethnology as to concepts of social groups.

A claim brought in behalf of the "Chippewa Nation" before the Court of Claims was directed to be broken down into separate band claims. Since the claims were not settled in the Court of Claims, the Chippewa then brought their claims before the Indian Claims Commission and the designation by separate bands was retained. The bands enjoyed political autonomy but contiguous territories and cultural and linguistic similarities. The ethnologist can consider that the legal emphasis is on functional social entities.

However, in other instances Congress has created "statutory groups" for the purpose of establishing jurisdictional provisions in acts permitting claims by Indians to be brought before the Court of Claims. Such a group, "The Indians of California," was created in 1928. When a claim of these same Indians was later brought before the Indian Claims Commission they remained as "The Indians of California," but are actually, of course, a collection of the most politically autonomous and culturally and linguistically varied groups living within any given area of the United States. Although ethnological data were presented for the separate tribes in turn, the identity of the total group is in striking legal contrast to other cases where it is possible and even necessary to establish identity solely on the basis of ethnological criteria regarding social organization and other features.

Many tribes are not organized with a formally recognized council, and some do not even have reservations. Yet, they may be identified on the basis of social self-consciousness and recognition by outsiders that they constitute distinct societies with characteristic cultural traits. The problem is not disposed of easily, however, when even semantic features and conventional terminology obscure identifiability. To mention just a few examples, there are several "Upper" and "Lower" varieties of given terms, such as Kalispel and Kutenai. These have less in common and are more clearly distinct tribes than subgroups of individual tribes each enjoying their own particular names such as Quinault and Queets. Tribes such as the Winnebago and Potawatomi are now divided into reservation and non-reservation enclaves living in widely separated areas, whereas at the time of the origin of any claim involving aboriginal conditions they were single entities. If each group is represented by its own council, identifiability is confused for the period of land loss. The situation is even more confused in cases such as the Winnebago where the group in Nebraska is readily identified as a reservation group having its formally organized council while the Wisconsin Winnebago who have continued to occupy the northern portion of their old territory and who maintain many more traditional aspects of culture had to hold a special meeting to elect representatives to meet with the Nebraska council and retaining attorneys.

The identifiability of such diverse groups must be decided by the Commissioners on the basis of the legal and ethnological evidence presented. Had ethnological and historical considerations been recognized by the framers of the Act, they might have avoided ambiguous phrases such as, "any tribe, band or other identifiable group of American Indians" some of which may be identified by tribal organizations and some by other criteria. To the ethnologist it is preferable to use definitions which grow out of native variations on given themes, but this is precluded in some instances by the common organization of several tribes or the partial organization of a single tribe. Thus, the Act does not permit the development of ethno-legal concepts of general application in terms of an accretive definition of a society. When the ethnologist is asked whether a group in question is a fragment of a tribe he is not certain what is intended by these terms. Studies such as the paper by Dr. Kroeber are greatly needed to help define for general use the concepts and terminology which the ethnologist understands in their various contexts, but does not consider in larger scope. At any rate, there is now no consistent terminology for a matter which could be reduced to essentials and applied as any similar generalization; for example, the previously cited accretive definition of marriage which includes such forms as polygyny and monogamy, but is limited to the extent of being a socially sanctioned type of mating.

The existence of a justifiable claim is based on the remarkably broad jurisdictional provisions of the Indian Claims Commission Act.

These may be reviewed briefly as they are set forth in Section 2:

(1) claims in law or equity arising under the Constitution, law, treaties of the United States, and Executive orders of the President; (2) all other claims in law or equity, including those sounding in tort, with respect to which the claimant would be entitled to sue in a court of the United States if the United States was subject to suit; (3) claims which would result if the treaties, contracts, and agreements between the claimant and the United States were revised on the ground of fraud, duress, unconscionable consideration, mutual or unilateral mistake, whether of law or fact, or any other ground cognizable by a court of equity; (4) claims arising from the taking by the United States, whether as a result of a treaty of cession or otherwise, of lands owned or occupied by the claimant without the payment for such lands of compensation agreed to by the claimant; and (5) claims based on fair and honorable dealings that are not recognized by any existing rule of law or equity.

The first four provisions for grounds for a claim can be assessed by people trained in the law, familiar with precedents and legal decisions, and with a sufficient background of historical and ethnographic facts provided to them to carry out the letter of the law. It is the spirit of the law, as enacted and reflected in the fifth provision, that puzzles ethnologists, and probably attorneys as well. Unless lawyers with whom the ethnologist is associated ask him about certain possibilities of fair and honorable dealings, he may possess data that are never utilized. Nor is the ethnologist in a position to judge what this phrase might apply to; he points out, perhaps naively, that the first four provisions are stated neutrally or negatively; "arising under the Constitution. . ." or "unconscionable consideration." To be consistent, the fifth provision should read "claims based on dealings that are not recognized by any existing rule of law or equity," or "claims based on unfair or dishonorable dealings . . ." The ethnologist thinks of broken cultures, of grievances against the Government not for loss of property in economic terms but the loss of a way of life, of social and psychological inadequacy which resulted from fair, honorable and even benign motives on the part of the Government.

Ethnologists can point to the abolition of polygyny which in some instances led to a crumbling of whole socio-economic structures. Indian children were practically kidnapped at times and sent away to boarding schools with devastating results, now so well known, to the societies from which they were derived; the intent of the Government had been to civilize and aid the Indians. Or, the Government, unable to control the pioneering proclivities of its White citizens, endeavored to remunerate the Indians fairly and honorably for lost lands. Treaty minutes from many areas contain statements by Indians to the effect that they did not want or need money, but wished their lands to be restored to them. Any ethnologist can think of dozens of examples of losses not recognized by any rule of law or equity, but any of these claims would require peculiar interpretations in the attempt to gain restitution.

The Indian Claims Commission is frequently referred to mistakenly as the Indian Land Claims Commission which reflects the necessity that claims can only be based on highly tangible losses such as land, or matters regarding payment for such land and administration of material needs of the Indians once placed under Government supervision. However, the legislators who wrote the Indian Claims Commission Act recognized that all grounds for just grievances did not stem from material sources, although it is doubtful if there was a conscious recognition in the fifth provision of the Act that many such grievances derive from the results of misplaced philanthropy. It may be argued that the Wheeler-Howard or Indian Reorganization Act sought to remedy the situation created by the peculiar management of Indian affairs, and that the Indian Claims Commission merely seeks to offer financial remuneration for tangible losses. However, there remains that bothersome phrase, "fair and honorable dealings," which indicates a social awareness on the part of legislators but lack of social scientific facts to develop constructive legal measures for the alleviation of the gnawing bitterness on the part of Indians and satisfaction of the sense of national obligation that led to the enactment of the Indian Claims Commission.

No one takes the unrealistic view that time can be reversed or that we should give the country back to the Indians. Furthermore, ethnologists are clearly aware that many Indian grievances are habitual expression relied upon to excuse as a fault of the Government, any personal inadequacy or disappointment. Yet, had the wording of the Act been less emotionally weighted in terms of fair and honorable dealings and concerned instead with ethnological concepts of cultural integrity and functional expediency it would permit objective presentation of facts on such matters and be no more far-fetched than such established legal precedent of claims based on "mental anguish" or "loss of companionship;" for example, the case where a spouse is confined to a hospital for long periods of time as the result of an accident deriving from the defendant's negligence or intent to do harm.

In view of the foregoing, the ethnologist should be aware not only of the complications incident upon testifying as an expert witness, but also alert to power situation on a world wide scale where legislation similar to the Indian Claims Commission Act is likely to be enacted. When Micronesians are already complaining about the illegal taking of their land, when various European powers can misunderstand nativistic movements as thoroughly as the United States misunderstood the Ghost Dance and like developments, and when versions of our reservation system are being repeated throughout the world with similar shortcomings and problems arising therefrom, it is reasonable to assume that the growing political awareness of native peoples will have them clamoring for restitutive legislation. It may be objected that in the above cases we are dealing with colonialism, the abolishment of which will automatically solve native problems in other parts of the world. However, a large proportion of Indian claims stem from a period when Indian tribes were dealt with by treaty as sovereign nations and were considered such before the law. It was due in great part to the difficulties arising from tribal claims that led to the establishment of a special Commission since the redress of ordinary citizens before the Court of Claims was fraught with complications for Indian groups because of their peculiar status as nations within the United States.

The United Nations need only be mentioned as a likely source of legislation on a world-wide scale affecting native peoples. Therefore, while there is little to be done about the Indian Claims Commission Act, unless it may be reconsidered if its duration is to be extended for another period of years beyond 1956, it does serve several useful purposes to the profession of ethnology.

First, we should be sufficiently aware of ourselves to make our data of real utility to people who require social and cultural information but do not have the basic understanding of ethnology as a science to give credence to our methods and assumptions unless we state and defend them explicitly.

Second, apart from ordinary concepts of applied anthropology, the ethnologist *qua* ethnologist should be cognizant of power situations in which legislation may be enacted relating to the use of social scientific data in court proceedings. Such legal measures may be greatly expedited if the profession makes its services available and interests known before an issue becomes law. In this way intelligent provision may be made for the use of impartial ethnological testimony without occasion of delay and misunderstanding of uncertain and unscientific terminology.

Finally, ethnologists presently in the field can benefit from the now sharpened alertness to significant details in routine data concerning territory, property, values, and designations of group identity both in the interest of increasing knowledge for its own sake and in the event of future significance of the ethnologists' observations for the societies in question.

Part Four includes four essays, each specifically aimed at a discussion of critical issues in anthropology — theoretical and applied. Ward H. Goodenough in Chapter 17 draws upon his experience in anthropology and public service to point up the needs of government for behavioral scientists' advice, and the implications of this for both the profession and government (see Parsons and Goodenough, 1964). Laura Thompson, also one of the most experienced of applied anthropologists, discusses other related questions, for example, the possibility of developing a "clinical" anthropology; and she concludes that applied anthropology plays a major role in the development of the science.

PART FOUR

ON ISSUES AND ETHICS

Guillermo Bonfil Batalla's discursive essay on conservative thought in applied anthropology represents a line of opinion common in some North American critiques of the field and prevalent among anthropologists, political figures, and others outside the United States. He argues that much anthropological advice works against the national interest of the countries in which anthropologists work. Precisely this same issue — the influence of the anthropologist's existential situation on his conclusions and recommendations — is taken up again but with fewer polemics by Jacques Maquet in his brilliant essay on objectivity in anthropology. Maquet discusses the reevaluation of the discipline occasioned by the emergence of the new states of Africa and examines the epistemology or cognitive values of anthropology.

213

17

The Growing Demand for Behavioral Science in Government: Its Implications for Anthropology

WARD H. GOODENOUGH

My remarks this evening do not reflect much inside information on governmental activities and interests as they relate to the behavioral sciences. My connections with the federal government are slight. So when I speak of a growing demand for behavioral science in government, I am giving voice only to a personal impression.

Because many of our national and international problems reflect social, cultural, and psychological processes, at least some of our nation's top policy makers are concerned to get a clearer picture of the extent of hard knowledge in the behavioral sciences that might be applied to these prob-

"The Growing Demand for Behavioral Science in Government: Its Implications for Anthropology" by Ward H. Goodenough is reprinted from *Human Organization* 21:172–176, 1962, by permission of the author and publisher.

lems. They want honest assessments, not big sales pitches, so that they can see what scientific resources now exist and how these resources can best be improved by further support. A highly significant step toward the promotion of closer working relations between government and the behavioral sciences was the publication in *Science* of the report of a subpanel of the President's Science Advisory Committee, entitled "Strengthening the Behavioral Sciences" (Science Advisory Committee, 1962). The highest office in the land, on recommendation of its scientific council, has indorsed the proposition that the growth and development of the behavioral sciences is in the national interest and has invited attention to certain recommendations regarding the furthering of that development. Those who have been trying to promote more extended involvement of the behavioral sciences in the governmental operations for which they are appropriate have been giving strong moral support.

Assuming, then, that there is and will continue to be a growing demand for behavioral science in government, what are its implications for anthropology?

There are several kinds of questions that we as behavioral scientists may appropriately be asked by government officials. Each type of question offers a different challenge to us. It is incumbent upon us to take stock of ourselves in relation to each of these challenges, for how we deal with them may seriously affect the future of our science.

The first kind of question that we are asked may be illustrated thus: What are the things we must consider in formulating a workable civil defense program? This question concerns the classes of phenomena that should be taken into account to develop a policy or program relating to a problem. It can be answered satisfactorily insofar as the problems of civil defense can be meaningfully related to a general theory of human behavior. In the absence of a general theory, decisions as to what are relevant considerations must be made on an informed common-sense basis, and the behavioral scientist *qua* behavioral scientist has little immediately to offer. What he can offer, of course, given his inability to answer the questions posed, is a special research program aimed squarely at the problem. The hope is that a working theory of the problem can thus be formulated to serve until such time as general theory has caught up with it. In connection with civil defense, for example, the Disaster Research Group of the National Academy of Sciences-National Research Council has supported research of this sort.[1]

As for the second type of question, after officials have decided what are the classes of phenomena that they must take into account in developing a program or policy, they may ask behavioral scientists to indicate what is known about these phenomena. In connection with civil defense, to continue my example, they might ask,

What do scientists know about panic behavior? What are the conditions under which it occurs? Is existing knowledge of these conditions adequate to provide guiding principles for civil defense planning?

Here we are asked not to determine whether or not panic behavior should be taken into account, but to marshall what we know about it and translate our knowledge into operating principles that are applicable to the problem at hand. If our knowledge of the class of phenomena in question is insufficient, we may then be asked to determine the magnitude of research needed to correct this deficiency.

The third kind of question involves specific information about the actual settings in which applications are to be made, or are being made. Here answers require field study. We may know the conditions under which panic behavior occurs, but we cannot decide on how to meet the civil defense needs of any specific community until we have reliable information on its physical layout, the bottlenecks it presents for escape to places of safety, and so on. This is analogous to the problem of an agronomist, who cannot determine how to apply his general principles in order to improve the crop yields on a given farm until he has analyzed soil samples from that farm to see just what the specific conditions are to which he must apply his principles. When we are asked as behavioral scientists to assay the range of sentiments in the United States about a given issue or problem, we are being asked to supply reliable information on the actual conditions to which political or other kinds of decisions are going to apply. The same, of course, is true when anthropologists are asked to provide information on the culture of a community whose economic development has become a matter of administrative concern. Another problem calling for specific information about concrete situations arises when an action program fails to go as expected. In community development projects, for example, anthropologists have been used as trouble shooters to find out what is wrong and why. Specific information is needed, again in connection with pilot projects, which seek to test the efficacy of alternative applications and to reveal unforeseen bugs in program designs. Much of the government's research needs has to do with some form of intelligence gathering that calls for the behavioral scientist's professional skills in data collection and interpretation.

Obviously, we are challenged by all three kinds of questions. I submit, moreover, that the challenge in each instance is good for us. What it implies for behavioral disciplines other than anthropology, I cannot, of course, say. But I do have a few thoughts about its implications for cultural anthropology.

The first kind of question that we are asked forces us to face our general theoretical shortcomings. Some years ago, for example, I was asked to prepare a manual for agents of social and economic development in which I was to take up the "human" considerations affecting the course of development. For each of these considerations I was then to go on to answer the second type of question, indicating what was known and formulating guiding principles for its application. The book was to be done in two years. It is now ten years later, and I am only just finishing it. Nor does it come very close to achieving its original purpose. After I started to look over the literature ten years ago, it soon became evident that the book could not be written in the absence of a general theory of social and cultural change, and no theory worthy of the name existed. Here and there a beginning towards the construction of such a theory had been made in connection with acculturation and nativistic movements. There were Margaret Mead's insightful application of anthropological wisdom to development problems (Mead, 1955) and Spicer's valuable casebook (1952). But by and large, what passed for theory did not come fully to grips with the fact that men are the significant actors in the change process. It did not relate private motives to public values in any systematic way, or either of these to customs and institutions. We anthropologists were talking about the systemic integration of customs and the consequent chain-effect of change, but we had no developed theory of how customs are actually integrated systemically. There were no conceptual tools that would indicate how to go about predicting the course that a chain reaction to a particular change would follow in a given case. Since then, some useful works have appeared, notable among them Homer Barnett's important book on innovation (1953) and, more recently, Erasmus's intriguing contribution toward a theory of economic motivation in change (1961). Of course, I hope that my own efforts will have helped to carry things along as well (1963).

The point is that as the government demand for behavioral science increases, we are going to find ourselves forced more and more to face major theoretical issues squarely. For us in anthropology this can be highly embarrassing, but in the long run it can only be a blessing. When we stop to consider that we have not yet operationally defined any of the major concepts with which we deal in our research — such as custom, culture, status, role, institution, religion, etc. — we can only welcome our being asked questions that compel us to try to do so. As of now, I think that we must admit that there are few questions of the first type that we are likely to be asked for which there is much in the way of established general theory. What we have are good beginnings, broad outlines suggestive of the rich and complex interrelationships of human phenomena to guide our research, but little beyond them.

As for the second type of question — what do anthropologists know about specific subject matters — are we much better equipped? We can point to the existence of all kinds of cultural and social phenomena of which the nonanthropologist has never heard. A botanist can point to the existence of many out-of-the-way species of plant of which the layman is ignorant, too. But what bodies of verified knowledge do we have about the phenomena we have recorded? Have we established the conditions under which different kinds of descent groups emerge, to take an area where we have concentrated a lot of our scientific attention? In part, perhaps. What can we say about the functions of sorcery, about the conditions promoting concern with witches, about the ways in which culture is effectively transmitted, about the extent to which values are shared cross-culturally, about the status of women under polygyny and monogamy, to name a few of the subjects that we anthropologists have debated?

We have accumulated a great deal of information about specific societies, essential spadework for the development of a cultural science. Out of our ethnographic experiences we have demonstrated the inadequacy and error of many behavioral hypotheses and we have formulated many new ones. But only occasionally have we taken the next step and systematically reviewed the ethnographic evidence with an eye to validating our hypotheses or to isolating and defining general social and cultural processes, distinctive natural human syndromes, as objects for further study. We can point to Murdock's efforts in kinship and kingroups (1949), to Eisenstadt's work on age grading (1956), to Hoebel's study of law (1954), and to Wallace's extensive review of the literature that led him to isolate the revitalization movement as a distinctive and widespread syndrome in human affairs (1956). There is the work of Whiting and Child on theories of disease (1953), Swanson on religious beliefs (1960), and Roberts investigation of games (Roberts and Sutton-Smith, 1962). But the list is not very long, and the work done has been largely exploratory. We are quickly forced to go back two generations to the work of such men as Frazer (1890), van Gennep (1960), and Westermarck (1891), many of whose concepts are alive today only because no one has bothered to carry on where they made a start.

Obviously, careful comparative study is essential in order to develop bodies of verified knowledge concerning human phenomena. The practical obstacles to such study are immense. But how many of us have seriously tried to take advantage of the one major facility that has been developed to overcome some of these obstacles, The Human Relations Area Files? Even more important, how many of us have been sufficiently concerned about the matter to try to promote improvements in the files or to develop additional facilities for comparative study? We cannot get very far with the questions we are likely to be asked if we do not seriously face up to how we are to break away from anecdote and make the development of a rigorous comparative method possible. The White House report, "Strengthening the Behavioral Sciences" (Science Advisory Committee, 1962), specifically recommends that a study group be appointed to look into the whole problem of information on societies other than our own with a view to improving the present facilities for comparative study. Until these facilities are improved and used, most of our answers must be expressions of "informed opinion" rather than deductions from verified knowledge.

When we come to the third and last type of question, we feel much more confident. One thing we do know how to do is to get reasonably reliable information about the cultures of specific societies. Much of our work as applied anthropologists, moreover, has been of the intelligence-gathering sort. Our appeals to the Agency for International Development and the Peace Corps for anthropological research in connection with community development have this intelligence-gathering function primarily in mind, especially as it relates to program planning, pilot projects, and program evaluation. Although it is doubtful that once we have the relevant cultural information we will always know how best to use it, in trying to use it we can learn much. Nor does the record lack instances in which cultural knowledge has been successfully used to accomplish objectives that would have been unattainable without it. The Vicos project in Peru is currently a very visible example (Holmberg, 1960; see also Chapters 6 and 7). The Army is another potential market for the ethnographic skills of anthropologists. The successful conduct of modern guerilla warfare obviously requires both extensive and intensive ethnographic intelliegnce. At present, it is impossible to say what requests, if any, for our ethnographic services may emerge from governmental agencies, but there are straws in the wind suggesting that we may be called upon. If this should happen, how are we to respond?

I do not have an accurate count, but I doubt that the number of professionally trained ethnographers in this country exceeds three hundred. When we consider the increased demand for cultural anthropologists by universities and colleges in the past two years, it is clear that in the foreseeable future government agencies will be unable, without a general mobilization order, to recruit more than a handful, at most, of competent ethnographers. Although we have the skills to provide answers to some of the questions that we may be asked, we are "out of stock" in trained personnel.

There is, I feel, only one solution to this problem. It is to establish special training programs with the object of producing people who are not anthropological scholars in the academic sense, but who are able to do competent ethnography and who have some background in the cultural and psychological aspects of social process. A master of science program in practical ethnography suggests the sort of thing I have in mind. Agencies that feel a need for anthropological skills could send some of their own personnel for a year or two of training under such a program. What I have in mind, in fact, is something akin to the Summer Institutes of Linguistics, where missionaries are trained to do technically competent descriptive linguistics. I see no reason why those who already work in government agencies and who have overseas assignments that require close collaboration with the common people in underdeveloped areas cannot be trained to do fairly reliable ethnography in much the same way.

Suppose that we were encouraged to undertake such a training program. It sounds all right in principle; but just what would we teach? What kind of ethnography has the greatest utility for people engaged in overseas action programs that require the cooperation of local populations in order to succeed? Those who lack experience with cultural anthropology and its applications tend, I think, to assume that what they need is information on a community's conditions; its standard of living, technological resources, customary recipes for getting things done. The degree to which these fail to fit the community's needs as defined by a program's objectives indicates what must be changed in order to achieve those objectives. From this point of view, intelligence is needed in order to know what must be changed. Those with experience, however, know that this is an entirely inadequate view. It is essential to know *how* things *can* be changed. What is vital is not the material state of affairs that characterizes a community as a more-or-less self-contained system, but the ideas and values of the people in the community. The kind of ethnography needed is one that seeks to isolate and describe the categories in whose terms the local people perceive their material and social world, the values they place upon the things they perceive, their aspirations for themselves, the principles by which they construct procedures for getting things done, all of the things, in short, that we must attribute to their heads and hearts in order to make sense of what they do. A description of a culture, in this sense of that term, is a statement of what one has to know in order to understand events in a community as its members understand them and to conduct oneself in it in a way that they will accept as meeting their standards for themselves. It is vital to know these things if one is to enlist people's cooperation in economic development or in guerilla warfare, and if one is to assess reliably the way in which people are likely to respond to changed conditions in the future.

The analogy with descriptive linguistics is clear. I can describe all sorts of things about a language without ever telling you what you have to know in order to generate meaningful utterances in it and understand the utterances of others, even when you have never heard those particular utterances before. Most ethnography in the past has been largely of this inadequate sort. Language descriptions that tell a person what he needs to know in order to speak the language effectively represent the sort of thing that practically useful ethnography has to aim at. What we need are descriptions that tell us how to live and act a culture.

These are things that the members of the Society for Applied Anthropology know very well. I mention them in order to invite thought about how we are to train people to learn and describe culture in this sense of the term. We have to do more than just tell them to go live with the people they are studying, to take censuses, genealogies and other inventories, to participate in as many activities as they can, to try to learn the language, to get a good informant, and to keep notes on it all. For years I have been struck by the answers budding anthropologists give on grant application forms to the question about "methods to be followed in your research." The answer hardly ever varies, stating,

> I will employ the usual anthropological methods of participant observation, intensive interview, census taking, etc.

This in effect states that the approach to be followed is about the same as the one that a highly competent journalist would use. Most discussions of method amount to the swapping of tactical gimmicks for eliciting certain types of information that have proved useful in circumscribed situations. A course in ethnographic method is not unlike a course in how to keep order in a fifth grade classroom. The wisdom of experience has its place, of course. Indeed, I would be the last to disparage it, but it does not constitute a scientific method.

The essentially journalistic approach to ethnography that we have tended to follow in the past has produced much crucial information of practical value. But it falls short of supplying the kind of ethnographic intelligence that is often needed in action situations. So, also, does the approach to ethnography exemplified by some members of the sociological school of anthropologists, who describe what they observe in terms of a general theoretical system of a logico-deductive sort, using the community under study to exemplify their ability to apply the concepts of their *a priori* frame, and to demonstrate that, whatever one studies, it is possible to find a way of interpreting it so as to make it appear that in some respects it contributes to the continuity of the community. Both practically and scientifically, the value of such exercises is dubious. All kinds of designs can be constructed for describing what goes on in a community. The validity of a particular design, however, is established when it enables one to interpret events as others in the community interpret them and to act in a way that others in the community accept as their own. The problem of ethnographic method is to develop explicit procedures by which we can inductively formulate a design for a given community that will meet this test. Some ethnographers have succeeded in developing designs or models of a people's culture, or part of it, that meet this test, but they have done so intuitively without making their inductive operations explicit for replication. All men do, in fact, learn cultures. The problem of ethnographic method is to objectivize the steps by which we learn them, converting the haphazard subjective process into a set of explicit procedures by which inductively to formulate a valid model or design of a society's culture. The journalistic approach, as I have called it — with the consequent disparaging view of ethnography as "mere description" without scientific interest as such — has generally failed to produce cultural descriptions of either high scientific merit or of more than limited practical value. Descriptive ethnography must be faced as posing a genuine scientific problem, calling for the development of a rigorous methodology for inductively oriented model construction. There is nothing "mere" about good cultural description.

To illustrate, let us consider one of the things that A.I.D. wants very much to get from anthropologists, namely good accounts of the local codes of manners and etiquette, the kinds of roles that people can play in dealing with one another, and the acts and avoidances symbolic of these roles. What they want, so to speak, is a "dictionary" and "grammar" of social conduct. They search the ethnographic literature for anything like this in vain. But suppose their need should stimulate us to face up to the problems involved and to develop ethnographic method so that the preparation of grammars and dictionaries of this sort becomes routine. This would represent a major "break-through" in anthropological science.

It would appear, then, that if we are effectively to fill our government's need for our ethnographic skills by developing training programs in practical ethnography, we are again challenged to develop methods of descriptive ethnography capable of producing the kind of ethnographic intelligence that is practically most needed. A new generation of anthropologists is fortunately beginning to formalize methods that will better enable us to provide this kind of ethnography. I am confident, therefore, that a suitable curriculum for a master of science degree in practical ethnography can be devised. Having to devise it will help make us even more concerned with problems of inductive method, and this in turn will help us to operationalize our concepts.

In emphasizing the challenges that a government demand for behavioral science poses for anthropology, it is easy to make it appear that anthropology has little to offer of a practical nature. Actually, of course, it has much to offer. It would be unfair, moreover, to belittle our past achievements in laying the foundations for a general science of man. We have come a long way in the past hundred years, clearing a vast territory of its dense growth of misconception and ethnocentric bias. We have learned a lot about the resources of the territory we have cleared. We have gathered many of its wild fruits as we cleared. We have started a few trial gardens, here and there, and we have reaped a few small, promising harvests. But we have yet to start cultivating on a large scale. That, it seems to me, is a fair estimate of where we stand as an emerging science.

It is in the light of this estimate that we must evaluate what the growing demand for behavioral science in government implies for the future of our discipline. In my opinion, its implications are positive. Rather than being diverted from the paths of "pure" science, we will be stimulated to take the next necessary steps toward formalizing our methods, broadening the scope of what we know, and building toward an empirically based general theory of socially learned, human behavior.

NOTES

1. See the series of fifteen Disaster Studies published to date by the National Academy of Sciences-National Research Council.

18

Is Applied Anthropology
Helping to Develop
A Science of Man?

LAURA THOMPSON

INTRODUCTION

In his review of Mühlmann's collection of theoretical essays, Honig-mann (1963) calls attention to the current peak of brilliance in cultural anthropology. We have but to pause a moment to note the high caliber and originality of much work by anthropologists today. This applies not only to cultural anthropology but to virtually all fields of the discipline:

"Is Applied Anthropology Helping to Develop a Science of Man?" by Laura Thompson is reprinted from *Human Organization* 24:277–287, 1965, by permission of the author and publisher. A short version of this paper was presented at the Twenty-third Annual Meeting of the Society for Applied Anthropology in San Juan, Puerto Rico, March 25, 1964.

human genetics, linguistics, archaeology, ethnography, and psychiatric anthropology, for example. Applied anthropologists, working at a fast pace amid the complexities of the midcentury, may not fully appreciate the extent to which our specialty is involved in the current productive period.

This paper is concerned with one phase of recent developments in applied anthropology. I shall consider briefly whether applied anthropology is playing a role in helping to develop a science of man. I shall not discuss whether a science of man is emerging since this question has been treated at length elsewhere (Thompson, 1961). Assuming that such a science is imminent, the question here is: What if any role is applied anthropology playing in the birth process?

Many anthropologists take the position that applied anthropology has little if anything to contribute to theoretical anthropology. As late as 1959 Kroeber wrote:

> I consider the development of fundamental science, whether of human relations or of anything else, a different matter from the solution of pragmatic problems. The practical problems can no doubt be solved more wisely if there exists genuine science to draw on. But the science as science will not develop better or faster for having its pursuit mixed with problems of application (1959:291).

Shortly before his death Clyde Kluckhohn told me that he found it virtually impossible to interest his best students in a career in applied anthropology. They simply did not regard this subdivision of the discipline as one worthy of their attention. Several very good government jobs in this field went begging, he said, because these students could not be persuaded to accept them (see Chapter 17, Goodenough).

In view of these facts and assumptions an attempt to clarify certain aspects of the role of applied anthropology in today's world would seem timely.

APPLIED ANTHROPOLOGY: CLINICAL VERSUS ENGINEERING TYPES

There is considerable agreement among social scientists that two contrasting schools of applied social science have emerged recently. Gouldner (1956) calls these the engineering type and the clinical type.[1] He finds these types represented not only among applied sociologists but also among applied anthropologists. In this paper I shall not discuss applied anthropology as a whole but only that subdivision of the discipline which falls within the category of clinical anthropology.

Clinical social scientists may be distinguished from the engineering type in terms of role. From this standpoint a clinical anthropologist, as the term is used here, interprets his role in relation to that of his client, whether the client be an administrator or a citizen group, as one of scrupulously refraining from the decision-making function and leaving that function to the client. The clinical anthropologist's role is seen as one of providing the client with decision-making tools, including relevant information concerning the probable consequences of alternate possible choices. Since this role requires that the clinician predict the probable behavior of the group under consideration from a long-range viewpoint under alternate pressures, including those implemented to induce change, the clinical anthropologist must understand the group in an explanatory way, including the interrelationships between all variable sets operating significantly in the group's situation relevant to the prediction problem.

By contrast, the role of the engineering anthropologist, from this viewpoint, involves formulating specific recommendations for his client regarding the implementation of specific policy objectives, or even regarding policy and other objectives as such. The engineering role may also involve controlling, guiding, and accelerating adaptive change (Richardson, 1962:61). While these roles require the engineering anthropologist to be cognizant of the group's system of interpersonal relations, and even in certain cases of its ideology (Shepard and Blake, 1962) and economic resources (Dobyns, Monge, and Vasquez, 1962), they do not prevent him from directly intervening in the lives of community members and from attempting directly to guide or change the pace of culture change processes in directions he or his client consider appropriate.

By the term clinical anthropology, in sum, I refer to projects in applied anthropology which attempt to investigate, by means of a scientific approach, whole human groups as organismic units in the context of their ongoing, constantly changing life situations, for purposes of prediction. The life situational approach of the clinical anthropologist forces him to experiment with a multilevel methodology reflecting the multidimensional nature of the real life situations he is trying to elucidate. I shall try to clarify the point further in the following pages.

STATEMENT OF THE THESIS

Since space is limited, the discussion will focus on five propositions regarding the successful practice of clinical anthropology. Although obviously no single point is unique to applied anthropology, my thesis is that, considered as a whole, they reveal and illuminate the unique, positive role which clinical anthropology is currently playing in directly helping to develop a science of man.

(1) The practice of professional applied anthropology forces the anthropologist to concentrate on dynamic, real life problematic situations rather than on academic or pure research problems.

(2) The problematic situations with which applied anthropologists concern themselves relate primarily to human groups rather than to human individuals.

(3) Such group problematic situations are usually critical ones with human lives and welfare at stake, in urgent need of resolution within relatively fixed limitations of time, space, and available resources. Hence the conscientious clinician is motivated to succeed in his endeavor over and above the challenge afforded by projects of a more orthodox, academic type.

(4) Resolution of such problematic situations, translated into scientific problems, demands of the investigator demonstrable skills in forecasting probable changes and future trends in human group behavior under certain limiting conditions and potentialities. The development of such predictive skills depends not only on professional training and experience but also and crucially on the use of a mature scientific approach involving refinements in theory, method, and professional role.

(5) Success in the practice of applied anthropology involving predictive skills is measured in the long run by the empirical test, not by consensus of professional colleagues, administrators' preferences and prejudices, political expediency, or any other nonscientific criterion. In turn the empirical test may serve as a corrective to theory and a spur to greater refinement of method.

I shall discuss briefly each of these propositions in turn.

FROM THE STUDY OF CULTURE CONTACT
TO THAT OF CULTURAL CHANGE

(1) The practice of professional applied anthropology forces the anthropologist to concentrate on dynamic real life problematic situations rather than on academic or pure research problems.

A good deal has been written about the relation between the rise of applied anthropology and the shift in focus in anthropology from culture contact to culture change (Peattie, 1958:4–8). Nevertheless, since the shift is critical to the development of my thesis, I shall dwell on a few of its salient features.

The emphasis of Keesing, one of the earliest administrative anthropologists, on problems of acculturation (Keesing, 1934, 1945, and 1953; and Siegel, 1955) compared to that of most earlier anthropologists may serve to illustrate the point. Indeed, obviously a rigid, mechanical approach toward the diffusion and linkage of culture traits and trait complexes, often treated out of context, grew primarily out of an academic, museum-oriented or library-oriented study of cultural phenomena, especially material culture, detached from the real life situations and problems of the peoples concerned. The term "culture carriers," still applied occasionally to human groups manifesting a particular culture in their behavioral habits, well expresses the essentially static, sum-total, non-biological, nonpsychological model of culture which characterized many anthropologists both in Europe and in the Americas half a century ago and carries over to some extent today.[2]

As soon as applied anthropologists began to work on the actual life problems of real people we found that we had to change our models of the group and its culture from static to dynamic ones in environmental context in keeping with the changing clinical "problematic situations" that required elucidation. This change in conceptual approach characterizes most applied social science research, according to Gouldner (1956: 171).

CHANGE OF PERSPECTIVE TOWARD THE UNIT OF RESEARCH

A situational approach, with historical as well as ecological dimensions, developed by Bronislaw Malinowski while he was attempting to deal scientifically with problems of culture change and applied anthropology in Africa (Malinowski, 1945), illustrates the point. The model of a cultural institution which Malinowski formulated in his later years (Malinowski, 1944, Ch. 6) may profitably be contrasted to Radcliffe-Brown's paradigm of a social system. In Radcliffe-Brown's model the investigator seeks out and focuses on a so-called natural system in the Durkheimian sense by attempting to isolate it conceptually and to ignore everything else in the universe as environment (Radcliffe-Brown, 1957; M. N. Srinivas, 1958). He attempts to study the social event so conceived as though it were a reality external to him. On the other hand, the investigator using Malinowski's model in the field must explicitly observe, describe, and relate to the behavior of the human group (i.e., the personnel of the institution) relevant aspects of the environment in their natural context. He does not attempt artificially to separate social relations or structures of the human group under consideration from either the world of nature with which it is transacting or from its human components as human organisms.

Comparing these approaches we gain insight as to why Radcliffe-Brown formally eschewed applied anthropology (Radcliffe-Brown, 1930: 267–280; see also Evans-Pritchard, 1946:92–98), while Malinowski fostered and encouraged it (Malinowski, 1940). Radcliffe-Brown's model is a construct far removed from the many-faceted everyday problematic situations with which real people living out their lives must cope, and removed from the practical problems they must resolve more or less successfully or lose their identity as a human group (Nadel, 1957:158). Malinowski's model, also a construct, of course, is one which reflects and includes, rather than obscures, ignores and excludes, the multidimensional nature of the problems with which the successful clinical anthropologist must deal. Indeed, despite the fact that Radcliffe-Brown had worked in the field himself, his theoretical and methodological tools seem to have been fashioned primarily to solve academic problems. Those of Malinowski, on the other hand, were sharpened operationally during the course of his professional lifetime to cope successfully with real life (in the clinical sense) problems on a scientific basis. Thus it is no accident that Goodenough uses Malinowski's model of an institution in his general book on applied anthropology (Goodenough, 1963:347, f.n. 1).

When an anthropologist accepts a position on the staff of a local community administrator, whether the latter official be a community development project director, a public health or anti-poverty worker, a Peace Corps official, an educator, a mental health director, or a dependency group commissioner, he may attempt to project an academic type model of the community, small group, culture, or society under investigation. But a field administrator has constantly to deal with the group's actual problematic situations of every day experience, whether they be of community organization, poverty symptoms, schooling, housing, sickness, mental hygiene, crime, resources conservation or economic development. The applied anthropologist soon discovers that to do his job successfully he too must concern himself with these situations and tune in on the same wave-length, so to speak, as his objects of study including his client.

HOW TO DESIGN THE PROJECT SITUATIONALLY?

How to design this complex situation scientifically has, of course, presented the greatest obstacle to the development of clinical anthropology as well as other social science disciplines. For example, how shall we formulate the problem?

D. P. Sinha (Sinha, n.d.) shows, in a case study of Birhor resettlement, that the clinical problem may be approached fruitfully from at least three dimensions:

(1) as a practical problem of the tribal welfare administration of the Government of Birhor, India;
(2) as a problematic situation of the community of Birhor, before, during, and after resettlement; and
(3) as an analytical problem of scientific anthropolgy

Thus it appears that the clinical anthropologist may fruitfully perceive his problem from three different perspectives simultaneously: that of the administrator or client; that of the local community in time and space depth; and that of himself in the role of professional scientist.

Now, the question is how does he proceed with this three-prong perspective?

First, he must translate the community's changing problematic situation, including the client-administrator's practical problem, into a scientific problem (Thompson, 1963:354–355). The task requires that he extend his frame of reference to encompass all the variables relevant to the group's problematic situation. If necessary he may carry out a pilot field project in order to collect sufficient empirical data about the group so that he can formulate a heuristic working hypothesis on the basis of the facts, to be verified by subsequent field research (Little, 1963:367). Since the group under consideration is involved with the limitations and potentials of its bio-physical environment, the anthropologist may not ignore these aspects of the environment nor slight them. Neither may he leave out the group's history, demography, social structure, psychology, core values, or any other dimension of the whole relevant to the problematic situation with which the community is critically concerned.

Then he must select the significant unit of research in relation to the scientific problem. He must seek out, adapt, or develop a dynamic, multidimensional model of his research unit which reflects the existing, changing realities of the group under consideration. Thus, to resolve the scientific problem successfully, with the approach and methods of science, the investigator is forced by the action aspects of the experiment, to consider actual problematic situations of living, ongoing human groups, not merely academic problems.[3]

ROLE OF THE CLINICAL ANTHROPOLOGIST

Finally, if the clinical anthropologist is to operate professionally in the role of an applied scientist he may never under any circumstances, as a scientist, assume an administrative role or accept the position of an administrator-client. As Rapoport (1963; also Anon, 1954) has noted, policy and action, frequently the dominant preoccupation of the subjects as well as the clients of the applied anthropologist, imply value decisions. The applied anthropologist must assiduously avoid commitments to values other than those of the scientific method and translate his scientific findings in a value-neutral framework into specific action alternatives.

This means that in his professional role, the applied clinical anthropologist must strive to resist all pressures, whether hidden or overt, to assume responsibility for the selection, from his findings, of appropriate alternatives and for the implementation of a client-selected course of action. In other words, his role of doctor of society should be limited to that of diagnosis.[4]

On the other hand, it is generally accepted in the profession of applied anthropology that

> the ideal of presenting all possible alternatives and then permitting an unrestricted selection fails to take into account the realities of the socio-political constraints and the biases of the suggester (Barnett, 1958; see also Keesing, 1945:84–85 and Nadel, 1957:54–55).

I take the position, however, that in the emerging profession of applied scientific anthropology, a firm statement of the professional role of the applied scientist, in contradistinction to that of the administrator-client, is imperative. The Tanganyika experiment (Brown and Hutt, 1935) and others indicate that such a distinction is not impossible. Moreover, only within such a strict division of labor can the "natural experiment," emerge (Brown and Hutt, 1935:xvii, xviii, 4, and Ch. 4).

A FRESH LOOK AT ACTION RESEARCH

Within this context the action research methodology frequently recommended as an efficient and economical method of implementing social change, and the role of the applied anthropologist in action research programs, should be reexamined and clarified. Equipped with specialized knowledge of certain aspects of the community's problematic situation, especially in regard to the finding of modern science concerning the history of the community, its relation to the larger regional, national, and world scene, and the extensiveness of and demand for its resources, the applied anthropologist may qualify as an expert. Certain anthropologists who were engaged by American Indian tribes to undertake basic research and to testify in Indian Claims Commission cases (Macgregor, 1955), did so qualify and, by supplying basic data relevant to the questions at issue, helped to win favorable legal judgments for the tribes. It is in such a role that the anthropologists may be best qualified to function with a group of community members who have organized themselves as an action research team. He may also function with team leaders in the delicate role of catalyst of group planning and action potentialities (Kimball, Pearsall, and Bliss, 1954:5–8). It would not seem appropriate, according to the present thesis, however, for the applied anthropologist in cooperation with the people to be affected to set the goals of community action in an action situation, either on a trial basis or by advance planning.[5] He may train and even supervise volunteers in special skills, as Leighton did young Japanese volunteers in the Poston WRA center, for example (Leighton, 1945:375–378). But he should scrupulously refrain from actually setting goals for the group either overtly or covertly.

SHIFT IN FOCUS FROM INDIVIDUAL TO GROUP

(2) The problematic situations with which applied anthropologists concern themselves relate primarily to human groups rather than to human individuals.

This basic point is often overlooked. Many of the disciplines which focus on man, such as medicine, psychology, psychiatry, psychoanalysis, human development, learning theory, and social work, developed their approaches by concentrating primarily on the individual rather than the group. By this I mean that the scientific problems for whose solution their traditional concepts and methods have been developed are geared to the individual as the significant unit of research. Realization of the importance of the group has come late, if at all, to most investigators in these disciplines. A change of focus from individual to group, or an extension of the research unit to include the group or aspects of it, patently has been difficult.

A certain success in this direction was achieved by Durkheim and his followers. But we should not forget that, in seeking to isolate sociological events conceptually from the rest of the universe for purposes of analysis, and to discover sociological explanations for these events which may be used as a basis for formulating sociological laws of universal validity, Durkheim and his followers removed their models from their clinical contexts. Thus their usefulness in resolving practical problems was greatly reduced. Goldenweiser's critique of this school of thought, based on anthropological field findings, suggests that it exaggerates the importance of social factors while underrating the role of nature in everyday life (Goldenweiser, 1922:371–381). Thus he points out a pitfall to be avoided in clinical anthropology.

When a measure of success in understanding group behavior has been achieved within the traditionally individual-oriented disciplines, as in social psychology, social psychiatry, culture and personality approaches, group work and community development, it has usually involved the borrowing of approaches, concepts, and methods from one or more of the disciplines which focus traditionally on the group. Examples of such donor disciples are cultural anthropology, certain schools of sociology, Gestalt psychology, and ecology.

ANTHROPOLOGY TRADITIONALLY STRESSES THE GROUP

Anthropology is one of the disciplines focusing on man which has grown out of an interest in understanding primarily whole group phenomena such as are expressed, for example, in the concepts of culture, race, community, society, and small group. With anthropologists, interest in the individual has come late and principally as a component of the group, that is, as a clue to the nature and dynamics of the group (Sapir, 1949:569–577).

Since *Homo sapiens* is a group species, progress toward developing a science of mankind seems to depend on the development of heuristic operational hypotheses, concepts, and methods which focus primarily on whole groups. Especially does the type of conditional prediction of change and future trends, involved in the successful solution of every problem in clinical anthropology, necessitate forecasting probable group behavior in a changing situation under certain stimuli such as individual leaders in a certain group context may provide (Mead, 1964:Ch. 8, 233–234; and Little, 1963:367) but not the behavior of every separate individual member. The crucial prediction problem in clinical anthropology is discussed in section 4.

Here we note that clinical anthropologists, because of the nature of the practical problems with which their clients are concerned, have to concentrate on whole human groups. Moreover, since a situational approach which attempts to take into consideration all relevant factors of the problem including the group's effective environment (Allee, 1949:1), is indispensable to forecasting the probable behavior of the group under certain changing conditions, clinical anthropologists have had to develop dynamic operational models adequate to the complex phenomena involved.

SEARCH FOR AN ADEQUATE MODEL OF THE COMMUNITY

Realization that the smallest unit of research adequate to the solution of such changing group behavior problems is the changing local community or breeding population in effective environmental context has come slowly through trial and error (Hockett and Ascher, 1964:136). First, the difference between, and noninterchangeability of, the concepts of culture and society had to be spelled out. This was effectively done by Kluckhohn and Kelly (1945:78–106), etc. The role of the little local community, long the object of research by field anthropologists seeking to understand cultural phenomena, had to be formulated as object and sample (see Arensberg, 1961; Arensberg and Kimball, 1965; and Redfield, 1955). The role of the near isolated local population transacting with an evolving ecosystem had to be investigated by means of several disciplines, including ecology, geography, demography, human genetics, and anthropology (Fosberg, 1963). And finally a dynamic multilevel model of a community undergoing change under pressure had to be produced — a model which afforded a niche for all aspects of the change process involved in the clinical prediction of the probable behavior of the group under certain conditions.

From an operational standpoint the model had to include both an ecological dimension and a psychic dimension, as well as dimensions to accommodate descriptions in depth of the community viewed as a social system, as a breeding population, and as a symbol-creating and symbol-transmitting unit.

An example is afforded by the model of a local community under strong externally instigated pressures to change developed experimentally by the research staff of the Indian Education, Personality and Administration project, in order to solve a problem in clinical anthropology. In this case the key relationship activating change is conceived as that between contact agents belonging to two quite different community systems. These were the local community system under observation *in situ* and the intrusive community system, represented by agents of purposive change who are displaced from their native habitat. According to this model, reflecting a purposive acculturation situation wherein the agents from the intrusive system are seeking aggressively to change, and in certain ways to displace, the local system, the key influences are represented as at the points of contact between two juxtaposed psychosomatic and symbolic sets — the local set and the intrusive set. An attempt is made to represent this view of the contact situation diagrammatically in Figure 3.[6]

The multilevel model depicting variable sets involved when the behavior of the members of a local community is changing under pressures from missionaries and other agents representing an alien or exotic cultural community may have certain advantages as a field tool. Its twelve variable systems reflect the complex field situation operationally and attempt to show their interrelations as experienced by human components of the two communities involved. The model contains a niche for findings derived by means of techniques from many disciplines (e.g., ecology, social anthropology, genetics and physical anthropology, linguistics and the humanities, psychology and psychiatry) used simultaneously on a single unit of research; and it focuses on the local community (viewed as a population in environmental context) as the primary significant unit of research in this type of scientific investigation.

Transactive processes within each community system, resulting from either externally (cross-cultural) instigated pressures or internally (intra-community) derived stresses are represented by two-way arrows. Contacts between the two supersystems in contact as represented by individual agents (each viewed as a psychosomatic-symbolic system reflecting the culture of his community idiosyncratically, including its core value system) are shown by two-way dotted line arrows. The model obviously depicts several levels of abstraction but it focuses the central inner covert position of the core value system as the most stable set of variables reflected in the structure of each of the other five systems and in the structure of the community supersystem as a whole. This major finding

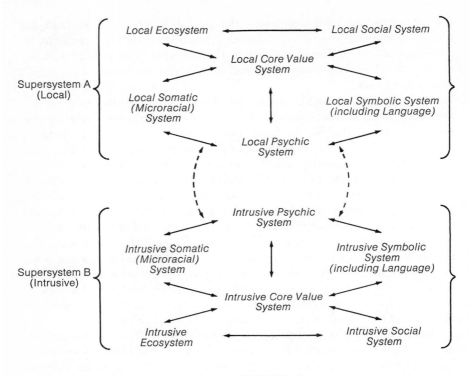

FIGURE 3

Model of Major Variable Systems in Contact Situation
Between Two Community Supersystems: A) Local and B) Intrusive

of the project (Thompson, 1951:183) is being validated by subsequent research (Ablon, 1964:296–304).

In sum, it is suggested that insofar as the problems with which clinical anthropologists concern themselves involve whole human group problematic situations, and insofar as such problems may be resolved successfully by means of a sharpening of theoretical and methodological field tools relating to whole groups, applied anthropology is helping in a critical manner to develop a science of man.

(3) Such group problematic situations usually are critical ones with human lives and human welfare at stake, in urgent need of resolution within relatively fixed limitations of time, space, and available resources. Hence the conscientious clinician is motivated to succeed in his endeavor over and above the challenge afforded by projects of a more orthodox, academic type.

THE CULTURAL FACTOR IN A RAPIDLY CHANGING WORLD

We live in an age when rapid, critical social change characterizes most of the world's communities. The rise of scores of new nations since the war and concomitant changes in the balance of global political power may serve as one outward sign of this change. Life goes on and decisions are made. Are they to be made on the basis of the available facts and clinical relationships?

Probably the most crucial facts usually omitted today from decision-making considerations at all levels relate to the cultural factor. I refer to national and international deliberations including especially those concerning development and anti-poverty activities at home and in so-called underdeveloped nations, to military strategy, to treaty formulations, and to other fundamental aspects of war, cold or hot. So long as this situation is not remedied we find ourselves unable to forecast probable changes in the behavior of national groups undergoing change, including our own, and hence frequently surprised and frustrated by errors of judgment.

RESPONSIBILITY OF THE ANTHROPOLOGIST

Who shall supply the missing ingredient if not the anthropologist? By training and experience he is equipped to discover, describe, and relate cultural facts and processes to relevant contexts. Indeed, the anthropologist's central concern, his stock in trade, is generally considered to be culture, including the analysis of cultural change and conflict (Kroeber, 1953:361–362 and Mair, 1957:71). It is true that many of our theories, concepts, and methods at present are inadequate or barely adequate to the scope, depth, and subtleties, in terms of human lives, resources, and welfare, of the tasks we face. Regardless of how we delimit our problems and sharpen our tools, we tend to feel overwhelmed by the magnitude of the challenge in terms of the world's exploding billions, the urgency of the time factor, and the complexities of the historical, biological, physical, and cultural realities.

Nevertheless, probably never in the history of the discipline have anthropologists operated effectively in positions of such responsibility in human terms. But applied anthropologists, as well as others with heavy human group responsibilities (see Chapter 6, Holmberg) and Mayer and Associates, 1962), have noted that the very difficulties of the problems confronting applied anthropologists and other applied social scientists operate as a strong motivation to meet the challenge and overcome obstacles, to develop concepts, methods, and operations as the projects progress, to learn by doing, and to persevere until the task has been accomplished. Out of this work, which seems at times to verge on dedication

(Tax, 1958), apparently are emerging the tools and the rules for the approaches and behavior which are moving clinical anthropologists and the discipline of applied anthropology in the direction of success as an applied science.

(4) Resolution of such problematic situations, translated into scientific problems, demands of the investigator demonstrable skills in forecasting probable changes and future trends in human group behavior under certain limiting conditions and potentialities. The development of such skills depends not only on professional training and experience but also and crucially on the use of a mature scientific approach involving refinements in theory, method, and professional role.

THE "IF . . . THEN" PREDICTION FORMULA

The "if . . . then" construction of a proposition which appropriately expresses the findings of a social scientist in the role of applied anthropologist, as contrasted to the role of administrator or client group, always embodies a prediction (Shepardson, 1962:748). According to this position, it is the function of the applied anthropologist to formulate his findings in a series of statements projecting the consequences, in terms of community action, to be expected as a result of the implementation of several policy and program alternatives (Barnett, 1963:382–383). He would aim to indicate to the administrator or client group the implications of alternative policies and programs so that the administrator or other decision-maker might make an informed choice between them (Mair, 1957:15).

Keesing was one of the first anthropologists to appreciate the importance of this mandate for professional applied anthropologists and to insist on its usefulness as an indispensable means of protecting the anthropologist in the delicate political situation engendered by his employment by a government or other client agency. Illustrations of the "if . . . then" construction as used by anthropologists may be found in Keesing's work as well as that of Elkin, Firth, Fischer, Joseph and Murray, Spindler, Thompson and others (Keesing, 1945:299–300; Elkin, 1964:114; Firth, 1936:416–417; 589–599; Fischer, 1963:528; Spindler, 1963:257; Joseph and Murray, 1951:315, 322, 325; Thompson, 1951:167). Their infrequency in the professional literature should, however, be noted.

Use of this formula for embodying the findings of the anthropologist insures that responsibility for policy and program decisions will fall on the client and not on the anthropologist. The latter is thus free to operate in a situation which protects his role as a scientist and fosters his objectivity. It also reduces the importance of the problem of the professional ethics of the applied anthropologist.

CASE OF THE PACIFIC TRUST TERRITORY

Barnett (1956, Chs. 3 and 4) has shown how difficult it is, under certain field conditions as, for instance, those operating in the Pacific Trust Territory, to maintain a strict division of labor between anthropologist and administrator, even though their roles are formally spelled out. Here the District and Staff Anthropologists' work assignment was stated as follows:

> In most general terms . . . the Staff Anthropologist's duties are, either directly or indirectly, to organize and conduct research in the field and to maintain professional relations with outside specialists interested in research in the Territory. The District Anthropologist engages in research and reports to his District Administrator on the latter's authorization or on the request of the High Commissioner. His special obligation is to know the native language and customs of his district. The Staff Anthropologist's responsibilities in this respect are more generalized since they cover the Territory as a whole. Both specialists are regarded as technical experts, and as such they are expected to function as impartial intermediaries between the administration and the Micronesians. Neither has executive status and the value of both lies in their objectivity and in their abstention from policy determination and implementation. As experts on Micronesian attitudes and behaviors, they are expected to devise and recommend techniques to accomplish the objectives settled upon by the administration. In short, they are responsible for means, not ends (Barnett, 1956:87–88).

Despite this carefully worded professional charter it is reported that persistent and often unwitting attempts on the part of administrators occurred to maneuver the anthropologists into a position of endorsing and advocating goals or ends to be sought (Barnett, 1956:129).

Barnett (1956:129–130) clearly points out that this charter does not relieve anthropologists of responsibility but rather places on them a different kind of responsibility, namely the "unenviable responsibility of forecasting human behavior." Since in social science the ability to predict changing group behavior under certain describable conditions may be accepted as the measure of scientific maturity, success in applied anthropology actually should depend on skill as a mature scientist.

THE METHOD OF CLINICAL PREDICTION

It should be noted that predicting group behavior under certain conditions as a consequence of change, as practised by clinical anthropologists, usually does not depend *primarily* on statistical methods or extrapolation. It thus differs markedly from probability forecasting as usually worked out by sociologists, demographers, economists, and others. By contrast, the applied anthropologist usually employs a clinical method which is as yet inadequately understood. It is based on understanding in depth of the changing culture of a community in historical and geographic perspective, including the community's covert attitudes and implicit values (Kluckhohn, 1943). Frequently the method involves knowledge of the community's unconscious group personality or psychic system. It also demands a refined concept of culture as an emergent out of the past *with direction* into the future, and specification of an *activity* unit of analysis as significant in relation to the scientific problem. Goodenough attempts to explain the method which he calls "forecasting the course of change" in his *Cooperation in Change* (1963).

A FRUITFUL TRAINING GROUND IN SCIENTIFIC ANTHROPOLOGY

Thus the practice of clinical anthropology affords a much-needed training experience for anthropologists who are concerned with learning to predict group behavior clinically with the degree of precision required to resolve problems in applied anthropology. It should be noted that once a series of alternate "if . . . then" propositions concerning the behavior of a community are formally submitted to his client, the applied anthropologist is "on the spot," so to say. He is publicly committed. Implementation of any one predictive proposition by the client can afford, in the long run, a situation whereby the student may test his maturity as a scientist. It is the only field situation, I suspect, which affords an anthropologist this type of opportunity for professional growth through self-correction.

USES OF STUDIES IN CLINICAL ANTHROPOLOGY

(5) Success in the practice of applied anthropology involving predictive skills is measured in the long run by the empirical test, not by consensus of professional colleagues, administrators' prejudices, political expediency, or any other nonscientific criterion. In turn, the empirical test may serve as a corrective to theory and a spur to greater refinement of method.

During the early years when new and more adequate operational models were being developed to cope with complex problems that were challenging applied anthropologists, it was fashionable to assume that the findings of applied anthropologists "really didn't matter" since their work, far from being used, would probably be ignored. Speaking of the use of anthropology in the United Nations, Métraux stated in 1953 that, although anthropologists were employed in several capacities, very little attention was paid to their recommendations (Métraux, 1953:354–355). Without doubt such statements were based on facts.

However, now that several decades have elapsed since the publication of the first significant studies in applied anthropology, it may be rewarding to take a fresh look at the situation regarding application. For example, we note that twenty years after publication of the Leightons' classic study of Navaho health and medical problems, *The Navaho Door* (1944), is basic to the theory behind the administration's public health program on the Navaho Indian Reservation (Adair, 1964). Ten to twenty years after publication of studies by anthropologists regarding educational, mental health and administrative problems in Guam (Thompson, 1947) and the Pacific Trust Territory (Oliver, 1951) many of the findings have been used. Almost twenty years after the Indian Education, Personality and Administration project was officially terminated the volumes (Havinghurst and Neugarten, 1955; Joseph, Spicer, and Chesky, 1949; Kluckhohn and Leighton, 1946; Leighton and Kluckhohn, 1947; Leighton and Adair, 1965; Macgregor, 1946; Thompson, 1950; Thompson and Joseph, 1944; Thompson, 1951) reporting factual findings from the research are recommended reading for Indian Service trainees and reservation personnel. The action research methodology, introduced and taught to reservation personnel and administrators by the project staff (Thompson, 1950); is advocated by the Education Division of the Service as basic to both policy and program. Approaches and information acquired by teachers, school principals and administrators during the project's training seminar and field work have become basic to in-Service training programs for many years. At least one member of the Indian Service who was trained and apprenticed by the project staff has become an executive for Bureau headquarters where he is creatively implementing project findings. He writes:

> I fear my literary skill is not good enough to put into words the very strong feelings I have about the Indian Education Research project on which I was privileged to have a small part. My evaluation is based on the profound and beneficial impact this study and others have had directly on the kind and quality of the total Indian education program.
>
> It seems so perfectly obvious now that if any program is going to be effective the operating personnel must have an understanding of the recipients to be served. It is surprising how many people involved in work with Indians do not realize that most reservation Indians have a different set of values which motivates and directs their life activities. Public school officials with whom I work are puzzled at why children drop out of high school on an average of 50 percent or more than non-Indian children and say to me, "We treat them just the same as all other children. It is here for them if they just come and get it." Unfortunately, many Indian children do not just come and get it and for the basic reason that they and their parents have not yet realized the utilitarian value in what we call modern education.

It was through the study sponsored by the Bureau and the University of Chicago that I feel I gained a basic understanding of Indian people to the point that it has made a difference in whatever I have attempted to do in directing the educational process involving reservation Indian children (Pratt, 1962). . . .

It should also be noted that the methods developed to resolve the problems faced by the staffs of these projects have been borrowed as a whole or in part by subsequent projects faced with similar problems in many parts of the world. A well-known example is Lewis' analysis and restudy of a Mexican community (1951) which demonstrates brilliantly the potentialities of the method of community analysis developed by the staff of the Indian Research project mentioned above, under whom Lewis trained before starting his field work at Tepoztlán.

UNIVERSAL APPLICABILITY OF FINDINGS IN
CLINICAL ANTHROPOLOGY

It should perhaps be emphasized that the approaches and findings of projects in applied anthropology, to the extent that they are scientifically valid, are of general, universal applicability. Translated in terms of the practical problems faced by anti-poverty workers, technical consultants, and community development workers on economic development projects, some lessons learned from the above-mentioned projects may be formulated as follows:

> If their work is to be effective in terms of the ends sought, most technical consultants, anti-poverty and community development workers need not only more knowledge about the communities with which they work, but also a different kind of knowledge. Facts assembled by economists, sociologists, population statisticians, etc., are essential to our understanding of these communities, but still more important perhaps to a more effective relationship between technical assistance workers and recipients of assistance is understanding at a deeper level. Reference is made to the level of implicit community goals and core values.
>
> The term core values may be defined as the group's concept of the world, of nature, animals, plants, microorganisms and man; its concept of social order, community, the relation between the sexes and social classes; its way of thinking about the ego and its extensions, if any, beyond death and before birth; its attitudes about time, space and direction. To improve significantly the relations between assisting group and recipient community we need more knowledge of the cultures of both interacting groups at this deeper level. And it is the assisting group rather than the recipient that must seek out, learn, or in some way acquire this knowledge.
>
> If the technical consultant or community worker were to build into himself such an understanding of the recipient community vis-à-vis his

own, he would be better equipped to participate in the contact situation in a creative way. He would be prepared to regard not only the contact situation flexibly but also the directions and goals of group activity, both immediate and long-range, as emerging rather than fixed. He would be in a position to perceive the "development" process as an attempt to help the receiving community members to build new structures — economic, social, psychological, perhaps within limits even ideological — on the basis of traditional ones, as contrasted to an attempt to superimpose upon the recipient community a preconceived, blue-print type plan accompanied by preconceived techniques for its implementation toward preconceived rigid goals.

The findings from projects in clinical anthropology indicate further that it is very important to train technical assistants on development missions toward sensitivity in regard to the actual problematic situations which the recipient community is facing and resolving more or less successfully. Blindness to biotic, ecological, and geophysical realities at the community level, for example, is a major factor in the failure or near failure of many technical development programs. A multidimensional view of community process, including the organic, ecological, socio-cultural, and psychological levels, should be projected in a training program for community workers, if enhancement of local human welfare is the goal.

USES OF THE NATURAL EXPERIMENT

A last point to be noted is that, a specific policy having been implemented by the administrator of a local group, this may be used by the clinical anthropologist as a natural experiment for testing theories and methods. This point has been made by Collier, Holmberg, Leighton, Lewis, Thompson, and others (Collier, 1945; Holmberg, 1958; Lewis, 1951; Lewis, 1953; Thompson, 1956).

As defined by Festinger and Katz,

> the "natural experiment" involves a change of major importance engineered by policy-makers and practitioners and not by social scientists. It is experimental from the point of view of the scientist . . . [since] it can afford opportunities for measuring the effect of the change on the assumption that the change is so clear and drastic in nature that there is no question of identifying it as the independent variable . . . (1953:78)

The argument for the natural experimenter is explained by Freilich to be

> that this type of change can be treated as an independent variable in an experimental setting and its effect can be observed and recorded. Or, differently put, the socio-cultural system in which a clear and dramatic

change has occurred is, for a given time, a natural laboratory, where given variables are in a state of control so that the effects of an independent variable (the change) can be studied. Thus, the argument would here continue that it hardly matters how control is achieved, what is important is that it is there and can be used for experimental purposes. The role of the researcher using the natural experiment is then to opportunistically capitalize on situations which exist. The opportunism of the researcher lies in searching for situations where change of a clear and dramatic nature has occurred and using such situations as "natural laboratories" (Freilich, 1963).

Thus the significant unit of research in this type of investigation is perceived in the context of a natural "laboratory" under natural conditions in time and space. Hence all the variable sets relevant to the solution of the scientific problem may be assumed to be present, overtly or covertly, including ecological, physical, and historical ones, and the burden of identifying them falls clearly upon the investigator. In other words, successful solution of the problem has not been ruled out by the investigator's misidentification of the significant variables and therefore his failure to include them in a contrived laboratory set-up. Solution of the problem has been drafted by nature into the unit of research. Its discovery depends entirely on the training, experience, sensitivity, and ingenuity of the investigator.

SUMMARY

In this paper I have tried to show that applied anthropology is playing a major creative role in helping to develop a science of man. First, the discipline affords a strong stimulus for developing new heuristic theories, concepts, and methods. It also provides an ideal proving ground for hypothesis testing. And finally it affords a difficult training experience for field workers concerned with learning to understand human groups in depth so that they may predict probable group behavior under changing conditions within certain limiting conditions and potentialities, with the degree of precision needed to resolve practical problems.

By providing the challenge to sharpen theoretical and methodological tools for the scientific solution of local group problems of broad scope, and the crucial natural experiment for their testing, applied scientific anthropology affords the means and the motivation to move the several subdivisions of anthropology systematically and logically from their natural history phases to an empirically-based mature phase; from inductive, fact-based generalizations to heuristic deductive working hypotheses which give promise of holding up under the empirical validation test. Thus applied anthropology is helping in a positive way to develop a science of man.

Applied anthropologists have apparently failed to project an image of their discipline which reflects its significant role in present-day anthropology, not to mention its true potential in today's world. This seems to be directly responsible for loss of talent to the discipline.

These considerations seem to me particularly relevant to workers in development projects of all types, including anti-poverty programs at home. For development projects afford the opportunity simultaneously to test theoretical concepts and to formulate new ones. This suggests the promising scope for theoretical research in development. Technical assistance, anti-poverty, and community workers who successfully assume the role of scientists are thus directly helping to create a science of man.

NOTES

1. For a somewhat different approach see Lee, 1955; Ulrich, 1949; and Warren, 1956.
2. See, for example, the work of Fritz Graebner, Ankermann, Clark Wissler, and Harold Driver.
3. For an attempt to illustrate a method of presenting a community's problematic situation systematically see Laura Thompson.
4. For a different point of view, see the works of A. H. Leighton, Allan Holmberg, and Sol Tax.
5. For a different view see Sol Tax, 1958 (see Chapter 8); and Gouldner, 1956:174–175. My position on this issue has been misread by Barnett, 1963:383.
6. Taken from Thompson, 1951:182.

19 ....

Conservative Thought in Applied Anthropology: A Critique

GUILLERMO BONFIL BATALLA[1]

Most of the people in Latin America countries live in an actual state of unrest which frequently manifests itself in outbursts of violence. This is a reflection, without doubt, of a growing demand from large sectors of the population to achieve a rapid and complete satisfaction of their established needs, as well as of the new ones which arise from contact with forms of modern urban life. Even with national and international efforts undertaken to raise the living standards of millions of Latin Americans, our region continues to be one of the poorest in the world. This fact cannot be ignored by those who work applying social science knowledge to the integral development of our countries. Do the social sciences, particularly anthropology, possess the theoretical equipment necessary to understand Latin American problems and to propose effective solutions

"Conservative Thought in Applied Anthropology: A Critique" by Guillermo Bonfil Batalla is reprinted from *Human Organization* 25:89–92, 1966, by permission of the author and publisher.

246

for them? Undoubtedly the social sciences are indeed prepared to con-tribute their part in such tasks, even though, of course, the contribution of other disciplines is needed.

Now then, the body of theory used in applied anthropology possesses a conservative trend of thought, whose influence is wide and manifest. In my opinion, this current not only prevents the proposal of effective solu-tions, but it also represents a tendency which goes against the national interests of our countries.

The characterization of this conservative thought in anthropology is a decisive and inevitable task which has been fruitfully undertaken by various investigators. The ideas outlined in this paper are intended only to stimulate the already proposed discussion. I shall attempt to present briefly but not exhaustively some of the fundamental theoretical premises of this conservative tendency. For such purposes I have carefully ana-lysed a number of studies in applied anthropology, particularly those which refer to problems of nutrition and public health in Latin America. Even though the topic for which I have analysed bibliography is a very specific one, I believe that the conclusions of this analysis can be validly applied in their essence to other areas in which attempts have been made to apply anthropology.

This paper is largely based on the theoretical postulates included in my work *Diagnóstico sobre el Hambre en Sudzal, Yucatán. Un Ensayo de Antropología Aplicada.* (Diagnosis of Hunger in Sudzal, Yucatan: An Essay in Applied Anthropology.) The complete bibliography from which conclusions have been drawn may be consulted in that publication (Bonfil Batalla, 1962).

To speak of the existence of a conservative trend of thought does not necessarily imply that a group of anthropologists shares belief in the complete set of premises which characterizes that tendency; it is rather, that the conservative point of view in the theory of applied anthropology has influenced the thought of many anthropologists to a greater or lesser degree. The central problem, therefore, is not who are the conservative anthropologists, but, what are the conservative ideas of anthropologists.

In broad terms, the conservative trend in applied anthropology may be characterized by accepting the following postulates, not listed in hier-archical order:

First: A heavy psychological emphasis, not only in the selection of problems for study, but in the interpretation of research results. In the selection of topics for study, one need only review the bibliographies, on problems of public health, and the essays which classify anthropological studies on the subject, such as those prepared by Caudill in 1953 and by Polgar in 1962, as evidence that most of them refer to subjects such as ideas and beliefs on health and illness; concepts and rationalizations about nutrition; stereotypes carried by the community about the personnel in charge of sanitation programs; communication problems derived from differences in cultural traditions, and other subjects. The need and value of such studies is unquestionable; but it is more important still to point out the fact that greater attention has been paid to these subjects than to the study of basic causes of public health and malnutrition problems in our countries. In general, the problems studied have secondary importance as causal elements; that is, they are not primary factors in the alarming state of chronic malnutrition and poor health which affects most of the people in Latin America. At least in many cases, the selection of topics responds to a trend which interprets social realities in purely or largely psychological terms. The phenomenon is well known and it has been consistently criticized (Mills, 1959). It may be sufficiently illustrated with Dr. George Foster's observations (Foster, 1955:20):

> It appears as if *the most important* categories of culture that should be more or less completely understood to carry out successful health and hygiene programs are *local ideas* about health, welfare, illness, their causes and treatment. (translation — author's italics)

If field materials are interpreted according to Dr. Foster's proposal, then the basic structure of a society, the low levels of technology, and the inadequate and unjust social organization, are factors which take second place in the explanation of the problems that are supposed to be analyzed. The solutions that might be proposed with the above-mentioned study emphasis will not produce the improvement of life conditions, because they do not suggest any alterations in the structures that have determined their existence. In summary, the psychological manifestations of a problem have been taken as its causes.

Second: Another basic postulate of the conservative trend of thought in applied anthropology is the almost axiomatic affirmation that the main function of the anthropologist is to avoid rapid changes, because of the resulting maladjustments and conflicts which frequently produce social and cultural "disorganization." This affirmation implicitly carries with it the idea that all societies present resistance to directed changes; to avoid conflict, anthropologists must try to promote development and general welfare programs which adjust to the local culture, respecting the established social structure, the value systems and the norms of behavior of the population to which programs are directed. Consequently, the anthropologist takes the position of favoring slow and long-term changes, he promotes small and partial reforms, and consequently rejects and condemns radical changes which are the only ones that affect the basic institutional structures of a society. At times this fear of radical change goes to such an extreme that the anthropologist pays little attention to the fundamental processes of social dynamics. Thus, Dr. Richard N. Adams writes:

> Basically, there are two different types of cultural changes: the first is a slow, gradual and evolutionary type . . . ; the other is rapid and revolutionary, caused by the efforts of societal members who wish to produce immediate alterations, of far reaching consequences. Applied anthropology can and must focus concern, principally on the first of these types of change (Adams, 1955). (translation)

With such an emphasis, the knowledge proper to the field of applied anthropology is limited and mutilated.

Third: One must now refer to the form in which the concept of cultural relativism is usually handled in applied anthropology. The obvious existence of various value systems, of differing cultural alternatives to satisfy the same needs, frequently leads to a theoretical position that rejects the possibility of pronouncing value judgments in relation to societies and cultures. Edwin Smith points out:

> As men and women we may have our opinions about the justice or injustice of certain acts and attitudes, but anthropology as such can pronounce no judgment, for to do so is to invade the province of philosophy and ethics. If anthropology is to judge and guide it must have a conception of what constitutes the perfect society; and since it is debarred from having ideals it cannot judge, cannot guide, and cannot talk about progress (Smith, 1934).

When the meaning of cultural relativism is taken to such extremes, one enters into a basic contradiction with the very claim of applying anthropological science to the solution of human problems. That is, the *raison d'être* of applied anthropology is denied.

I believe that lack of historical focus is one of the reasons for adopting such a mistaken position. Knowledge of social and cultural history is, in my opinion, an absolute requirement for any attempt to apply anthropology. The study of history gives origin to outlines, patterns, and laws of changes which should be used in the promotion of development programs.

Fourth: The multiple causation theory, according to which all phenomena are a product of countless small and diverse causes, is another common postulate of this trend. C. Wright Mills aptly concludes that according to this position, as long as it is impossible to know all the causes of a phenomenon, the anthropologist must confine himself to the proposal of small modifications of little consequence (Mills, 1959). On the other hand, this postulate points to the impossibility of enunciating general societal laws; the function of the anthropologist thus reduces itself to the mere description of each particular case. Richard N. Adams is quite clear in this respect when he states:

> One thing is to make generalizations in a monograph or article for discussion among colleagues, and it is quite a different matter to make such generalizations when these are to be used as a basis for the action in a specific region and have real effect on the way of life of the people inhabiting such an area. Applied work deals directly with specifics; in opposition to science, it does not formulate generalizations (Adams, 1955:219, 222). (translation)

Anthropologists who think in this form emphasize the necessity for making careful research in each particular case, because, according to Dr. Foster's assertion,

> there are no two groups of population with the same needs (Foster, 1952). (translation)

It is an opinion that, on the other hand, increases our employment possibilities. By this path, one unavoidably arrives at a denial of science itself, of which one characteristic and specific function is, precisely, to find regularities in order to establish general laws.

In passing, we shall mention another postulate, very much related to the above-mentioned: Research in applied anthropology is usually undertaken at the community level, and on many occasions, only one sector of the community is studied; so, because according to the multiple causation theory it is impossible to generalize, the results obtained have validity only for the small sector of the population that the anthropologist studies directly.

On the other hand, as Prof. Ricardo Pozas (1961) has pointed out, focus on the community as the unit of study has led, on occasions, to underrating the importance of relations maintained by a community with external influences. That tendency is clearly seen in many monographs with an "Indianist" orientation, which consider indigenous communities as isolated societies, outside the spheres of national society; we believe that, at least in many cases, such a stand is erroneous. Essentially, communities must be understood within a wider framework: at regional, national, and in certain cases, international levels (as in the case of the community of Sudzal, whose basic crop, sisal, is assigned in its totality to the international market (Batalla, 1962). The relevance of such a problem cannot be underestimated, particularly by the growing importance given to community development programs.

According to this conservative trend, the problems of marginal societies with traditional culture have their origin in the very existence of just these kinds of societies. This is, in my opinion, an illogical point of view, a naive one at best, because it is exactly the existence or survival of these groups that needs to be explained. In focusing on the problem, it is completely useless to apply conservative assumptions; it would be better to study similar situations with the aid of some other analytic concepts like the "internal colonialism" proposed by Dr. González Casanova (1963:15–32).

Fifth: Almost all the social problems in the so-called underdeveloped countries are related in a direct fundamental manner with low levels of income. These in turn are the result of a type of social organization that prevents an increase in productivity at the necessary pace, and also conditions an unequal distribution of wealth. Such a fact cannot be reasonably doubted. However, most anthropological investigations connected with development and welfare programs seem to consider level of income as a phenomenon that can be modified only in a slow and long-term manner. Anthropologists who like to call themselves realists and practical frequently attempt to raise levels of living without touching the institutional structures that cause and permit the existence of large numbers of people who grow more impoverished day-by-day. In short, this refers to an "anthropology of poverty": attempts are made to modify but not to eradicate conditions which give rise to poverty.

Sixth: Even though one could still point to other theoretical premises that characterize this conservative trend in applied anthropology, I shall mention only one more: the consideration that diffusion is the most important, and for some, the only process which must be brought to play in efforts to promote change in the communities under study. This tendency may possibly be related to the fact that many investigations have been undertaken in connection with international assistance projects, in which, one naturally searches for the best way of applying external aid. In few cases is there an establishment of goals to accelerate the internal dynamics of the societies studied. The problems which preoccupy anthropologists are related with greatest frequency to the action forms needed so that the population receiving the aid program benefits may use it profitably. The intention is a valid one; but by no means may it be considered as a statement of the whole problem.

In summary, we have presented in broad terms the theoretical postulates which characterize the trend of conservative thought within applied anthropology. I must repeat that I do not conceive this trend as a school of thought that has thus far identified its total body of postulates with great clarity. Nevertheless, it is a trend followed to a greater or lesser extent by a number of anthropologists; some only hold implicitly or explicitly to one of the above mentioned postulates, and at times, even reject the rest. Others orient their professional activity closely following the above-outlined model, and separating from it only fortuitously.

Now then, in my opinion, the realities of the countries usually called underdeveloped, like those of Latin America, require that the anthropologist interested in the application of this science separate himself consciously from this conservative trend. The type of applied anthropology required by our countries must begin with premises which are very different from the ones we have singled out. The magnitude of the problem with which we are faced and the scarcity of our resources place us in a situation far different from that of wealthy and highly industrialized nations, like the United States of America. We need to establish hierarchies for our problems; we cannot permit ourselves the luxury of turning our efforts to the acquisition of knowledge about inconsequential aspects of problems. Thus, as we do not believe that our poverty has a psychological origin, nor that it results from the ideas and images peculiar to our cultural tradition, nor that our basic problems can be explained by "deficiencies in channels of communications"; so, we do not believe that studies on these themes will give us the knowledge that we fundamentally need to face our problems.

These are not opportune times to deceive ourselves into thinking that efforts should be limited to the promotion of small changes, shielding ourselves with the fear that radical changes will produce disorganization. On the contrary, we believe that it is the task of the anthropologist to point to the very frequent uselessness of timid development programs, and that it is also his task to demonstrate with scientific rigor the need to carry out radical changes, that is, changes which get to the root of the problems themselves. Sometimes it looks as if those who work along the road of slow evolution intend to achieve only minimal changes, so that the situation continues to be substantially the same; this is, in other words, *to change what is necessary so that things remain the same.* Those who act according to such a point of view may honestly believe that their work is useful and transforming; however, they have in fact aligned themselves with the conservative elements who oppose the structural transformations that cannot be postponed in our countries.

The Latin American anthropologist needs to learn to work well and rapidly. In Mexico there are more than 100,000 localities; I do not believe that any locality wants to be the last studied by anthropologists, so that it may then receive scientifically dosed attention. If we are not capable of generalizing and proposing efficiently and uniformly applied measures, then we must recognize that our discipline is not prepared to respond to the pressing actual needs of our countries.

To state that science is universal is only part of the truth, because science is also an institution and a cumulative tradition, and, after all, a social product; as such, it necessarily reflects in some way the conditions, values and orientations of the society that produces it. To date, the theory of applied anthropology has been one of the items imported into the underdeveloped countries — an imported item, as many others. We receive from producing countries (such as the United States, England, France, and other European nations) many well-elaborated theoretical postulates, some of them perfectly adjusted to our reality and our needs; but others are infused with a different spirit, foreign to our interest and on occasions, decidedly contrary to them. This is the conservative thought, before which there must arise a dynamic and progressive conception of applied anthropology, whose proposals correspond to the deep and urgent needs of Latin America and the rest of the impoverished and backward areas.

Others before me have discussed these subjects with greater authority and with better documentation, such as Dr. R. A. Manners (1956), when he studied the influence of political interest in foreign aid programs of the United States, or Dr. Max Gluckman (1963), as he critically analyzed the applied anthropology proposed by Malinowski, in the light of British colonial interests. After them, little can be added; however, I have found myself in the need to do so, because in addition to my responsibility and interest as an anthropologist, I have the responsibilities and sentiments of a Latin American.

NOTES

1. Translated from the Spanish original by Lucy C. Cohen, Ph.D. candidate, Department of Anthropology, Catholic University, Washington, D.C.

Objectivity in Anthropology

JACQUES MAQUET

Is the "science of man and his works" a real science? We anthropologists like to think of ourselves as social scientists, and we understand "social scientists" as being not merely students of social phenomena but specialists dedicated to the building of a scientific knowledge of culture and society. Is this view supported by our productions: our books and our articles?

The problem is not new but has not been satisfactorily solved. To contribute modestly to its elucidation, it may be useful to consider in the light of the epistemology of anthropology a new situation in which some anthropologists find themselves directly confronted with this old irritating problem.[1]

The anthropologists directly concerned are those whose research area is tropical Africa. During the last decade, this area has seen the emergence of independent states. Africanists had usually been considered very liberal-minded by colonial administrations; they had prevented traditional cultures from falling into oblivion and had stressed the value of ways of

"Objectivity in Anthropology" by Jacques Maquet is reprinted from *Current Anthropology* 5:47–55, 1964, by permission of the author and the publisher.

life alien to the West. Anthropologists expected that their discipline would be well received in the newly independent nations, particularly by the university trained Africans who usually constitute the political and administrative elite. The very term "anthropology" and its French counterpart, *ethnologie* (more common in French-speaking Africa than *anthropologie sociale*), are frowned on in many quarters; they are suspected of being tinged with colonialism. New research projects are not always encouraged, and some African authorities manifest more distrust than enthusiasm when asked to support or facilitate anthropological field work. Some African intellectuals feel that earlier anthropological studies were biased in favor of the colonial regime, and they fear that new studies would also have an undesirable orientation.

One answer to these criticisms is to point out that scientific studies, precisely because they are objective, are not likely to please everybody (and particularly every government, colonial or independent); it is natural enough that African authorities feel suspicious about everything of European origin, particularly as researches are usually carried on by citizens of the former dominant power. Another reaction to these criticisms is to consider them as an interesting phenomenon likely to shed light upon the epistemology of our discipline. This view amounts to the affirmation that anthropology in Africa has been influenced by the colonial situation, and not only by its object of study, as is usually expected in a scientific discipline. Thus an unforeseen consequence of the decolonization process is to throw doubt upon the scientific character of anthropology.

We shall start from a hypothesis set forth by the sociologists of knowledge. The existential situation of a group within a larger society is a factor which conditions the knowledge acquired and used by the group. We take "existential" as a word referring to the multiplicity of the social, economic, and related determinants (such as prestige, power, standing) which account for the everyday existence of a group.

THE EXISTENTIAL SITUATION OF ANTHROPOLOGISTS IN THE COLONIAL SYSTEM

During the colonial period, professional anthropologists worked in Africa under the auspices of universities, museums, research institutes, and scientific foundations. These institutions were located in Europe or in the United States, or were African branches of organizations whose boards of directors, administrative offices, and advisory bodies were located in Europe, or else African institutions without European headquarters but with close ties to similar European institutions. In the first case (the arrangement used most frequently by Americans), anthropologists were usually scholars who had received grants for specific investigations in Africa. In the other two cases, anthropologists were permanently attached to the African bases of their institutions, as were the colonial civil servants and the local executives and staffs of commercial and industrial enterprises. Scientific institutions followed the usual colonial pattern: direction in the home country, execution in the colony.

When in Africa, anthropologists received what amounted to a fixed salary, somewhat higher than that of persons doing similar research in the home country (all colonial salaries for Whites were higher than in Europe). To the extent that it was related to professional achievements, promotion depended on the judgment of colleagues outside Africa and was expected to follow the Western hierarchy of scientific and academic institutions.

From this description of the economic situation of anthropologists, it appears that they were integrated into the colonial system, whose frame of reference was external to the dominated country and in which rewards were measured in terms meaningful only in the outside society. Consequently, the end of the colonial system was likely to have important consequences for anthropologists; and it did.

What was the place of anthropologists in colonial society? The borders of a colonial society are difficult to establish. If one includes in a society all the persons who interact with each other economically and politically, it would include both established and transient Europeans as well as all African inhabitants. If one gives priority to psychological criteria (feeling of belonging, distinction between insiders and outsiders, recognition of persons with whom it is normal and proper to have face-to-face relations), then the colonial society would be limited to the white minority living in it at a given time (Balandier, 1963:15–22).

Although they studied African groups, and in spite of the very frequent friendships between them and some Africans, anthropologists were not assimilated to the African layer of the society. They were members of the white minority. They lived according to the same patterns, spoke the same language, and were assigned a certain status within the European group. The small white caste of a colony was divided vertically and horizontally into several subgroups. The main vertical subgroups were (a) administrative officers with some public authority, (b) specialized personnel of government and semipublic agencies (medical, veterinary, agricultural services) and nonprofit institutions (scientific research organizations, welfare agencies), (c) executives and staff of industrial and commercial companies, and (d) settlers. These four vertical groups were also hierarchies whose main levels were: (1) the highest local authority in each vertical group (for example, in the colonial capital, the governor, the head of the medical service, the directors of the institutes, the general agents of foreign commercial firms, the president of the chamber of commerce, and so on; similar enumerations could be made on a smaller scale for each province and district), (2) the middle level characterized by various criteria such as supervision of other European workers under them, medium salary bracket, and university education, and (3) the level of petty white-collar employees, manual workers acting as foremen for African unskilled laborers, shopkeepers, and the like.

In spite of their rather marginal activities, anthropologists were situated in the (b) vertical group and in the (2) horizontal layer. Others falling into this group were the middle level specialized personnel of public and semipublic institutions which organized practical or fundamental research, agricultural development, public health, and related activities. This strongly hierarchical society (there was little social intercourse between the three horizontal groups) was also very fluid in the sense that the membership was constantly renewed; of the several vertical groups, only the settlers who had invested capital and labor were firmly rooted.

The existential situation of anthropologists may thus be characterized as follows: They were scholars whose material and professional interests lay in their home countries but who participated in the privileges of the dominant caste during their stay in Africa. Their stay might last for a few years or for all their active life, but, ultimately they returned to Europe. Their group interests were not significantly different from those of other middle level specialists. These characteristics of their existential situation were perfectly compatible with holding progressive views: anthropologists were not settlers and were not under constraint to view phenomena which led to increases in wages — for example, advances in education — as threats, as were the agricultural settlers. The anthropologists' existential situation was also compatible with the participant-observer attitude that some of them assumed, not so much for purposes of research but rather out of their deep sympathy for the society they were studying. Moreover, since their activities were marginal, relative to those of the production-conscious European caste, who looked on the anthropologists' work as a romantic waste of money, the anthropologists were oriented toward non-comformist attitudes critical of the colonial order.

Nevertheless, in actuality, the socioeconomic situation of anthropologists in Africa depended on the stability of the European domination pattern. Europeans of the first three vertical groups (all those who were not definitely settled in Africa) were not likely to feel that the granting of independence would mean a catastrophic personal loss. Afterward, most middle level specialists would probably remain in unchanged capacities: as experts. Or, if that proved impossible, they could without too much difficulty pursue careers in Europe. To sum up, the interests of the group of the white population to which anthropologists belonged were best served by a position of mild conservatism. The colonial order was not worth fighting for, but as long as it lasted, it was a most satisfactory system for those who profited moderately by it.

It should be stressed that in the hypothesis we follow here, the determination of the existential situation of a group within a global society is arrived at by a sociological analysis and not by a public-opinion survey of the group members. The stated opinions of group members as to their existential situation are phenomena of another level and may differ substantially from the results of a sociological analysis; in this instance, they did. Mild conservatism was not advocated, so far as I know, by members of the group whose interests would have been well defended by such a view. On the contrary, many were in favor of maintenance of colonial rule, even by coercion. Individuals are often unaware of the collective interests of their stratum, or if they are not, do not always perceive the relation between existential conditions and political views. Nevertheless these "objective" conditions, according to an important school of sociology of knowledge, are reflected in the mental productions of the group.

ANTHROPOLOGICAL STUDIES DURING THE COLONIAL PERIOD

But really, are they? Was what Africanists wrote "useful" to the colonial order? Did it, in fact, help to maintain it? Most anthropological books and articles published during colonial times focused on traditional cultures, certainly for scientific reasons. The discovery of ways of life, beliefs, and art forms completely foreign to Western patterns had important implications for anthropology. Consequently, the traditional cultures had to be studied, and the sooner the better, as they were disappearing. During the whole colonial period in tropical Africa (beginning, in the various regions, in the interval from 1885 to the beginning of the twentieth century and ending during the period from 1957 to the present — the process not complete for all territories), interest in the genuine traditional cultures has been dominant in anthropological literature. However, the image of these traditional cultures has varied. We can distinguish very roughly two periods, separated by the First World War.

Let us consider the most recent period first, because it is principally during the last four decades that the existential situation of anthropologists has been as described above. The functional theories of Malinowski and Radcliffe-Brown, different but essentially similar, renewed anthropology in 1922 and had an important effect on African studies (Malinowski 1922; Radcliffe-Brown 1922). Traditional cultures were seen as integrated wholes — systems of adaptation of a group to its environment, and delicately balanced units. Africanists made their readers aware of the value of these ways of life, which provided adequately for the universal needs of individuals and societies. This high appreciation of the African past and emphasis on preservation of the traditional cultures were well received by African intellectuals. One may say that the proud affirmation of fidelity to *négritude* and *africanité* was made possible by anthropological studies.

In acculturation studies, anthropologists went further, asserting that the Western impact on African societies and cultures was mainly negative. Acculturation studies stressed the disruptive effects of industrialization, money economy, and Western administration on the harmonious structures of precolonial societies. From acculturation studies to applied anthropology, the distance is short. At the request of colonial governments and on their own initiative, anthropologists acted as advisers on proposed or implemented reforms. In either case, the anthropologists have urged that the reforms be as acceptable to the people and as little disruptive of the social fabric as possible.

These activities at first sight appear to reflect a very enlightened stand, as indeed they did to the anthropologists concerned. But in fact these activities were conservative, in the sense that they contributed to maintenance of colonial rule.

Around 1920, the conquest period was over in Africa, and military commandants were replaced by administrative authorities. It was a period of stabilization. Under the diversity of the British, French, Belgian, and Portuguese colonial policies, there was a common concern for economic development geared to the metropolitan economic system. To succeed, the economic growth of the overseas territories had to be accompanied by a general and gradual development of other sectors such as education, public health, and urbanization. But what mattered more was the gradualness of the evolution. If the process were not slow, political and social disorder might prevail. Urban labor was indispensable, but it could not take on undue importance and its force had to be counterbalanced by that of the peasant masses.

Valorization and idealization of the traditional cultures were, for the colonial regimes, socially useful trends in spite of the apparent oppositions. Indeed, there were contradictions between traditional political organization and administrative bureaucracy, between customary law and ordinances, between old methods of cultivation and new ones recommended by government agronomists, between ancestors' cults and Christian rites, and the like. But the conservative forces of tradition were less dangerous for the colonial order than the progressive forces emerging in the industrial regions commercial towns, and middle or higher education institutions. The real or fictive "legitimate heirs" of the precolonial authorities, included in the colonial administrative hierarchy at the lower levels, had become bound up with the colonial order and were usefully counterbalancing the progressive group.

In another connection, the stress on the interest of the traditional culture emphasized the differences between the European ways and the African ones, and this was an effective barrier preventing "natives" from entering European groups. Traditional costumes, dishes, languages, and the like were constant reminders that the cultural distance separating the dominant European minority from the dominated autochthonous population was not to be easily bridged. Here again, sympathy for African folklore was genuinely and sincerely felt by many whites; but as a group attitude, it was at least ambiguous.

I do not mean that anthropological writing, by enhancing African traditional values, has had a significant bearing on the upholding of the colonial system. This is not our concern here. What matters is that anthropology was oriented as though it wanted to preserve the existing situation.

The picture anthropology gave of Africa from the beginning of colonization up to the First World War was different. Isolated institutions (e.g., marriage, kinship), specific religious beliefs (e.g., animism, polytheism), and particular types of material objects (e.g., bows, arrows, drums) were more often studied than whole cultures. Evolutionists attempted to build temporal sequences of stages of development, and diffusionists were interested in contacts and borrowings. The reader of the ethnological literature of that time was under the impression that "savages" were very different from Europeans, that they had queer if not repugnant customs, that they lived in a prelogical world of curious superstitions, that their strange behavior — deemed a submission to instinctive impulses — was explainable only by a theory of racial inferiority, and that their ways of life were therefore inferior to "civilized" ones. All ethnographic books were far from blunt in expressing these ideas, but of the writings of that time, most were more or less explicit in their assertion of these views.

At that time there were not many professional anthropologists working in Africa south of the Sahara. Most field reports came from explorers, missionaries, and traders and were used by library anthropologists who had no firsthand knowledge of the people they wrote about. For them, the "savage" was an abstract concept; a culture was not a reality lived by a group but was made of separate items which were compared with similar items from another society; the distinction between race and culture was not clear. These conceptions, reflecting the level of the developing discipline of anthropology, account for the image Africanists then gave of traditional Africa. But again, that picture was just the one corresponding to the needs of the first stage of colonization.

Western Europe was at its peak, self-confident and in a conquering mood. Its industrial development and its economic system required an expansion beyond its borders. Cheap raw materials were necessary for the European transforming industries, and new markets were needed for manufactured low-quality goods. These requisites for the prosperity of the European bourgeoisie were found in Africa and other tropical regions of the world. The partition of Africa into "spheres of influence," military expeditions into the dark continent of "cannibals," and establishment of colonial rule were made morally acceptable — even virtuous activities — since the colonized peoples were so different, so inferior, that the rules of behavior for intercourse with civilized peoples were obviously not applicable. Indeed, the "savages" were considered fortunate to be put under the rule of a Western country, to be obliged to work, and to be forbidden to engage in their immoral practices. The colonial expansion required that a certain image of the nonliterate peoples be accepted by Western public opinion. On a more refined level, ethnology supported that picture.

The existential situation of the two groups, which was partly responsible for that image, was obviously related to the Western expansion. The amateur field reporters were directly committed to the colonial enterprise by their main activities in Africa, and the library anthropologists had professional interests in sources of information unavailable in the precolonial period, while their academic institutions shared in the growing common prosperity of the colonial powers.

In these few paragraphs, we have attempted to indicate the relevant trends which are exemplified in a considerable portion of the literature on colonial Africa. Although many exceptions could certainly be pointed out, it seems not unfair to say that during the colonial period, most anthropological studies were — unwillingly and unconsciously in many cases — conservative: first, in that Africans were described as so different from "civilized" peoples and so "savage" just at the time that Europe needed to justify colonial expansion; and second, in that later on, the value of the traditional cultures was magnified when it was useful for the colonial powers to ally themselves with the more traditional forces against the progressive Africans. We do not believe that these parallels are mere coincidences.

ANTHROPOLOGY AND SOCIOLOGY

We are not concerned here with the distinctions between social and cultural anthropology, ethnology, and ethnography. We take "anthropology" as a general term for the different viewpoints expressed by these four categories, and we distinguish it from sociology. Anthropology is the study of nonliterate societies and their cultures. Why do we have a special discipline for "primitive," "simple," preindustrial, nonliterate, small-scale societies? Why have we reserved the term "sociology" for "advanced," "complex," industrial, literate, large-scale societies? Is it justified to distinguish so sharply as to make of them different disciplines between two approaches to the same kind of phenomena (social and cultural) seen from the same angle (man as a social being)?

There is a justification. Although sociology and anthropology both study social phenomena, the characteristics of nonliterate societies have made it necessary to devise special research techniques (interviews, indirect observation of behavior, long stays in the field, and the like), since the techniques used in literate societies were not applicable (written answers to questionnaires, study of archives and other literary sources, and so forth). A new attitude has also been required of the student; there is a great difference indeed between the study of one's own society where the whole culture is taken for granted, and the study of another one, for which one has to cross a cultural barrier. The significant contributions of anthropology to the study of man — the notion of culture, the conception of the integrated character of the ways of life of a social unit, the universals of human societies — have largely originated in the situation of the anthropologist as carrier of an outside culture.

Whatever the validity of these reasons, anthropology emerged in the nineteenth century as the discipline devoted to peoples considered by evolutionists of that time as "primitive" and "inferior," whereas sociology has remained the study of "higher" societies. In recent decades most anthropologists have avoided the use of terms such as "primitive" and "savage" or, if they use them, they have implicitly indicated that they did not imply a judgment of value; all of them have made serious efforts to strip anthropology of its normative connotations; some have, with Professor Herskovits, gone so far as to propose a philosophical position, cultural relativism, which denies the possibility of finding criteria permitting establishment of a hierarchy of cultures (Herskovits, 1948:61–78; Maquet, 1946:243–56).

In spite of this, societies studied by anthropologists have tended to view the attention of this discipline as a sign of implicit discrimination; to be an object of research is never pleasing, and if one feels, as many educated Africans do today, that selection for study by the "science of savages" expresses the European conviction of difference and superiority, the unpleasantness becomes painful.

This impression is now strengthened as the matter considered the distinctive province of anthropology no longer exists in Africa. There are still many African illiterates but I doubt that a single nonliterate society remains. Everywhere people are reached by the written word, if only through administrative relationships with their governments. There are still many peasants tilling the soil according to traditional techniques, but no place is completely free from the influence of money economy, road, rail, and air transportation, commercial exchange, industry, and cash crops. It is an illusion to believe that one can still study today an African society living as if modern techniques and institutions did not exist. With the disappearance of the conditions considered the matter of anthropological study in Africa, it is likely that the study of preindustrial societies will be taken on by the historical disciplines, whereas contemporary societies will be studied by sociology.

Whatever the outcome of this situation, it seems clear that the existence of a particular discipline dedicated exclusively to the study of non-Western cultures reflected the Victorian sense of superiority of 19th century Europe and was perfectly consistent with, and useful to, the colonial expansion of that period. Is it not striking that this situation persisted in Africa as long as did the colonial system and had to wait the decolonization process to be questioned?

THE SOCIAL PERSPECTIVE OF ANTHROPOLOGY

For many of us who were anthropologists in tropical Africa, it required an effort to become aware of these disturbing correspondences between our discipline and the colonial regime. Certainly psychological resistances prevented us from perceiving a function of anthropology that we did not like. Because of our existential situation, certains aspects of our work remained in the shadows. On the other hand, many educated Africans — not only social scientists — noticed these close relations between anthropology and colonialism. This confirms the importance of the "point of view," of what Karl Mannheim called the "perspective" in the apprehension of social phenomena (Mannheim, 1946:243–56). From our "perspective," some facts were difficult to see, whereas they were plainly visible from the "perspective" of African nationalists.

The term "perspective" seems particularly well chosen because of the visual simile it calls to mind. When a photograph of a house is taken, the resulting image depends not only on the building, but also on the angle, that is to say, on the position of the camera. Someone familiar with the house and its surroundings can, just by looking at the picture, determine the exact spot where the camera was set up; even a person who has never seen the building will note whether the photographer was on the left or the right side, at street level or above it. There is no picture without a perspective, that is to say, not taken from a definite point.

This is just an analogy, but it helps to understand what is meant by "perspective" in anthropological studies. It is the fact that the anthropologist perceives the social phenomena he studies not from nowhere but from a certain point of view, which is his existential situation. To define adequately an anthropological study, it is not enough to indicate its object, e.g., "the social structure of the Mundang;" one should add "as seen by an anthropologist belonging to the socioeconomic middle stratum of the white colonial minority."

This addition is not just one more welcome instance of precision, comparable, for example, to details of the interviewing techniques used. In the most acute manner, it raises the question of the scientific nature of anthropology. If the anthropologist's perspective has to be mentioned, it means that the observer's subjectivity is taken into account. And is not subjectivity just what science eliminates? To be scientific, should not an assertion be verifiable by any scientist? And how can an anthropologist verify what another has written about a certain society if the description or analysis is determined not only by the object (the society studied) but by the subject (the anthropologist) as well?

Before attempting to answer these thorny questions, we shall follow the different stages of the elaboration of an anthropological study from beginning to end to see where and how the existential perspective may be relevant.

INDUCTIVE ANTHROPOLOGY

On arrival in the field, the anthropologist first looks for facts; that is to say, for facts which are relevant to the matter he wants to investigate (e.g., economic and political organization) and to his research hypothesis (e.g., a specialized and permanent body of governing individuals appears when there is surplus production of consumer goods). This is the first step in any scientific research.

However, a difficulty arises immediately in relation to observation of the facts. Social phenomena, even when reduced to their simplest components, differ from physical phenomena in that the former have one or several meanings as integral parts. The social fact to be observed is not "a man making utterances in front of a wooden statue" but rather, "a sorcerer trying to kill somebody by magical means." Or is it "a lineage head paying respects to his ancestors"? Thus two completely different social phenomena, an act of magic and an act of ritual, may have, as it were, the same behavioral manifestations. Without its meaning, an observable behavior is not a fact for the anthropologist. And the meaning of such behavior is rarely obvious; it requires interpretation — often, much interpretation. The observer's general knowledge of anthropology, his intellectual skill, and his imagination are important assets in that interpretation. At the very first step, individual characteristics and social perspective get into the research process.

At this point, it would be well to note that in our sketchy survey of African anthropology we have singled out the affiliation of the anthropologist in a socioeconomic group as the only determining influence on the subject's knowledge. As we were considering only general trends, the individual characteristics of the observer were not mentioned. They constitute, however, another important determinant pertaining to the subject, and influencing knowledge. By "individuality," we understand what Kluckhohn and Murray describe as the product of countless and successive interactions between the maturing constitution and different environing situations from birth onward, that is to say, the innate equipment developed by different educational processes and moulded by the personal history (Kluckhohn and Murray, 1948:35–48). It is by his individuality that the anthropologist (the subject) reads into the gestures he observes (the object) the meaning that makes of them social phenomena. In the remainder of this paper, individuality will often be mentioned side by side with social perspective because both are subjective factors conditioning knowledge; but we shall keep our interest focused on the existential situation.

Then we reach the second step, the factual generalization which synthesizes in a general statement the numerous cases observed, without, in principle, adding anything to them. However, the effect of generalization is to amplify subjective factors. An anthropologist who describes witchcraft as entirely dominating the life of the society he studies may rightly assume that this is a factual description which simply sums up all the observations he has made. At the same time, the subjective component of each particular observation is, so to speak, magnified in the generalization.

The subject's influence on observation and generalization makes it difficult to verify if the picture given by an anthropologist conforms to the facts. The test would be that other anthropologists come and observe the same facts, or rather, similar facts — in human action, there is never more repetition, as in physical science — and compare their descriptions. To my knowledge, this comparative procedure has never been really carried out. Had this been done, it is highly probable that anthropologists would have evolved a set of techniques facilitating comparison like the ones commonly used in social surveys (e.g., scales of attitudes, sociometric scales of behavior). Such techniques do not give the final answer to the problem of observation and verification of the social phenomena: too many important and significant facts pass through the too widely-meshed net of impersonal techniques. But they constitute an effort toward elimination of the individual factor in observation. Such an effort has not been made in anthropology because research has not been oriented toward this aim. Up to now anthropologists do not seem to have been bothered by the influence of their individual characteristics on the collection of facts. Incidentally, I do not imply that they should have been bothered; we shall return to this point below.

The third step in the inductive stage of anthropology is to draw logical inferences from the descriptive generalizations. The logical inferences then combine into one or more constructs. The construct asserts more than do the observations and generalizations, and is not directly verifiable: it is the theory which explains the observed facts by relating them to more general principles. For instance, from the observation of a high level of witchcraft in a society and of an egalitarian repartition of wealth, a theory may be induced which explains witchcraft as a regulating device acting as if it were meant to insure a certain economic equality in the society.[2]

The importance of a theory is not limited to its explanatory value. It also summarizes in a convenient form a certain number of separate generalizations which had appeared up to then to be completely unrelated. Finally, with the assumption that the principle will be applied to other behavior than that observed, a theory has predictive value.

In the building of a theory the imagination, the *esprit de finesse*, even the intuitive insight into an alien culture, play a very important part, because the logical inductions constituting the theory are not logically necessary inferences from the observed facts. From observations of witchcraft and economic behavior, one could induce a different hypothesis from the one just mentioned; for instance, that there is a positive correlation between sorcery and economic insecurity. On logical grounds, this theory is as good as the other. The other basis on which the anthropologist chooses one theory rather than the other, is his total perception of the society he studies and of the social reality in general.

Does this personal and creative intervention of the subject prevent a theory from being valid? Not at all. The first criterion for judging a theory is its explanatory value. The best theory is the one which makes the facts intelligible; that is to say, the one that is most satisfactory to the mind. This rather flexible way of judging takes into account the simplicity of the theory, its logical consistency, and its coherence with a more general conception of society. The second criterion leads us back to the facts: the deduction of the consequences of the theory which constitutes the deductive process of anthropology.

DEDUCTIVE ANTHROPOLOGY

If a theory is valid, we may expect that other facts than the ones from which the theory has been inferred conform to it. If in Society A, economic insecurity has produced a high level of witchcraft, in Society B, where the economic situation is satisfactory, sorcery should not be developed. Or if witchcraft is linked to economic insecurity, it is very likely that other forms of insecurity will also produce it; thus we should examine social situations breeding personal anxiety and determine if sorcery is important. These examples are very crude and obviously are not representative of the richness and complexity of anthropological deductions;

they are mentioned merely as illustrations of the often-used and well known logical process of deduction.

Now again, it is easy to see where individuality and perspective may enter. Like inductive reasoning, deductive inference is not logically necessary. In his famous theory, Max Weber claimed that the doctrine of predestination is at the focus of the origin of the spirit of profit in capitalistic society, because success in trade was considered a sign of divine election (Weber, 1930:112–16). Sorokin remarked very aptly that the doctrine of predestination could just as well lead to passivity and inactivity: From the premise that human action has no bearing on salvation, it is logical to conclude that it is useless to struggle (Sorokin, 1937: 503). This means that the anthropologist has a certain leeway in deducing new consequences from the theory he has constructed. As various propositions may be deduced from a premise, he has a choice; thus he is led by other considerations than strict logical reasoning.

But, it may be argued, uncertainty disappears when the consequences deduced from a theory are verified, that is to say, confronted with the facts, surely, but to a variable extent, depending on the kind of factual consequences deduced. If an anthropologist postulates for some theoretical reason that in a certain society cross-cousin marriage should exist, it is not too difficult to determine if this is true. But if he postulates that these marriages are "frequent" or "very frequent," it will be much more difficult to verify these affirmations. And it will be almost impossible to check a deduction such as "there should be a high level of intrafamily tensions in a given society." The verification of the deduced consequences of a theory confronts the difficulties already mentioned in discussing anthropological observation of social phenomena. Thus, at the end of this schematic analysis of an anthropological study, we encounter the same obstacle met in the very first step: subjectivity in observation.

IS ANTHROPOLOGICAL KNOWLEDGE SCIENTIFIC?

From this short survey of the different stages of an anthropological study, it appears clearly that anthropology follows the general pattern of any Western knowledge, as explicated by Northrop: careful observation of data, explanation of the data by an induced theory, and then indirect verification of the theory by examining if the facts are in accord with the deductive consequences of the theory (Northrop, 1947:294–97). This is also the pattern of scientific knowledge.

Like any other knowledge, anthropology results from an activity in which a subject thinks about an object distinct from it and says something about the object. The object is supposed to have an existence independent of the subject (i.e., to be "real"), and what is said of it is supposed to correspond to the object (i.e., not to be projected onto it by the subject). The aim of the knowledge-seeking activity of the mind — as opposed, for instance, to its artistic or ethical activities — is objectivity, that is to say, conformity with the object.

Anthropology is, like other knowledge, concerned with objectivity. We have seen that each step is assessed with reference to the final goal, which is to express the social reality. Thus, if anthropology is distinct from science, it is not because they differ as to their ultimate value, objectivity.

But the content of knowledge is never entirely independent from the subject; rather it is the result of the meeting of the subject and the object. This is true for scientific knowledge as well as for anthropological knowledge. If they have to be distinguished, it is not on the ground that scientific knowledge can reach complete independence from the subject whereas anthropology cannot. Neither of them can. This point deserves some elaboration.

In discussing science, we have in mind not the natural, biological, historical or social sciences, but physics, because it is in this field that scientific methods have been applied most thoroughly and most successfully, thus affording a more useful contrast. Physical scientists attempt to suppress individual differences in their perceptivity: the observer's perception is limited to the reading of a few figures provided by an instrument, or resulting from a mathematical treatment of data. Under these conditions, agreement among different observers is easily secured. The image of physical reality built by science presents characteristics which may be checked by anybody knowing the proper techniques. This impersonal verification should not be confused with objectivity; that is to say, independence from the subject. The using of techniques in which neither the individuality of each observer nor his social perspective play any part eliminates any clue as to the personality and social affiliations of the scientist. But this does not mean that the object is the only determinant of knowledge. The impersonal subject determines the aspect of the reality which is perceived. The same camera, fixed in front of the same object illuminated by a constant light, focused at the same distance, with time and aperture remaining the same, will give identical pictures even when operated by different photographers, but only if each exposure is made on emulsions having the same characteristics (such as color sensitivity, speed, graininess, contrast). The pictures will be different if the film sheets used are ortho or panchromatic, color or infrared. Although perceived by an impersonal instrument, the object will produce different images. All of them are "objective" in the sense that they are partly determined by the object but not in the sense that the participation of the subject is eliminated.

Anthropology is not constructed by an impersonal subject. It is in this sense that anthropology differs from science. As mentioned before, anthropologists in fact have not attempted to elaborate techniques suppressing the personal factors in observation, in spite of the general trend, based on a high appreciation of achievements in the physical disciplines, to adoption of impersonal techniques in other fields. Anthropologists have refrained from doing so because the meaning which is an essential part of any social phenomenon is an obstacle to the development of impersonal methods of observation; anthropologists have even refrained from developing impersonal techniques in the restricted field of anthropological phenomena in which it seems that such methods can be applied.

Other disciplines of knowledge — history, political "science," art criticism — are in the same situation for similar reasons. Unfortunately, there is no name covering all the disciplines of knowledge which have not eliminated the personal subject. The old term "humanities" is very close to what we are looking for, but it has a broader scope than we wish: It includes creative disciplines such as literature or poetry and normative ones such as rhetoric and ethics. The supreme value of some disciplines included in the humanities is not objectivity.

Whatever the category in which anthropology should be put, it is certain that it does not provide an impersonal view of social reality. What our African critics had noticed has been confirmed by our short survey of the process of an anthropological study. A first conclusion to be drawn from this is that our studies have too often been presented as though they were based on impersonal procedures: The anthropologist seems to be an ubiquitous, detached, even abstract observer; sometimes he disappears altogether as an observer. We do not proceed in this manner with the intention of concealing our perspectives, but because of the high valuation of science, we are led to adopt the impersonal conventions of a scientific report.

Finally, the crucial question has to be faced: granted that anthropology aims at objectivity as much as does science, but by other methods than impersonal techniques of observation, does it attain it in some measure? That is to say, are individual and social perspectives obstacles that hopelessly prevent us from progressing toward objectivity?

On a general level, the answer is deceptively simple. The object in its independence from the subject influences the knowledge that the subject has of it, even if the subject has an individual and social situation which limits his possibilities of perception and thus partly determines his knowledge. The picture of a house is not devoid of objectivity because it is taken from a certain angle; that view gives only one aspect of the building and not all of them. It is similar in the case of the sensitive properties of films: The picture of a landscape taken with an infrared emulsion is very different from the one taken with a panchromatic one, and yet both have been affected by external light and tell us something objective about the landscape.

Unfortunately when we leave photographic comparisons, the precise assessment of viewpoints, perspectives, and perceptive sensibilities becomes much more difficult. It is easy to determine the spot where a camera is placed and to understand how it affects the picture; it is easy to analyze how the emulsion has reacted to the external light in order to produce the print we look at. But individual and social perspectives of an anthropologist are not easy to evaluate. Many more factual investigations of the relations between anthropologists and their studies have to be carried on before we have at our disposal the analytical tools and categories permitting us to indicate more adequately the variables of the observer's situation.

Nevertheless, we should not minimize the positive conclusion reached: A perspectivistic knowledge is not as such nonobjective; it is partial. It reflects an external reality but only an aspect of it, the one visible from the particular spot, social and individual, where the anthropologist was placed. Nonobjectivity creeps in when the partial aspect is considered as the global one. Any knowledge, even that obtained through an impersonal subject, is partial, thus inadequate to the external reality. In science, the characteristics of impersonal techniques and instruments are well known, since procedures have been invented and equipment has been built by scientists. Therefore, there is little chance of mistaking the incomplete view they produce for the global one.

Several perspectivistic views of the same social phenomenon help to describe more precisely each view point and consequently to determine how each of them affects the resulting knowledge. It is just the intervention of a new perspective, the African nationalist one, which has permitted us to become conscious of the bearing of the previous socioeconomic situation of Africanists on their studies. More is to be expected from the confrontation of a multiplicity of perspectives than from the quest for "the best one." If there were a priviledged one, it should be the anthropological. Even in the colonial situation, anthropologists were comparable — more so than any other group — to what Alfred Weber called the "socially unattached intelligentsia" (Mannheim, 1946:137). However, their existential situation has influenced their knowledge. It is from the comparison of different existentially conditioned views, and not by the futile attempt to cleanse one's view of any social commitment, that more complete knowledge of the object will be obtained.

PROSPECTIVE CONCLUSIONS

In this paper, what African anthropology was and is has been considered, not what it will or should be. Let us conclude with some tentative remarks on probable future developments.

In the former colonial countries which have recently become independent states, it is very likely that more and more studies will be devoted to present-day social phenomena, particularly to those giving rise to urgent problems. The parts of the cultures which remain influenced chiefly by traditional patterns will no longer be studied as if they existed in isolation, in a sort of timeless present, but rather as parts of the modern, literate, and industrial global society to which they now belong. Several recent publications have taken this approach. The discipline concerned with these contemporary phenomena will probably be called "sociology" instead of "anthropology" or "ethnology." As for societies of the past, traditional and colonial, they will be studied by history, using its specific methods and techniques.

This does not mean that the distinctive approach associated up to now with anthropology will disappear. Social phenomena with their meaning, depth, and complexity will still be approached in Africa — as well as everywhere else in the world, in nonliterate or industrial societies — by the methods best adapted to them, those in which objectivity, the supreme value of knowledge, is conquered by a sociologist endowed with imagination and insight. Limited by his individual characteristics and his existential situation, he will not pretend to offer impersonal knowledge but will claim that his results are valid and perspectivistic.

This approach is neither new nor exclusively characteristic of anthropology. It is to this approach that we owe nearly all our knowledge of man and society. The impersonal approach characteristic of the physical sciences — so successful there and already used in some social fields — can be very usefully extended to the few aspects of social phenomena which are liable to be apprehended by their use. No doubt, some sociologists will be inclined to work on the development of such devices.

An unexpected consequence of the decolonization process and of the emergence of new states in Africa has been to lay bare, for some Africanists at least, the perspectivistic character of their discipline and, consequently, to draw their attention to the problem of objectivity in anthropology. Some outcomes of this reexamination have been outlined here; some others will perhaps show themselves in the future. They are themselves another example of the influence of society on knowledge.

NOTES

1. "Epistemology of anthropology" is understood here as the critical assessment of the cognitive value of anthropology whereas "sociology of anthropological knowledge" refers to the study of the social or existential conditioning of anthropology. The influence of the existential situation on anthropology has

obviously a bearing on the cognitive value of our discipline but it seems useful to keep distinct the viewpoints of epistemology and of sociology of knowledge (Maquet, 1951:75–78).

2. A theory is understood here as a mental construct from which one can deduce (a) the observed generalizations, and (b) hypotheses, that is to say its logical consequences formulated in such a way that they can be confirmed or infirmed by observation (Maquet, 1951:236–240).

21

Statement on Ethics of the Society for Applied Anthropology

The following statement was unanimously approved at the twenty-second annual meeting of the Society.

(1) An applied anthropologist may not undertake to act professionally with or without remuneration, in any situation where he cannot honor all of the following responsibilities within the limit of the foreseeable effects of his action. When these responsibilities are in conflict, he must insist on a redefinition of the terms of his employment. If the conflict cannot be resolved, or if he has good reason to suspect that the results of his work will be used in a manner harmful to the interests of his fellow men or of science, he must decline to make his services available. *To Science* he has the responsibility of avoiding any actions or recommendations that will impede the advancement of scientific knowledge. In the wake of his own studies he must undertake to leave a hospitable climate for future study. With due regard to his other responsibilities as set forth here, he should undertake to make data and findings available for scientific pur-

"Statement on Ethics of the Society for Applied Anthropology" reprinted from *Human Organization* 22:237, 1963, by permission of the publisher.

poses. He should not represent hypotheses or personal opinions as scientifically validated principles.

(2) *To his fellow men* he owes respect for his dignity and general well-being. He may not recommend any course of action on behalf of his client's interests, when the lives, well-being, dignity, and self-respect of others are likely to be adversely affected, without adequate provisions being made to insure that there will be a minimum of such effect and that the net effect will in the long run be more beneficial than if no action were taken at all. He must take the greatest care to protect his informants, especially in the aspects of confidence which his informants may not be able to stipulate for themselves.

(3) *To his clients* he must make no promises nor may he encourage any expectations that he cannot reasonably hope to fulfill. He must give them the best of his scientific knowledge and skill. He must consider their specific goals in the light of their general interests and welfare. He must establish a clear understanding with each client as to the nature of his responsibilities to his client, to science, and to his fellow men.

Bibliography

ABLON, JOAN
1964   Relocated American Indians in the San Francisco Bay Area: Social interaction and Indian identity. Human Organization 24:296–304.

ADAIR, JOHN
1964   Personal communication to Laura Thompson.

ADAMS, RICHARD N.
1955   Notas sobre la aplicación de la antropología. Suplemento No. 2 del Boletin de la Oficina Sanitaria Panamericana, Washington, D.C.

ALERS, J. O.
1960   Population and development in a Peruvian community, Mimeographed, Cornell University Comparative Studies of Cultural Change, Ithaca, N.Y.

ALLEE, W. C., ET. AL.
1949   Principles of animal ecology. Philadelphia, Saunders and Co.

ANON
1954   Editorial, Role of the consultant. Human Organization 13:3–4.

ANTHROPOLOGICAL REVIEW
1866a   Race in legislation and political economy. 4:113.
1866b   Race in religion. 4:289.

ARENSBERG, CONRAD
1961   The community as object and sample. American Anthropologist 63:241–264.

ARENSBERG, CONRAD AND SOLON T. KIMBALL
1965   Culture and community. New York, Harcourt Brace.

ARENSBERG, CONRAD AND ARTHUR H. NIEHOFF
1964   Introducing social change. Chicago, Aldine.

ARISTIDE, ACHILLE
1958–59 Le destin et l'avenir des cultures noires dans le monde. Bulletin du Bureau d'Ethnologie, Series 111, Nos. 17–19:21–40, Port-au-Prince, Haiti.

BALANDIER, GEORGES
1963   Sociologie actuelle de l'Afrique noire (2e éd.). Paris, Presses Universitaires de France.

BALFOUR, H.
1903   Anthropology, its position and needs. Man 33:11–23.

BARNETT, C.
1960   Indian protest movements in Callejon de Huaylas. Cornell University Ph.D. Thesis.

BARNETT, H. G.
 1953 Innovation: The basis of cultural change. New York, McGraw-Hill.
 1956 Anthropology in administration. Row, Peterson and Company, Evanston.
 1958 Anthropology as an applied science. Human Organization 17:9–11.
 1963 Materials for course design in the teaching of applied anthropology. *In* American Anthropological Association Memoir 94.

BERREMAN, GERALD D.
 1968 Ethnography: Method and product. *In* Introduction to cultural anthropology, James A. Clifton, ed. Boston, Houghton Mifflin Company.

BERREMAN, GERALD D., G. GJESSING, AND K. GOUGH
 1968 Social responsibilities symposium. Current Anthropology 9:391–435.

BONFIL BATALLA, G.
 1962 Diagnóstico sobre el hambre en Sudzal, Yucatán (un ensayo de antropología aplicada). Instituto Nacional de Antropología e Historia, México.

BRAUNHOLTZ, H. J.
 1943 Anthropology in theory and practice. Journal of Royal Anthropological Institute 73:1–8.

BRODIE, SIR B. C.
 1856 Address. Journal of Ethnological Society 4:294–97.

BROKENSHA, DAVID
 1966 Applied anthropology in English-speaking Africa. Society for Applied Anthropology Monograph No. 8.

BROWN, G. GORDON AND McD. B. HUTT
 1935 Anthropology in action: An experiment in the Tringa district of the Tringa Province, Tanganyika territory. London, Oxford University Press.

BUCHER, K.
 n.d. Arbeit und rythmus.

BUXTON, L. B.
 n.d. Primitive labor.

BUXTON, TRAVERS
 1929 Slavery. Encyclopaedia Britannica 14th ed. 20:781.

CAUDILL, WILLIAM
 1953 Applied anthropology in medicine. *In* Anthropology today, Chicago, University of Chicago Press.

CHAPPLE, E. D. AND C. S. COON
 1942 Principles of anthropology. New York, H. Holt.

COLLAZOS, CH. C., ET. AL.
 1954 Dietary surveys in Peru, Chacan, and Vicos: Rural communities in the Peruvian Andes, Journal of the American Dietic Association 30.

COLLIER, JOHN
1945   The United States Indian administration as a laboratory of ethnic relations. Social Research 12:265–303.

CUNNINGHAM, D. J.
1908   Anthropology in the 18th century. Journal of Royal Anthropological Society 38:10–35.

DALTON, GEORGE AND PAUL BOHANNAN
1961   Review of Rostov, The stages of economic growth. American Anthropologist 63:397–400.

DOBYNS, HENRY F., CARLOS MONGE AND MARIO C. VASQUEZ
1962   Community and regional development: The joint Cornell-Peru experiment. Summary of technical-organization progress and reactions to it. Human Organization 21:109–115.

DRUCKER, PHILLIP
1951   Anthropology in the trust territory. The Scientific Monthly 72, No. 5.

EGGAN, F. (ED.)
1955   Social change of North American Indian tribes. Chicago, University of Chicago Press.

EISENSTADT, S. N.
1956   From generation to generation. Glencoe, The Free Press.

ELKIN, A. P.
1964   The Australian aborigines. New York, Doubleday Anchor Books.

ERASMUS, CHARLES
1952a   Human Organization 11:20.
1952b   Southwestern Journal of Anthropology 8, No. 4.
1961   Man takes control. Minneapolis, University of Minnesota Press.

EVANS-PRITCHARD, E. E.
1946   Applied anthropology. Africa 16:92–98.

FESTINGER, LEON AND D. KATZ (EDS.)
1953   Research methods in behavioral sciences. New York, Dryden Press.

FIRTH, RAYMOND
1936   We, the Tikopia. London, Allen and Unwin (Boston, Beacon Press, 1963).
1959   Social change in Tikopia. London, George Allen and Unwin.

FISCHER, J. L.
1963   The Japanese schools for the natives of Truk, Caroline Islands. In Education and culture, George D. Spindler, ed. New York, Holt, Rinehart and Winston.

FLOWER, W. H.
1884   On the aims and prospects of the study of anthropology. Journal of the Anthropological Institute 13:May 488–501.

FOSBERG, F. R. (Ed.)
1963   Man's place in the island ecosystem: A symposium. Honolulu, B. P. Bishop Museum Press.

FOSTER, GEORGE M.
1952   Papel de la antropología en los programmas de salud pública. Boletin de la Oficina Sanitaria Panamericana 33, No. 4. Washington, D.C.
1955   Análisis antropológico intercultural de un programma de ayuda técnica. Instituto Nacional Indigenista, México.
1962   Traditional cultures and the impact of technical change. Harper and Row, New York.
1969   Applied anthropology. Boston, Little Brown and Co.

FRAZER, J. G.
1890   The golden bough, 2 Vols. 1st Edition. London, Macmillan and Co.
1900   The golden bough, 2 Vols. 2nd Edition. London, Macmillan and Co.

FREILICH, MORRIS
1963   The natural experiment: Ecology and culture. Southwestern Journal of Anthropology 19.

GARIGUE, P.
1956   French Canadian kinship and urban life. American Anthropologist 58:1090–1101.
1958   Les sciences sociales dans le monde contemporain. Université de Montréal.

GEARING, F., R. McC. NETTING, and L. R. PEATTIE
1960   Documentary history of the fox project. Department of Anthropology, University of Chicago.

GLADWIN, THOMAS
1960   Technical assistance programs: A challenge for anthropology. Fellow Newsletter, American Anthropological Association 1:6–7.

GLUCKMAN, MAX
1963   Malinowski's "functional" analysis of social change. *In* Order and rebellion in tribal Africa. London, Cohen and West.

GOLDENWEISER, ALEXANDER
1922   Early civilization. New York.

GONZÁLEZ, CASANOVA, P.
1963   Sociedad plural, colonialismo interno y desarrollo. América Latina 6:15–32, Rió de Janeiro.

GOODENOUGH, WARD H.
1963   Cooperation in change. New York, Russell Sage Foundation.

GOULDNER, A. W.
1956   Explorations in Applied Science. Social Problems 3:169–181.

GREENBERG, DANIEL S.
1967   The politics of pure science. New American Library, New York.

HADDON, A. C.
1934   History of anthropology. London, Watts.

HAILEY, LORD
1944   The role of anthropology in colonial development. Man 44(5): 10–15.
1955   American Indian and white children: A sociopsychological investigation. Chicago, University of Chicago Press.

HENRY, JULES AND JOAN WHITEHORN BOGGS
1952   Child rearing, culture, and the natural world. Psychiatry 15:261–271.

HERSKOVITS, MELVILLE J.
1948   Man and his works. New York, Alfred Knopf.

HOCKETT, CHARLES F. AND ROBERT ASCHER
1964   The human revolution. Current Anthropology 5.

HOEBEL, E. ADAMSON
1954   The law of primitive man. Cambridge, Harvard University Press.

HOGBIN, H. IAN
1957   Anthropology as public service and Malinowski's contribution to it. In Man and culture: An evaluation of the work of Bronislaw Malinowski, Raymond Firth, ed. Harper and Row, New York.

HOLMBERG, ALLAN R.
1952   Proyecto Peru-Cornell en las ciencias sociales applicadas. Peru Indigena 5 & 6:158–66.
1955   Participant intervention in the field. Human Organization 14:1 (Spring, 1955), 23–26.
1958   The research and development approach to the study of change. Human Organization 17:12–16.
1960   Changing community attitudes and values in Peru. In Social change in Latin America today, New York, Harper and Brothers, pp. 63–107.
1965   The changing values and institutions of Vicos in the context of national development. American Behavioral Scientist March, 8:3–8, No. 7.

HONIGMAN, J. J.
1963   Review of W. E. Mühlmann, Homo creator. American Anthropologist 65:1360.

HUNT, JAMES
1863   On the study of anthropology. Anthropological Review 1:1–20.
1865   President's address. Anthropological Review 3:lxxxv-cxvii.

HUNTER, EVAN
1954   The blackboard jungle. New York, Simon Schuster.

JOSEPH, ALICE AND V. MURRAY
1951   Chamorros and Carolinians of Saipan. Cambridge, Harvard University Press.

JOSEPH, ALICE, R. SPICER, AND JANE CHESKY
1949   The desert people: A study of the Papago Indians. Chicago, University of Chicago Press.

KEESING, FELIX M.
1934   Taming Philippine headhunters: A study of government and of cultural change in northern Luzon. London, Allen and Unwin.
1945   The south seas in the modern world (revised ed.) New York, John Day.
1953   Culture change. An analysis and bibliography of anthropological Sources to 1952. Stanford, Stanford University Press.

KEITH, SIR ARTHUR
1917   How can the institute best serve the needs of anthropology? Journal of Royal Anthropological Institute 47:12–30.

KELLY, ISABEL
1959   Technical cooperation and the culture of the host community. Community Development Review, September.

KIMBALL, SOLON T., MARION PEARSALL, AND JANE A. BLISS
1954   Consultants and citizens: A research relationship. Human Organization 13:5–8.

KLUCKHOHN, CLYDE
1943   Covert culture and administrative problems. American Anthropologist 45:213–227.

KLUCKHOHN, CLYDE AND WILLIAM H. KELLY
1945   The concept of culture. *In* The science of man in the world crisis, Ralph Linton, ed. New York, Columbia University Press.

KLUCKHOHN, CLYDE AND DOROTHEA C. LEIGHTON
1946   The Navaho. Cambridge, Harvard University Press.

KLUCKHOHN, CLYDE AND HENRY A. MURRAY
1948   Personality formation: The determinants. *In* Personality in nature society and culture, Clyde Kluckhohn, Henry A. Murray, and David Schneider, eds. New York, Alfred Knopf.

KROEBER, A. L.
1953   Concluding review. *In* An appraisal of anthropology today, Sol Tax, *et al.*, eds. Chicago, University of Chicago Press.
1959   Critical summary and commentary. *In* Method and Perspective in anthropology, R. F. Spencer, ed. Minneapolis, University of Minnesota Press.

LASSWELL, HAROLD
n.d.   Law, science and policy papers. Mimeographed, Yale University, New Haven.

LEE, A. MC.
1955   The clinical study of society. American Sociological Review 20: 648–653.

LEIGHTON, ALEXANDER H.
1945   The governing of men. Princeton, Princeton University Press.

LEIGHTON, A. H. AND D. C. LEIGHTON
1944   The Navaho door. Cambridge, Harvard University Press.

LEIGHTON, DOROTHEA C. AND CLYDE KLUCKHOHN
1947   Children of the people: The Navaho individual and his develop-
        ment. Cambridge, Harvard University Press.

LEIGHTON, DOROTHEA C. AND JOHN ADAIR
1965   People of the middle place. New Haven, Human Relations Area
        Files.

LEWIS, OSCAR
1951   Life in a Mexican village: Tepotzlán restudied. Urbana, University
        of Illinois Press.
1953   Controls and Experiments in Field Work. *In* Anthropology today,
        A. L. Kroeber, ed. Chicago, University of Chicago Press.

LITTLE, KENNETH
1963   The context of social change. In American Anthropological Asso-
        ciation Memoir no. 94.

LUGARD, LORD FREDERICK J. D.
n.d.   The dual mandate in British tropical Africa. London, F. Cass (cf.
        also 5th Ed., Hamden, Conn., Anchor Books, 1965).

LURIE, NANCY OESTREICH
1966   Women in early American anthropology. *In* Pioneers of American
        anthropology, June Helm, ed. University of Washington Press,
        Seattle.

MACGREGOR, GORDON
1946   Warriors without weapons. Chicago, University of Chicago Press.
1955   Anthropology in government: United States. *In* Yearbook of
        anthropology-1955. New York, Wenner-Gren Foundation.

MACKENZIE, K. R. H.
1866   On popular errors concerning anthropology. Popular Magazine of
        Anthropology 2:60–71.

MAIR, LUCY P.
1957   Studies in applied anthropology. London, Athlone Press.
1968   Applied anthropology. International Encyclopedia of the Social
        Sciences, Vol. 1:325–330.

MALINOWSKI, BRONISLAW
n.d.   The present state of culture contact studies. Africa 12:1.
1922   Argonauts of the western Pacific. London, Routledge.
1926   Crime and custom in savage society. New York, Humanities Press.
1938   Methods of study of culture contact. Memorandum 15, Interna-
        tional African Institute, London, Oxford University Press.
1940   Modern anthropology and European rule in Africa. Reale Academia
        D'Italia Fondazione Alessandro volta, Instituita Dalla Societa
        Edison de Milano, Rome.
1944   A scientific theory of culture and other essays. Chapel Hill, Uni-
        versity of North Carolina Press.
1945   The dynamics of culture change. New Haven, Yale University
        Press.

MANNERS, R. A.
1956   Functionalism, realpolitik and anthropology in underdeveloped areas. América Indigena 16.

MANNHEIM, KARL
1946   Ideology and utopia. New York, Harcourt, Brace & Co.

MANNONI, O.
1956   Prospero and Caliban (Translated from the French), London, Methuen & Co.

MAQUET, JACQUES J.
1951   The sociology of knowledge. Boston, Beacon Press.
1958–59 Le relativisme culturel. Presénce Africaine 22:65–73; 23:59–68.

MASON, LEONARD
1950   The Bikinians: A transplanted population, Human Organization 9, No. 1.

MAYER, ALBERT, AND ASSOCIATES
1962   Pilot project India. Berkeley, University of California Press.

MEAD, MARGARET (ED.)
1955   Cultural patterns and technical change. New York, New American Library.

MEAD, MARGARET
1964   Continuities in cultural evolution. New Haven, Yale University Press.

METGE, A. J.
1959   Maori society today (mimeographed). Auckland, Adult Education Centre, University of Auckland.
1960   Maori Komiti in Action in New Zealand's Far North. Mss. to be published in a symposium on capital, savings and credit in peasant societies, Ed; Raymond Firth.

METRAUX, ALFRED
1953   Commentary. *In* An appraisal of anthropology today, Sol Tax, *et al.*, eds. 354–355. Chicago, University of Chicago Press.

MILLS, C. WRIGHT
1959   The sociological imagination. New York, Oxford University Press.

MURDOCK, GEORGE P.
1949   Social structure. New York, MacMillan Company.

MYRES, SIR JOHN L.
1931   Anthropology in the British association for the advancement of science. Man 31:205.
1944   A century of our work. Man 44(4):2–9.

NADEL, S. F.
1951   The foundations of social anthropology. Glencoe, The Free Press.
1957   The theory of social structure. London, Cohen and West.

NIEHOFF, ARTHUR H.
1964   A casebook of social change. Chicago, Aldine.

NORTHROP, F. S. C.
1947   The meeting of east and west. New York, Macmillan.

OLIVER, DOUGLAS
1951   Planning Micronesia's future. Cambridge, Harvard University Press.

PACIFIC SCIENCE BOARD
1950   Fourth annual report, Pacific Science Board, National Research Council, Washington, D.C.
1951   Fifth annual report, Pacific Science Board, National Research Council, Washington, D.C.

PALL MALL GAZETTE
1866   Popularized ethnology. Jan. 17, 1866. Reprinted in Popular Magazine of Anthropology, 1866, 80–82.

PARSONS, ANNE AND WARD E. GOODENOUGH
1964   The growing demand for behavior science in government. Comment, reply, and rejoinder. Human Organization 23:93–98.

PAUL, BENJAMIN D.
1955   Health, culture and community. New York, Russell Sage Foundation.

PAYNE, E. H., ET. AL.
1956   An Intestinal Parasite Survey in the High Cordilleras of Peru. American Journal of Tropical Medicine and Hygiene 5: 696–98.

PEAKE, N. J. E.
1921   Discussion. Man 21(103):174.

PEATTIE, LISA REDFIELD
1958   Interventionism and applied science in anthropology. Human Organization 17:4–8.

PIDDINGTON, R.
1957   An introduction to social anthropology, Vol. II. Edinburgh, Oliver and Boyd.

POLGAR, S.
1962   Health and human behavior: Areas of interest common to the social and medical sciences. Current Anthropology 3.

POPULAR MAGAZINE OF ANTHROPOLOGY
1866   Anthropology a practical science. 1:(1):6–9.

POZAS, R.
1961   El desarrollo de la comunidad. Téchnicas de investigatión social. Universidad Nacional Autonoma de México, México.

PRATT, WAYNE
1962   Personal communication to Laura Thompson.

RADCLIFFE-BROWN, A. R.
1922   The Andaman islanders. Cambridge, Cambridge University Press.
1930   Applied anthropology. Report of the Australian and New Zealand association for the advancement of science, Section F. 20:267–280.
1957   A natural science of society. Glencoe, The Free Press.

RAPOPORT, ROBERT N.
  1963   Aims and methods in the teaching of applied anthropology. *In*
          American Anthropological Association Memoir 94.

REDFIELD, ROBERT
  1953   The primitive world and its transformations. Cornell University
          Press, Ithaca, N.Y.
  1955   The little community. Chicago, University of Chicago Press.

RICHARDS, AUDREY I.
  1935   Tribal government in transition. Supplement to Journal of the Royal
          African Society, October.
  1939   Land, labour, and diet in N. Rhodesia. International Institute.
          Oxford University Press.

RICHARDSON, F. L. W., Jr.
  1962   Forward. *In Major issues in modern society,* R. J. Smith, ed.
          Human Organization 21:61.

ROBERTS, JOHN M. AND BRIAN SUTTON-SMITH
  1962   Child training and game involvement. Ethnology 1:166–185.

ROSTOV, W. W.
  1960   The stages of economic growth. New York, Cambridge University
          Press.

SAPIR, EDWARD
  1949   Why cultural anthropology needs the psychiatrist. *In* Selected
          writings of Edward Sapir in language, culture and personality.
          Berkeley, University of California Press.

SCHWIMMER, E. G.
  1958   The mediator. Journal of the Polynesian Society 67:335–351.

SCIENCE ADVISORY COMMITTEE
  1962   Strengthening the behavioral sciences. A Report of a Sub-panel of
          the President's Science Advisory Committee. Science 136:233–241.

SHEPARD, H. R. AND R. R. BLAKE
  1962   Changing behavior through cognitive change. Human Organiza-
          tion 21:88–96.

SHEPARDSON, M.
  1962   Value theory in the prediction of political behavior: The Navajo
          case. American Anthropologist 64.

SIEGEL, B. J. (ED.)
  1955   Acculturation. Stanford, Stanford University Press.

SINHA, D. P.
  n.d.   Resettlement of a semi-nomadic tribal community in Bihar, India:
          A problem in applied anthropology. Mss.

SJOBERG, GIDEON (ED.)
  1967   Ethics, politics, and social research. Cambridge, Schenkman.

SMITH, E. W.
  1934   Anthropology and the practical man. Journal of Royal Anthropo-
          logical Institute 54:xiii-xxxvii.

1956   Anthropology and the practical man. Journal of Royal Anthropological Institute 64:xxxiv-xxxvi.

SMITH, SIR G. ELIOT
1935   The place of T. H. Huxley in anthropology. Journal of Royal Anthropological Institute 55:199–204.

SOROKIN, PITIRIM A.
1937   Social and cultural dynamics, Vol. II. New York, American Book Co.

SPATE, O. H. K.
1959   The Fijian people: Economic problems and prospects. Suva, Fiji, Government Press.

SPICER, EDWARD H. (ED.)
1952   Human problems in technological change. New York, Russell Sage Foundation.

SPILLIUS, J.
1957   Natural disaster and political crisis in a polynesian society: An exploration of operational research. Human Relations 10:3–27 and 113–125.

SPINDLER, GEORGE D.
1963   The role of the school administrator. *In* Education and culture, George D. Spindler, ed. New York, Holt, Rinehart and Winston.

SRINIVAS, M. N. (ED.)
1958   Method of social anthropology: Selected essays. Chicago, University of Chicago Press.

STARKEY, MARION L.
1949   The devil in Massachusetts. New York, Knopf.

SWANSON, GUY E.
1960   The birth of the gods. Ann Arbor, Michigan University Press.

TAX, SOL
1958   The fox project. Human Organization. 17:17–19.

THOMPSON, LAURA
1947   Guam and its people. Princeton, Princeton University Press.
1950   Action research among American Indians. Scientific Monthly 70: 34–40.
1950   Culture in crisis: A study of the Hopi indians. New York, Harper and Brothers.
1951   Personality and government: Findings and recommendations of the indian administration research. Mexico City, Instituto Indigenista Interamericano.
1956   U.S. Indian reorganization viewed as an experiment in action social research. Estudios antropologicos publicados en homenaje al Doctor Manuel Gamio. Mexico City, Direccion General del Publicaciones.
1961   Towards a science of mankind. New York, McGraw Hill.
1963   Concepts and contributions. *In* American Anthropological Association Memoir No. 94:354–355.

THOMPSON, LAURA AND ALICE JOSEPH
1944   The Hopi way. Chicago, University of Chicago Press.

TRUNDLE, G. T., JR., ET. AL.
1948   Managerial control of business. New York, Wiley.

TYLOR, E. B.
1871   Primitive culture. London, John Murray.
1881   Anthropology. London, Macmillan.

ULRICH, DAVID M.
1949   A clinical method in applied social science. Philosophy of Science
        16:246–249.

VAN GENNEP, ARNOLD
1960   The rites of passage. Chicago, University of Chicago Press. (First
        Published in Paris, 1909, Les rites de passage; also by Phoenix
        Books, 1961).

VASQUEZ, M. C.
1952   La anthropologia y nuestro problema del Indio, Peru Indigena 2:
        7–157.
1964   The varayoc system in Vicos. Mimeographed, Cornell University
        Comparative Studies of Cultural Change, Ithaca, New York.

WALLACE, A. F. C.
1956   Revitalization movements. American Anthropologist 58:264–281.

WARREN, ROLAND
1956   Toward a reformulation of community theory. Human Organiza-
        tion 15:8–11.

WEBER, MAX
1930   The protestant ethic and the spirit of capitalism. New York, C.
        Scribner's Sons.

WESTERMARCK, EDWARD
1891   The history of human marriage. 1st Edition, London, Macmillan
        and Co., 1921, 5th Edition.

WHITING, JOHN W. M. AND IRVING CHILD
1953   Child training and personality. New Haven, Yale University Press.

WILSON, GODREY
n.d.   The constitution of Ngonde. Rhodes-Livington Paper No. 3.